D1271105

Cupids and Chaos

DARBY CUPID

CUPIDS & CHAOS
Hands of Fate

ISBN: 978-1-80068-407-2

For Kallie
Be the creator and master of your own fate.

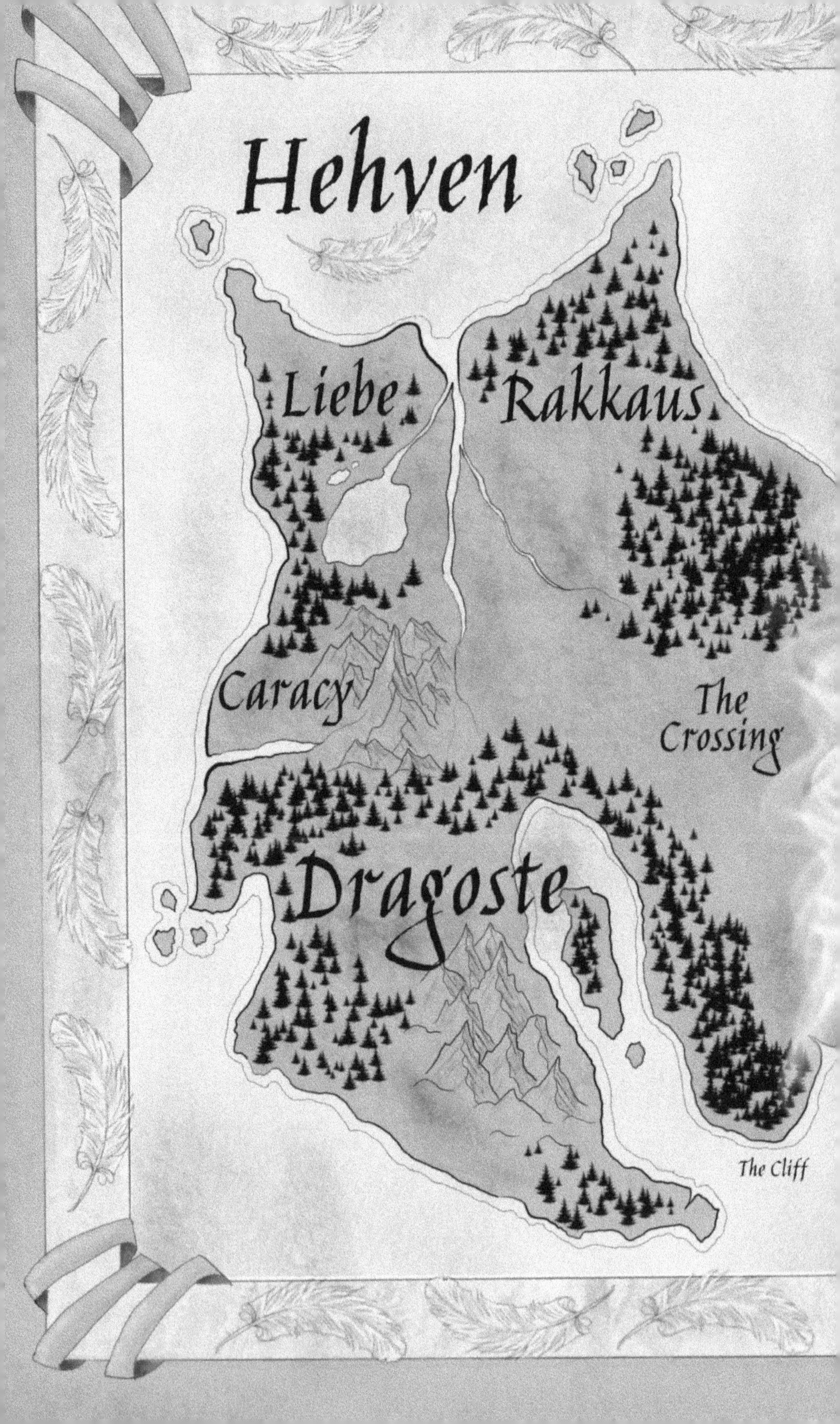
Hehven
Liebe
Rakkaus
Caracy
The Crossing
Dragoste
The Cliff

e of Fate
Helle
Hadeon
Arazo
Nefret
Devland

The Wendell Islands

Liridona

N
W
E
S
Dalibor
Newbold

Fate leads him who follows it, and drags him who resists.

~ Plutarch

1
Pace

Freedom was salt air in my lungs, and the dark stern of the galleon rising from the silvered morning mist before me. I'd waited nineteen and a half years for a taste of it, and as we flew closer, the cold air filtering through my wings, it didn't disappoint. As we descended, a single small white feather landed on the sea-soaked deck, and I stooped to pick it up, only to find Dariel had beaten me to it.

"That is exactly why this was a bad idea." He thrust the feather in my face, his ice blue eyes narrowed. "I still can't believe I let you talk me into this."

Snatching the feather from his fingers, I shoved it in my pocket. "Like you never shed when you land." Dariel swept his arms out to the side in answer, gesturing dramatically to the empty deck, and I rolled my eyes. "Sorry we can't all be as perfect as you, Captain."

"Can you two be quiet?" Tiesa hissed. "If the humans found it, we all know they would just assume it was from a bird. A large bird, but a bird nonetheless."

Dariel folded his arms across his broad chest, a smirk on his lips. "My cousin, the oversized pigeon."

Mirroring his stance, I lifted my chin as I stared him down. "Say that again."

"Are you seriously trying to wake the entire ship?" Tiesa looked between us, her green eyes wide enough to crease the gold tattoo on her forehead.

Dariel's answering frown caused his own gold markings to wrinkle against his dark skin. "Like I said. This is a terrible idea."

Ignoring him, I returned my attention to the ship and the steady pulse of excitement thrumming in my chest. For too long, I'd made do with fragments and titbits of tales from my friends' assignments in the human world. Now, I was finally experiencing it for myself. Folding my wings, making sure not to shed any more feathers, I gripped the damp wooden rail and peered over the side of the ship.

Mist caressed the heaving grey waves, making it difficult to tell where the sky ended, and the sea began. On the horizon, a pale pink glow was creeping through the dusky clouds as the sun began to rise, ready to burn away the freezing fingers of fog. Beneath my feet, the ship creaked and groaned, and I looked up, straining my neck to see the top of the tall mast amidst the clouds. I'd read about ships in books, and there were fishing boats in Hehven, but this was something else entirely.

"Stop gawking." Tiesa grabbed my arm, tugging me towards the cabin. "You're going to get us caught."

I winced as the action stretched the bruising on my torso and she shot me a look, which told me she knew exactly why the bruise was there, and she wasn't impressed. Pretending I hadn't noticed, I focused on trying to quell the pounding anticipation in my chest. I was going to see humans. Tiesa had told me countless times that they looked just like Cupids without wings but that thought alone blew my mind. How could anyone live without wings? Without flying? My own white wings, the long feathers tipped with the faintest hint of gold, shuddered at the thought.

Tiesa and Dariel pressed close together, peering through the murky cabin window and I edged in beside them, grateful for the warmth as icy wind whipped around the ship. Several long white strands had been tugged free from Tiesa's braid, and as they hit me in the face for the third time, I reached out and tucked them behind her ear.

"There," Dariel muttered, his eyes fixed on the other side of the window.

A lamp was lit, causing the room to glow. The flickering light illuminated a long wooden table at the far end of the cabin, maps and instruments strewn on its surface and strange pictures and drawings adorning the walls. A movement pulled my focus and I stared as a woman seemed to materialise from the shadows. She sat at the table, pulling long dark braids woven with different colours over her shoulder as she spread papers out before her. *No wings.* I had been expecting it, but the sight was still jarring.

A door opened and a woman holding two steaming cups and wearing a strange wreath of material around her neck appeared. She handed one of the cups to the first human, earning a warm smile in response, and I realised what I'd initially thought was perhaps a scarf, was in fact a scaled creature curled around her shoulders. My fingers tightened their grip on the window ledge as I watched the creature stretch—its burgundy tail encircling the woman's neck as a steady stream of smoke filtered from its nostrils. Tiesa had told me tales of the dragons that lived in the Wendell Islands but until that moment I had thought she'd been joking.

"The woman with the braids is Cove," Tiesa whispered. "That's our mark."

Cove reached out and scratched under the dragon's chin, causing it to momentarily open its slitted yellow eyes before resuming its slumber. The second woman pulled out a chair and began gesticulating at the papers on the table with a frown. Who were these humans that the Fates were intervening in their lives? I tried to identify anything special or unique about them, but as they were the only two humans I'd ever seen, my frame of reference was rather limited.

The second woman reached out and linked her fingers with Cove's. Her straight black hair skimmed her chin in sharp lines and her dark eyes were a tilted shape I'd never seen before. In fact, it was the first time I'd seen anyone with hair that wasn't white. I pressed closer to the window to see more clearly.

"You're fogging the glass," Tiesa hissed, shoving me back.

Ignoring her, I leaned forward again, unable to tear my eyes from the humans inside. I wanted to know who they were. I wanted to know why the Fates had sent Hands to deliver an arrow to them.

"Time to go." Dariel stood, the morning light catching on the quiver of golden arrows on his back as he extended his wings and launched himself into the air toward the folded sails.

Tiesa straightened and followed, but I allowed myself one last fleeting glance at the two humans before spreading my own wings and leaping into the air.

Taking a seat amongst the damp rigging, the unrelenting wind whipped and snapped at me and I fastened the top button of my shirt, wishing someone had warned me to dress warmer. Although the sun had burned away most of the mist—the sea rippling out endlessly around us as we waited, watching—it was still uncomfortably cold.

Dariel's intricately carved golden bow was ready in his hand, the feather shaped limbs glinting, but he hadn't yet selected his arrow.

"Thank you," I said, causing him to turn, an eyebrow raised. "For bringing me."

Dariel huffed in response, returning his gaze to the cabin

below. As a captain, he had dozens of Hands under his command, including Tiesa, but if anyone found out he'd allowed me, the second prince, through The Crossing . . . If my parents found out . . .

I shuddered at the thought. "How do you know when to shoot her?"

Dariel reached into the pocket of his brown leather tunic and handed me a piece of paper. Orders direct from the Fates. Gripping tight to stop the wind from snatching it, I pored over the words written in swooping gold ink.

Cove is meeting with other humans today and the meeting must go well.

Dariel's arrow would ensure that. My gaze drifted to the quiver tucked between his wings as I handed the paper back.

"I warned you it wasn't as exciting as you thought." Tiesa nudged me with her shoulder. "Most of our assignments are waiting around, freezing or sweating our feathers off."

She was wrong. This *was* exciting. Even the breeze felt different—sounded different—in the human world. A gust of wind buffeted us, and I flexed my wings, my hands gripping the smooth wood to keep my balance. Once it passed, I pushed the strands of white hair from my eyes and Tiesa snorted.

"What?"

Shaking her head, she pointed at my face. "You've smudged your markings."

It took me a moment to realise what she meant and, glancing down at my hands, I found traces of gold paint on my fingertips. Cupids' faces were tattooed when they were ordained as Hands of Fate, the gold markings worn with pride. It was Tiesa's idea to paint them on me, saying it would help to disguise me. Of course, Dariel had been quick to point out that there was no Cupid in Hehven who wouldn't recognise the second prince, but she had insisted anyway. Reaching out, I wiped the gold paint on her nose with a grin. She gasped, lifting her hands to shove me, but I gripped her wrists.

"Let go," she huffed.

"You should know better." I smirked, holding on for a moment more before releasing her. "You haven't landed a hit on me since we were smallwings."

She snorted. "Well, someone has."

"Excuse me?"

Tiesa jutted her chin towards my torso. "I saw you wince. You've been fighting again, haven't you?"

I shifted, straightening my shoulders, aware of Dariel's narrowed gaze. "You make it sound so sordid."

"If it's not sordid, why isn't it happening in the training rooms?" she asked, her eyebrow arched. "Why don't your parents know about it?"

I exhaled, squinting at the horizon. "You know why. It's more than training. It's the best of the best. Besides, if you're so concerned, why don't you fly off and tell the king and queen?"

"You know I'd never." Tiesa gasped, her eyes wide. "Pace, you're my best friend."

"Then back off."

She frowned. "Just because I don't approve of what you get up to, doesn't mean I'd betray your trust."

I pressed my lips together, wondering whether I was imagining another layer to her comment but before I could question it further, a movement on the deck below drew our attention.

The cabin door opened, slamming in the wind, and Cove strode out, a frown creasing her brow. The other woman followed close behind, the small dragon beating its deep red wings as though protesting at being brought out into the cold. Part of me waited for them to look up and see us, but I knew they wouldn't. There was something in a human's subconscious that told them not to. We were nothing more than a flicker in their peripheral vision.

Cove pulled a long cylinder from her belt and held it to her eye, facing out to sea. I watched curiously, trying to follow where she was looking but, from high up in the rigging, I saw it instantly. Another ship had appeared on the horizon. Cove offered the cylinder to the other woman and as she took it, she leaned forward and kissed her.

"Hey look, Pace," Tiesa teased. "A tutorial."

I narrowed my eyes, glaring as I considered shoving her off the rounded wooden pole, but she just wiggled her pale eyebrows. Teeth gritted, I focused on the approaching ship instead. Cupids embodied the highest level of purity, saving all intimacy, including their first kiss, until marriage. *Marriage.* My stomach rolled at the thought. When my parents informed me that they had arranged my betrothal, I'd almost bitten my tongue in half in an attempt to keep my mouth shut. Clenching my jaw, I turned my head and tried to appreciate the soft shades of pink and orange the sea was turning as the sun moved higher above the horizon, warming my frozen skin.

"Sorry," Tiesa muttered.

I shook my head, knowing she was talking about more than teasing me. "It's fine." It wasn't.

"The Rakkaus are a good family," Dariel offered as he set about re-plaiting his long white braid. "Caitland's brother is a well-respected Hand."

Although well intentioned, his words did little to soothe the burning in my gut. It was because of my engagement I had managed to persuade Dariel to bring me—a last taste of freedom before I was expected to start taking on more responsibility. Before I married on my twentieth birthday that winter. My brother wasn't expected to marry until taking to the throne and he would get to choose his partner. It was almost enough to make me wish I had been the first born, but not quite. Ruling Hehven was a responsibility I was glad would never fall on me.

The sun had risen high enough for its rays to caress the world with warm fingers, and I closed my eyes as it heated my skin, stretching my wings a little to allow the breeze to filter through my feathers. Flying was everything to me. From my very first flight, I'd been reluctant to ever set foot on the ground again. A small smile curled my lips as I remembered exploring the mountains near the palace with Tiesa as smallwings. We had spent hours climbing to the top and then riding the downslope winds to the valleys below. Every flight, every taste of freedom since my parents had announced my engagement, felt like my last.

"It'll be okay," Tiesa offered, as though reading my thoughts. "Marriage isn't the end of the world."

"Like I said. It's fine." I ran a hand through my hair, sitting up straighter. "At least once I'm married, all the eligible females will finally get the message. I'm running out of drawer space for all the love letters."

Instead of teasing me for my arrogance, Tiesa stared at me, sadness swimming in her pale green eyes.

I frowned and looked away. "Do we know who Cove's meeting with?"

"No," Dariel replied as a handful of crew members appeared below us, preparing for the arrival of the other ship. "It's not our place to know the details. We only know what the Fates allow."

Shouts carried up to us as the other ship drew closer and we watched as it dropped anchor, lowering a rowboat to the choppy sea below. It was still too far to see the humans it was carrying, but I noted Dariel nocking an arrow beside me. Crew members unfurled a ladder over the side, and I turned my attention to Cove and the other woman. Watching their mouths moving, their body language strained, curiosity itched beneath my skin. I needed to know what they were saying.

Before I could think better of it, I leaned backwards, falling from the rigging. I arched my wings as I flipped, gliding silently down to the quarterdeck. Dariel's soft cursing reached me on the wind, and I grinned as I landed. The quarterdeck was deserted, with everyone's attention on the main deck and the approaching guests. Tucking my wings in tight, I crouched behind a stack of crates and barrels and listened.

"Fates and feathers," Tiesa growled as she landed beside me. "You are a liability, Pace. What do you think you're doing?"

"I want to know what they're saying."

I ignored her answering glare, my attention fixed on the two women.

"Stay calm," the woman with the short hair soothed, her fingers trailing through Cove's braids as the dragon nuzzled her cheek. "You know what Marlowe said."

Cove shook her head. "If this meeting is so important, my brother should be here himself."

"You know it's too risky for him to leave the islands."

"But it's okay to risk us instead?" Cove turned, taking the woman's hands in hers. "Shanti, if things go bad, you need to get yourself out of here. Promise me."

"I'm not going to promise that, and you know it."

I watched as the two women rested their foreheads together, eyes closed. It was a simple action, but the love between them was almost tangible. The dragon mewled a cry, swapping to Cove's shoulders and wrapping around her neck as smoke plumed into the air.

Laughter broke through the cold morning as the crew helped a man over the side of the ship. He dusted off his long blue velvet coat, the silver embroidery at the sleeves and hem setting him apart from the others that followed. He was a tall slim man, his hair and neatly trimmed beard silvered with age.

"I swear that used to be easier," he boomed, striding across the deck. "I must finally be getting old."

As Cove and Shanti turned to him, I could see wariness smeared across their faces. A flash of gold sliced through the air, piercing Cove's heart, happening so fast, the humans didn't even blink. As Dariel's arrow melted into nothing, the trepidation faded from Cove's face, replaced by a warm smile.

"Lord Bickerstaff," she said, dipping into a graceful bow. "It's been a long time."

"Emeric, please." He smiled back, his arm extending as he sketched his own bow. "It's even longer since I've seen your brother. How is Marlowe?"

"He's in good health, thank you. I'll pass on your regards."

The change in Cove was subtle, but noticeable enough that Shanti regarded her with narrowed eyes.

"Come on." Tiesa nudged me. "Time to go."

"Your dragon is quite the specimen," Emeric said. "I heard they'd begun to repopulate successfully on your islands, but I hadn't dared believe it."

The dragon opened an eye, staring at him in what could only be described as disdain, before huffing a cloud of smoke and returning to sleep.

"Have you considered my proposal?" the older man asked. "I've received word that Lord Diarke is rebuilding his armada. Liridona would be eternally grateful for your support."

I knocked Tiesa's hand away as she poked me again. "Just a minute more."

"Liridona's gratitude is not the issue," Cove said. "Who will protect the Wendell Islands if our defences are destroyed?"

Emeric shook his head. "If we are to stand against Diarke and the Midnight Queen, we must unite."

"The Midnight Queen is dead," Shanti said, causing Cove to snap her head towards her. "No one has heard from her in years."

"Just because no one has heard from her, does not mean she's dead," Emeric replied. "I have it on good authority that she and Diarke are joining forces. If we face them separately, we will be decimated. We only stand a chance together."

My head spun at the onslaught of information, and I scrambled to piece together the names and places. There were four human lands and every Cupid worth their feathers knew they had been at war for centuries. It was only thanks to the intervention of the Fates that humans hadn't wiped themselves out completely.

"Pace," Tiesa hissed. "This is none of our concern. We must get back to The Crossing."

I turned to look at her. "How is it not our concern? The Fates sent us to ensure this meeting went well, which means it must be important. Don't you want to know whether it worked?"

"First of all," she said, her wings ruffling. "The Fates sent Dariel, not you. And no, it doesn't matter if it worked or not. We carry out our orders and leave."

I raised an eyebrow. "Sounds boring to me."

"I don't care if it sounds boring. If we don't get going, Dariel is going to shoot you. I can feel him glaring at you from here."

"Oh, calm your wings," I said. "What's a few minutes?"

Tiesa huffed beside me and out of the corner of my eye, I saw her gesticulate her frustration up towards where Dariel was still perched. He'd be furious, but I couldn't find it in myself to care as I grasped at the sliver of freedom with both hands.

"Fine. Let's stay," she said, sarcasm dripping from every syllable. "Let's stay until dark and the demons arrive."

"Will you relax? It's still morning." I tried to keep my voice even. "A few more minutes, that's all I'm asking for. Then you and Dariel can drag me back to Hehven."

Something softened in her eyes, and she shook her head. "Fine. Five minutes. Not a second more."

Giving her a wink, I tugged her braid. "Thanks, Tee."

"Give me some facts and figures," Cove said. "How many ships you have. How many soldiers. The extent of your arsenal. I'll go back to Marlowe and we can decide whether your alliance stands a chance in Hell of working."

My ears pricked up at the mention of the lands fabled to exist on the other side of The Crossing—a dark world filled with demons. I hadn't realised humans were aware of its existence.

Emeric gestured to the man and woman waiting a respectful distance beside him, clutching scrolls and books. "I came here prepared to be transparent. Perhaps you can now understand the severity of our situation."

"Thank you," Cove said, motioning to two of her own crew members to come forward and take the stacks of documents. "Your transparency is appreciated."

Emeric dipped his head in response. "When do you think we might be able to meet again? I don't want to press you, but I fear time is not on our side."

"Perhaps you would come to the Wendell Islands for the Festival of Fates?"

An audible gasp slipped from Shanti's mouth and Cove shot her a warning look.

"I would be honoured," Emeric replied. "It's been many years since I last visited your islands."

"War has a funny way of interfering with holiday plans," Shanti muttered.

Cove placed a hand on her shoulder, squeezing. "Hopefully we are at the beginning of putting war behind us once and for all."

"My sentiments exactly," Emeric said, a beaming smile lighting his face. "I will bring additional offerings and hope our steps toward peace please the Fates."

"That's it," Tiesa hissed at my ear, her fingers digging into my arm. "We leave. Now."

Knowing I had already pushed my luck, I reluctantly followed her lead as she stepped back from our hiding place and launched herself into the air without looking back.

I rode the current, soaring high above the dark blue waters until the ships were dots beneath us. The sun was almost directly above and, as I dipped my wing, its rays caused the gold marking my feathers as royal to glow. Something huge and solid barrelled into me from the side and I plummeted, my wings beating hard as I regained my balance.

"You promised." Dariel snarled, grabbing the front of my shirt, and hauling me to him.

Taking his fist in my hands, I growled as I shoved him away. "What's your problem?"

"My problem is you," he replied, blue eyes blazing. "You begged me to bring you and promised you'd be no trouble."

"How exactly was I trouble?" I argued. "You completed your mission, and we weren't seen."

Dariel stared at me, his jaw set, before pulling a large hand over his face. "If anything happened to you, Cousin . . ."

I clasped his shoulder. "Nothing happened."

"Was it worth it?" he asked, his eyes searching mine as his wings pounded the air behind him. "Risking our safety? My position as captain? Did you satisfy your curiosity?"

"Come on," Tiesa called, swooping past. "We've still got to get through The Crossing without anyone seeing him."

Dariel stared at me a moment longer before shrugging off my hand and following her. I pushed down the feeling of guilt, sharp in my gut, as the wind whipped around me. The truth was, I wasn't satisfied. I had nothing but questions and my moment of freedom was over.

2
Sirain

Sweat stung my eyes as I roared with the effort of swinging my blade. It smashed against the gleaming metal of my opponent's sword and the impact shook my bones, reverberating violently through my teeth. I barely had time to catch my breath before he struck again. Stumbling backwards onto one knee, I raised my weapon above my head to block his next blow.

"Come on, Sirain," Kwellen jeered, shaking sweat-soaked strands of long dark hair from his eyes. "Is that all you've got?"

Gritting my teeth, I extended my black wings, pushing up off the ground as I charged, forcing him backwards. My next swing sliced across his shoulder, and he bellowed a filthy curse. I only had a second to grin before he turned his gleaming black blade in his hand, determination flashing in his midnight blue eyes. Already aware of the small crowd we'd drawn as the other Hands paused their training to watch, I launched into the air, flying high above the arena. Kwellen's wings were a looming shadow as he followed.

Nestled in the base of the mountains, beneath Hadeon Castle, the training grounds consisted of several flat circular patches clustered around the main arena where crowds would gather to watch the best of the best battle it out for entertainment. The air was ice cold as it blasted through the snow-tipped mountains, and from so high up I could see the rock fade into green forests trailing all the way to the ocean.

"Get back to the ground!"

I raised my eyebrows at Kwellen's command, turning my blade in my hand as I caught my breath. "Why? Worried I'll beat you up here?"

His dark eyes narrowed, and I forced myself to hold his gaze. A beast of a male, he was currently at the top of the list of Chaos fighters, besting warrior after warrior, even with the single arm he was born with. I'd been beaten by him more times than I could count since we were smallwings, although it was always close. He never took it easy on me.

"Because," he said, "I don't feel like being executed by the king for sending the future queen plummeting to her death."

I looked pointedly at the blood trickling from his shoulder. "I'm not the one bleeding."

With a roar of frustration, he dove for me, his wings booming against the air with the effort. I twisted out of the way, which was a mistake, as his blade nicked the edge of my wing causing me to cry out. There was barely a chance to prepare myself before his fist flew at my face. I managed to bend just in time, his knuckles only just grazing my jaw, but it was still enough for the tang of blood to coat my tongue.

"Have you had enough, Princess?"

I glared at him, trying to hide the fact that I could no longer extend my right wing without a jolt of searing pain. "No."

"Don't make me knock you out," he said with a sigh. "Your father already hates me."

"He hates everyone."

Kwellen rotated his shoulder, his muscles flexing beneath his pale skin as he adjusted the grip on his sword. "That might be true, but I'm pretty sure knocking you out isn't part of my job description as your personal guard."

"I wish my father had never given you the job. You're no fun anymore." I rolled my eyes and sheathed my sword. "Fine. Let's call it a tie."

"A tie?" He bellowed a laugh. "You're about a minute from falling out of the sky. I can see how much that wing is hurting you."

Flinging a rude gesture over my shoulder I dived back down to the ground. I'd barely gathered my wings before a healer rushed over to tend to my wound.

"See to Lord Devland first," I said, pointing to Kwellen. "I'm not even bleeding that much."

The healers ignored my request, slathering a foul-smelling ointment on my black feathers as my friend watched and grinned.

"I can't believe you went for her face, Kwellen."

I snorted as my cousin sauntered over, his face red from the exertion of his own match. "When have you ever known him to go easy on me, Odio?"

"Good point." He chuckled. "Most of the Hands are fighting with a no faces rule this week."

Kwellen's booming laugh echoed around the arena. "I wouldn't expect anything less from you preening pretty boys."

I couldn't keep the smirk from my face as Odio scowled at him. Even covered in cuts and bruises, Kwellen was never short of female attention. "High hopes for my brother's birthday then, Cousin?"

"Always," he said with a smirk. "Fin's been shouting from the mountain tops that the Spring Festival of Fates will pale in comparison to the celebration."

My answering laughter filled the air. "Modesty is not one of his strong suits."

The very idea that my little brother's eighteenth birthday could compare to the Spring Festival of Fates was absurd. An entire day of music, food, dancing, fighting and anything else that might take your fancy, Festivals allowed every citizen of Helle to give thanks to the Fates and let off steam. There were no rules on Festival days and just the thought of the upcoming celebration made my blood tingle.

Of course, I didn't get to blow off steam with quite the same recklessness as my friends. Being Crown Princess came with certain responsibilities. Even more so when I turned twenty in a few months.

"Why do you look like someone just shoved your face in Kwellen's armpit?" Odio asked, something close to concern in his garnet-flecked eyes.

"It's the stench of that Fated ointment," I lied. "It's turning my stomach."

Kwellen stepped over, peering down at the wound from his great height. "Barely a scratch. Nothing to worry about."

"I didn't say it was," I snapped, testing my wings. It still stung but not enough to stop me from flying. "I'm going to get cleaned up."

Without awaiting a response, I spread my wings and pushed off into the air. Hewn from the same dark rock as the mountain, the castle was as foreboding as it was beautiful. My rooms were in one of the towers in the east wing, with windows large enough I could fly in and out with ease, and the view from them was one of the few things that calmed me, no matter what was on my mind. On a clear day, I could see all the way to the wastelands of Nefret, with the undulating waves of colour that formed The Crossing lingering just beyond the water.

Hoisting myself through the peaked window, I smiled at the view over my shoulder before propping my sword against the wall with the others and kicking off my boots. Servants had already filled my bath, anticipating my return from training, and I trailed my fingers through the steaming water, groaning as I inhaled the soothing scent of lavender. Leather clunked to the floor as I quickly shed my layers and lowered myself in, a hiss escaping my lips at the heat. My muscles were still uncoiling when a knock sounded at the door, causing me to tense.

"Your Majesty? Would you like assistance with your wings?"

"No."

Listening to the footsteps as they retreated down the stone stairway, I waited for silence before finally closing my eyes and sinking back against the marbled rim of the bath. My water-logged feathers tugged me beneath the water, and I let them, sinking below into blissful silence. There was something numbing about the muted stillness of being under water. I stayed submerged until my lungs burned.

Bursting to the surface with a gasp, I pushed the strands of soaking hair from my face and rested against the edge, breathing heavily. I wasn't sure how long I lay there replaying my sparring session with Kwellen over and over, searching for ways to better myself, but it felt like mere seconds before the water turned cool enough to draw a shudder. Quickly soaping myself down, I washed the sweat from my long black hair, my fingers trailing through the faint purple sheen as it caught in the firelight.

It was almost laughable that my father had assigned my best friend as my personal guard. On a good day, the king didn't care where I was or what I did. Which was fine with me, as he certainly wouldn't approve if he ever found out where I was most nights. Shivering in the cool afternoon air, I climbed out and dried myself before pulling on a simple black dress.

As I turned my back to the fire to dry my wings, I realised that the foul-smelling ointment the healers had applied to my wing had worked faster than anticipated because, as I tested them, stretching them out to their full length, the sting had completely gone.

Once my feathers were dry, I grabbed an apple from a bowl on the dresser, and took up my favourite perch at the window, staring out at the view. I had only taken my first bite when an enormous, winged figure dropped down into view, causing me to fall backwards into my room.

"What do you think you're doing?" my father barked.

I scrambled to my feet, the apple rolling under the bed. "I was having a snack and then you tried to kill me."

My father landed on the wide ledge, folding his wings as he stepped down into my room. His pale, cruel face twisted into a sneer as he looked around. "If I'd wanted to kill you, you'd be dead."

"Comforting words, Father. To what do I owe this pleasure?"

"Where have you been?" he asked, raising an eyebrow at the cold bath water. "Why are you bathing at this time of the day?"

I folded my arms across my chest, my fingers digging into my skin. "I trained with Kwellen this morning."

His lip curled but he said nothing. He didn't approve of the amount of time I spent training, but I suspected somewhere beneath his sneer, there was a part of him that respected my strength.

"People are asking where you are," he said, turning to look out of the window.

I stared at his back, wondering if he saw the same view I did. "Which people? And I'm here. I'm always here."

My father whirled, his flowing black robes an extension of his wings as he flew across the room. There was no time to react before his hand wrapped around my throat knocking me from my feet. Dragged through the air, my hands flew to his, trying to prise myself free, but then my back smacked against the stone wall, wings splayed, as the breath was shoved violently from my lungs.

"You will speak to me with respect," he snarled. Flecks of spittle hit my face, causing me to turn my head, but he gripped my chin, turning me back to face him. "If you were not my daughter, I would have had you killed in the arena years ago."

"I love you too, Father," I gritted out, knowing full well the defiance in my eyes might push him over the edge. I didn't care.

He glared at me, the dark red swirling in his eyes clear at such close quarters. I forced myself to meet his stare, preparing for whatever came next, but he let go and I sank against the wall.

"The lords and ladies of Helle are reporting to me in an hour," he said, striding back to the window. "Be there."

Without waiting for a response, he plummeted, the snap of his wings carrying into my room on the wind. I rubbed my jaw, my stomach already coiling with dread at the thought of sitting through hours of lords and ladies giving meaningless reports from their cities. I decided to keep on the simple dress I was wearing but added a bodice of silver chains. My gaze flitted to the tiara on my dresser, but I ignored it. He said to be there, but he didn't say I had to dress up.

An hour. I hastily braided my hair over my shoulder as I made my way through my rooms. Just enough time to find food to get me through the presentations. I decided to take the stairs as there was less risk of running into my father again, but quickly realised my mistake as I reached the bottom of the tower. My attempt to melt into the shadows failed as my brother halted his stride, pinning me with a sneer eerily identical to our father's.

"There you are," he said, his dark eyes narrowed as he looked me up and down. "Father was looking for you."

The finger marks on my chin throbbed in response. "Yeah, he found me."

I descended the final couple of steps and made to continue to the kitchen, but Fin stepped in front of me, his black wings flaring wide enough to block the entire corridor. Even at almost two years younger, he was beginning to tower over me. In a fair fight, he knew I would win, but cornered in a dark corridor without weapons . . . I swallowed and schooled my face into a sneer to match his. "The Hands are excited about your birthday, Brother. I hear it's going to rival the Festival."

"What can I say?" He took the smallest step closer, his wings lifting to block me against the stairwell. "The people are excited to celebrate the birth of their favourite royal."

The way he looked at me sent shards of ice through my bones and I fought the shudder rising in my gut. His closely shorn hair only served to accentuate the sharp angles of his cruel face and I tensed, as though preparing for a cold blade to slip between my ribs. I wouldn't put it past him.

"Favourite royal?" I echoed. "Was there a vote no one told me about? Does our beloved sister know?"

He stepped closer, leaving me no choice but to move backwards. My ankles knocked against the bottom step, and I stumbled.

"Where is your guard?" Fin asked, his eyes never leaving mine as I tried to stand my ground.

"Do I need a guard?"

He shrugged. "I'm just being observant. He's not doing a very good job. Perhaps you should hire one that has all their limbs."

"You know damn well, Kwellen is the best fighter in Helle. And I didn't hire him. Father did." My jaw clenched and my fingers flexed at my sides, itching to wrap themselves around my brother's neck.

His eyes flitted to the movement, and he smiled. "Maybe the old male is losing his grip on reality."

"Move out of the way, Fin. Don't make me knock you to the floor."

He laughed, cold and quiet, and the hairs on the back of my neck rose in response. "You're coming to the presentation."

It was more of a statement than a question, so I held his stare. Waiting.

"I've been attending the presentations for months," he said, his voice barely above a whisper. "It's a travesty that you were first born. Helle deserves so much better."

My fists clenched at my sides, and it took every ounce of strength not to connect one with his sharp jaw. Instead, I used the sides of the stairwell to propel myself forward, my wings flaring as I reached out and shoved him out of the way. He moved without resistance, and I stalked off, refusing to dignify his words with a response. His cold laughter echoed off the stone walls, chasing me all the way to the kitchens.

A familiar figure was already seated at one of the large wooden tables, a mountain of bread and butter before him. I smiled at the stripe of black-red hair; the sides shaved.

"Hungry, Cousin?"

Odio glanced over his shoulder, his cheeks bulging. "Mmhm."

I slid onto the bench beside him, snatching a hunk of bread from his plate. He reached out and plucked it from my fingers before it could reach my mouth.

"Get your own," he snarled.

A servant placed a plate of fresh bread and cheese in front of me before I could respond, and I grunted my thanks. "Have you got orders tonight?"

Odio paused in his chewing, his eyebrows raised in question. "Why? You want to come?"

I looked away, focusing on the bread as I shredded it between my fingers. "Of course."

"What happened?"

"My father. Fin. Take your pick."

Odio stared at me for a moment before leaning closer, his face close enough that I could smell the salted butter on his breath. "I could kill him if you wanted."

Something cold settled in my stomach. "Who?"

He blinked as though it was obvious. "Fin."

With no idea whether he was being serious or not, I turned my attention back to my bread. "Do you have orders or not?"

"Yes."

I breathed a sigh of relief. "Kwellen will want to come too."

Odio swore around his mouthful of food, and I laughed. Despite the constant teasing, I was sure they liked each other, but with my cousin, you could never be sure.

"I'll meet you at The Crossing at dusk, like usual," he said, dusting crumbs from his tunic and dragging the back of his hand across his mouth.

"Do you require anything else, Lord Hadeon?" a servant asked, bowing low as my cousin stood.

He dismissed her with a wave of his hand, his attention focused on me. "Don't be late or I'll leave without you."

I gave him a withering look before returning to my food. I was never late. It had been almost a week since I'd last travelled through The Crossing to the human world, and it was eating away at me like an addiction. Excitement fizzled in my gut. I had been accompanying Odio on his Hand missions for a little over a year and even though I was fairly certain most of the Hands in his division knew, none of them would be foolish enough to tell the king. Not when they knew I'd be queen one day and their name would be one I would certainly remember. And not favourably.

Shoving a chunk of bread in my pocket and another in my mouth, I dusted off my hands and made my way toward the throne room. At least now, I had something to look forward to.

3
Pace

This was a bad idea. A really bad idea. The air was like water, flickering in blinding green and blue as it wrapped around my limbs, filling my lungs, and smothering my senses. Beating my wings harder, I propelled myself forward, knowing the rippling folds of The Crossing couldn't go on forever. When I'd passed through them with Tiesa and Dariel earlier that day, I hadn't paid much attention to direction, too awed at being inside the mysterious curtain of lights I'd stared at from afar my whole life.

Pity. That had been the only reason Dariel relented, allowing me to accompany him to the human world after months of asking. We both knew it. A growl of frustration rippled in my throat, and I tensed my shoulders, pressing harder through the shimmering air. Returning to the human world alone and after dark was reckless, even for me, but after forcing my friends to stay longer on the ship, I knew I'd ruined any chance of a repeat visit with them. If I wanted answers, my only choice was to go alone.

Steadying the pounding of my wings, I turned a wary circle, trying and failing to see anything around me but undulating colour. From a distance, The Crossing was beautiful, a mass of shimmering columns of multi-coloured light. Being inside, it turned out, was a wholly different experience. All sense of direction had vanished, and I couldn't have turned back if I'd wanted to. There was nothing to do but fly and hope for the best. Bowing my head against the disorientating lights, I pushed forward.

When I felt the light thinning, hints of dark sky appearing in patches, I didn't dare believe my senses. Bursting from The Crossing, my senses screamed at the sudden return of their use, and I blinked as my eyes adjusted to the darkness. The sky was littered with bright stars, looking so much like Hehven, I couldn't help but wonder whether after everything, I was back home. Even as I allowed my gaze to fall from the full moon and smattering of stars, the sound of waves and occasional caw of a seabird told me I wasn't. Below me, the sea was vast and black, the moonlight painting the wave tips silver as they were pushed, shimmering, by the breeze. There was nothing but water in all directions and, for a moment, I was as disorientated as I had been inside The Crossing.

Once again, I was confronted by what a profoundly idiotic idea this was. I should have worn Tiesa down instead. I could even have tried to find another Hand to bring me. There were a few female Hands I'd flirted with often enough; I could likely have persuaded one of them to help me. As I took in the foreboding darkness both above and below, however, I shoved the thought away. My hand moved to the hilt of the golden sword slung at my hip. If I was going to be reckless, it was better not to involve anyone else. With the sea dark and endless below me, I chose a direction and flew.

One thing I hadn't considered was the distance. I'd been flying for hours and with the journey that morning, combined with a few hours of training that afternoon, I hadn't allowed myself enough time to rest. The honed muscles in my back groaned in protest, and I dipped a little lower to the surface of the sea. Gritting my teeth, Tiesa's face filled my mind, a knowing smile on her lips telling me I was too cocky for my own good. I had no idea how long it had taken me to make my way through The Crossing, but it had felt twice as long as it had the first time. I needed a break. Whether it was an island, a boat, or even a piece of driftwood, I needed to find somewhere to rest my wings.

Minutes or hours later, I couldn't be sure, I found myself dipping lower still to the choppy surface of the sea. My exhaustion was so thorough, that when I spotted the silhouette of a ship on the horizon, I was certain it was my mind playing tricks on me. The sensation of my feet dragging in the icy water jolted me and, my heart pounding with renewed adrenaline, I forced my wings to beat harder to regain some height. My hands clenched into fists at my side as I fought against plummeting into the freezing waters, hoping against hope the vision was real.

Somewhere behind me, the sound of wings disturbed the silence and my hand moved to my sword, hoping it was just a trick of my mind. If it really was wings, it couldn't be anything good.

"Are you going to make it?"

I started at the sound of Dariel's voice and looked up to find him flying just above me, his face dark with rage. Glancing at the ship, I nodded. "If that's a real ship, yes."

"Good."

He flew on toward the vessel, swooping over it in loops, checking to see whether it was safe. Summoning the last of my strength, I soared up the side of the ship and over the railing before collapsing unceremoniously on the quarterdeck. I leaned my head back against the cold, damp wood, my chest aching with every ragged breath as I stared up at the gathered sails. I realised with surprise, it was the same boat as that morning. Cove's ship.

Dariel descended before me on silent feet, watching, waiting as my breathing evened. "Why?"

I swiped at my brow, shoving my sweat-soaked hair from my face before sitting up and resting my forearms on my knees. "How did you know where I was?"

"You could have died."

I suppressed a shiver as I stared up at him, jaw clenched.

"Tiesa went to your place to talk to you." Dariel sat down beside me with a heavy sigh, his eyes continuously searching the skies. "She was worried you'd do something stupid. It turns out she was right."

"Where is she?"

"Waiting to raise the alarm if I don't come back with you in the next couple of hours."

I rolled my aching shoulders, the muscles earned through hours of combat training barking in protest.

"Why?" Dariel repeated. "Why would you go through The Crossing alone? At night, no less. Are you actually trying to get yourself killed?"

I frowned at the deck, painted silver by the moonlight, wondering how many humans were slumbering below. "It seemed pretty straight forward when I came through with you and Tiesa. I thought I could get my answers and be back before anyone realised. And, yes. As soon as I flew into The Crossing, I realised what a monumental mistake it was."

"You should have asked—"

"There's no way you would have let me come with you again."

Dariel stared at me, and I held his gaze defiantly. He looked away first, his attention falling to the gilded sword at my side. He raised his eyebrows. "Please don't tell me you were planning on killing a human."

"What? Of course, not. It's for protection."

The corners of Dariel's mouth twitched as he returned his

attention to the clear night sky. "How exactly was the sword going to protect you from drowning?"

I reached out and shoved him as he chuckled. The reality wasn't lost on me, though, and I relented. "Sorry."

Dariel huffed a laugh. "Whatever. You've been apologising for stunts like this since you learnt to fly."

"What are you talking about?"

"The time you convinced me to climb the highest peak in Dragoste on the coldest night of the year? The time you decided it was a good idea to jump off the cliffs and see if we could pull up before we hit the water. The time you—"

"Okay, okay, okay." I held my hands up, leaning my head back against the railing. "I get it."

"As soon as you feel strong enough, we need to head back."

The idea of flying over the vast ocean, through The Crossing and across Hehven to the royal city of Dragoste sent my shoulders into a slump. "Can't we just hide until morning?"

"If we do that, Tiesa will raise the alarm and we'll have every Hand under my command flying through The Crossing to look for you."

I groaned. "Great."

After a moment's silence, Dariel turned to me. "What answers did you want that were worth risking your life for?"

"You wouldn't understand."

"Try me."

Countless stars were splashed across the sky above us and as I tried to gather my thoughts, I wondered whether anyone had ever tried to count them. "The humans were talking about the war," I explained. "They mentioned the Festival. And Helle. I need to know whether they know about Hehven too. Whether they know about us."

Dariel's answering silence stretched on for longer than I could bear, and when I looked away from the sky, I found him frowning. "What?"

"How would you get answers to those questions, Pace? Were you planning on talking to the humans?"

"No. Of course, not."

"How, then?"

I fumbled for the words to explain my plan, but I didn't really have one. "I was going to watch and listen."

"Do you honestly think you would have found all your answers in one night?"

He wasn't expecting an answer, so I didn't give one, glaring at the mast jutting up from the centre of the ship instead. Maybe I had planned on coming back more than once. I honestly hadn't thought past getting through The Crossing.

"This is exactly why your parents arranged your marriage," Dariel muttered.

I tensed, turning to him. "What are you talking about?"

"You know I love you, Pace—you're like a brother to me—but you leap first and think second." He shook his head, causing his long white braid to slip over his shoulder. "If the king and queen found out about the tournaments . . ."

I leaned my head back and closed my eyes with a sigh. "You honestly think they don't already know?"

"Why isn't it enough to train with me?" Dariel pushed. "Is it that different?"

"You should live a little and come to a tournament, Cousin." I smiled. "Training is pretty. It's conditioning. The tournaments are a true test of skill and strength. When you're fighting someone who's actually trying to wound you . . . Yes, Dariel. It's that different."

"Well, morally questionable fighting aside, you know there are other concerns," he continued. "Your timekeeping, your attitude, the amount of time you spend unaccompanied with females—"

"Now you sound like my parents." I opened my eyes and

looked at him. "And they really think marriage will remedy that impressive list of faults?"

Dariel rubbed his hands over his face, his gaze returning to the sky. I wondered whether it was because he was still scanning for danger, or because he couldn't bring himself to look at me. "Caitland is sweet, sensible. Dedicated. Level-headed. They're hoping she balances you out."

I choked a laugh, but before I could respond, Dariel threw out an arm, pressing me backwards against the side of the ship.

Three black-winged figures swooped over our heads, silent against the inky blanket of sky. Dariel clasped my arm, tugging me behind the same crates I had watched the humans from that morning. It felt like a lifetime ago.

"Tuck your wings in as much as you can," he whispered, his eyes fixed on the figures as they circled above us. "Fates save us. We might as well be waving at them."

The moonlight caught the creatures as they turned, and my stomach lurched. Their faces were spiked twists with small obsidian eyes and red horns, their bodies clad head to toe in black leather and dark metal. *Demons*. I noted the large blades two of them carried strapped to their backs. The third demon carried a black bow, a quiver of onyx arrows between his wings.

Tales of demons were used to stop children straying into the woods or wandering into The Crossing. I had never really believed they were real. But there they were. The stuff of nightmares.

They landed on the deck, soundlessly creeping toward the cabin, where a faint amber glow flickered beyond the window. Someone was still awake, or had perhaps fallen asleep with the lamp still burning. A million questions twitched on my tongue, but I forced my lips together. From the look on his face, Dariel didn't have any more answers than I did.

The demons huddled together in a mass of black wings, and I could make out voices, but not words. The one with the arrows strode across the deck, stooping to pick something up. I couldn't tell what it was and as Dariel's hand clamped down on my shoulder, shoving me backwards, I realised I'd risen from our hiding place to better see what was going on. I shrugged off his hand, my body tensed. Were the demons going to harm the humans? Something hard and hot burned in the pit of my stomach at the thought and my hand moved to my sword.

Two of the demons flared their wings, shooting up into the rigging while the third threw the object at the window. As it bounced off the glass, falling to the deck with a clatter, he launched himself upwards out of sight, perching amongst the ropes with the others. Their backs to us, they were almost invisible against the night sky. With our white hair and feathers, I was painfully aware that if they turned around, there was no way they wouldn't see us.

The cabin door swung open, and Cove strode out, sword in one hand, lamp in the other. She looked around, eyes narrowed, searching for the source of the noise. A faint whistle filled the air and my wings flared as a black arrow pierced Cove's heart. She shuddered, a frown overcoming her features, before turning and striding back into the cabin, slamming the door behind her.

I stared at the cabin, my head spinning. What had that arrow done? I turned to Dariel, but his gaze was fixed on the demons. Their mission apparently complete, they extended their wings, shooting up into the night sky. I watched for a second as they swooped in and out of each other's way as though playing. For a second, I swore I heard laughter, but it must have been a bird. As soon as they were far enough away, the questions tumbled from my lips.

"What in the Fates was that?" I demanded. "What does a demon arrow do?"

Dariel shook his head, his dark brown skin glowing almost

blue in the moonlight. When his eyes met mine, I saw nothing but confusion. "We need to get out of here."

Nodding in agreement, I stood, stretching my wings. I was still exhausted, but launching myself into the air, I hoped the adrenaline coursing through my veins would be enough to get me home. My wings had barely unfurled in their second beat against the cool night air when a shout rang out across the water. Dariel glanced back at me over his shoulder, his face the picture of dismay as he watched whatever was behind us. I didn't need to look to know what he saw.

I straightened my body, streamlining myself, as I rode the wind to catch up with my cousin. Only when I drew level with him did I push every ounce of strength into flying as fast as I could. It was all I could do to focus on beating my wings instead of lingering on the questions roaring in my head. What would they do if they caught us? Could they follow us into The Crossing?

"Come on, Pace," Dariel urged, his features lined with fear as he shot a glance over his shoulder again.

Bowing my head against the wind, I pushed myself harder. My wings beat relentlessly, my muscles taut as I worked them despite their painful protest. No matter how much I tried, I didn't seem to be going fast enough. On a good day, I was faster than Dariel, but I realised with a sickening jolt that now, I was the one holding him back. If only one of us could survive the demons, he had the better chance. The beating of my wings slowed as I tried to find the words to tell him he should go on without me and get help.

"Don't even think about it," Dariel snapped, reading the resignation on my face. "Come on. We're almost there."

He was surely lying. I had flown further than this before. Something hard and black slammed into my side, knocking the breath from my lungs and I fell from the sky, plummeting towards the inky sea. Dariel shouted something but it was muffled by the blood roaring in my ears as I struggled to right myself. I twisted, the tip of my ivory wing tracing the freezing water as I swooped upwards, only to find myself face to face with the largest of the demons.

"Who are you?" he boomed, his midnight wings merging with the darkness.

I tried to fly around him, but he blocked me, anticipating my move. My hand went to my sword, but before my fingers could grasp the hilt, the demon had his own obsidian blade in his hand.

"Don't even think about it," he growled.

I realised with a start, he only had one arm, his left coming to an end just before his elbow. If only I could draw my weapon, I was confident I could beat him. The clash of metal on metal filled the air and I looked past him to find Dariel, sword drawn, fighting the other demon.

"Leave him alone," I demanded. "We're no threat to you. Let us go."

The demon snorted. "We'll decide who's a threat and who's not."

"Lower your weapon," another male voice called from the darkness.

I looked up to find the archer, an arrow nocked and pointed at Dariel. My cousin glanced between us all, weighing the situation before reluctantly lowering his blade.

"There's a small island just over there," the demon with the bow called out.

Squinting into the darkness, I could just about make out what looked like a smattering of rocks. "Why?" I asked. "If you want to talk, why not here?"

The large demon drifted closer; his blade almost close enough to touch my chest. "Because I can tell you're about to drop out of the sky and dead males don't speak."

An answering snarl curled in the back of my throat. There

was no denying it. I knew the beating of my wings was unsteady but the idea of the demons thinking of me as weak set my blood on fire.

"Let's go," the demon with the bow called.

Dariel met my gaze with a slight nod, and I knew he was thinking the same thing. We'd be stronger on land and although it was nothing more than a collection of sand and rocks, every second of rest my wings could get would improve our chance of escape. If we were going to have to fight our way out, this was our best option.

"Fine," I said, glaring at the dark holes I assumed were the demon's eyes.

The archer kept back, his arrow trained on Dariel as we flew to the island, while the larger demon flew beside me, his sword steady in his meaty hand and pointed at my throat. I landed beside Dariel, and together we faced the demons as they advanced towards us, weapons raised.

"Who are you?" the biggest demon repeated, his deep voice reverberating in my bones. "Or even better, *what* are you?"

I raised my chin. "I was wondering the same thing about you."

"The ones with the sharp pointy things get to ask the questions." He stepped toward me, his blade angled at my throat.

Dariel moved to block him, but I threw out an arm, keeping him back. I knew he would lay down his life for me in an instant, but I didn't want the demons knowing that. I didn't want them knowing anything about us.

Every sinew of my body tensed as I wondered whether we could take out all three of them. Possibly, if I'd been at full strength. Looking at them, it felt safe to assume demons were strong warriors. Our best bet was to try and take down the archer and simply outfly the other two. First, however, I'd have to disarm the big guy.

"Fine. We'll tell you who we are," I said, looking pointedly above his head, "as soon as our friends land."

He turned, glancing over his shoulder, but by the time he snapped his head back with a snarl, we had our weapons drawn.

My lips curled into a grin. "I suppose we can add gullible to the top of the list of things we know about demons."

With a roar, the demon lashed out with his sword. It took both my arms to absorb the blow and I was still drawing a breath when he struck again. The smallest demon slipped forward, launching gracefully into the air before bringing his blade down on Dariel. He blocked it, swinging his sword with enough force to push the smaller demon backwards.

The rocks were slippery, and I alternated between standing and hovering as I found myself being pushed across the barren island by the one-armed demon. Sweat trickled down my back as I tried to land a blow, a whisper of panic settling in my gut. I was good. I was more than good. But I was running on empty, and as the behemoth tried to separate my head from my body, I realised the demons were fighting as though their lives depended on it. Letting loose a snarl, I swung at the brute with all my strength.

He parried my blow, and I stepped back, my legs smacking against a cluster of waist-height boulders. As he swung his sword, I tucked in my wings and twisted to the side, leaving his blade to smash into the rocks. The demon was still pulling his weapon free, mid yell, when I slipped around him and raised my sword. I hesitated for the briefest of seconds. They were demons, but could I bring myself to kill one? With a growl of frustration, I smashed the hilt of my sword down onto the back of his head.

The continuing clash of metal on metal rang out across the rocks and I sprinted over to where Dariel was fighting both the archer and the smaller demon. The archer had tucked his bow between his wings and was wielding a long knife. I launched myself forward, swinging my blade at his weapon in hope of disarming him but the smaller demon whirled at me, the tip of his sword slicing across my chest.

I cursed and Dariel used the distraction to knock the knife from the archer's grip, slamming the hilt against the side of his head and sending him to the ground. I could tell the wound to my chest wasn't deep, despite the warm wetness soaking through my shirt, and for the first time since the demons had found us, I felt an inkling of hope. We both turned on the smaller demon, who backed away, sword raised.

At the sound of an intake of breath behind me, I turned just in time to block the giant demon's blow before it sliced through me. He swung again and I bent out of the way, tucking my wings in tight. Dariel launched at him, but the beast was too fast. Too strong. He swung at my cousin, the blade slicing along his upper arm. Dariel roared as blood splattered against his wings, the red stark against the ivory and gold. I lifted my sword to strike, but the smaller demon launched at me, drawing me away.

Despite the smaller demon's size, his movements were like water, rippling with such speed and agility it took all my concentration to block the onslaught of attacks. My wounded chest throbbed in time with my rapid heartbeat as I clenched my jaw and tried to disarm my opponent. To my left, the grunting and clanging of swords were my only indication that my cousin was still standing.

The small demon slipped on a seaweed covered rock and I seized my chance, bringing the hilt of my sword down on his wrists before thrusting it up into his jaw. The demon stumbled backwards, his head flying from his shoulders and landing on the rocks. I backed away, my eyes wide, as I took in the crumpled face lying on the moonlit ground. It was only when I turned back, horror-struck, to the demon, I realised my mistake. The demon's head remained firmly on his shoulders. *Her* shoulders. My arm dropped to my side as I watched the female in front of me stoop to pick up her weapon. *They're wearing masks.* I couldn't do anything but stare as she turned to me, swiping an arm across her bleeding mouth.

My sword was knocked from my hand with a blow that sent shrieking pain across my wrist right before an arm wrapped itself around my throat, pulling me backwards. I shoved and pulled but the larger demon held me tighter, his grip tensing until I felt my wings on the verge of snapping between us. Gritting my teeth, I stopped struggling and tried to catch my breath.

"Let him go," Dariel barked, his eyes fixed on the archer demon, who had his bow back in his hands, an arrow trained on him.

"Put down your sword or I'll snap his neck," the large demon snarled in response.

He tightened his grip, his bicep swelling against my throat, and I clawed at it, gasping for air. I couldn't bring myself to look at my cousin, but I heard the exhale of defeat followed by the clink of metal on stone as he laid his weapon on the ground.

The female stepped forward, her sword angled at my face. "What were you doing on that ship?"

I stared, unable to form a coherent response. She wasn't a demon. At least, not like any demon I had ever imagined. Her skin was like moonlight, her eyes as dark as the surrounding sea, and her face a graceful symphony of cheekbones and pale pink lips. Although braided back, I could see from the strands that had worked themselves free, her hair was as black as her wings. She was beautiful. My gaze drifted lower, and she took another step forward, pressing the tip of her sword to my chest, right at the top of the wound.

"Have you never seen a female before?" she sneered, her eyes narrowed.

She might not have been an actual demon, but as she

pressed the tip of the sword harder, I reminded myself that she may as well be. "What were *you* doing on the boat?"

"I'm asking the questions. What were you doing on the boat? Tell us or I'll start taking slices until one of you feels like talking." I pressed my lips together and she sighed. "I was really hoping you'd be cooperative."

"Start with his fingers and when you run out, we'll hack off his wings," my captor growled, his breath uncomfortably warm against my ear.

Panic began to flicker in my chest, and I tried once more to struggle free, my hands prying at the enormous forearm against my windpipe, but his vice-like grip didn't falter. Instead, he tightened it, causing my vision to swim.

"I like that idea," she said, tilting her head as though considering. "We can leave his pretty face for last. Although, if he passes out, he won't be able to say much at all."

The grip around my throat loosened and I gulped at the cold night air.

"Three questions," she said. "What are you? Where are you from? What were you doing on the ship?"

"Go back to Helle," I snarled.

Her lips curled in amusement. "We'd love to. Just as soon as you answer my questions. It seems unfair that you know where we're from, but we know nothing about you. Unless . . ." She paused, eyes widening. "No."

"Don't tell them anything," Dariel bit out.

The female stepped closer, angling her sword between us as she peered at me. "It couldn't be," she whispered.

"No," the archer said, barking a cruel laugh. "I know what you're thinking and there's no way."

I tried to swallow, my mouth bone dry, as her gaze slowly trailed over every inch of me.

"Cupids," she murmured.

The demon holding me snorted. "Don't be ridiculous. Cupids are a myth."

"Do I look like a myth?" I snarled.

The female's face lit up in triumph and Dariel groaned.

"Well, I never," she said, pressing her sword hard enough to make my jaw clench as she leaned closer. "What a turn of events."

She was so close I could smell her—a mix of leather and something familiar—something floral I couldn't place.

"Get away from him," Dariel warned.

Turning from me, she raised her dark eyebrows. "You're not in a position to make demands. You're very protective of this one. What is he? Your brother? Lover?"

Dariel glared at her but said nothing.

"Interesting." She pressed the tip of her sword into my wound, drawing a hiss from my lips. Pulling the blade back, she peered at the bloodied end. "They bleed red as we do."

"What are you?" I asked, my voice thick with disgust.

She shrugged. "You called us demons. Let's go with that."

"Let us go," I tried again. "We're no threat to you."

"Clearly." She smirked as she looked me up and down, trapped against her companion.

Gritting my teeth, I decided to up the stakes. "If you don't let us go, others will come looking for us and—"

"Stop!" Dariel barked.

The female's eyes lit up. "Why would they come looking for little old you?"

Ice cold dread coated my skin as I realised my mistake. I had hoped the threat of numbers would deter them, but instead I'd shown them just how valuable we were. The sea lapping at the pitiful excuse for an island was the only sound as she slid her sword up my chest, its tip coming to a rest against my heart. Leaning into it, her face was close enough I could feel her breath. I turned my face away.

"Are you scared of me?" she asked, pressing the tip of her blade hard enough to send a fresh trickle of blood down my chest.

"You're pressing a sword against my heart," I gritted out. "What do you think, demon?"

She withdrew the sword but stayed close, rising up on her toes to inspect me closer still. Her hand reached out to touch my face and I jolted away from her fingers with such force the demon gripping me tightened his hold.

"Don't touch me," I hissed.

Even with everything that had happened, the blood soaking into my shirt, the bitter disappointment of my cousin—even my possible death—I refused to let a bloodthirsty demon touch me. The thought alone turned my stomach, and I glared at the dark-eyed female, forcing every possible inch of hatred into the act.

"It's not just my sword, is it?" She laughed. It was a cruel, cold sound. "What are you scared of, Cupid?"

My blood was on fire, every inch of skin fizzing and burning, wanting to tear these creatures apart feather by feather. As she smirked in my face, it took all my self-control to keep my mouth shut.

"Just let us go," Dariel pleaded. "We were doing nothing on the ship, I swear."

The female's eyebrows rose at his confession, but her eyes stayed fixed on me. "Why are you here, then?"

"We were curious," Dariel said. "We won't do it again. It was stupid."

His shame-laden words were daggers in my chest. I'd never heard my cousin beg before.

"Yes, it was," she said. Her gaze dropped to my mouth, and I swallowed.

"Let him go," Dariel tried again.

"But we were just beginning to have fun." The female

pouted, her dark gaze returning to mine. "You know, I don't think the king will believe we encountered actual real-life Cupids. I'll have to take a souvenir as proof."

Her breath was warm against my skin as she leaned in, and I tried to turn my head, but this time the meaty forearm around my throat kept me locked in place. My jaw clenched at the blatant mix of mischief and curiosity in her eyes, and I watched transfixed, as she dragged her teeth over her bottom lip. My heart hammered in my chest. Was she going to kiss me? A bark of protest gathered in my throat but then released in a roar as searing pain shot along the arch of my wing and down my spine. The female demon stepped back twirling one of my long white feathers between her fingers.

Anger flooded through me, my teeth bared, as I watched her in disbelief. Feathers were not taken. They were given. Different to moulting, the very act of giving someone your feather was intimate—an act of trust and commitment usually performed on a couple's wedding night. My breath came in ragged bursts as I tensed against my captor, but my hate-filled gaze was fixed solely on the female demon in front of me.

Staring at the unbridled rage twisting my features, uncertainty flickered across her face, and she took a step back. It wasn't fast enough. I brought my knees up to my chest, pushing back against the large demon, and my feet collided with her ribs. She flew backwards, her sword skittering along the rocks.

My vision edged with pulsing red as I threw my head back with as much force as I could muster, smashing into the one-armed demon's face. His grip faltered enough for me to twist and kick him between the legs. Roaring in pain, he released me, and I picked up my sword, the waves lapping at the rocky island drowned out by the seething rage roaring in my ears.

The female demon watched wide-eyed, her arm wrapped around her waist, as I took a step toward her, my weapon raised. She spread her sleek black wings and leapt into the air.

"Let's get out of here," she commanded.

The archer leapt up after her, instantly blending in with the night sky. I whirled, my sword raised for retaliation from the largest demon, but he grunted at me before unfurling his own wings and soaring up into the sky after the others. I watched, my chest heaving, until I could see nothing but darkness and stars.

"Pace?"

I turned, my teeth still bared, to find Dariel sheathing his sword.

"We can't stay here. If we don't get back soon, Tiesa is going to raise the alarm." He exhaled, looking up at the sky in the direction the demons had disappeared. "I won't tell anyone."

I tore my gaze from the empty blanket of darkness above us. "About what? Me sneaking to the human world? Almost getting us both killed? Or having my feather taken by a demon? Which one, Cousin?"

He stared at me, releasing a slow breath. "All of it."

A cold, hard laugh echoed in my chest as I sheathed my blade. I'd never felt such anger in my life. I couldn't bring myself to look at Dariel, sensing the wariness pouring off him. Trembling with rage, I tested my wings before shooting up into the night sky.

Every inch of me ached, but the worst pain of all was the burning sensation on the arch of my left wing. Perhaps things were different in Helle. Maybe they shared feathers like ripe fruit at harvest time. My fingernails dug deep crescents into my palms as I pushed myself forward. Exchanging one of our long, primary feathers was an important part of our wedding ritual and that demon had torn one from me with the same care my little sister plucked wildflowers. Whether Dariel told anyone or not, it didn't matter. A slither of my purity was gone forever. Maintaining my purity was one of the only things I'd done right as far as my parents were concerned, and if they found out about this . . . A low growl rumbled in my throat.

"I think they got enough of a head start that we won't run into them again," Dariel said, searching the horizon as he glided beside me.

"They'd better hope we don't."

Dariel watched me for a moment before asking, "What do you mean?"

"If I ever see that demon again," I said, my words little more than a snarl, "I'll kill her."

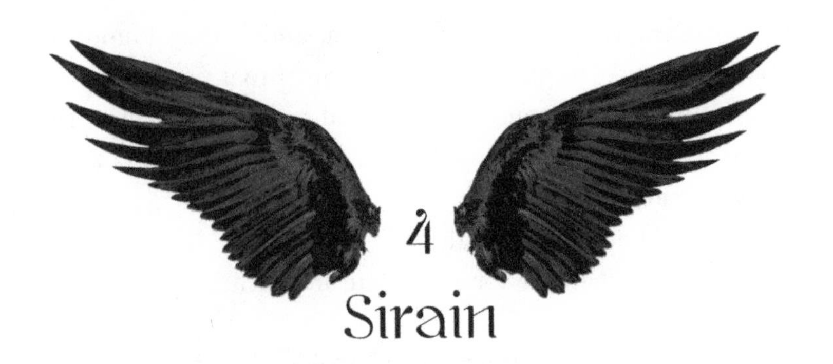

4
Sirain

C*upids*. The thought repeated on a loop in my brain as I allowed the currents of The Crossing to guide me home. Even though I couldn't see them through the densely coloured air, I knew Kwellen and Odio were nearby. My ribs ached from where the pretty one had kicked me, but I didn't think anything was broken. There was probably more damage to Kwellen's pride.

The Crossing tugged me to the left, and I allowed it to take me. Mere moments later, the familiar dark skies of Helle appeared and I inhaled the cool night air, letting it wash the feeling of The Crossing from my feathers. Kwellen and Odio emerged beside me, and I swooped low over the night covered forests toward the foreboding mountains of Hadeon and the castle etched into its side. I needed to sit down and process everything.

"Are we going to talk about what happened back there?" Odio asked, frowning as he tried to keep up with me.

I shot him a glare. "Obviously."

"Don't you think we should do it before we get to the castle?" he said. "Or are you actually planning on telling the king about our discovery?"

I took a deep breath, closing my eyes for a second. He was right. "Fine."

Tucking in my wings, I dove down toward a clearing. The towering pines were black in the moonlight, casting shadows on silvered grass. Odio landed beside me, tugging off his mask and shoving it in his belt. He surveyed the area for a moment, then perched on a tree stump, his wings not quite tucked, as though ready to leave at a moment's notice.

Kwellen landed last, most likely having circled the area first to check for unwanted eavesdroppers. Usually, I'd tease him, asking who he thought would be loitering in the depths of the forest in the middle of the night, but after what had happened in the human world, I was grateful for his foresight. He shoved his mask up on top of his head and put his hand on his hip as he watched me. My stomach sank as I realised, I'd left my mask on that pathetic excuse for an island. I couldn't sit. Stooping to pick up a pinecone, I paced across the glen trying and failing to order my thoughts.

"Stop staring," I snapped.

"I'll stop staring when you stop acting so strange."

"Do you really think they were Cupids?" Odio asked.

I threw my hands in the air. "What else could they have been? They certainly weren't human."

"I thought Cupids were small fluffy things that humans wished on for happiness," Kwellen offered.

Odio frowned. "I think you're getting confused with dandelion puffs."

My hand twitched at my hip, my lip curling. "I've got a lot of rage to work out right now. Don't push me with your stupidity."

"If The Crossing is our access to the human world," Odio continued, drawing my attention from a seething Kwellen. "Do you think they travelled through it too?"

My head ached with unanswered questions. "Unless there's

another way to access the human world. Is that what you think?"

He shrugged. "I don't know. I've been through The Crossing a thousand times, and I've never seen or heard anything to suggest Cupids use it, but that doesn't mean it's not possible."

"Helpful."

"Why haven't we crossed paths with them before, though?" Kwellen asked, pushing his long hair up off his face and tucking it under his mask. "They stand out a mile with those white wings."

My hand lifted to my chest, where the Cupid's feather was tucked safely against my skin. "It sounded like they don't usually go there. The long haired one was saying they'd made a mistake."

"Well, we only visit the human world at night," Odio reasoned. "Perhaps Cupids only visit during the day."

I stared at him, my mind struggling to cope with the endless possibilities. "Why were they there tonight, then? Why were they on that ship?"

Kwellen and Odio looked at each other with a shrug. The adrenaline coursing through my veins gave way to exhaustion and I slumped down against a tree, leaning my head against the rough bark. *Cupids.* I'd never seen anything—anyone—like them before. Even in the moonlight, their skin had glowed in shades of brown and gold, a stark contrast to their snow-white hair. And their wings . . . Reaching inside my leather flight tunic, I pulled the long, ivory feather free, holding it up in front of me. The traces of gold along its edges reminded me of his eyes. I sucked in a sharp breath as I recalled the pure, burning hatred in his gaze and my ribs throbbed in a painful reminder of the line I had so clearly overstepped.

"You okay?" Kwellen asked.

My hand stilled where it had been rubbing the spot where he'd kicked me. "Yes. I'm just annoyed he took me by surprise."

Odio chuckled. "I think you're the one who took him by surprise."

"Hilarious." Snatching up a nearby pinecone, I chucked it at him.

"I can't believe you took one of his feathers," Kwellen said, trying to hide a grin. "You're lucky he didn't cause some real damage."

I focused on the grass beneath me. Why had I taken a feather? I certainly hadn't planned to. There had been something about the way he'd seemed so scared when I got close, as though my touch might burn him. Something had pulled me, wanting to test the boundaries—to see how far I could push him. Perhaps I'd felt insulted. Taking someone's feather without permission was rude, of course, but his reaction had been dramatic to say the least.

"Are you telling your father, then?"

Odio's voice jolted me from my thoughts, and I shook my head, climbing to my feet. "No. I want to try and find out more first."

Kwellen groaned. "Do I want to know?"

"As my friend or as my personal guard?"

"Both."

I flashed him a smile before extending my wings and launching into the air.

The sun was still hiding beyond the horizon when I leapt from my bedroom window and glided down the mountainside. It was so early, the training arenas were still empty; the world painted in shades of pale grey. I'd barely slept. How could I? Shivering, I tugged my hood tighter around my face as I left the Crown City of Hadeon behind. Below me, the fields were draped with dew, the morning mists still lingering amongst the tops of the forests like dense spiderwebs. I leant to the side, riding the breeze toward the sea. Vast and grey, it stretched out as far as the eye could see; the Isle of Fates the only thing marring its rippling surface.

Shivers ran down my spine at the sight of the small island shrouded in mist a few miles off the coast. A temple of jagged grey stone jutted from its centre, surrounded by nothing but rock and fog. Only the Fated were allowed on the island, receiving their orders from the immortal beings, and relaying them to the Captains of Fate. Tearing my gaze from the misted isle, I pushed forward, my lungs aching from inhaling the freezing air as I soared over the edge of the cliff and out over the open sea.

After a few minutes, I slowed, my wings beating steadily as I turned and hovered, panting. The cliffs extended all the way to The Crossing, where they were enveloped by the dense columns of blue, green and purple light. There was nothing but water on the other side. Clenching my fists, I bowed my head and flew back inland. I didn't stop, following the length of The Crossing as it split Helle from the sea.

The thoughts that had plagued me as I'd lain in bed continued to race around my mind as I wove my way across the fields and valleys. If Cupids existed, why didn't we know about them? Surely the Hands should know in case they needed to protect themselves. If they'd had equal numbers last night, things might have ended differently. They certainly knew how to wield a weapon.

"Why were they there?" I muttered, almost hoping The Crossing might answer me.

Why weren't Chaos allowed to go to the human world during the daytime? Could it have something to do with the Cupids? Maybe it was as simple as the reason we were given by the Fates: we blend in better with the darkness.

After an hour or so of flying, I spotted the sandy wastelands of Nefret across the sea to my left and knew I was almost at my destination. Just as before, I continued flying right over the edge of the cliffs and out into open waters. The same sight awaited me. There was nothing on the other side of The Crossing but water.

Gritting my teeth, I tried to fly around to the other side of the shimmering haze, but I was pushed back. A roar of frustration burst from my throat as I flapped my wings harder, but it was akin to flying against gale force winds. I stopped, breathing heavily as I stared at the invisible barrier that appeared to stretch across the sea.

"Fine."

Flying back inland, I swooped upwards, climbing high into the sky. If I couldn't go around The Crossing, I'd go over it. The iridescent sheets of light seemed to stretch on forever and before long, the air grew thin, and my head spun. Only then, did I allow myself to fall back down, spreading my wings and gliding to the ground.

Standing on the edge of the cliff, I stared at where The Crossing faded into nothing and reached out my hand. My fingers slipped between the shards of rainbow light easily, but when I tried further out over the edge of the cliff, a hard wall of air met my palm.

Heaving a sigh of frustration, I slumped down onto the long unkempt grass, my feet dangling over the rocky ledge. I knew that part of my irritation was due to the fact I'd never questioned it before. How complacent had I been, that I'd never wondered what else was out there?

There was no way I could ask my father about it. If he found out I had been visiting the human world . . . I swallowed. Perhaps my mother would be more open minded. I wondered if there was a way I could ask her without actually telling her what had happened. My mother, the queen, had always been a bit of an enigma to me. To my father, my siblings, and the rest of Helle, she was as cold and cruel as she appeared. Once, when we were children, Kwellen asked me if she ever laughed or smiled. His question had puzzled me. She was always laughing and smiling. It wasn't long after that, I realised. She only laughed and smiled when it was just the two of us.

As a child, I had been too scared to ask her about it in case it made the smiles stop. More often than not, her secret embraces were the best part of my day. Now, as an adult, it would feel strange to bring it up. I decided to try and broach the subject the next time we were alone together and play it by ear. After all, how was I supposed to rule Helle if I didn't know everything there was to know about The Crossing?

Extending my wings, I allowed the breeze to sift through my feathers and my lips curled in a smile. It was peaceful on the clifftop. I inhaled deeply, closing my eyes as the sea air filled my lungs. The feeling of contentment vanished as quickly as it had begun as I realised what day it was. Today was the birthday celebration to end all celebrations. As Fin's sister and Crown Princess, I would be expected to attend, and I could only hope it wouldn't be for too long. As soon as the night descended into the drunken debauchery it was bound to, I would slip away. My brother's taste in entertainment was questionable at best and I was more than content to wait and let myself loose at the Festival the following month.

I lay back on the damp grass spreading my heavy wings and stared up at the sky as the rising sun burned away the last of the morning mist. To my right, the churning sheets of rainbow light that formed The Crossing, shimmered at the edges of my vision. The stories called their land 'Hehven'. Was that also true? Did they have seas and forests, mountains and cliffs? Did The Crossing border their land like ours, or did it come and go as it did for the humans? Helplessness overwhelmed me as I scrambled for a way to find answers. Perhaps I could persuade someone to let me talk to the Fates themselves. The thought pulled a frown between my brows. No one had spoken directly with the Fates for as long as anyone could remember.

The thought of the small sacred island, just off the coast of Devland, where Kwellen's family ruled, reminded me that my best friend and guard would be looking for me if I wasn't back soon. There was no doubt he'd think I'd gone through The Crossing in broad daylight, and I couldn't risk him going in after me. Shaking out my wings, I leapt into the air and started the flight home, already missing the quiet peace of the clifftop.

5

Pace

"Can you see it?" I asked, arranging the buttons on my shirt.

Tiesa wound a thin white braid around her finger, her eyebrow arched. "No. And to be honest, you deserve a much bigger scar. In fact, I wish she'd chopped an ear off."

"Thanks a lot, friend," I huffed, rubbing my thumb over the raised edge of the almost healed wound across my chest.

"I don't know why you're asking anyway," she continued. "We both know you're a seasoned expert at hiding injuries. I saw that massive bruise on your side."

I paused as I held her gaze. "I thought we'd settled this. You promised you were going to stop guilting me about the tournaments."

Hopping down from where she had been perched on my dresser, Tiesa wrenched open my bedroom door. "Fine. But if you ever decide to break such a monumental rule again, please make sure you take me with you."

I hummed a noncommittal response as I followed her out of the room and down the hall. Considering I was the second prince of Hehven, my place was small and simple; but it was mine. My parents had pitched a fit when I'd told them I wanted to move out of the palace at eighteen—after all, Dashuri still lived there, so why would I want to leave? They'd thought it was suspicious. I snorted at the thought. Even if I'd had an entire wing to myself, I couldn't have sneezed without someone telling the king and queen. They had eventually relented when I'd found a small cottage on the shore facing the palace. Still close enough they felt like they could keep an eye on me, but far enough away I felt I had some semblance of freedom.

Closing the front door behind me, I turned and stared across the water at the towering marble palace. I'd managed to avoid my family for the past few days. The wound on my chest was easy enough to hide beneath clothes, but the couple of hits I'd taken to the face had resulted in bruises I really hadn't wanted to explain. The missing long primary feather was only noticeable when my wings were stretched to their fullest, but the ghost of the sensation still haunted me. My blood heated as I replayed what had happened on the island. I had lain low long enough. I needed to talk to my brother. Checking my shirt a final time, I spread my wings and launched into the air, Tiesa beside me, as I headed toward the training rooms at the back of the palace.

Even as we soared over the sparkling blue waters, it was hard to ignore the side eye my friend gave me as we flew. When Dariel and I had flown through my bedroom window and fallen to the floor in a heap of bloodied feathers, Tiesa had been seconds away from raising the alarm. My cousin had relayed most of the night's events and I was grateful he had stayed true to his word and left out what the demon had done to me. The arch of my wing ached at the thought and, even though I knew it was almost impossible to tell, nerves began to swell in my gut at the thought of seeing my family—as if they might be able to sense that that sliver of purity had been ripped from me. Visions of their horrified, disappointed faces swam before me and I sucked in a gulp of cool air, rolling my shoulders, and dipping lower over the water.

Tiesa had been furious that I'd put myself, and Dariel, in so much danger but she'd soon realised I was in no mood for being reprimanded. Anger had pulsed through me with such ferocity that night, I could barely breathe. It had taken both of them to restrain me, halting me from razing my room to the ground. Tremors of rage crept forward at the memory, but I knew a large part of that anger was at my own stupidity for going through The Crossing alone. At night. I hadn't been able to stop thinking about the demons. Their masked faces taunted me in my dreams and haunted every waking second. And *her* . . . my nails pressed crescents into my palms.

"Pace!"

My concerns melted away at the sound of my little sister's voice as we came into land. Sprinting toward me, her white curls streamed out behind her as she half ran, half flew until her arms were squeezing me tight enough that I wheezed.

"Amani! Too tight."

She laughed and squeezed harder before releasing me.

"Where have you been?" Slipping her delicate hand into mine, she stared up at me with pale gold eyes. "I haven't seen you in days."

My heart tugged at her words, but I grinned and ruffled her hair. "I've been busy doing grown up stuff. Speaking of which, I think you've grown since I saw you last."

Straightening her shoulders, she smiled proudly. "Well, it is almost my birthday."

"Is it?" I feigned surprise, my eyes wide. "How old will you be? Seven? Eight?"

Amani laughed and my heart warmed at the beautiful sound. "Ten, Pace. You know that."

"Ten?" I repeated, winking at Tiesa. "Surely not."

"Where are you going? Can I come? I missed you."

Her innocent words layered guilt, heavy on my chest. In avoiding my parents and my brother, I'd avoided her too.

"I'm going to the training rooms," I said, causing her smile to turn to disappointment. "Have you seen Dash today?"

Amani giggled, her eyes bright. "Don't call him that. You know he hates it."

I looked around, peering behind a bush. "He's not here, is he?"

"I think he's at the training rooms too," she said before turning to Tiesa, pouting. "Why are boys so boring?"

Tiesa laughed. "You're talking to the wrong female. I love the training rooms. Although, give it a couple more years and you probably will too."

Amani looked between us in confusion, and I elbowed my friend's ribs in warning. "Stop it."

"You know it's true." Tiesa wiggled her eyebrows. "There's a reason hordes of giggling smallwings cluster in the viewing sections. Especially on days you're training, Pace."

"I can't help it if my skill with a sword draws crowds," I said, chin lifting as I rested a hand on the golden hilt at my side.

Tiesa snorted. "Your sword skills aren't *that* good."

I pulled a face at her, but the clashing of blades had already filled my ears, the scent of sea salt and sweat permeating my senses. My muscles tensed at the memory of wielding my sword against the demons, wondering whether I'd live to see Hehven again.

"Oh! I know why they're there," Amani squeaked, her voice tugging me back to the present.

Tiesa tilted her head in question, but I forced a smile and shrugged. "Like I said, they're there to see the swordsmanship. Tiesa, stop filling my baby sister's head with nonsense."

"I'm not a baby," Amani huffed. "And I do know why they're there. They want to be your princess."

A cold shiver ran the length of my body, my shoulders tensing, but I forced a smile and took her hands in mine. "Look, why don't we do something later? We could go look for mountain goats."

"Mountain goats?" She wrinkled her delicate nose. "How about wildflowers?"

"Fine. I'll come and find you after I've spoken to Dash."

With another squeeze around my middle, and a hug for Tiesa, she skipped away, disappearing between the curves of the sculpted palace gardens.

"What was that?" Tiesa asked.

"Nothing."

"It wasn't nothing. When she mentioned princesses, you went as white as wings—"

"You know why," I snapped, cutting her off.

Tiesa's face fell at my tone, but I couldn't bring myself to tell her the truth. I was damaged. The Rakkaus family would never agree to their daughter marrying a prince who wasn't pure. I clenched and unclenched my fists at my side. I couldn't tell Tiesa about the demon. With only Dariel knowing, I could almost pretend it hadn't happened. If Tiesa knew, she'd want to talk about it. And that would only serve to make it real.

Huffing a sigh, I strode toward the training rooms, my friend falling into step beside me in silence. I was itching to find out if Dashuri knew anything about the demons. Six years older than me, he had been training to step into my mother's footsteps since he was my age. If there was anything to know, surely my parents would have told him. The real question, however, was would he tell me?

The training rooms weren't really rooms. Large, sanded circles in one of the three palace courtyards, covered seating surrounded each one, with pathways between so they could be used in all weathers. The circles themselves weren't shielded and years ago, I'd asked my father why. He'd told me there was no shield from the elements in battle. Of course, I'd then asked when Cupids had last battled, which had resulted in my being confined to the palace under a no-fly ban for two days.

Despite the chill winter air, the warmth of spring had begun to sink its tendrils into the breeze whipping between the training rooms. The smell of blossoms only served to remind me that the Spring Festival of Fates was but a few weeks away. My thoughts were no longer of the banquet, reflection, and ceremony but of what would happen when Cove met with Lord Bickerstaff. Had the demon's arrow changed things? If it had, what would that mean? My fingers twitched at my side, and I turned, searching the perimeter of the training rooms for my brother. It didn't take long to find him. Surrounded by his usual crowd, he was watching a sparring session while his advisors leaned in, whispering in his ear. With his white wavy hair kept short, and his dark brown skin, he looked more like our mother than I did. Amani and I took after our father.

I turned to Tiesa. "Why don't you go and find Dariel?"

It was clear it wasn't a request and she stared up at me, her mint green eyes flashing with annoyance. I held her gaze until she relented and walked away with a slight shake of her head, her feathers brushing the ground. Guilt swirled in my gut at shutting out my friend, but it wasn't fair to drag her into this. Once I knew what we were dealing with, I'd explain. Straightening my wings, I strode over to the Crown Prince and his entourage.

"Brother!" I announced as I entered the viewing area.

Dashuri turned, his golden gaze taking in my casual outfit before landing on the sword slung at my waist. "You're still alive I see. Are you training today, Brother?"

I shrugged. "Haven't decided yet."

His face was impassive as he turned back to the fight he and his crowd seemed so enthralled by. It annoyed him that I dressed in shirts, tunics and trousers instead of the flowing robes worn by the royal family, but they just seemed so impractical. His own robes that morning were ivory with golden feathers embroidered along the hem and sleeves.

I stepped closer, people parting with half bows to let me through. "I would like to talk to you, Brother."

Dashuri didn't take his eyes from the fight. Two males were sparring, the golden metal of their blades glinting in the morning sun. Judging from the slick gleam of their torsos, they must have been quite evenly matched, as neither was showing signs of winning. Watching their graceful movements, I tried not to sneer. This wasn't fighting. It was little more than dancing. My fingers gripped the hilt of my sword as my blood tingled in my veins, craving the sweat soaked adrenaline of a real fight.

"I think I have some free time later this afternoon," Dashuri said. "Perhaps after lunch."

"It won't take long. Just a few minutes."

With a sigh, he turned to look at me. "What is so urgent, it cannot wait a few hours?"

My jaw ticked at his tone; insinuating that nothing I had to say could be of importance. My brother was shorter than me, and I couldn't help but draw myself to my full height, my wings flexing as I folded my arms across my chest. "Give me five minutes of your time and you'll find out, *Dash*."

His eyes flashed at the nickname he despised but after a moment of holding my stare, he relented. "Fine. What do you want to talk about?"

"In private."

Dashuri sighed again, gesturing at the crowd surrounding us. "Leave us." The advisors, and whoever else my brother liked to surround himself with, wandered off to watch other matches. "Talk."

"Don't speak to me like I'm one of your pets," I snarled. "You might be the future king but I'm still Second Prince. If anything happens to you, it'll be me on that throne."

Dashuri turned to face me fully, his white eyebrows raised in amusement. "Is that a threat, Little Brother?"

"Of course not. You know full well I have no interest in putting my ass anywhere near that throne. You're welcome to it."

He chuckled, returning his gaze to the fighters. "So, what do you wish to talk to me about?

"What do you know about Helle?"

Dashuri stiffened. "Helle is none of your concern."

"So, you do know something."

"I said, it was none of your concern."

"Where is it?" I pressed. "Can the demons pass through The Crossing to Hehven?"

Dashuri whirled, his gold eyes flashing. "What are you talking about? What demons?"

"Tell me what you know."

"I know nothing more than you do," he hissed, looking around us as though someone might overhear. "Helle is a land of demons who prey on humans. They are nothing to do with us."

"What if our Hands encounter one in the human world?"

Dashuri stepped closer, his white wings ruffling. "What are you talking about?"

"It's purely hypothetical, Brother."

His voice was dangerously low, his eyes dark pits of golden flame. "If it were purely hypothetical, why would you need to discuss it as a matter of urgency?"

My shoulders tensed as I held his accusatory stare. "I thought demons were purely myth—a smallwing's bedtime story—until I heard someone mention them. I thought as heir to the throne, if anyone would know, it would be you."

He raised his hand, fingers tensed as though making to grip my shirt, but he took a small step back, letting it fall to his side instead. "Who did you hear speak of demons?"

"I'm not sure. It was someone while I was training." I held his stare. "A conversation I heard in passing."

Dashuri exhaled, turning back to the fight, but the training circle was now empty. "Why not go to Mother or Father with your questions?"

"Like I said. I thought it to be little more than myth. I didn't want to waste their time."

"But you thought it acceptable to waste mine?"

"I knew you would tell me the truth," I said, not meaning a word. "I ask because I'm worried about Dariel and Tiesa. If demons are real, what if they encounter one on a mission?"

Dashuri gestured to the circles spreading the length of the courtyard. "Our Hands are well trained in combat."

I bit my tongue, swallowing my disdain. "What if they were outnumbered?"

"For Fates' sake, Pace," Dashuri said, shaking his head. "Fine. I will tell you what I know, but you must swear it goes no further."

I nodded. "Of course."

Dashuri stared at me for a moment, as though reconsidering, but then drew a deep breath. "They're not demons. They're called Chaos. You don't need to worry about our Hands meeting them as they are only allowed through The Crossing at night. That part of the stories is true, at least."

"So, where is Helle?" I asked, trying to school my expression into one of nonchalance, although I was sure I was failing miserably. "Can it be accessed through The Crossing?"

"Enough, Pace. I've told you all I know." Dashuri turned and began to walk away from me. "Let it be. It is of no concern to us here in Hehven."

My hands clenched at my sides, but I forced myself to shake them out, watching as my brother was swallowed once more by his group of admirers. *Chaos*. I blew out a slow breath. He wasn't much, but at least I had confirmation of my suspicions.

Before I could question whether or not it was a good idea, I swung myself over the railing into the uncovered training circle and launched into the air. Spreading my wings, I soared upwards until I was above the palace. From up there I could clearly see the curtain of multicoloured lights that formed The Crossing. If the Chaos entered the human world the same way we did, surely Helle was on the other side.

"I really don't like that look on your face."

I kept my eyes on The Crossing, squinting against the sun as I tried to make out where the lights ended. "What look, Tiesa?"

A second pair of wings sounded a steady rhythm on my other side. "Please tell me you're not considering going back," Dariel said, his voice weary.

"I spoke to my brother."

Tiesa gasped. "You told him you went through The Crossing."

I rolled my eyes. "Of course not."

Before she could bombard me with more questions, I dove, swooping across the water that separated the palace from the mainland, bypassing my home and heading for the foothills of the Dragoste Mountains. Dariel and Tiesa flew silently at my side, but I knew as soon as we landed, they'd be expecting answers.

Setting down on a grass covered peak, I sank to the ground and drew my knees to my chest, facing The Crossing. I closed my eyes, allowing the sun to warm my face despite the brisk breeze. "Go on, then."

Tiesa slumped down at my right. "If you didn't tell him you went through The Crossing, what did you tell him?"

"I told him I'd overheard people talking of demons and Helle and I was concerned for your safety."

"And?" Tiesa prompted. "What did he say?"

"He said they aren't demons. They're called Chaos." I

waited to feel guilt at betraying my brother's trust so readily but felt nothing. "He also said they were none of my concern."

There was a shuffle of wings and a slow exhale as Dariel sat on my other side. "You know he'll be suspicious now. He'll probably tell your parents."

"I don't think he will. But he will be suspicious. You're right about that."

Tiesa leaned against me, bumping my shoulder. "You know you can't go back."

"I know." We sat in silence for a moment before I asked my next question. "I want to know about your missions."

"What about them?" Dariel asked.

"I want to know who you've been targeting. What are the Fates trying to achieve? I don't understand why you would be assigned an arrow for Cove, only for it to be undone by a Chaos hours later."

"We don't even know if that's what happened," Dariel reasoned. "We have no idea what a demon—Chaos—arrow does."

"Even so," I pressed. "Tell me. Is it always Cove?"

Tiesa muttered under her breath and Dariel groaned. "It's a bit late for you to show an interest in the inner workings of the Hands now, Cousin."

"Remember when we completed training," Tiesa said, a smile tugging at her lips. "We were itching to tell you all about our first mission and you wouldn't hear a word of it."

"I was jealous!" I protested. "My best friends were off on adventures, visiting the human world and I was stuck at the palace learning how to be a backup for my brother should the Fates turn on him."

"It's not always Cove," Dariel relented. "There are hundreds of Hands, most of whom are targeting everyday humans. I will admit, however, most of my missions as of late have been either leaders of the human countries or those close to them."

I looked up in interest. "Why do you think that is?"

Tiesa snorted. "You know why. You heard Bickerstaff talking about it. Yet another human war is brewing."

In the distance, The Crossing shimmered in constantly moving sheets of white, green and purple, and I stared, entranced by its hypnotic rhythm. The last human war had been twenty years ago. The older Hands still talked about it as the busiest time of their existence. I could believe it. Surely love, peace and joy were needed more than ever in a time of war. Questions fired inside my brain like shooting stars, but I pushed them down, knowing there was a limit to how much my curiosity would be tolerated. There was one question however, I kept coming back to, and it blazed across my brain like a flaming comet.

"How do the Fates know who to target?"

Tiesa flopped backwards on the grass, her white wings splayed. "Feathers and Fates, are you serious, Pace?"

"Please tell me you're not questioning the Fates themselves?" Dariel asked.

"No, of course not," I lied. "I'm merely curious."

Dariel sighed. "I think it's time to put your curiosity in a box and hide it under your bed."

"Yeah." Tiesa huffed a dry laugh. "I hope you're not planning on bombarding your wife with this many questions. She'll fly for the hills."

My mouth snapped shut, my teeth clenching hard enough to crack. Before Tiesa could draw breath to apologise, I was on my feet and in the air. She knew. They both did. Tiesa knew how frustrated I was about the marriage, but she continued to taunt me with it. Frustration curled in my shoulders as I sped towards my home. Perhaps if she knew about my damaged purity, she'd be more considerate. Her shouts carried to me on the wind, but I rode the currents down the mountain, my body like an arrow as the wind snatched at my feathers. By the time my cottage came into view, I decided it didn't matter. As my closest friend, she should be on my side. She should know better. I dropped down to my front door, only to find one of my parents' messengers standing, waiting. He jolted to attention as I landed.

"Yes?" I demanded, not bothering to mask my irritation.

"Your Majesty." He bowed low. "The king and queen request your presence in the main hall."

"When?"

"Now, Your Majesty."

I stared at him for a moment, trying and failing to find a way out of meeting with my parents. "Fine."

Watching as the messenger turned and flew away, I contemplated going inside to change, or even just tidy my windswept hair, but if I was heading into an interrogation, my appearance didn't really matter.

It only took minutes to cross the water to the palace and, as I strode down the gilded corridors, I made a list of possible reasons for the meeting. Had Dash informed them of my line of questioning? Perhaps someone had seen me coming or going from The Crossing. I sucked in a readying breath as two guards heaved open the heavy doors to the throne room.

I hated the main hall. By far the largest room in the palace, the domed marble ceiling was decorated with delicate paintings and carvings of male and female Cupids adorned with bows and arrows, intertwined in movements somewhere between dancing and fighting. Naked, of course. As young boys, Dariel and I had lain on the floor of the main hall addled with giggling curiosity. Now, I saw it for what it was: a garish romanticism of the dangerous and thankless task of being a Hand.

My parents were not on their thrones, the dais empty. Instead, they stood side by side at one of the towering arched windows overlooking the mountains. Unease was slick on my skin as I realised, they had a direct line of sight to my home.

Had they watched me fly in? My footsteps echoed on the polished marble floor as I drew closer, and they turned to face me, their expressions more neutral than I'd expected.

"Pace, my darling. It's been too long." My mother glided toward me, her dark blue gown billowing in sheets of silk around her. Large gold earrings swayed from her ears and her white hair was shaved closer than when I'd seen her last.

"It has," I said. "I'm sorry."

She wrapped her arms around me, her fresh citrus scent enveloping my senses and melting away my trepidation. When she pulled back, her hands remained on my shoulders. "You look sad. Why are you sad?"

"I'm just a little tired. That's all."

She studied me, her large golden eyes filled with concern. "Are you sure?"

"I'm sure, Mother." I glanced at my father who remained by the window. "What did you want to speak to me about?"

"The Festival," my mother replied.

Relief flooded through me. Of course. As Second Prince they would want me to recite something or take part in one of the many rituals that made up the festivities. "What am I needed for?"

My father gave me a once over, followed by an almost imperceptible shake of his head. "I've arranged with Lord Rakkaus for you to meet Caitland at the Festival."

I choked on my intake of breath. "What?"

"Her father and I think it would be best for you to marry at the Winter Festival of Fates, just after your birthday. It will give you time to get to know each other and for Hehven to prepare for the biggest celebration since your mother and I wed."

The floor dropped away at my feet, my wings flaring as though trying to halt my fall. My mother was saying something, but I couldn't hear over the roaring of blood in my ears.

"Pace?" my father asked. "Do you understand?"

I nodded, my mouth utterly and entirely dry. "Yes."

"This isn't a punishment, Pace," my mother started. "It's the—"

"I have to go." I took a step backwards. "I promised Amani I would search for wildflowers with her."

Pain flashed across my mother's face as she reached for me, but I was already backing towards the door. I spread my wings and flew from the room, too shaken to walk. I could barely see, barely think, as I burst out of the nearest open window, gulping at the cool air. Wingbeats sounded nearby but I ignored them, trying to put as much space between me and the palace as possible while my heart threatened to hammer its way out of my chest.

A strong hand wrapped around my forearm, tugging me to a halt and I tried to pull away, whirling to see who might be stupid enough to try and drag me from my spiral. *Dariel.*

"Come with me," he said, his grip firm.

Unable to think of a reason not to, I allowed him to pull me away. I was so lost in my own thoughts, stumbling over my father's revelation, that it took me a minute to realise he was taking me to the training rooms. It was much quieter than before, with only a handful of Cupids training. Even so, Dariel took us to the furthest circle. He reached for my sword, pulling it from its scabbard, and thrust it in my hand.

"Let's go," he said, drawing his own sword. "Show me this 'proper' fighting."

I stared between the sword in my hand and my cousin, who was crouched, tensed and ready. How had he known where I was? What did he think this would achieve?

"Come on, Pace." He gestured to me with his free hand. "Let me have it."

I opened my mouth to tell him not to be ridiculous, ready to throw the blade to the ground, but instead my grip tightened, and I spun, bringing my blade down on his with such force it rattled my teeth.

Dariel didn't retaliate, instead focusing all his attention on blocking the onslaught of attacks that followed. I was so tired. Tired of being a disappointment. Tired of the way Dashuri looked at me. The way my father looked at me. The way I had caught my friends looking at me since the engagement. How was I such a liability that they thought marrying me off would improve me? I noted the pity in Dariel's pale blue eyes, even as he gritted his teeth against my attack and a rumbling rippled in my chest, building until it burst from my throat in a rasping roar. Wielding my sword with two hands, I slashed and swiped at my cousin with renewed vigour.

Caitland would be disappointed. Of course, she would. I wouldn't even be able to exchange feathers with her on our wedding night without it being a lie. She was expecting a prince. Centred, calm, and pure. Instead, she was getting me: a tainted, angry excuse for one. She deserved better.

My chest heaving, I stabbed my sword into the sanded ring and stepped back, sweat stinging my eyes. Dariel stared at me in question, but I just shook my head and launched up into the sky. I had promised to go and pick wildflowers and I refused to disappoint anyone else.

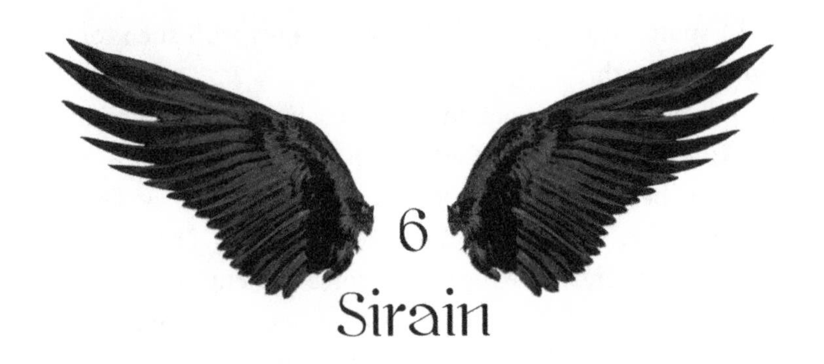

6
Sirain

Music was playing somewhere, but the steady, pounding beat of the drums was the only sound discernible over the laughter and cheering echoing throughout the castle grounds. Taking a deep sip of my wine, I cast my gaze along the rows of sprawling tables around the vast courtyard. Stacks of towering black candles sent cascades of glistening wax down toward the mountains of roasted meat and sugared fruit and, glancing at my own heaped plate, I pushed it away, my appetite lacking. A cry rang out overhead and I tilted my head back to find a group of Chaos drunkenly racing each other between the draped black, red and purple banners hanging above the courtyard. Although outwardly rolling my eyes as I watched their black wings whip between the billowing folds of material, my chest warmed with memories of taking part in similar antics with Kwellen and Odio when I was younger.

A servant sauntered past, laden with jugs of wine, and I lifted my glass without looking up. The deep red liquid sloshed over the side, staining my fingers, and the servant spluttered a frantic apology, but I waved them away. Perhaps Fin would have inflicted punishment for a splash of wine on his sleeve, but the thought alone exhausted me. I had more pressing things occupying my mind.

The light spring breeze picked up, sending the rippling strips of gauze fluttering, and with it the smell of the sacrifices. Wrinkling my nose at the vague scent of rotting meat, I glared at the platform that had been erected to present the offerings brought across from the human world. The day before a Festival, humans sent rafts of offerings out on the sea to appease the 'demons' that might steal their children or harm their loved ones. Each of the four human countries seemed to favour a different type of offering, with some sending food, some jewels and clothing and others the hearts of sacrificed livestock. At least, I hoped it was livestock. I'd heard stories of human sacrifices centuries ago. I shuddered at the thought. The pile was beginning to fester and smell. None of it would be touched in case it had been tampered with, although I knew some Chaos would root through the pile for jewels and trinkets before the morning. What would the humans think if they knew their offerings sat in a heaping pile—a stinking symbol of our power over their world?

It had been four hours since the Festival began and most Chaos were already worse for wear, some dancing and stomping on the tables and some indulging their more primal urges. Something nudged my foot and I shifted backwards in my seat, unable to escape the glimpse of tangled bare limbs beneath the table as I did so. A few tables away, my parents were watching the celebrations, their faces impassive as they sipped their wine. My sister, Malin, sat beside them, wide eyed as she watched two men go from dancing to fighting on the top of a nearby table, sending food and cups tumbling to the stone floor in a frenetic symphony. At only sixteen, she was allowed to attend but required to stay with my parents. A smile pulled at my lips. I remembered the frustration well. Although I had found more than one way of sneaking off.

A small cluster of servants surrounded my sister, tending to her every need, while a crowd of her peers lingered nearby. The Chaos adored her. Petite and delicate, she favoured stunning robes and complicated hairstyles, looking every bit the future queen I didn't.

A wing brushed my calf and I huffed a sigh, resisting the urge to kick the grunting pair at my feet. Instead, I stood, moving toward the source of the cheering. The arena was packed with Chaos, all dressed in their finery and sprawled along the stone seating as they ate, drank and watched the entertainment. A few hours ago, dancers and performers had opened the ceremony, but now the arena floor was open to anyone who wanted it.

Leaning against the wall at the top, I watched as a shirtless, sweat-soaked Kwellen raised his arm in triumph, yelling a roar that echoed around the arena. The crowd screamed their appreciation as the Chaos he had defeated limped from the ring, blood dripping from his mouth and nose. Another opponent rose from the stands and flew down to the ring, their sleek black blade raised and ready. Kwellen grinned, his teeth stained red. Whether it was from blood or wine, I had no idea. I glanced across the stands looking for Odio, but I couldn't see him anywhere. Chances were he'd already found some company for the evening.

I was restless. Despite looking forward to the Festival for weeks, now it had arrived, I found it lacking. The noise and crowds irked me, and the wine was doing little to quell my frustration. I considered flying back to my rooms, but I knew there was no chance I'd be able to rest, and it was still far too early to sleep. As the breeze picked up, rippling through my feathers, and causing the thin black material of my dress to wrap around my legs, an idea began to form. My lips curled into a grin and anticipation tingled in my limbs as I began to make my way to the edge of the castle grounds, where I would be able to take off without being questioned.

"Having fun, Sister?"

I stilled, my skin prickling and my shoulders tensing at the sound of Fin's voice. Taking a readying breath, my fingers moving to rest over the dagger strapped to my thigh beneath my dress, I turned to him, my smile frozen. "Always, Brother. Are you?"

Despite the slight sway to his stance and the glass of wine in his hand, he still managed to maintain his cold and cruel, dark prince demeanour; tall and lean in an embroidered tunic and pants of black and silver.

"You shouldn't stray so far from the crowds without your guard," he slurred.

"Oh, really? Why is that, Fin?"

He stepped towards me, red liquid sloshing over the edge of his glass. In the late afternoon light, his pupils were imperceptible, making him look every bit the demon the humans thought we were. "Something might happen to you. It would be a shame if you didn't live long enough to see the Royal Rites. Although, the chances of you successfully completing them are slim at best."

"Oh, don't you worry, Brother," I said, my hands curling into fists. "I'd never give you the satisfaction of seeing me dead."

He held my gaze for a moment, the breeze rippling his feathers. Then he threw his head back and laughed—a rasping, choking sound that sent a shudder down my spine. Knowing he was likely too drunk to fly, I spread my wings and launched up into the sky, the dregs of his laughter chasing me on the wind.

We had never liked each other. My earliest memories of Fin were as a small child throwing things at me or pulling at my wings. He was born hating me. The thought had never really bothered me as I was always taller, stronger, and a much better fighter. Then last year, almost overnight, he grew. Now, he was taller than me. Broader than me. I had no doubt I could still best him in a fight, but Fin didn't fight fair. I had almost two decades of 'accidental' injuries to prove it.

Gritting my teeth, I beat my wings harder, trying to put as much space between me and the Festival as possible. It wasn't the first time he'd brought up the Royal Rites, his words dripping with threats, and the constant looking over my shoulder was exhausting. My father made no efforts to hide the fact that he favoured him, and I was certain he would prefer Fin to take the throne. If I failed the Royal Rites, they'd both get their wish. They were so similar, my father and Fin. They shared, not only the dark royal red in their wings, hair, and eyes, but the same ice-cold ruthlessness. And their apparent hatred of me.

The air whipped at my dress as I dipped and soared towards the coast—towards the little slice of peace I'd claimed as my own. I had been back to my clifftop a few times since discovering it, and every time I returned, a tremor of trepidation shuddered through me. What if someone else had found it? What if someone had followed me? Glancing over my shoulder, there were no wings to be seen as I soared down towards the grassy ledge overlooking the sparkling sea. The sun was sinking lower, casting shades of rose and orange over the rippling waves as I landed, but my heart was still frantic, my blood coursing with so much anger, that even the beauty in front of me couldn't soothe it. It wasn't fair. The last few Festivals had all ended the same way. Either my father or brother twisting their verbal knives in my gut until I was forced to leave or hide at the bottom of a bottle of wine. I was strong. Until it came to them. Picking up a rock, I hurled it off the edge of the cliff with a scream that tore at my throat.

"Why?" I yelled into the emptiness. "Which Fate did I so desperately offend to deserve this?"

Tears burned my eyes, as I lobbed another rock into the waves below with a shriek.

An awkward cough, distorted and distant, as though underwater, sounded beside me. "I should probably let you know someone's here before you get too carried away."

I was so startled I almost fell off the edge of the cliff, my wings flapping frantically to help me regain my balance. Wide-eyed, I turned in a circle searching for the voice, but there was no one in sight.

"Where are you?" I demanded. "Come out."

"I could say the same to you," the voice replied.

Although the words were clear, the tone was so distorted, I couldn't discern whether they were male or female. I frowned, my heart hammering as I turned to stare at the wall of light beside me.

"Where are you?" I repeated, my command wavering despite my best efforts.

There was no reply. I pressed my hand to the shimmering light, dipping my fingers through the waves. Pushing further, I hit the same solid blast of air that had prevented me from flying around to the other side.

"Are you in The Crossing?" I tried again. "Because if you're spying on me, that's really creepy."

The voice laughed. "No. I was just sitting here minding my own business when you showed up screaming and shouting."

My cheeks burned. "Where are you, then?"

"On a cliff looking out at the sea," the voice replied, the words bubbling like a stream. "The sunset is going to be stunning. What about you?"

My breath caught in my throat, and I turned to stare at the wall of light, eyes wide. "Me too."

Was this being, whatever they were, looking at the same view? Hardly daring to breathe, I stepped off the cliff, hovering over the water. My wings beat steadily as I tried to see around to the other side of The Crossing but just as before, the wall of wind pushed me back. Gritting my teeth in frustration, I returned to the cliff, slumping down on the cool grass.

"Okay," I tried. "Where is your cliff?"

My heart was a steady drumbeat as I waited for the voice to answer. I already knew what I was hoping for. Could it be a Cupid? If so, would it be so bad if they knew I was in Helle? I didn't need to disclose more than I wanted. I could fly away at any time.

"Beyond the forests and next to the sea," the voice replied.

Despite the warped effect, I could hear a teasing tone to the words that nudged my lips into a smile. "Hilarious," I responded. "What land is your cliff in? Answers for answers?"

The following pause was longer. Long enough that I wondered if I'd pushed too far. I plucked another stone from the ground and tossed it off the edge of the cliff. It was a drop so steep, I didn't hear it fall.

"Hehven."

I stilled, my hand closed around a rock, ready to throw. I'd hoped, but I hadn't realised how much I'd needed the confirmation.

"Where are you?" the voice rippled. "That's the deal, right? Answers for answers."

My mouth was dry as I swallowed. I could leave now, knowing my suspicions were right. Hehven was on the other side of The Crossing. If I did, however, it would be the only answer I'd get. The price, of course, was giving up information of my own. Although, I could lie. How would they ever know?

"Helle," I replied, the truth surprising me as it tumbled from my lips.

Again, the silence stretched out and I wondered whether the Cupid was processing the information with the same awe as me.

"Why are you here?" the voice asked, the question surprising me.

I reached out and ran my fingers through the lights, watching the blues and greens dapple my pale skin. "I was tired of the Festival."

"Wait. The Festival of Fates?"

My eyebrows shot up in surprise. "Yes. Is it the Festival of Fates in Hehven?"

"It is."

"The Spring Festival?"

The voice laughed. "Yes. It seems the seasons are the same in Hehven and Helle."

"Why are you not at the Festival?" I asked.

I wanted to know so much, but I knew I had to tread carefully. One wrong question and I might scare the voice away. Silence. Perhaps it was too personal a question. Fates only knew what the Festival was like in Hehven. Probably a stuffy tea party of pomp and circumstance followed by an early night.

"I could ask the same of you," the voice replied. "What is the Festival like in Helle?"

It didn't escape me that the Cupid had avoided my question, but I decided that maybe if I offered more information, it might build some level of trust.

"It's long and loud," I said. "A full day of eating, drinking, dancing and giving in to all our basic desires. Exhausting."

"Really? Ours is a day filled with speeches, sermons and reflection, followed by a banquet. There is dancing, but not until after sunset."

"So, you came to the cliff because you're bored?" I snorted.

Silence.

"What's it like in Hehven?" I tried.

A sigh rippled through the light. "It's the only world I know, so I wouldn't know how to describe it. Grey mountains, green forests, blue lakes. What about Helle?"

I glanced over my shoulder at the forests sprawling in the distance. "Sounds about the same."

"What does it smell like on your side?"

A laugh burst from my lips. "Excuse me? What kind of question is that?"

"It's a good question," the voice replied defensively.

"No. It's an awful question. I don't know. I can smell the sea; the pine of the forests." I inhaled deeply. "I can smell jasmine too. It's blooming a little early this year."

"Jasmine only grows in the far north of Hehven," the voice replied. "I can smell the sea and the forests and something feminine, but I don't know what type of flower it is."

I choked on a laugh. "Something feminine? You're male, then."

"Just because I think a flower smells feminine doesn't mean I'm male. Name me a masculine smelling flower."

"Flowers don't smell like a gender," I said, shaking my head. "They just smell like flowers."

"If they don't smell like females, why do they have such feminine names?"

Chuckling, I lay back in the grass, spreading my wings. The sun had painted the clouds peach and gold as they drifted across the pale blue sky. "Flowers don't have feminine names. They just have names. If a rose was called a thorn, it would still smell the same."

"I suppose."

"You didn't answer me," I said, carefully. "Are you male?"

"Would it make a difference?"

I considered the question. Would I be speaking any freer if I knew?

"No, I suppose it wouldn't."

"Are you male or female?" the voice asked.

"Would it make a difference?"

A laugh echoed through the barrier of light, and I smiled.

Watching the clouds in silence, I wondered whether the Cupid on the other side was doing the same. Were they seeing the same clouds? The idea made my head hurt. There was a whole world on the other side of The Crossing. A world filled with white winged Cupids. I'd closed my eyes, trying to imagine what their world might look like, when I realised something.

"You never told me," I started, hoping the voice was still there. "Why are you not at your Festival?"

The silence stretched out around me, punctuated only by the occasional cry of seabirds. I tried to quell the disappointment lying heavy in my gut.

"I'm hiding," the voice said.

I sat up, my heart pounding with relief. "From whom?"

The Cupid snorted. "My future wife."

My mouth fell open. It was not an answer I had been expecting. "Oh. Congratulations?"

The voice huffed. "I'm supposed to meet her tonight."

"You haven't met?" I asked, sitting up straighter.

The thought tied my stomach in knots. If my father tried to marry me off to a stranger . . . I didn't know what I'd do.

"We're supposed to meet at sunset," the voice admitted.

I looked at the semicircle of orange slipping below the horizon. "I think you're going to be late."

"It certainly seems that way."

"Here was me thinking my day was bad just because my brother threatened to kill me."

"Ah. The reason you were cursing the Fates?"

My face burned as I recalled the screaming rage the being on the other side of The Crossing had overheard. "Yeah. He's pretty awful."

"My brother is a piece of work too."

I laughed, the sound surprising me. "I can guarantee my brother is worse than your brother."

"Were you being serious? Did he really threaten to kill you?"

The blade of grass I'd wrapped around my fingers snapped as I pulled it tight. "It's not the first time and it won't be the last."

"Okay. You win. My brother is a pompous ass, but no matter how much he dislikes me, I don't think he would kill me."

"Lucky you. You don't sound thrilled about your future wife. Is she horrible?"

"I don't know. She's probably lovely."

I chewed my lip thoughtfully. "Perhaps it won't be that bad."

"It's not me I'm worried about," the voice admitted, quieter than before. "It's her. She deserves better."

My curiosity piqued, but I bit down on my lip. The conversation felt like watching a deer in a forest clearing. One wrong move and it would startle and run away.

"I'm sure that's not true."

A hollow laugh echoed through the light. "You don't know anything about me. I might be a cold-hearted killer."

"Are you?"

"Of course, not."

I smiled. "There we go, then."

"What if she hates me?"

The uncertainty was clear, despite the distortion and my heart ached a little for them. "I'm sure she won't. Unless perhaps you're a terrible kisser."

My joke was met with silence, and I wondered whether I had touched a nerve. Had I finally scared away the deer? "Sorry," I offered. "I'm sure you're excellent."

Just as the silence became unbearable, the voice rippled through. "Cupids remain pure until marriage."

"What?" My eyebrows shot up as I stilled. "Not even a kiss?"

"Not even a kiss."

In Helle, kisses meant nothing and beds were shared without a second thought. Bile rose in my throat, and I swallowed as I remembered the hatred in that Cupid's eyes. I could still feel the anger radiating from him. Had I affected his purity by taking one of his feathers? Feathers played a part in marriage ceremonies in Helle, of course, but if things got a little heated in a fight or in the throes of passion, and a feather got pulled out, it wasn't the end of the world. My dismay faded to annoyance and I frowned. There was no way I could have known. I considered asking the voice, but it was clear it was already a sensitive subject.

"I assume it's different in Helle," the voice said.

"Just a little."

A comfortable silence settled between us and I exhaled, the tension that had been stored in my shoulders and wings melting like the last rays of the sun on the horizon. I smiled as I kicked off my shoes and dug my toes into the grass.

"Can you see that cloud?" the voice rippled. "The one that looks like a fish?"

Tilting my head back, I squinted at the slow-moving puffs of white and grey, the warm colours of the setting sun replaced by the muted blues of dusk. After a moment, I saw it—a large cloud with fins and a tail—and my pulse quickened at the thought that we were looking up at the same sky. A whole world existed mere strides away on the other side of The Crossing. Staring up at the wall of undulating light, curiosity and determination prickled beneath my skin as I realised, things had just changed forever.

7

Pace

It was no use. I tried for the third time to fly around the edge of the cliff, beyond the lights of The Crossing, but the wall of air pushed me back. The sun had long since disappeared beyond the horizon and I knew my parents would be furious with me for embarrassing them, but I still couldn't bring myself to leave. In the weeks following my chat with Dashuri, I'd tried to come to terms with the fact that I would never find out about Helle, but now, here I was chatting to a real-life Chaos. The thought alone was enough to make me laugh.

"What's your name?" I asked.

"Jasmine," the voice replied, muffled as though underwater. "No. Wait. Thorn."

I laughed. I'd known I wouldn't get a proper response. "Nice to meet you, Thorn."

"What's your name, then?"

My lips curled into a grin. "Rose."

Laughter echoed through the barrier, and I tried to ignore the warmth spreading across my chest. This Chaos seemed friendly, but I knew better. They were ruthless and cruel in Helle. The scar across my chest tingled in agreement. At least I knew why the female Chaos had been so surprised by my reaction to the feather she'd stolen. It appeared that intimacy meant nothing in Helle. It was hard to imagine a world on the other side of the rippling wall of light. A world that looked like Hehven but filled with black-winged Chaos who, it seemed, lived as viciously as they fought. My family annoyed me, but the idea of fearing for my life at their hands sent a shudder down my spine.

The lights of The Crossing glowed brighter as night fell, and as we chatted, I trailed the tip of my wing through the colours, watching my white feathers turn purple and green. The conversation flowed with such ease, it was easy to forget who, or what, I was talking to.

As I pushed the thought aside, the air filled with the sound of beating of wings and for a moment, I wondered if the Chaos had found a way around The Crossing to Hehven. I turned, looking over my shoulder to find that the approaching wings were white.

Tiesa landed beside me, staring at me in disbelief. "What are you doing? I've been looking everywhere for you!"

I cast a glance at The Crossing. I had to get Tiesa out of there before she said something that might give away more than I wanted to share. More than that, I didn't want Tiesa to know about Thorn. I was already bitterly disappointed that she now knew the whereabouts of my clifftop hideaway.

"Sorry," I said. "I was just trying to prepare myself."

"You've been gone for hours, Pa—"

"I said I'm sorry," I cut her off. "I'm coming. Okay?"

She stared at me, hurt flashing in her sea green eyes. "I should warn you. Your parents are not happy."

I exhaled. "I can imagine. Just give me a second. I'll be right behind you."

She didn't leave, continuing to stare at me as though I'd lost my grip on reality.

"I promise," I tried again.

Shaking her head, Tiesa launched into the air. I waited until she was a safe distance away before turning to The Crossing.

"I have to go," I said.

"Sounds like you're in trouble, Rose."

I smiled. "Yeah. I think my night is about to get a lot worse."

"Good luck."

"Thanks."

I pressed my fingers to the light for a second, then before I could lose my nerve, spread my wings and flew back towards my parents, the Festival, and my responsibilities. Tiesa hadn't got far, and I caught up with her after a minute or two. Falling in beside her, I tried to find the right words to apologise for being so brusque.

"It's okay," she said, her eyes focused ahead. "I forgive you."

"Forgive me for what?"

"Being a jerk."

I snorted. "Thanks."

"You're welcome." She turned to look at me, the tiny braids she'd put in her hair coming loose in the wind. "You should practise your apologies, though. You've got quite a few to make when we get back to the palace."

My stomach sank. "I lost track of time."

It was true, in a way. I had only meant to step away for an hour to clear my head and mentally prepare for meeting my future wife. The world tipped slightly at the thought, and I swallowed hard. I hadn't expected to meet anyone at the cliffs. Let alone a Chaos.

"I'm worried about you, Pace."

The gleaming ivory spires of the palace came into view on the horizon, and I blew out a breath, dipping lower. "I'm worried about me too."

The lush green grounds of the palace were decked out in white and gold, with flashes of peach and pale blue between.

Long tables had been set up in two of the courtyards, draped with white cloth and lit by candles in delicate glass orbs. Music played softly as people reclined on chairs and piled cushions, chatting and laughing. Every Cupid in Hehven was invited to the Festival, although cities hosted their own smaller events for those who preferred not to travel to the capital.

As I landed on the outskirts, straightening my gold embroidered tunic and running a hand through my hair, I wondered what the Festival would be like in Helle. I tried to imagine people shouting and laughing, drunk and dancing. What had Thorn said? People giving into their basic desires. My heart stuttered.

"Are you okay?" Tiesa asked, frowning up at me. "You look like you're going to be sick."

"Is it that hard to understand, Tee?" I replied. "I don't want to get married. I don't want any of this."

Startled by my honesty, she grabbed my sleeve, dragging me further back from the outskirts of the crowd. "I do get it," she said. "But it's happening. You can't fly away from it."

"I wasn't trying to fly away from it. I just . . ." I pressed my fingers to my eyes. "Let's just get this over and done with."

I started to move forward but Tiesa kept hold of my arm, her grip tugging me back until I stopped to look at her.

"It's going to be okay, Pace," she said. "I know you're not happy about it, but it's going to be okay."

I managed a tight smile, then slipped out of her grip and headed into the crowd towards where my parents were watching over the proceedings. I barely acknowledged the murmured greetings and half bows as I made my way through the heaving mass of wings. My stomach was in knots and my heart was pounding so fiercely it was all I could do not to turn and fly away. Or vomit. I wasn't sure which would be worse.

My father saw me first. Dressed in robes of flowing pale blue to match his eyes, a circlet of jewelled wings rested, sparkling, atop his long white hair, which he wore loose around his shoulders. His pleasant expression faded into one of familiar dissatisfaction as he watched me approach.

"Pace. You've decided to grace us with your presence."

My mother turned, the smile on her face fading to sadness upon hearing my name. "Where were you? Poor Caitland is devastated."

Devastated. The word tore through me like a jagged blade. I hadn't stopped to think about what she might have felt. Did she *want* to marry me? I had assumed she'd been forced into the marriage as I had.

I bowed low, folding my wings. "My sincerest apologies, Mother. Father. I stepped away for some quiet and fell asleep."

My father shook his head with a grunt before motioning to someone at a table nearby. My heart rate rocketed as a tall, slim male stood, a young female rising beside him. Was that Caitland? I could hardly breathe as they moved towards us. She was pretty. Tall and slender, with elegant wings, her white hair was tied up in sweeping thick braids, with wisps framing her soft features. Her flawless brown skin had a golden glow to it, enhanced by the candlelight. I watched until she was only a few steps away, but she didn't look up once, facing my parents instead, and sinking into a curtsey.

"I'd like to extend our sincerest apologies once more, Lord Rakkaus," my father said. "My son has promised to improve his timekeeping before the wedding."

My neck was hot as I met Lord Rakkaus' wary expression, dipping into a small bow. "Please accept my humblest apologies. It was never my intent to keep you and your daughter waiting. I've been looking forward to meeting her."

The lie rolled off my tongue with little effort and I hated myself for it. Caitland kept her eyes on the marble paving stones and guilt burrowed a little deeper into my chest. I'd hurt her. What a great first impression.

"Perhaps you and Caitland would like to take a little walk and get to know each other," my mother suggested. "Not too far, of course."

"An excellent idea, Mother."

Lord Rakkaus gave me a nod of approval, although I could see the reluctance in his eyes. He had probably been beside himself when his daughter was offered a prince and now, he was stuck with me. I stepped to Caitland and offered my arm. She took it but kept her gaze downcast and, as I led her away from the scrutinising gaze of my parents, I wondered whether she would ever look at me. I didn't even know what colour her eyes were.

People murmured as we walked by, heads dipping in respect. I was used to it, but I doubted Caitland was. Had she even noticed, with her gaze fixed on her feet? On the outskirts of the celebrations, I found a pair of empty chairs and gestured for her to sit, sinking down onto the one opposite.

"I really am sorry," I said. "I didn't mean to keep you waiting. I could give excuses but none of them would be good enough. I was rude and inconsiderate, and I'll do everything I can to make it up to you."

Caitland dipped her head a little, her gaze now focused on her hands, folded in her lap. "Thank you, Your Majesty. It really is okay. I forgive you."

"Please, call me Pace."

I frowned, resting my chin on my fist as I stared at her. *My future wife.* At the words, every fibre of my being wanted to launch into the sky and fly until my wings gave out. The truth was, I'd never given much thought to who I'd marry until it was decided for me.

"If we're to be married," I said, "you're going to have to look at me at some point."

Her hands tightened in her lap, but then her head started to lift. Her eyes were an unusual shade of silvered grey. I scarcely dared breathe as I quickly took in the delicate angles of her face, but Caitland held my stare for all of two seconds before returning it to her lap. I noticed that her cheeks had pinkened significantly, even beneath her bronzed skin, and I exhaled with the realisation. She was nervous.

"I promise I don't bite," I joked. "There's no need to be nervous."

She made a small sound, and I wasn't sure if it was a giggle or a whimper. Pulling a hand over my face, I stared at her through my fingers. It was like pulling teeth. With an uncomfortable jolt, I realised how much easier it had been to talk to the Chaos on the cliff. Although perhaps that had been because we couldn't see each other. I chewed the inside of my lip as inspiration sparked.

"I have an idea." I took my chair and moved it behind hers, placing them back-to-back, before sitting down once more. "There we go. Is that better?"

"I'm not sure what you want me to say, Your Majesty."

I grimaced. "Please. Call me Pace. And I want you to say whatever you'd like. We're supposed to be getting to know one another."

"What would you like to know, Your—Pace?"

Leaning back in the chair, I rested my ankle on my knee. "What do you enjoy? What do you do for fun? I've never seen you at a Festival before. Is this your first time in Dragoste?"

Caitland was silent for a moment, and I realised I'd bombarded her with far too many questions in my desperation to get her to talk.

"I enjoy poetry and embroidery," she answered, her voice quavering a little as though worried she was getting the answers wrong. "I haven't been to Dragoste before. This is my first time leaving Rakkaus. My father is quite protective."

Fates. "I can imagine this must all be rather overwhelming, then," I offered. "Was it a long flight?"

"We travelled by carriage."

My eyes widened. Only small children and the elderly travelled long distances by carriage. Perhaps her father was unwell. "Do you enjoy flying?"

"I like it as well as any other."

As well as any other. What did that even mean? Flying was everything. The feeling of soaring on the wind, muscles stretching, and feathers caressed by the sun—I couldn't live without it. I cast a subtle glance over my shoulder at her wings. The elegant appearance I had noted on her approach, I now realised was a lack of muscle definition. She wouldn't have been able to fly here from Rakkaus even if she'd wanted to. I doubted she could fly to the top of the palace.

"What about you, Your Ma—Pace?" she asked. "What do you enjoy?"

"Flying," I answered without hesitation. "I enjoy flying, sword fighting, reading, and spending time with my friends."

"Reading?" she asked. "What do you enjoy reading?"

I sank back in my chair with a smile. "Adventure. Stories of far-off lands and epic battles."

"That sounds very exciting."

My hands gripped the arms of my chair, wanting to turn it around to face her, but now I had her talking, I didn't want to startle her. "You said you liked poetry? What type of poetry?"

"Any, really," she said. "I'm particularly fond of poems about nature and flowers."

Something in my chest unravelled just a little and I smiled. "You'd like my sister, Amani. She knows the name of every flower there is."

Perhaps Tiesa and Dariel were right. Maybe this wouldn't be so bad. Caitland certainly wasn't exciting, but she wasn't awful. Maybe in time, I could get her to enjoy flying as much as I did.

"I think perhaps we should return to our parents," she said quietly.

"Oh." I frowned. "If that's what you wish."

"I don't mean to offend," she added hurriedly. "It's only that my father and I are returning to Rakkaus tonight and it's a long journey."

Of course. Guilt tightened its grip around my heart once more. I had wasted more than an hour of the time we could have spent together. "Would you and your father prefer to spend the night at the palace? We have plenty of rooms."

"Oh, no, Your Majesty. Thank you for your kind offer but we must return to my mother and sisters."

I stood and circled her chair, offering her my arm once again. She lifted her eyes to mine for a second, before blushing profusely and returning her gaze to the floor. Swallowing my frustration, I walked her back to where her father stood talking to my parents.

"Did you two have fun?" my mother asked.

I dipped my head. "Caitland is most lovely. We had a wonderful conversation. I tried to convince her to stay longer, but she informs me you must leave tonight."

Lord Rakkaus nodded. "Indeed. I must return to my family. I have just confirmed with the king and queen that we will return a week before the Winter Festival of Fates in preparation for the wedding."

My eyebrows shot up in surprise. "Wait. I won't get to see her again before the wedding?"

"Pace," my mother warned.

I stared at her in disbelief before returning my attention to Caitland's father. "I had hoped to get to know your daughter better before the wedding. Would you not be able to return for the Summer Festival?"

Lord Rakkaus glanced at my parents before shaking his

head. "There is much to do in Rakkaus with the planting season and the harvest."

"You will have plenty of time to get to know each other once you are married," my mother said, her tone signalling the end of the discussion.

I was still struggling to process as Caitland and her father bid their farewells before disappearing into the crowd. As soon as they were gone, I turned to my parents, but the king cut me off before I could draw a breath.

"If you'd wanted to get to know her, you should have been here on time."

"I didn't know it would be the only chance I had," I snapped.

My father shook his head. "It shouldn't have mattered. You were rude and thoughtless."

"She is lovely, though. Is she not?" my mother asked.

I sighed, pinching the bridge of my nose. "Yes. She is."

"Don't worry, Pace," she soothed. "You're a good match. I'm confident you'll be very happy together."

There was no point arguing, so I gritted my teeth and bowed. "I'm sure you're right, mother. If you'll excuse me, I'm going to go and find Dariel and Tiesa."

Avoiding my parents' gaze, I turned and started back between the crowded tables, heading for the outskirts of the celebration. Music wove its way between the masses, as delicate as the spring breeze that carried it. Now that the sun had set, tables had been moved to make space for dancing, although it was mostly married Cupids who took up the opportunity.

A cluster of white wings caught my eye at the edge of the crowd, and I slowed my escape. Three young males who couldn't have been more than fifteen, were huddled around something, casting furtive glances over their shoulders. Curious, I took a step closer.

"I said, no."

At the sound of a young female's voice, my wings flared, and I strode over to the group. "What's going on?" I demanded.

The young males turned, annoyance sliding from their faces as they realised who had interrupted them. I regarded them with narrowed eyes before finding the source of their attention. A female stood before them, her arms wrapped around her shoulders and tears staining her dark cheeks.

"I'm going to ask one more time," I bit out, anger tightening my jaw. "What is going on here?"

"Nothing!" one of the males protested. His friend elbowed him in his gut and he winced. "Your Majesty."

I turned my attention to the female, softening my tone. "Are you okay? Were they hurting you?"

She sniffled, her long white hair sliding over her shoulders as she shook her head.

"We swear on the Fates, we weren't doing anything bad," another of the young males insisted. "Our friend Koa told us she'd—"

"She said no," I snarled. "It doesn't matter what your friend said."

"But—"

I reached out and gripped his tunic, lifting him off the ground. "There is no 'but'. If someone says no, it means no."

The young male's silver eyes were wide as his wings flared behind him. "I'm sorry, Your Majesty. We won't do it again."

I took my time, searing the other two males with my gaze before lowering him to the ground. "If I hear of you doing anything like this again, I'll tell the queen and order your wings clipped. Do you understand?"

"Yes, Your Majesty," they stammered in unison.

"Get out of here," I barked. Shaking my head as they scattered amongst the crowd, I turned back to the young female. "Are you all right? Did they touch you?"

"No," she said, her voice barely above a whisper. "They were just mean."

I exhaled in relief. "Do you have family or friends nearby?"

She nodded. "My parents are dancing."

"Would you like me to take you to them?"

She looked up at me, her blue eyes wide. "No. I'm fine. Thank you for getting rid of them, Your Majesty."

"My pleasure." I smiled. "Go and enjoy the rest of the Festival."

I watched as she fluttered off in the direction of the dance floor, only looking away once I was sure she was okay. Anger continued to course through my veins, however, even as I continued to make my way toward the outer edge of the courtyard. What if someone behaved like that toward Amani?

"Pace!"

I looked up, spotting Dariel and Tiesa making their way towards me. Both wore matching wary expressions.

"How did it go?" Dariel asked.

Tiesa grimaced as she looked up at me. "We watched the whole thing."

"Great. So, you know exactly how awkward it was."

Dariel frowned. "Why, for the love of Fates and feathers, did you move your chair behind hers?"

We sank down onto seats at the end of an empty table. "She couldn't look at me," I explained. "It was bizarre. I thought perhaps it might help her to talk to me."

"Did it work?"

I shrugged. "Sort of. I found out she likes poetry and embroidery, and doesn't fly." The look of horror on Dariel's face was laughable. "She was so nervous," I continued. "I know I was an ass for keeping her waiting, but it's not as if I'm scary, right?"

Tiesa turned her face away, chortling into whatever was in the glass she was holding. I glanced at Dariel, but he shrugged.

"What's so amusing?" I asked, folding my arms. "Please share."

Tiesa shook her head, still snickering. "Nope. Your ego is big enough."

Lifting my foot, I kicked her thigh, shoving her off her seat. Her wings flared, stopping her from hitting the ground but most of her drink landed in a puddle on the floor. As soon as she'd steadied herself, she rounded on me, eyes blazing.

"Prince or not, I will not hesitate to knock you on your ass."

I leaned back, my eyebrows raised. "Tell me what you found so funny."

Muttering under her breath, Tiesa reclaimed her seat. "I was laughing because it was clear why she was nervous and you're an idiot for not seeing it."

My wings ruffled at the insult, and I sat up straighter. "I know she's nervous for the same reasons I am. Meeting the person you're supposed to marry isn't a normal social situation."

Tiesa rolled her eyes. "You're really going to make me spell it out for you, aren't you?"

I turned to Dariel in frustration. "What is she talking about?"

"I think, Cousin," Dariel offered. "What Tiesa is trying to say, is that Caitland was intimidated."

I frowned. "Because I'm a prince?"

"Because you're a very attractive prince," Dariel corrected, amusement flashing in his pale blue eyes.

"What am I supposed to do about that?" I huffed. "Is she just never going to look at me?"

Tiesa snorted. "Maybe you could wear a mask?"

"Or you could just always stand back-to-back." Dariel laughed.

"You know," I said, getting to my feet. "I remember a time not so long ago when you two were on my side."

"Oh, come on," Tiesa said. "We're only teasing."

"And I'm not in the mood. I'll be in the training circles in the morning."

Before they could respond, I stepped away and shot into the air, not caring that my wings caused candles to flicker out and glasses to overturn. I flew with the intent of putting as much distance between me and the palace as possible and, as my wings beat hard against the cold evening air, I didn't realise where I was flying to until I found myself back at the cliffs. Breathing hard, I stared out at the inky ocean.

"Thorn?" I called out, instantly regretting it.

The only reply was the sound of the waves crashing against the rocks far below. I pressed my fingers to the emerald and sapphire lights of The Crossing, contemplating the world on the other side. Was the Chaos who'd taken my feather enjoying their version of the Festival right now? My jaw clenched as I pictured her drunk and dancing, my long white feather grasped in her hand. Perhaps she was as bored by it as Thorn. I still had so many questions. Sinking down to the ground, I stared out at the water and wondered whether the Chaos would return to the cliff knowing that they might talk to me again. I huffed at the horizon. It had been a fluke, and the chances of us ever meeting again were a million to one.

Our conversation had felt different. I loved Dariel and Tiesa, but as of late, our interactions had left me feeling raw and tense. I thought of my talk with Caitland and snorted. Speaking to Thorn had been like taking a deep breath. They didn't expect anything from me. They didn't want anything from me. I couldn't disappoint them.

Looking up at The Crossing, I knew I wouldn't be able to let it go. Chaos or not, I wanted more. Needed more. The evening breeze ruffled my hair and feathers, and I closed my eyes, trying once more to picture the world on the other side of the lights.

8
Sirain

Entering the human world was different this time. I'd accompanied Odio on countless missions, but never had I scoured the night sky looking for white wings—nor endured the fear of waiting for an arrow to pierce my flesh. They may have been Cupids, fabled for spreading love and peace, but there had been no mistaking the naked hatred in those honey-gold eyes. I knew in my soul that if we ever met again, he would try to kill me.

"Everything okay?" Kwellen called out as we soared over the ocean.

I flipped onto my back, gliding effortlessly beneath the slither of silver moon. My new mask was itchy, and I pushed my hand up under the leather to scratch my nose before pulling it back in place. "Never better."

Tonight's mission was taking us to Dalibor, my favourite of the four human countries. Already I could see the long white beaches lining its shores, melting into rich emerald jungles and thick winding rivers that embraced towering snow tipped mountains. It was as though someone had combined all the best parts of the human world in one magnificent thriving landmass.

We soared through the darkness, heading toward the sprawling stone palace built into the side of the tallest mountain. Although it reminded me a little of Hadeon, the architecture was starkly different. Where my home was hewn from dark rock, wrought into jagged spikes and spires, Dalibor's palace was a collection of smooth pale domes and curved arches, draped with flowering vines. We alighted on the tallest dome to catch our breath, staring down at the expansive cobbled courtyard bustling with humans.

Odio signalled toward another tower and a light flickering inside the open window. I nodded and he leapt from the dome, his wings carrying him in a sweeping arc before landing soundlessly on the vine wrapped balcony. Our wings were so large, the sound of them beating risked drawing attention, so wherever possible, it was vital we allowed currents of air to carry us. Kwellen gestured for me to follow, so I pushed myself forward, letting the wind lift me in a silent glide between the towers. Voices carried through the open window and as Kwellen landed beside us, Odio leaned back against the stone wall, his hand clutching his chest.

"I love her," he whispered.

Kwellen sneered. "She's old enough to be your mother."

"Age means nothing when it's true love."

Kwellen groaned and I grinned. My cousin's inappropriate crush on the ruler of Dalibor was longstanding.

"Why do you think she only comes out at night?" I mused, listening to the murmur of voices beyond the window.

Odio sighed. "Isn't it obvious? It's because she knows that's the only time I can visit. It's Fated."

"As if a queen would be interested in you." Kwellen snorted.

Before they could start fighting, a shout carried up from the courtyard and, pressing back against the stone, I peered down. The guards were changing shift. I watched, fascinated, as they marched in unison, their smart, midnight black uniforms reminiscent of the rippling sea at night.

"The coach has been spotted, Your Majesty."

A voice sounded at the window, and my heart leapt into my mouth.

"Excellent. Let's go and greet our guest."

Odio slid down the wall, his hands gripping his chest at the sound of the Midnight Queen's rich, velvet tones. I gave him the briefest of glances before turning my attention to the road that wound its way up the mountain to the palace. Two horse-drawn carriages could be seen between the gaps in the dense forest and before long, the steady clattering of hooves on the stone path carried on the wind.

The black-clad soldiers in the courtyard had arranged themselves in a neat semicircle in preparation for the visitors and, as the ornate carriage made its way up to the towering iron gates, the Midnight Queen emerged from the main doors. Six aides held the hem of her long velvet train as she gracefully descended the marble steps, and the soldiers shifted their swords, feet stomping as they acknowledged their revered leader. Her black diamond crown sparkled under the light of the flaming torches adorning the courtyard and her long dark hair, woven with accents that caught the light, trailed down her back. She might only come out at night, but she certainly knew how to make an entrance.

Tearing my gaze from the scene below, I peered at the other domed turrets for the hundredth time, searching for any sign of white wings. Only when I was satisfied we were alone, did I return my attention to the courtyard. A tall human male had stepped from the carriage, and it took me a moment to place him as the ruler of Liridona. I recalled his name being something pompous and ridiculous, but it had been a while since Odio had been assigned to his lands. *Tumeric Snitcherton? No.* I shook my head and tried to concentrate, intrigued by their tense body language.

"Do you ever wonder what they're saying?" I asked as Odio selected an arrow from his quiver.

He shook his head and lined up his shot. "It's inconsequential. What do we care what the humans get up to? Besides, straying from orders might incur the wrath of the Fates." He released the bowstring. "No, thank you."

The arrow arched gracefully down into the courtyard piercing the Midnight Queen's heart. A perfect shot. I considered my cousin's words. What exactly would the wrath of the Fates involve? My stomach squirmed uncomfortably. Did the Fates know about our run in with the Cupids? Did they know we had drawn blood? Did they know I had stolen a feather?

"Sirain," Odio hissed. "Come on. Time to go."

Kwellen extended his wings and dropped from the balcony swooping behind the palace to the mountainside, where he pulled up at the jagged treeline, soaring back towards the sea. I followed, with Odio just behind, but I found myself taking in more than just the scenery. The large, curved harbour was crammed with looming wooden winches and pulleys alongside the skeletons of mammoth ships in various stages of construction.

Drifting away from the others, I flew over the silent harbour, my brow furrowed as I tried to make sense of what I was seeing. Only the Midnight Queen and her court slept during the day, the rest of her country rising with the sun, so the harbours were all but deserted. Further along the coast, I spotted another similarly repurposed harbour and frowned.

"What are you doing?" Kwellen asked, joining me as I continued along the shoreline of the vast country. "We need to get back."

"Why are they building so many ships?"

"Who cares? What the humans get up to is their own business."

I pressed my lips together. There was no point pushing the matter.

"You're not looking for *them*, are you?"

My head snapped round. "Looking for who?"

"Cupids."

Before I could stop myself, my eyes lifted, scanning the sky for white wings as though the mere mention might force them into existence. I breathed a sigh of relief when I found nothing but Odio flying high above us. "No. I was just curious about the ships."

Kwellen stared at me, but I couldn't read the expression behind his mask. He shook his head. "Come on. We can't linger, you know that."

I did. Tearing my gaze away from the human world below, I headed out to sea and back towards The Crossing. *Was Rose a Hand*? The thought came out of nowhere and I blinked in surprise. It had been a week since the Festival, and I hadn't been back to the cliffs. I'd thought about it, of course. I just hadn't had the time. I swallowed the lie as we reached the shimmering air of The Crossing, the thought now a niggling itch beneath my skin.

I was still lost in thought when I flew through the open window of my bedroom. Tucking my mask away in the jagged slit hidden in my mattress, my fingers brushed the Cupid feather stashed there and I pulled it free, my heart pounding. It was so white it seemed to glow in the darkness and, stroking along the ivory vane, I revelled at its softness. A hint of shimmering gold lingered at its edges, and I touched my finger to it in awe. Against my better judgement, I dragged the silken edge against my cheek, my eyes drifting shut. I swore I could smell him—warm and light like a summer's breeze. Shaking my head, I shoved the feather back into its hiding place.

Almost as though it was calling me, I moved to my window and stared out at The Crossing, glowing green in the distance against the star flecked sky. My mind wandered to thoughts of the cliffs. Rose wouldn't be there. Not so late at night. It had been a one in a million chance the first time. What if they *were* there, though? I'd never know if I didn't try. My pulse throbbed as I gripped the window ledge.

A sharp knock sounded at my door, and I paused, considering ignoring it. Before I could decide, it opened, and I froze as my brother strode in as though the room was his own.

"Excuse me," I snapped, stalking across the room towards him. "You can't just barge in here."

Fin raised his dark brows and looked around. "It would seem I just did."

"What do you want?"

He looked pointedly at the window before taking in my black leathers. "Where have you been, Sister?"

"None of your business. Get out, I was about to take a bath."

"It doesn't look like you were about to take a bath," he drawled, his eyes flitting from the empty tub before returning to the window.

Perhaps it was the lingering adrenaline from visiting the human world, but before I could think better of it, my knife was in my hand and pressed to my brother's throat. "I don't give two feathers what you think it looks like, Fin."

His garnet eyes blazing, he leaned into the blade, sending a small bead of blood down the smooth black surface. "What are you going to do, Sirain? Slit my throat?"

My grip tightened but I held my ground, refusing to let him intimidate me in my own space. "If you get out, I won't have to."

For a moment, I thought he might push further forward, leaving me no choice but to withdraw or risk slicing into his throat, but he stepped back. I kept the bloodied blade raised, my eyes fixed on his, as he moved to the door.

"I know you're hiding something," he said, his hand on the handle. "I'll find out what it is soon enough."

"Ugh. Why do you have to be so creepy?" I shuddered. "Go annoy your friends. Oh, wait. You don't have any."

Fin smiled, knowing he'd ruffled my feathers, and stepped

out into the reception rooms beyond, closing the door behind him. I threw the knife with all my might, and it embedded in the wood almost up to the hilt. My brother's chuckle echoed under the door, and I swallowed my scream of frustration. Grabbing my sword from the wall, I ran and leapt from the window, heading straight for the training grounds—all thoughts of visiting my peaceful cliff forgotten.

9

Pace

Colour stained my cheeks as I got to my feet, my legs stiff from sitting for so long. I was a fool. The chances of both Thorn and I being there at the same time were a million to one. I'd thought perhaps trying at night would have increased the odds, but it seemed I was wrong. It was the first time I'd been back to the cliffs since the Festival, although I'd thought about returning several times. Each time I'd convinced myself I was remembering it wrong. I hadn't laughed. I hadn't delighted in the easy conversation. I certainly hadn't enjoyed the company of a Chaos. The only reason I'd finally given in was because I needed to find out more about Helle. Thorn was nothing more than a source of information. The fact they weren't here was definitely the only reason for my disappointment. Rubbing my hands over my face, I took one last look at the black waves dancing under the crescent moon and launched into the sky. If I couldn't get answers from Thorn, it left only one option.

The palace island was shrouded in darkness, with only a handful of Cupids keeping watch, their lanterns flickering. What were they watching for? Chaos? I'd never stopped to wonder before. Was there any chance of the so-called demons getting into Hehven? Dipping my wing, I rode the cool evening breeze past the palace toward the towering mountains on the other side of the water. Spring had melted most of the snow, but the peaks of the Dragoste Mountains still glistened like jagged teeth beneath the moonlight. I kept going until I saw a small cluster of buildings nestled in the foothills—a village with red slate roofs presided over by a large stone building. Chateau Dragoste.

My cousin would likely be asleep, but I headed to the north wing of the building regardless and landed on the wide window ledge, gripping the stone frame. The room inside was dark, the glass closed against the cool night air. I hesitated, pulling my lip under my teeth as I considered my options. My dishevelled reflection stared back at me, and I frowned. I should have waited until morning. This was exactly what Dariel had meant on Cove's ship. I acted first, thought later. It was why my parents had matched me with quiet, sensible, non-flying Caitland. I leaned forward and rested my forehead against the cold windowpane. My sigh fogged the glass and I spread my wings, ready to return to the palace. I'd speak to him tomorrow.

My fingertips were just letting go when a lamp flickered on. Dariel pushed himself up in bed, his sharp blue eyes finding my silhouette instantly, and I lifted my hand in a half wave. He threw back his covers and stalked to the window. Even in undershorts and sleep mussed hair, he cut an intimidating figure and I braced myself as he opened the window.

"Get inside," he said, his voice thick with sleep.

Jumping down from the ledge, I savoured the warmth of his room as he closed the window behind me. "I'm sorry for visiting so late."

"I'm assuming it's important." He lay back on the bed with a groan, his wings splayed out on either side.

"I was just about to leave when you woke up," I offered. "I hadn't realised how late it was."

Dariel dragged a hand over his face. "You know what? I'm glad you came. I've been wanting to speak with you."

"Really? About what?"

"What you said at the Festival," he began. "It stayed with me. I haven't been the greatest of friends recently and I want to apologise."

"Dariel, seriously. It's fine. I—"

"No." He sat up and pulled his fingers through his long hair. "I need you to hear this. Your father approached me months ago about arranging your marriage. He convinced me it would be good for you. I should have put our friendship first. I should have warned you."

My mouth ran dry. "What did you do?"

"Caitland was my suggestion." Dariel pinched the bridge of his nose. "Her brother is a friend of mine. We were talking, and when he described how quiet and sensible his sister was, I knew she was exactly the kind of female your parents were looking for. I told the king about her, and he agreed."

I stared at the floor, the intricate blue and yellow patterns on the diamond-shaped tiles swimming as I tried to process what my cousin was saying. "*You* chose Caitland for me?"

"I'm sorry," Dariel said. "I knew you wouldn't be thrilled about the arrangement, but I clearly misjudged the situation. As soon as I saw how devastated you were, I went to the king and queen and asked them to reconsider—to wait until you were older—but they'd already made up their minds."

I looked up to find him watching me, his face pained.

"That's why I let you come with me to the human world," he said. "It wasn't pity, Pace. It was guilt. I knew it was a bad idea, but I thought perhaps I could offer you something, anything, to atone for my betrayal."

My head ached. "So, my father wanted to arrange my marriage with someone quiet and sensible, and you chose Caitland. Can't even look at me, couldn't fly to the top of an apple tree, Caitland."

Dariel winced. "I didn't know she didn't fly. She sounded sweet."

I turned and gripped the window ledge, unsure what to do with my cousin's confession as I stared out at the silent village below. He was expecting me to be angry, but I wasn't. Disappointed, definitely. But, not angry. I closed my eyes and exhaled. If he hadn't suggested Caitland, my parents would have chosen someone similar. Although maybe their choice might have enjoyed flying.

When I finally turned back around, I found my cousin with his head in his hands, his large wings cocooning his shoulders. Even though there were only four months between us, he had always been like a big brother to me—my voice of reason and the source for my advice.

I crossed the room, tucking my wings in tight so I could perch beside him on the bed. "It's okay, Dariel. I forgive you."

He shook his head. "You shouldn't."

"Cousin, I'm not going to throw a lifetime of friendship away because you made one questionable choice." I reached out and gently pushed his wing away so I could wrap my arm around his shoulders. "The marriage wasn't your idea. It would have happened either way."

Dariel exhaled and leaned into me. "I'm sorry, Pace. I'll do better. I promise."

I squeezed the hard muscle of his shoulder. The question I had gone there to ask formed on my tongue, although it tasted bitter enough to make me wince. "Will you take me on another mission?"

Dariel looked up. "Excuse me?"

"I want you to take me back to the human world."

"No."

I stood, folding my arms across my chest. "You said you were going to be a better friend."

Dariel laughed, his face the picture of disbelief. "How would taking you to the human world make me a better friend? If anything, it would make me a worse friend. I should never have taken you the first time. Look what happened! I'm not risking your safety again."

I stared down at him, my heartbeat thrumming in my throat. "If you don't take me, I'll go by myself."

"You'll get yourself killed."

I straightened my wings. "Not now I know what to expect."

"I'll tell your father." Dariel stood, his wings flaring. "I'll tell him everything."

The laugh that left my lips was cold. "And just like that, everything you said—everything you promised—has turned to dust. What of our friendship, Cousin?"

"I'll do whatever it takes to keep you safe."

"I'm not a child, Dariel," I bit out. "I don't need you to keep me safe. Take me with you or run and tell my father. Either way, I'm going to get my answers."

Dariel pressed his lips together so hard, they turned as pale as his hair. I shook my head and strode to the window, sliding open the latch.

"Wait."

I turned; my eyebrows raised.

"I have a mission in the morning," he admitted, his shoulders slumping in defeat. "I'll take you. Just promise you'll wait until then."

It took all my self-control to keep the grin from my lips. "Thank you."

Dariel snorted as he threw himself down onto the bed, reaching for the light. "What choice did you give me?"

I looked back at him, his figure now shrouded in darkness. "I could say the same, Cousin."

10
Sirain

Despite my complete and utter exhaustion, I was unable to get back to sleep. My dreams had alternated between Fin and the Cupid pointing sharp objects at me and plucking my feathers one by one. Even if I had managed to settle my racing mind and throbbing head, there was the matter of the rattling snores coming from the foot of my bed, loud enough to wake the humans through The Crossing. Cracking open a weary eye, I peeked at the window to find that the night had already begun to melt into a medley of soft pinks. I pulled my pillow over my face with a groan before admitting defeat.

Sliding out of bed with a grunt, I realised I was still dressed in my clothes from the night before. I had no recollection of returning to my rooms, let alone getting into bed. Wincing at the pulsing between my eyes, I padded over to where a long pair of black-clad legs were stretched out on the floor.

"Hey." I kicked one of the legs and the snoring momentarily stopped. "I'm getting up now, so you can use my bed if you want."

Odio muttered something unintelligible before rolling over and promptly returning to sleep. I stared down at him, marvelling at how my tall, lean warrior cousin looked little more than a scrawny teenager, curled up on my stone floor. My heart remained heavy from last night's ritual; but then Odio's birthday was always bittersweet as it was also the day his mother died.

His father made no secret of the fact he blamed my cousin for her death, which was also the reason we were so close. Odio had practically moved into the castle as a child, my uncle unable to stand the sight of him. I tugged the thick red blanket from my bed and draped it over him, tutting at his mud splattered boots. If there was any wine left in the cellar this morning, I would be very surprised.

Tugging on my boots, I crept out of my room, closing the door behind me. Servants were already milling around in the sprawling sitting rooms I never bothered using. A quick sweep of the chairs and corners told me that Kwellen had made it back to his own room this year. The servants didn't look up as I passed, instead curtseying low, their eyes downcast. My mother had caught me trying to talk to them once when I was younger. The threat of informing my father had ensured it was both the first and last time. My mind wandered to the feather stuffed in my mattress and I wondered whether there was a Cupid castle on the other side of The Crossing. Did they talk to their servants? I snorted. They probably didn't even have servants.

Opening the door to exit my rooms, every muscle in my body tensed. I was unlikely to run into Fin at this time in the morning, but I could never let my guard down. He was one of the reasons I hadn't been back to the cliff. If he ever decided to follow me—or more likely have one of his minions do it for him—it would be over. After listening for any sign of footsteps or rustling of wings and finding none, I stepped out into the corridor, making my way to the castle library.

It had been Odio's idea. Last night, halfway through the fourth bottle of wine, the Cupids had wound their way into our conversation. Although I'd managed to keep Rose to myself, I'd mentioned that I wanted to find out more about Hehven. My cheeks flushed at the memory of his obvious suggestion. Why hadn't I thought of it? Every footstep sounded like it was screaming my presence to everyone in the castle, and I cursed the high ceilings and thick stone walls.

"Sirain?"

My blood froze in my veins, every sinew of my body seizing at the sound of my father's deep scathing tones. I considered continuing on my way, pretending I hadn't heard him, but I had already paused too long. Steeling myself, I retreated a step and peered around the doorway I hadn't even noticed was open, the warmth of a roaring fire crackling out into the corridor. My father sat slumped in a large velvet chair, a wine glass in his hand. His dark eyes were fixed, unblinking on me; the shadowy circles around them, a sure sign he hadn't been to bed yet.

"Yes, Father?"

"You're up early."

I took another step into the room. "Odio's snoring woke me."

He pressed his wine-stained lips together and nodded. "I always think it's going to get easier, but it doesn't."

My heart throbbed in my stomach as I watched him. I had never seen him express any emotion besides disgust, disappointment and hate. Was this remorse? Sadness? Sinking back in his chair he took a deep swig of his wine and, as his eyes left mine, I felt air begin to seep into my lungs once more. Odio's mother, Mallou, had been my father's sister, but it had never once occurred to me that he might be sad about her death, even two decades later. I lingered, unsure what to do.

"How is Odio?" he asked.

I took a deep breath. "Same as every year."

My father nodded, his burgundy eyes fixed on the near-empty glass. I edged my way over to the low table at his side and picked up the bottle, offering it to him. His face remained expressionless, but he held up his glass, so I poured out the last of the wine.

"It wasn't his fault."

I froze, the now empty bottle in my hand, as the king drank deeply. Draining the glass, he set it down on the table and stood, his balance only wavering slightly. Without so much as a glance at me, made his way out of the room and into the corridor, his dark wings dragging on the floor, leaving me wondering what I'd just witnessed. Placing the bottle down, I followed after him, but he'd already disappeared. Of course, it wasn't Odio's fault. Even Odio knew that on some level. It was then I realised my father had never once blamed my cousin. I would have expected it of him, even more so than my uncle, but he never had. He'd accepted Odio's constant presence as I was growing up with barely a complaint.

Still reeling from possibly the most pleasant encounter I'd ever had with my father, I continued to the library. Consisting of two floors filled with books and three seating areas spaced between them, it was somewhere I hadn't visited since completing my studies at seventeen, and as I pushed open the carved wooden doors to find the large fireplace lit and a pleasant cinnamon smell in the air, I wondered why. The books were well organised, and I could hear the rustling of the librarian somewhere out of sight. I hoped I could find what I wanted without his help. Asking for books on the history of The Crossing and Hehven was something I didn't want getting back to my parents.

It didn't take me long to locate the shelves housing the historical texts, still in the same place I remembered from my studies, and I ran my fingers along the spines searching for titles that sounded promising. With gradually increasing disappointment, I realised I'd read most already and there was certainly no information about Hehven in them. That would have been something I'd have remembered.

"Can I help you, Your Majesty?"

My heart sank a little as the librarian appeared beside me, dipping into a bow. He was a short male who looked to be in his thirties, a long black ponytail over his shoulder. I ignored the unwelcome twinge of guilt I felt at the fact I had no idea what his name was. "I was just looking to brush up on my ancient history."

He glanced at the shelves with an approving nod. "Well, you've found the right place."

"Are there more?" I pressed. "Where are the really old books?"

"Old books?" he repeated, his brow furrowing.

I nodded. "Where are the oldest books in the castle?"

The librarian's face fell as he shook his head. "All destroyed."

"Destroyed? How?"

He glanced at me before turning to the books, straightening spines that were already perfectly straight. "A fire."

I blinked. "When?"

"Twenty-three years ago." He continued poking and prodding at the books for a moment before turning to me again. "All these books were commissioned and gathered by King Hadeon shortly after he took to the throne."

I opened my mouth to push further, but as the librarian shifted from foot to foot before me, shooting furtive glances over his shoulder, I realised there was no point. He would have been a child at the time. Certainly not the librarian. I gave him a grateful smile, which only served to make him tense further.

"Thank you," I said. "That'll be all."

He bowed again, turning on his heel and scurrying out of sight in a rustle of black feathers. My own wings drooping a little, I left the spiced warmth of the library and headed back to my rooms. With each step, my limbs grew a little heavier and I hoped that Odio had either stopped snoring or woken and returned to the room he usually used when at the castle.

There was no such luck, and I opened my bedroom door to find him still sprawled at the foot of my bed, his snoring louder than ever. I stared at him for a second before deciding I was too tired to care. Kicking off my boots, I collapsed onto my bed, pulling my pillow over my face. Questions swirled around my head, pulsing in time with the throbbing building there. Why had I never heard anyone mention a fire? How bad had it been? I would have to ask Kwellen and Odio later. Perhaps they'd heard something about it. I closed my eyes and this time, not even Odio's snores or the threat of bad dreams could keep the heavy pull of sleep from tugging at me, drawing me into darkness.

11

Pace

Keeping close to clouds tinged orange by the morning sun, clusters of golden sand and lush green trees stretched as far as the eye could see. Some islands were bigger than the one that housed my parents' palace and others were barely big enough to hold a village. The sapphire sea merged into rings of vivid turquoise around the gilded islands, and as the sun warmed my skin, my eyes drifted shut with bliss. The Wendell Islands were one of the most incredible things I had ever seen.

"Try not to look so damn happy," Dariel grumbled.

I opened my eyes and twisted, diving into a loop and allowing the warm air to caress my wings. "Why shouldn't I be happy? The scenery is gorgeous, the sunshine is divine, and I'm with my two favourite people."

Tiesa laughed. "Yes, well, let's hope it stays like that."

"Seriously, Pace," Dariel warned. "I'm in charge here. No flying off to eavesdrop like last time."

"I won't, I promise."

I meant it too. All I wanted was to see the humans again and enjoy a taste of freedom. Besides, the sunshine had burned away any fear of running into demons, although I noted Dariel scouring the skies a little more than usual.

"What's it like?" I asked. "Where they live?"

Dariel glanced at me before pointing at the city sprawling across the largest island. It was bigger than Hehven itself. "I've not been here before, but apparently it's on the outskirts, just inside the wall."

"You haven't been to the Wendell Islands before?"

"No. My past missions involving humans from these islands have been like the one you came on—taking place on ships and usually involving Cove. Today's mark is Marlowe, her brother."

I turned to Tiesa. "Have you seen Marlowe before?"

"Just once," she admitted. "It wasn't here though, and it was a while ago."

Before I could question them further, Dariel gestured again and dove toward the walled city. As we drew closer, patches along the towering wall that appeared newer than the rest of the weathered yellow bricks caught my eye—perhaps scars from the last human war. Watchtowers were dotted along the perimeter and my muscles flexed with anxiety. It was disconcerting flying over a city in broad daylight, even though it was still early morning, and the streets were deserted. We swooped, riding the breeze to avoid drawing attention with the beating of our wings, coming to a halt on top of an empty watchtower roof.

"Over there." Tiesa pointed to a five-storey building made of the same coarse yellow brick with dense forest to its back.

Its walls were peppered with small windows, big enough to let in the breeze but small enough to keep the hot air out. Squinting against the sun, I noted the royal blue banners hanging on either side of the door, a blazing golden sun at their centre.

"How do we find Marlowe?" I asked. The building wasn't as big as Hehven's palace, but it was still enormous, with unusual balconies wrapping each layer in staggered tiers. Finding a single human could take hours.

"We wait," Tiesa said, sinking down to the ground and bringing her knees to her chest.

"Wait," I repeated. "For how long?"

Dariel sat down beside her. "For however long it takes."

The sun beat down, becoming almost unbearably warm as it rose above the city, and I wondered whether we'd arrived early as some sort of punishment. Perhaps Dariel thought boredom would deter my curiosity or teach me a lesson. Well, it wouldn't. I lay down on my stomach, watching the city within the walls slowly come to life as the blazing sun rose in the sky. Before long, I'd unfastened the top few buttons of my shirt and wasn't far from considering taking it off completely.

"And this is spring?" I asked for the third time.

Tiesa groaned from where she was laid beside me, her large white wings curved to provide shade. "Yes. Summer in the Wendell Islands is like being inside an oven."

"Look," Dariel hissed.

I sat up, following his gaze to the staggered balconies. Each tier narrowed in width with the top balcony wide enough for a table, chairs and some potted plants, but not much else. A movement caught my eye and I saw what Dariel had spotted. Someone was standing between the balcony doors, their back to us as though talking to someone inside. The human took a step backwards and the sunshine illuminated familiar long dark braids interspersed with brightly coloured material. *Cove.*

"Let's get closer," Dariel said, his wings flaring.

Following his lead, I stretched and dove from the tower, soaring along the wall and up to the roof of the large building.

"Our intelligence is good," Cove's voice rose from the balcony below. "Bickerstaff met with the Midnight Queen."

A male voice sighed wearily. "That doesn't mean he's planning on moving against us."

"Why else would he visit Dalibor? To invite her to his birthday party?"

Moving closer to the edge, I could see that a man with short, tightly curled dark hair had joined Cove on the balcony. Leaning against the railing, his head rested wearily on his forearms.

"You were convinced the Midnight Queen was dead until recently. We have to give him the benefit of the doubt."

The man turned, bracing his tall muscular frame against the balcony, and I noted the twin blades at his hips. Glancing between the two humans, I was unable to deny the similarities in their appearance. Although younger than I'd expected, I was certain the man was Marlowe.

I turned to Dariel to find he already had his bow in his hands, the shot lined up. He let the arrow fly, and as it sliced into Marlowe's chest, a screeching cry echoed up from the balcony, so loud I winced. It was only then I noticed the red dragon coiled around Cove's neck, half hidden beneath her braids. Its yellow eyes were trained on us as it screeched and wailed. It could see us. My heart stopped.

"Go!" Dariel hissed, his eyes wide.

Cove and Marlowe turned to see what the dragon was screeching about and before any of us had time to spread our wings, a knife sliced through the air, a hair's breadth from my face. It embedded itself in the arch of Dariel's wing and he cried out, sinking to his knees on the baking hot roof, his bow falling to the tiles with a clatter. Cove reached for another blade, and it flew past, landing somewhere out of sight, the sound masked by Dariel's rumbling growl as he tugged the first knife from his wing.

"We need to get out of here," he grunted.

Cove's next blade didn't miss, embedding itself in Dariel's shoulder. He bellowed, wrenching the knife from his flesh, and throwing it to the tiled floor.

"Grab his arm," Tiesa shouted, no longer caring if the humans heard us.

Muttering an apology, I took Dariel's injured arm and pulled it over my shoulder, causing him to moan in pain as blood streamed down his chest. Tiesa mirrored me on his other side and together we lifted him to his feet.

"Stop!"

I barely heard the human's shout, my heart pounding a frantic beat as I realised we were going to have to carry Dariel all the way back to The Crossing. He was panting, teeth grinding through the pain as sweat beaded on his brow. What if his wing was damaged permanently? Bile rose in my throat, and I choked it down.

"I said stop!"

"Go," Tiesa grunted as she spread her wings.

"My bow," Dariel moaned. "We can't leave my bow."

"Yes, we can," Tiesa said, beating her wings. "It's your bow or our lives. Go!"

Gritting my teeth, I extended my wings, tightening my grip around Dariel's waist. It was almost impossible to fly, with Tiesa's wings brushing mine and Dariel's folded between us. The second we left the roof, we dipped down, the humans still shouting at us to stop. Even with two of us, he was too heavy. Tiesa cried out as Dariel's arm slipped from her shoulders, and then we were falling.

My muscles screamed as I tried to keep us in the air. I heaved, my fingers slipping on his bloodied skin. A growl of frustration ripped from my throat as gravity won, and we fell with a thud to the balcony below. Above, Cove and Marlowe were still watching, weapons drawn. I shoved Dariel off from where he had landed on my leg and got to my feet. Blood was running crimson rivers down his arm, staining his shirt and dripping onto the feathers beneath him, turning them a dozen shades of pink.

"Come on, Dariel," Tiesa pleaded, pulling his good arm. "Come on."

A whoosh of air accompanied by a soft thud sounded behind me and I turned to find that Marlowe had leapt from the balcony above, landing just a few strides away. I drew the golden sword from my side, the metal singing against the scabbard. My wings flared, snapping the air as they extended to their full width, the gold edges of my feathers glinting in the blazing sun.

"Angels." Marlowe's mouth fell open and he dropped to his knees, his sword clattering to the ground beside him. "Fates forgive me."

I frowned, about to ask him what he meant, when the balcony doors swung open and Cove stormed out brandishing two curved blades. She skidded to a halt, taking in my stance and her brother knelt before me.

"Angels," Marlowe repeated, dragging his eyes from me to address his sister.

Cove staggered forward, sheathing her swords, before joining her brother on her knees. The dragon was no longer around her neck, and I glanced up at the balcony half expecting to see it watching us with its amber eyes. Glancing over my shoulder, I found Tiesa still crouching by Dariel's side, pressing bloodied fingers to his wound. She stared up at me, green eyes wide, screaming the silent question: *What do we do?* I stared back, unable to give a response. I realised, this must not be something covered in Hand training.

"Fates forgive us," Marlowe pleaded. "We thought you were spies or assassins. Your wings . . . I didn't realise they were real . . . I couldn't . . ."

He bowed his head, and I lowered my sword, folding my wings.

"The Fates will never forgive this," he continued, shaking his head. "Is he alive?"

Behind me, Dariel groaned in response.

Cove got to her feet, keeping her head bowed. “Please, allow us to help him.”

My heart continued to pound a steady rhythm in my chest. Humans had seen us—were talking to us—but we couldn’t fly. Dariel needed help, and that left us with no choice. Making my choice, I slid my sword back into its scabbard and stepped to the side.

Marlowe scrambled to his feet, rushing past me to get to Dariel. “Help me lift him, please.”

I lifted his injured side, trying to avoid the wound, but a howl of pain still tore from between Dariel’s gritted teeth. Marlowe took his other side and Tiesa launched up into the air, I assume to retrieve his bow, as Cove watched, awestruck.

Dariel’s blood soaked into my shirt as we helped him, stumbling through the balcony doors into a large open room filled with dark wooden furniture and colourful cushions. Marlowe indicated a heavy wooden table, and we heaved him up onto it. I removed Dariel’s quiver and ruined shirt, while Cove flung open cupboard doors, dumping an assortment of bandages and ointments on the table. Marlowe offered Dariel a drink of something, but he pushed it away with a grunt.

“It’s just a herbal pain reliever,” Cove said. “It’s going to hurt when we stitch you up and this will help relax you. I swear on my brother’s life, we would never harm an angel.”

Marlowe dipped his head at the word, muttering something about the Fates under his breath. I wanted to question him about it, but my thoughts were muted by the sound of my cousin’s blood dripping a steady beat on the stone floor. When Cove offered Dariel the drink again, he accepted it with a resigned sigh and downed it before sinking back onto the cushions that had been placed beneath his head. I stood back, watching as the two humans cleaned and stitched the wound, binding it with white bandages and muttering apologies every time he flinched.

When they got to his wing, Marlowe looked up at me, his dark brown eyes pleading. "I've never treated a wing before," he said. "I don't want to hurt him."

Tiesa stepped forward and instructed him on how to treat it in a similar fashion to Dariel's shoulder. Hands were trained in case they were injured on missions, and I knew I shouldn't feel guilty about my lack of knowledge, but as I watched my cousin groan in pain, my fingers curled into fists regardless.

"Please," Marlowe said, once Cove had tidied away the bloodied cloths and supplies. "Have a seat."

He turned to his sister, asking her to make it known to their staff that they didn't want to be disturbed. I exhaled in relief. Perhaps if we could keep it to just two humans, the repercussions wouldn't be so bad.

Tiesa joined me as I sat down on a large blue cushion embroidered with the same golden sun as the banners hanging from the front of the building. Cove sat cautiously opposite us, but Marlowe remained on a wooden chair at the table, his gaze flitting between us and where Dariel's breathing had evened out into a gentle snore.

"It won't last for much longer," Marlowe explained, noting my frown. "He'll wake soon."

"Why were you on our roof?" Cove asked.

"Cove!" Marlowe hissed.

My eyebrows raised as I looked between them. "It's a fair question, but one I'm sure you'll understand if we refrain from answering."

Marlowe shook his head, his gaze fixed on where Dariel's wings draped over the edge of the table, mottled with blood.

"It's all so much to take in," he whispered. "Angels."

I tore my eyes from my cousin's sleeping form. "You keep calling us that. What are angels?"

"Angels are beings sent from Heaven by the Fates to watch over us," Cove explained, her gaze moving between us, lingering on our folded wings.

Marlowe leaned forward, resting his forearms on his knees. "You have no reason to trust us, but please know we will tell no one of what's happened here. We've undoubtedly angered the Fates by injuring one of their angels, and I don't want to risk offending them further."

I gave him a tight smile, calling on hours of lessons in diplomacy to quieten the anger still roiling in my chest at seeing my cousin injured. "I don't blame you for your reaction. It must have been a shock to see us armed and on your roof."

The human male's eyes fell to the intricately carved gold bow on Tiesa's lap before moving to the quiver of golden arrows at my side. "Why were you armed?"

"You tell me," I said. "What do you know of the reasons angels visit you?"

"Angels come to give guidance and spread peace." Cove raised an eyebrow as she eyed the quiver. "Your arrows don't look very peaceful, though."

"They're harmless to humans," I explained.

Marlowe's eyes shone with curiosity. "Then why do you have them?"

"They're how we deliver the guidance and peace you spoke of."

Understanding flickered across his face as his eyes widened. "So, you shoot these arrows, and they alter the mood of the human?"

I raised my eyebrows, aware of Tiesa shifting uncomfortably beside me. I hadn't known what to expect from humans, but Marlowe was clearly very intelligent. I waited for him to ask about the arrow Dariel had shot him with, but he gave me a nervous smile instead.

"Will you stay and eat with us?" he asked. "While your friend is resting? I'm sure you must be thirsty at the very least."

"We really can't," I said, although it physically pained me to say the words.

There was very little I'd like to do more than sit and talk to the humans, finding out about their lives and the upcoming war. It was the entire reason I'd insisted on returning to the human world. Although, I'd expected to find my answers from a distance. I might be considered reckless, but even I was aware of the dangerous ground we were on. If the humans drugged us or poisoned us and took us prisoner . . . My stomach turned at the thought.

"Look," Cove said with a sigh. "That jug of water over there has been here since you came into the room. The servants place water in every room in the house each morning during the warmer months. The vessel is made of a particular type of stone that keeps it cooler for longer. If it were poisoned, we would have had to have known you were coming."

I glanced at Tiesa. My mouth was drier than a mountain goat's beard, and if we were going to have to travel all the way back to Hehven with an injured Dariel, we could use the refreshment.

"I'll pour it," Tiesa said, getting to her feet.

The only sound was Dariel's restful breathing as Tiesa poured two cups of water. She brought one to her nose and sniffed, meeting my gaze over the rim. My eyes widened as I realised what she was going to do. Before I could open my mouth to protest, she took a sip. I ground my teeth together as I watched her, waiting. If anything happened to her . . .

After a minute had passed, Tiesa nodded and brought the cups over, handing one to me.

"You shouldn't have done that," I growled as I took it from her.

She pulled a face and sat down beside me, taking a large gulp.

"So, you're important," Cove said, smirking at me as she leaned back, crossing her legs.

I raised my eyebrows at Tiesa, who muttered into her cup. I was glad Dariel was asleep. He'd have knocked us both out by now.

"I could say the same about you," I parried, tucking in my wings and leaning back against the cushions. "Tell me Marlowe, how did someone so young come to rule the Wendell Islands?"

His eyes widened at the sound of his name, but he blinked, quickly regaining his composure. "My family has ruled the Wendell Islands since the Six-Year War, over three hundred years ago. My parents were killed at sea during the last war."

"My condolences," I offered. "That must have been difficult."

He inclined his head. "It was. I'm lucky I have Cove to help me steer the wheel."

Cove smiled, but the sadness in her dark brown eyes was clear. "Let's just hope there are fewer casualties in this war."

"You're certain there will be another war?" I asked.

Marlowe sighed, his shoulders sagging. "We're doing everything we can to prevent it—to barter peace between the other countries—but with such a bloody history, trust is scarce."

"What do you mean?"

"He means, when we say we won't attack, other countries think we're bluffing," Cove explained. "They suspect we're merely lulling them into a false sense of security so we can attack first."

A faint clatter sounded outside the heavy wooden doors, and I flinched, my hand going to my sword. Beside me, Tiesa was on her feet in an instant.

"It's just dinner," Cove said, smirking. "You might be too wary to eat, but I hope you don't mind if we do."

I glanced out of the window at the sun, finding it much lower in the sky than I'd expected. Tiesa stayed standing as Cove went to the door and opened it, lifting a large tray of food from just outside. As she took it to the table and placed it down, the rich aromas of spices permeated the air, causing my stomach to grumble. I hadn't eaten since our early breakfast, and my resolve was fading fast.

Cove picked up a plate, piling on food before offering it to her brother, who was yet to leave Dariel's side. He took it gratefully and I swallowed hard as the smell wafted towards us. Sitting down with her own plate, Cove scooped some yellow-coloured rice into her mouth, licking the spices from her fingers.

"There's plenty left," she said, tilting her head towards the table.

I decided I couldn't take it anymore. Ignoring Tiesa's gasp, I strode over to the table and scanned the bowls of rice and grains, breads and fruits.

"What are you doing?" she hissed, appearing at my side.

"Eating."

"What if it's poisoned?"

I picked up a plate that looked as though it was made of dark stone and began putting a little of everything onto its curved surface. "Then I'll die with a full stomach."

Tiesa looked longingly at the food but didn't pick up a plate. When I glanced at her, she pouted. "Dariel's asleep and you're set on getting yourself killed. Someone's got to stay alert."

Shaking my head, I returned to my seat. The food was delicious, and it took all my self-control not to groan with pleasure. I was considering a second plate when Dariel stirred. Leaping to my feet, I was at my cousin's side in an instant, helping him into a sitting position.

"Relax," Marlowe soothed, also getting to his feet. "Take it easy, you'll tear your stitches."

Dariel glanced at him before looking at me. I could read the question in his eyes as clear as day. *What do they know?*

"We've just had a bit of food," I said. "Do you want some? It's safe."

I could see Dariel weighing up the options. If he was going to attempt to fly back, he'd need his strength. He sighed. "Sure."

Marlowe's eyes lit up and he moved to fetch him some, but I held up a hand. "I'll get it."

"May I ask a question?" Cove asked, from where she was nibbling on a strange green fruit I hadn't seen before.

"You can ask," I said. "I can't promise we'll answer."

"Why do only two of you have gold markings on your face?"

"The 'angels' sent by the Fates have markings," Dariel replied, his answer startling me to the point I almost dropped the plate I was filling. "He's just tagging along."

Tiesa's mouth hung open. "Dariel!"

He gave a half shrug, a look of resignation on his face. "They've seen us. Humans have seen 'angels' hundreds of times over the centuries. I'm sure it won't be the last time."

I handed Dariel a cup and a plate of food and he crossed his legs, downing the water before digging in to the food with ferocious bites.

"Your arrows," Marlowe began. "You say they alter human's moods."

Dariel paused in his shovelling of food.

"I believe that's what *you* said," I corrected carefully. "I neither confirmed nor denied."

Marlowe scratched his chin, his gaze flitting between me and the quiver of arrows. "If that is, in fact, what they do, they could help stop the war."

It was as though someone had sucked the air from the room. Dariel froze, mid chew. Tiesa was tense enough to pass as a statue and Cove stilled, as though a sudden movement might startle us.

"What do you mean?" I asked.

Marlowe drew a deep breath. "I mean, if we could use the arrows on Lord Diarke and the Midnight Queen, we could avoid this war. We could make them trust us."

I shook my head. "No. The Fates decide who the arrows are for."

"The Fates are real," Cove murmured, more of a statement than a question.

Marlowe barked a laugh. "We have three angels in our home, and you're surprised that the Fates are real?" He turned to Dariel, a wry smile on his face. "I was always more of a believer than my sister."

"How are you feeling, Dariel?" Tiesa asked.

The underlying meaning was as clear as the day that was quickly fading beyond the windows. We needed to leave.

Dariel set down his plate and slid from the table. Rolling his shoulder with a wince, he moved to the open area in front of the balcony doors before carefully, slowly, extending his wings. They were so wide, they blocked most of the light, sending shadows stretching across the room.

"Your wings," Marlowe murmured. "They're beautiful."

I pressed my lips together in amusement at my cousin's resulting flustered expression.

"I think I'll be okay to fly as long as we make the most of the currents and don't go too fast," he said, refolding his wings.

"I can give you a shirt," Marlowe offered. "Although I'm not sure how it works with wings."

Dariel inclined his head. "Thank you for the offer. It's warm enough out, I'll be all right."

Getting to my feet, I cast my eyes over his bandages, where a hint of blood was seeping through. "Are you sure you're all right to fly?"

He nodded before turning to Marlowe and Cove. "Thank you for your help."

"We're the ones who injured you," the young ruler said, his eyes downcast. "I hope the Fates forgive us."

"Whether the Fates are angered or not," Dariel replied, a small smile on his lips, "I forgive you."

I narrowed my eyes as I watched their exchange. Cupids were a naturally forgiving race, but Dariel's behaviour was puzzling. Perhaps he hit his head when he fell.

"Please, at least consider my suggestion," Marlowe said, turning to me. "Hundreds of thousands of lives were lost in the last war. Countless men, women and children. Our countries have barely recovered. If there is any way I can prevent another war, I have to take it."

I held his gaze, my expression stern. "We can't go against the Fates. There's nothing to consider."

"Thinking about it will cost you nothing," Marlowe pushed. "Take a week. Or two. Or more. Then, please will you come back? To tell us your decision?"

"There is no decision to make," I insisted. "We—"

"We'll consider it," Dariel said, opening the balcony doors and allowing a gust of warm air to sweep into the room.

I opened my mouth to ask whether he was feeling okay, but he stepped out into the golden afternoon light. When I turned to Tiesa, she shrugged, her expression as baffled as mine.

It felt strange to say goodbye when we didn't even trust them enough to tell them our names, so I nodded my gratitude instead; the humans bowing their heads in reverence to the angels they thought we were as we launched into the sky.

"What was that?" I demanded as soon as the city was no more than a flickering dot on the horizon behind us.

Dariel kept his eyes forward, sweat already beading his

brow more than it should have been. "I told them what they wanted to hear."

My heart jolted. "So, you're not planning on going back."

"Of course, not."

It's only then, I realised how much I'd hoped he'd meant it.

"Marlowe will be disappointed," Tiesa said, swooping above us. "I think the leader of the Wendell Islands has a little crush."

Dariel muttered something under his breath, and she laughed. I gave a half-hearted smile, but my mind was still raking over what Marlowe had said. What if we could help? Would preventing a war really be a bad thing? As I considered the oranges and deep reds of the sunset unfolding on the horizon, I wondered how many arrows it would take to stop a war.

"Dariel!" I called out in realisation. "Your bow and arrows."

He reached for the quiver that wasn't there and bellowed in anger, the sound scattering a small flock of seabirds. "We need to go back."

Tiesa and I exchanged a glance. If we went back, it would mean travelling through The Crossing at night.

"I can't leave them there," Dariel said, dipping his wing to turn back towards the islands. "Not when we know they want to use them."

He was right, but as stars began to speckle the sky, the scar across my chest burned.

12
Sirain

The peach and cobalt remnants of the sunset had all but dissolved into the horizon as we burst from the bright lights of The Crossing. Wrinkling my nose in discomfort, I wished I could take off my mask and let the ocean breeze whip away the lingering residue of the day's events. My father had insisted I sit through another presentation from Helle's lords and ladies, and I swore my brain was numb from it. Hours upon hours of reports of births, deaths, marriages and complaints that were little more than village gossip. The only highlight had been when someone was brought forward accused of stealing. My father had sentenced him to death with barely a second's thought. His mood had been fouler than usual due to his late night, but if he remembered speaking to me that morning, he said nothing—and I certainly wasn't going to bring it up.

I'd asked Kwellen and Odio about the fire the first chance I'd got. Neither of them had heard anything about it. Tiredness and disappointment had weighed heavy on my chest until Odio received orders from the Fates and invited me to join him. I would just have to find someone old enough to remember the fire and see if they could tell me anything. The problem was, finding someone to ask who I could trust not to go running to my parents immediately afterwards.

"Who's the mark?" Kwellen asked as we swooped down, riding the blustery ocean wind.

"Marlowe Windward, leader of the Wendell Islands," Odio confirmed.

My interest piqued; thoughts of the fire momentarily forgotten. I had only been to the Wendell Islands once, a long time ago, but I remembered the archipelago vividly. As we approached, I noted the air was warmer, the islands always a milder climate than the other human lands. The capital city on the largest island was contained by a towering stone wall and within it, the buildings twinkled like gemstones as they lit their lamps for the evening. Odio seemed to be familiar with the city as he led us right to a large multi-storey building layered with unusual, tiered balconies. We swept up onto the topmost one, pressing against the wall and melting into the shadows.

The balcony door was ajar, the voices inside leaking out into the evening air.

"Surely you didn't think we'd try to use them?"

"We don't know you well enough to say."

"As I told you before, we would never risk angering the Fates. I already fear repercussions from our earlier actions."

"Good, because if you used arrows outside the orders of the Fates, that's exactly what you would be ensuring."

My eyes widened and I turned to Odio and Kwellen, sure that their faces must be wearing similar expressions behind their leather masks. Who was talking about the Fates? Did this Marlowe human know about us?

I edged closer, attempting to peer inside, but Odio gripped my arm, pulling me back. He was right. There were at least four people inside and we had no idea how close they were to the balcony doors. If they saw us, it would be catastrophic.

"We've received word that the Midnight Queen is building an army of ships. I fear that this time, the Wendell Islands won't be able to withstand the attack. Even if Bickerstaff truly does intend to join with us, Dalibor and Newbold have far more resources."

"The Fates will decide what course of action to take. You need to trust in them, as you always have."

"The Fates have stood by, allowing countless wars. Why should we expect them to intervene this time?"

I recognised the angry voice. A human woman named Cove. If I remembered correctly, she was Marlowe's sister. Another of the voices seemed familiar too, but I couldn't quite place it.

"Perhaps this was the work of the Fates," a male voice said. "Bringing angels to us, so we might work together to stop the war before it starts."

Angels? I glanced over my shoulder at Odio, and he shrugged. My skin itched, wanting to see who was inside the room. Perhaps there was another window I could fly to.

"We're not angels," a different male voice said with a heavy sigh. "We're Cupids."

My gasp was audible as I leaned forward, no longer caring whether I was seen. That voice. It was the Cupid I'd taken the feather from. My eyes widened as I stared through the open door, trying to make sense of what I was seeing.

There were three Cupids standing with their wings to us. I recognised the two males but there was a female too. The male with the braid appeared to be injured, with bandages stark against his dark skin and his wings speckled with blood. Cove stood before them, her arms crossed, beside a man I assumed was her brother.

"Cupids?" Marlowe echoed.

"Thank you for returning my bow and arrows," the injured Cupid said. "However, we must go. It's not safe to travel at night."

Damn right it wasn't. Bile mixed with bitter confusion as

Odio tugged me back, taking my place. What were they doing talking to the humans? Was it something they did often?

"We should have killed them the other night," Kwellen muttered.

In front of me, Odio had selected his ebony arrow and drawn his bow. He glanced over his shoulder at us. "As soon as I shoot, we leave."

I watched, horror-struck, as my cousin toed the door open wide enough to aim his shot through the gap. If anyone looked at the balcony, they'd see him clear as day. He let the arrow fly and a cry rang out from inside the room. I frowned as Odio swore, already reaching for another arrow.

"What happened?" I asked.

"That fateforsaken Cupid pushed Marlowe out the way."

I balked. "What? Is he okay?"

"Yeah, he's fine, unfortunately."

Kwellen grabbed my shoulder, pulling me back, his wings already spread. "Come on. Let's go."

"No. Roof," Odio commanded. "I still need to get my shot. We'll hide up there until they leave."

I spread my wings, soaring up to the roof, a million questions lined up on my tongue. The voices below had quietened, and I wondered what they were talking about. Had they known it was a Chaos arrow?

We waited on the roof for what felt like hours, the night air steadily losing the heat of the day and settling into a bitter chill. Beside me, Odio cracked his neck, and I flexed my freezing fingers as I listened for any sign of life below. When the balcony doors finally opened and the sound of beating wings filled the air, I swallowed a gasp. Scrambling back into the shadows, I watched as the three Cupids took to the air, their white wings stark against the night sky.

"Wait," Odio whispered.

I wasn't breathing as I watched them climb higher. They

must have assumed we'd already left. Sweat gathered at my brow under my mask and I pushed it up off my face, gulping in the fresh air. Relief swept through me, my shoulders dropping, as I watched them leave, realising how close of a call it had been. I took a step out of the shadows, and as though my thoughts alone had called out to him, the Cupid turned and looked over his shoulder. His eyes met mine.

He didn't wait for his friends as he turned, barrelling back toward the roof, already pulling his sword free from its scabbard. Kwellen stepped in front of me, his own sword drawn and ready as I watched, my heart in my throat.

Behind the Cupid, his friends were shouting, begging him to come back. I could see from the look of pure rage on his beautiful face that there was nothing they could say to deter him. He landed, his first blow already slicing down toward Kwellen as I watched in disbelief. His shirt was already stained dark with blood. What had happened to them? Even as my head spun with questions, I realised this fight wouldn't end well for him. Not against all three of us. I pulled my sword from its sheath between my wings and adapted a fighting stance as his friends landed on the roof, their weapons drawn.

"What are you doing here?" the Cupid growled in between strikes against Kwellen.

I stared, eyes wide, as he attacked with both grace and speed despite his fury. He was nothing like he'd been on the island. Then, he'd been hesitant and sloppy with his blade. My pulse quickened as I realised just how much I'd underestimated him.

"Why we're here is none of your business," Kwellen snarled.

"Pace!" the female Cupid pleaded. "Please. Stop!"

I started at the use of his name. *Pace.* He dropped to the ground, rolling out of the way of Kwellen's blade, before seamlessly jumping to his feet, his sword poised for his next attack. He wasn't going to stop until blood was spilled. I couldn't let it be Kwellen's. This was my fault. I'd made the wrong choice back on the island. I should have either killed them or let them go.

"Stop," I said, my voice calmer than I expected. "This is between you and me, Pace."

The Cupid turned to me, gold eyes blazing at the use of his name.

"No," Kwellen barked.

I gritted my teeth. "Yes."

Pace braced his sword, knocking Kwellen's blow to the side, the sound echoing against the tiled roof. He stepped back, his chest heaving. "Yes."

Still marvelling at his strength and skill against one of our best Chaos warriors, I met his golden gaze, soaking up the anger and resentment I found there. This would end tonight. I took a step forward, my sword readied.

Before I could reach him, a piercing shout sounded from behind, and I whirled to find Cove and another human I assumed must be Marlowe climbing up onto the roof via some sort of hidden door. They ran towards us, twin swords in their hands, and a battle cry in their lungs. Of course, they would choose to help the Cupids—we were merely the evil demons who had tried to shoot them. I rolled my shoulders and crouched, ready.

As Cove brought down her gleaming silver swords, pandemonium erupted on the roof. Grunts and cries mingled with the melodic clashing of blades, and I wondered how long it would be before Marlowe's guards appeared.

Tucking my wings in tight, I landed a blow to Cove's side, and she staggered backwards, quickly rolling out of the way of Odio's dagger. Sweat trickled down my back as I looked for Kwellen, only to find him fighting both Marlowe and the female Cupid. The long-haired Cupid was crouched nearby, gripping his shoulder as blood seeped from his bandages.

Feeling a presence behind me, I turned, my sword raised, only to find myself face to face with him. *Pace.*

The snarl that ripped from his lips was feral as he slashed his blade at me. I stepped backwards out of the way, but he'd already raised his weapon for another blow. Blocking it shook my bones, and I gritted my teeth as I moved on the offensive, pushing him back. It was different this time. The last time we'd fought, I could tell he was biding his time, trying to find a way to escape. This time, he was out for blood. My blood. He stumbled on a loose tile, and I seized the opportunity, angling my blade at his chest.

"This feels familiar," I said, breathing hard.

Pace growled. "Going to try and steal another feather?"

I opened my mouth to apologise, but found myself saying, "Maybe. I was thinking I could stuff a pillow."

His eyes flashed and he brought up his blade, knocking mine to the side. "You had no right."

It took all my concentration to block his blows, so I didn't answer. I needed to kill him before he killed me. If I didn't, I'd never be able to relax in the human world again. Taking a steadying breath, I honed my concentration on a killing blow.

A familiar whoosh sounded over my shoulder, and I darted a glance to my left in time to see one of Odio's arrows pierce Marlowe's chest.

"Go!" he shouted, launching into the air.

I looked around in confusion. The female Cupid was sprawled, unmoving, on the ground and the male Cupid was huddled against Marlowe, Cove at his side. Kwellen launched into the air, and I tightened my grip on my blade as I turned back to Pace.

I wasn't sure what I was planning to say, but as his lip curled and he raised his sword once more, I shook my head and stepped back. Spreading my wings, I launched into the sky. For a moment, I thought he might follow, his own wings flaring in the wind. But he didn't. As I climbed higher into the night sky, I watched as he fell to his knees at the female Cupid's side. What had Odio done to her? I looked at my friends for the first time, wondering what injuries lurked beneath their black leathers.

"Everyone okay?" I asked.

"I hate Cupids." Kwellen spat.

His voice was cold and hard, but I didn't blame him. The feeling was mutual. "We need to talk about what they were doing with the humans," I said.

"Tomorrow," Odio said. "Kwellen and I need to visit the healer and hope they stay quiet."

My stomach rolled. "You're injured?"

"Nothing they won't be able to fix."

I scowled.

"Don't worry," Kwellen said. "We got some good hits in."

He sounded gleeful as the shimmering lights of The Crossing flickered into existence on the horizon, but his words sank like stones in my gut. All we'd done was stoke the fire of hatred already burning in Pace's chest. I pictured the female Cupid lying bloodied on the roof and my stomach churned. I needed to ask, but the answer would mean the difference between a tentative truce and Pace attempting to tear The Crossing apart to find us and make us pay.

Taking a deep breath, I looked at Odio. "Did you kill her?"

13

Pace

Stalking back and forth along the cliff edge, I tried to steady my pounding heart. The evening air ripped from the sea in jagged bursts, clutching at my hair and clothes as if trying to distract me. Comfort me. I was beyond comfort. Thrusting my fingers in my hair, I released a yell of frustration across the dark waters.

I hadn't wanted to leave Tiesa and Dariel, but the healers had made it as clear as they could without causing offence, that they would prefer it if I left. After reassuring me several times that they both would live, they'd told me to return in an hour or so. The cliff was the only place I could think of to try and clear my head. I sucked in a deep breath, blowing it out slowly. Dariel had burst his stitches fighting the one-armed Chaos. On the way back to The Crossing, he'd told me how Marlowe had stepped in front of him and saved his life. Guilt roiled in my gut.

I'd sensed her. I'd known even before I looked over my shoulder that I would see her standing there. All common sense had evaporated as I'd drawn my sword and charged. I dragged a hand over my face. Once again, I'd put the people I cared about in danger.

Tiesa had been knocked unconscious by the Chaos archer, resulting in a deep gash across her forehead. Marlowe and Cove had patched her up as best they could and, once she'd woken, they had tried their hardest to persuade us to stay, but we couldn't. Too many questions would have been raised in our absence and we couldn't risk more humans seeing us. Bloodied and broken, we'd dragged ourselves back through The Crossing.

Another yell of frustration tore from my throat, and I sank to my knees. Beside me, the lights of The Crossing shimmered against the moonless sky, turning the grass a dark shade of blue. I dug my fingers into the indigo blades, my fists tightening as though I was trying to hold on for my life. Perhaps I was.

"Rose?"

My head snapped up. "Thorn?"

"Are you okay?"

"No." I sat back on the grass, breathing hard. "Are you?"

"No."

I snorted. "Great."

"Want to talk about it?"

Did I? Even if I wanted to, I couldn't. "Not really. You?"

"No."

I exhaled, my breathing finally evening out. "We don't have to talk."

"Okay."

"I mean. Unless you want to talk about something else?" I offered.

"Like flowers?"

A flicker of a smile crossed my lips. "If you want."

"How did things go with your future wife?" Thorn asked.

I huffed a laugh. "I thought we were talking about flowers?"

Silence settled between us and, closing my eyes, I lay back on the cool grass, savouring the freshness of the sea air and the quiet that only came with the dead of night, despite the roaring in my head. Pressing my fingers to my temples, I knew I had to let it go—the rage. The Chaos had insulted me, sullied me, humiliated me, but it wasn't the end of the world. No one knew what had happened besides Dariel. Even if I told Caitland, I was sure she'd understand. I blew out a breath. It had to stop, before someone got killed.

"I thought of a masculine flower," Thorn said.

I blinked as the sudden statement yanked me from my epiphany. "Oh?"

"Larkspur."

I laughed. "Well. That's certainly a good effort."

"Have you ever regretted something?" Thorn asked after a pause.

"Of course," I replied. "I'm sure everyone regrets something at one time or another."

Silence.

"What do you regret?" I prompted. "Do you want to talk about it?"

"I made a mistake and because I didn't deal with it, people I care about got hurt."

I frowned. "Is there not still time to deal with it? There must be something you can do."

"Perhaps."

"It'll be okay," I reassured them. "Just keep moving forward."

"Is that what you tell yourself?"

My mouth twisted into a wry smile. "Touché."

"Sometimes it all just feels insurmountable," Thorn said, huffing a pained sigh that rippled through The Crossing. "It's like I'm being crushed under the weight of it all and I can't catch my breath."

"This isn't just about the friends who got hurt, is it?"

"No."

Staring up at the endless stretch of obsidian sky, I thought of that morning. Flying to the Wendell Islands in the sunshine, my heart full. I had no idea what pressures they were under in Helle, but I knew that in time, my friends would recover and that they would forgive me.

"Fear not the night," I mused. "The sun will always rise."

"Excuse me?"

I smiled. "Sometimes hatred and fear feel like an endless night—suffocating and dark—but love and joy are as certain as the sun. You just have to be patient."

"So . . . you're a poet."

I grinned. "I'm saying, it's going to be okay. Find a glimmer of joy and hold on to it. This night will pass, and the dawn will bring hope."

"Wow. Do all Cupids communicate in prose, or is it just you?"

"I haven't met all the Cupids, so I can't answer that truthfully."

Thorn laughed. "Is that what you're going to do, then? Wait for the dawn?"

"Metaphorically, yes. In reality, I have to go back soon."

My gut twisted with unease at the thought of facing my friends. I may have begun to come to terms with my anger, but the damage was already done. I hadn't even told Tiesa about the feather. As soon as I'd seen her lying on the roof, her head bloodied, everything else had faded into insignificance. I closed my eyes, trying to ignore the burning I felt there. It would have been entirely my fault if either of them had died, and I knew I wouldn't have been able to live with that guilt.

What had scared me the most was how prepared I'd been to kill that Chaos. Even at the height of the most intense fights in tournaments, I'd never been pushed that far. I'd drawn more blood than I could recall, but the desire to end a life . . . A deep shudder ran through me, my blood running cold. Was I any better than a Chaos?

"Have you ever killed someone?" I asked, the question slipping from my lips, half formed.

"Excuse me?"

I sat up, the back of my neck suddenly warm. "I just mean—"

"Because I'm a Chaos, I must be a bloodthirsty murderer?"

I winced. "No?"

"No. I've never killed someone."

"You sound disappointed," I said, my brows raised. "Is there someone you want to kill?"

"Yes. No. Maybe." Thorn sighed. "I don't know."

"Has this person done something to deserve being killed?" I asked.

"They want to kill me."

I grimaced. "It's not your brother, is it?"

"No. Unfortunately."

I smiled at the huff of laughter that rippled through the barrier of light. "Why does this person want to kill you?"

"Does it matter?"

"If it's a misunderstanding, or something you can apologise for, it does," I said. "Step back and look at the problem as an outsider. Sometimes things get magnified in our own heads to the point we can't see around it."

A chuckle rippled through the light. "Another poem?"

"You bring it out in me, what can I say?" I grinned. "Turns out I'm much better at giving advice than taking it."

"Aren't we all?"

I got to my feet, stretching my wings, the air rippling through my feathers as I squinted at the horizon. "I need to go. My friends need me."

"Okay. Thank you."

"For my wonderful poetry?"

"Sure." Thorn laughed. "But also, for listening. I was a mess when I got to the cliff, but I feel like I can see again now."

I smiled. "Fear not the night; the sun will always rise."

"You know, you're all right, for a Cupid."

My eyes crinkled with the grin that painted my face as I shook my head. "Well, you're pretty okay for a Chaos."

"Goodbye, Rose."

"Goodbye, Thorn."

Lifting a hand, I pressed it to the undulating curtain of light, letting it wash over my fingertips. It was a strange feeling to have a connection with a faceless, nameless person, knowing they could be anything from a twelve-year-old male to a seventy-year-old female. I tried not to think about it, instead relishing the way they made me smile—made my soul feel lighter. It also gave me hope that not all Chaos were evil, blood-thirsty demons.

By the time I reached the healers' quarters, any lightness my soul had felt on the cliff had morphed into a thick pool of sludge. Standing outside the room, I shook my hands out at my sides, my thoughts colliding as I readied myself. Part of me hoped they were asleep as I took a deep breath and pushed open the door. A dim lamp illuminated the space, and Dariel and Tiesa looked up at me as I stepped into the room, my mouth dry. I winced anew at their bandages and the weary expressions on their faces.

"How are you feeling?" I asked, perching on the end of Tiesa's bed.

"Alive."

My smile didn't reach my eyes. "That's good."

"What happened, Pace?" she asked, sitting up with a wince.

I focused on my hands, curled in my lap. "There's no excuse. Seeing that Chaos standing there, I just saw red. I didn't think. I'm so sorry."

"What aren't you telling me?" Tiesa asked. "What did she do to make you so angry?"

I shook my head, my gaze lifting to the dressing across her forehead. "Nothing. I overreacted, and I'm so sorry you got hurt."

"No," she snapped, immediately grimacing in pain. "Your actions almost got us killed, I deserve the truth."

I stared at her, knowing she was right. She was my oldest, most trusted friend and I'd kept this from her. Perhaps if I'd told her from the beginning, she would have helped me see what I'd come to realise on the cliff. Maybe this could have been prevented. With a weary sigh, I extended my left wing, stretching it so that the missing primary feather was visible. It would take the best part of a year to grow back, and I exhaled, quelling the ripple of anger warming my chest.

"She took one of my feathers," I said.

Tiesa stared between me and my wing, her eyes wide. "She *what*?"

"She said no one would believe they'd seen Cupids, so she took a 'souvenir'." I didn't attempt to hide the bitterness of my words.

"Fated Fates, Pace," Tiesa whispered. "Your purity."

I folded my wing. "I know."

"No wonder you were so angry," she breathed. "What do you think she did with it?"

Dariel groaned, sitting up in his bed. "Not helping, Tiesa."

"It doesn't matter," I said. "It happened, and it was my own fault for going to the human world by myself."

Tiesa's green eyes blazed. "You have every right to be angry, Pace."

"Not enough to risk your life," I said, reaching out and placing my hand on hers. "I wasn't just angry at the Chaos. I was angry at myself. My purity is one of the only things I've managed to do right, and she took that from me. I gave her the opportunity to take it from me."

"Yes, well you're not the only one responsible for what happened tonight," Dariel said, his voice fatigued. "I shouldn't have interfered with the Chaos' arrow. It wouldn't have harmed Marlowe. I heard it and reacted before I could think."

A small smile lifted my lips. "Look at you, saving humans."

"Yes, well, I owe him my life now."

My stomach lurched at just how close I'd come to losing my cousin. "I suppose you could call it even, seeing as his sister tried to kill you this morning."

Tiesa chuckled but Dariel's face remained impassive. "If she'd wanted to kill me this morning, she would have. They are both clearly well-trained warriors."

"It was fortunate they came to help us against the Chaos," Tiesa said. "Things could have gone very differently otherwise."

I grimaced, knowing just how true her words were. "Once again, I'm truly sorry I put you both in harm's way and I know I can't ever go back to the human world, but—"

"I'm going back to speak to Marlowe and Cove," Dariel interjected. "You should come."

I stared, open mouthed, at my cousin, my words frozen in my throat.

Dariel glanced down at his shoulder, poking at the dressing. "We need to explain properly why we can't help them—why we can't cross the Fates. We owe them that."

"I agree," I replied carefully. "But we could just leave it. You could continue to carry out your missions unseen and the humans would just have to live with a little less faith in angels."

"I don't want them to have a little less faith."

An inkling of understanding settled over me and I glanced at Tiesa, only for her to shrug in response. "When?"

"When we're healed. Perhaps in a few weeks."

I nodded, trying not to let my eagerness show on my face.

Dariel wanted to visit the humans again and, whatever his reasons, I wasn't going to be the one to convince him otherwise. Despite our last two visits ending in disaster, I was confident the next time would be different. It was just a shame we were going there to tell them we couldn't help them stop their war.

Accept the things to which fate binds you, and love the people with who fate brings you together, but do so with all your heart.

~Marcus Aurelius

14
Sirain

I wasn't sure when it had changed from wistful thinking to a daily occurrence, but for the last week and half, I'd willed the day to pass quickly so I could get to the cliff in time for sunset. I wasn't there for the sunset, however, no matter how glorious the melting array of colours. Somehow, despite the odds, Rose and I had fallen into an unspoken routine and, more often than not, the time I spent sitting on the cliff at the furthest reaches of Helle was the best part of my day.

"What's one thing you couldn't live without?"

Rose's question tugged me from my thoughts, and I frowned as I considered my answer. "My wings, I think."

"You think?"

"Well, there are these small honey cakes—"

Laughter echoed through The Crossing and I smiled, my heart warm and light. It was a strange thing—to know someone's favourite colour, their favourite food, stories from their childhood and their innermost feelings—but not know what they looked like or their age. From Rose's stories, and the way they talked about their parents, I was fairly confident they weren't far from my own age. Two days prior, they had let it slip that their younger sister had just celebrated her tenth birthday and although it was entirely possible they were female, from the way they'd spoken about their future wife, I was fairly certain they were male.

"What about you?" I asked. "What couldn't you live without?"

"My wings. Flying," they answered without a lick of hesitation.

I chuckled. "I mean, take a second to think about it."

"There's nothing to think about. Tell me one thing that even comes close to the feeling of soaring above the mountains, riding the winds."

Drawing my knees to my chest, the smile on my face ached pleasantly. I thought perhaps I'd smiled more in the last week or so than in my entire life. "It is a wonderful feeling," I admitted. "Although the adrenaline of a well-matched fight is a close second."

"Fair enough," Rose conceded. "I can agree with that."

A bark of laughter burst from my lips. "I would wager the fighting that takes place in Helle is a little different to Hehven."

"You would be right. The training here is little more than fancy footwork and endurance. However . . ." Rose hesitated.

"Go on?"

"However, if you know where to look, there are more realistic alternatives."

I quirked a brow, turning toward the lights. "More realistic alternatives? Do explain."

Rose chuckled. "It's not sanctioned by the king and queen, and the royal guards regularly find and shut down establishments that allow it to take place, but there are fights that happen—tournaments—where, barring fatally wounding someone, there are no rules."

"Do you go to these tournaments?"

"Yes."

There was enough hesitancy in their response that I questioned, "What?"

Rose huffed a sigh. "My parents pretend they don't know, but I know they do. It's just one of the many ways I disappoint them."

My smile faded. "Why do you go to the tournaments if you care about what your parents think?"

"It's complicated."

"When is life not complicated?"

Rose mumbled something and I waited patiently. If they wanted to tell me, they could. I wasn't going to push. Instead, I returned my gaze to the ocean, the sun a distant memory as the dark waves rushed toward the cliffs. *Tournaments.* It clashed so violently with my idea of the peaceful do-gooder Cupids, yet my thoughts drifted to Pace—of the hard lines of his broad, muscled figure as he'd wielded his sword against Kwellen with deadly precision.

Swallowing hard, I closed my eyes, letting the jasmine laced sea breeze wrap around me as it lifted wisps of dark hair from my face. Many a night I'd lain awake replaying the conversation I'd overheard him having with the humans. I had so many questions. Did all humans know of Cupids? How long had it been going on? I'd almost asked my mother about the Cupids but changed my mind at the last moment. What if what they were planning affected the Fates? I knew I needed to go back to the human world for answers, and the thought rolled like a jagged rock around my gut.

"I go because I need to feel . . . something," Rose started, causing me to open my eyes. "Something *more.* Facing your opponent, knowing they're going to try and hurt you, not just disarm you . . . Sometimes it's the closest I feel to living."

I blew out a slow breath as I processed their words. "I can understand that, although if you had people trying to hurt you all the time, it would lose its appeal pretty quickly."

"Ah yes. How are things with your delightful brother?"

"The usual," I replied with a wry smile. "I mostly try to stay out of his way. I haven't seen him for a few days."

It was only a half lie. I'd seen Fin plenty of times. He just hadn't seen me. Shame painted my face as I contemplated how adept I'd become at slipping around corners out of sight. "Surely it can't be that big of a deal that you put yourself in danger of getting hurt."

"It's not just that," Rose said, their tone harder than I'd heard in a while. "It's just one item on a long list of ways I'm not as good as my brother."

My heart quickened a little. Over the last few days, our conversations had deepened but this was the closest I'd got to really finding out about Rose. I hadn't asked about their marriage for fear of upsetting them and they usually avoided talking about their family.

"What do you mean?" I asked.

Rose huffed a cold laugh. "My cousin gave me quite the summary a while ago. Let me see if I can remember. Besides the tournaments, my attitude towards the . . . family business . . . leaves a lot to be desired, there are concerns over the amount of time I spend unsupervised with females, and my punctuality is questionable at best."

Laughter rippled from me, and I clasped my hands to my mouth in surprise. "Excuse me?"

"Yes, apparently showing up late to meet my fiancée is not a desirable attribute."

"No," I said, shaking my head even though I knew they couldn't see me. "What in the name of Fate do you mean, being 'unsupervised' with females?"

Rose groaned. "Forget it. I shouldn't have said that."

"Oh no," I said, a grin stretching across my face. "You don't get out of it that easily. Explain. I thought Cupids were the purest of the pure. What exactly are you getting up to whilst unsupervised?"

"Just because I have to remain pure before marriage doesn't mean I can't enjoy spending time with females."

My mind reeled. "So, you're just sitting around . . . talking?"

Rose hefted a heavy sigh. "Is there any chance you're going to let this drop, Thorn?"

"Nope." I chuckled.

"Fine." Rose paused. "Fates and feathers, I'm glad you can't actually see me. I don't even know how to explain it."

I grinned so wide my jaw ached. "Try."

"Okay, okay. So, there's this thing called spacing."

"Spacing?" I echoed.

"Yes. Again, it's one of the things I'm sure my parents have heard rumours of, but they'd probably clip my wings if they ever found proof that I'd done it."

My skin prickled with curiosity, and I leaned closer to the lights. "What is it?"

"It means getting very close to someone without actually touching them."

I rocked back with laughter, tears stinging my eyes. "I knew it! I knew it would be nothing. Oh, Rose. You wouldn't last a day in Helle. There are people rutting against walls at every corner."

"You laugh," Rose said, ignoring my mirth. "But there's a lot to be said for the allure of self-control. Imagine standing close enough to someone, you can feel the heat of their skin and the soft warmth of their breath but knowing you can't touch them. Your mouth, barely a fraction from theirs, restraining, even as your heart pounds and your body begs you to close the gap. Fingers hovering above heated skin, never touching even as your breathing quickens. Knowing that if you breathe too deeply, you'd touch."

My laugh forgotten, I swallowed, my mouth suddenly dry. Heat curled low in my belly, and I tucked my hair behind my ears as I sat up with a cough. "Sounds . . . frustrating."

Rose laughed. "You have no idea. That's part of the pull, though."

"So, you like torturing yourself? Is this all part of trying to feel something? No pun intended."

"Perhaps."

A comfortable silence settled between us as I wrestled with my idea of Cupids and what Rose had confessed. I supposed the same was true in Helle. There were those like my brother and father who revelled in blood and violence and then there were those who were disinterested, content with a quieter, more peaceful life. I wondered where I would put myself within that divide.

"I know I shouldn't assume, but with what you've said," Rose paused as though reconsidering. "I mean, you—"

"You want to know about my purity?" I grinned at their discomfort. "Is that what you're trying to ask?"

"No. Yes. I mean," Rose stumbled. "I shouldn't have asked. I'm sorry. You might not even be old enough for this conversation. Fated Fates. Please forget what I said before."

Laughter tore from me and I shook my head. "I'm old enough. Don't worry. Helle might be loose on morals but even smallwings aren't allowed to hang around on cliffs after dark."

"Even so," Rose said. "It's a very personal question."

"It's fine," I replied. "Let's just say your parents would be very disappointed in me. I haven't had a shred of purity in years."

"What's it like?"

I blinked. "Sex?"

"Yes."

"Not always great," I admitted. "It depends a lot on who it's with. My first time was at a Winter Festival of Fates against a wall. It was freezing and he smelled of meat." I wrinkled my nose at the memory and shuddered. "There have been others since that have been more enjoyable."

My honesty surprised me, and I was struck by how liberating it was to talk to someone you knew you'd never meet. Although Kwellen and Odio had no qualms discussing their various conquests in front of me, I'd never opted to join in, even when Odio and I had discovered we had a lover in common.

"What if you have no choice over who it's with?" Rose said quietly.

My stomach sank. "I'm sorry. I didn't think."

"Don't apologise. It's not your fault."

Still cringing inwardly, I decided to ask what I'd wanted to for a while. "How did your meeting go with her? Is she nice?"

Rose sighed. "It was fine. She's quiet. Pretty. Doesn't like flying."

"What?" I exclaimed.

"Exactly."

I shook my head. "When do you see her next?"

"Not until the Winter Festival, when we're to marry."

My stomach lurched. "You only get to meet her once? Why?"

"Something to do with harvest and family. I mean, she couldn't even look at me when we met, so the Fates only know what our wedding will be like."

"What do you mean, she couldn't look at you?"

"She was too shy."

I blew out a slow breath. "I'm so sorry, Rose. That's really tough."

"It's fine."

"It's not though, is it?" I said, the unfairness of their situation prickling under my skin.

"I suppose in a way, it's my own fault."

I frowned. "How so?"

"If I'd behaved the way I should have, played the part of the perfect Cupid, my parents wouldn't have felt the need to arrange my marriage."

"Would you have been happy, though?" I asked.

Rose snorted. "I'm not happy now."

"So, you could have lived a basic, boring existence, but chosen your own partner when you were ready. Or, you could have lived your life the way you wanted but have your partner chosen for you." I shook my head. "I'm going to be honest. Both options suck."

"I wish it were as simple as choosing between two options," Rose said. "I haven't even chosen a path. Everything I do that makes me feel happy—alive—is something I have to keep hidden. My life has never really been my own."

I wrapped my arms around my bent legs, resting my chin on my knees. "Maybe it is that simple. I mean, you can't have it both ways. You can't be rebellious and pious. Either follow the rules like your parents want you to or burn it all down and face the consequences."

Perhaps I should have stayed quiet, but the words tumbled from my lips before I could stop them. I bit my lip, hoping I hadn't pushed too far.

"If I follow the rules, I'll be miserable," Rose said carefully. "If I burn it all down, I lose everything."

I sighed. "Like I said before, both options suck."

Silence settled between us again and I shivered as the air began to cool. A wave of sadness crept over me as I realised, whatever was going on between us had an expiry date. It was unlikely Rose would continue to come and meet me when they were married.

Consoling myself with the fact that it was still months away, I cocooned myself within my wings as I listened to the rhythmic crashing of the waves below. Besides, I had other things to think about. Like how I was going to persuade Kwellen and Odio to accompany me to the human world in broad daylight.

"I need to go," Rose said after a while. "Tomorrow?"

I smiled, anticipation wrapping itself tightly around my heart. "Tomorrow."

The dark corners and sharp edges of the castle were always jarring after spending time at the cliff. While much of Helle was lush green forest and golden desert, the mountains of Hadeon were eclipsed in permanent shadow—a looming presence over the rest of the land. I should have gone straight to my rooms, but my stomach pulled me toward the kitchens. The fire was still roaring, casting a warm glow over the cavernous stone room and most of the kitchen staff had retired for the evening. I wasn't surprised to see a familiar figure already seated at the chunky wooden table before the fire.

"Why don't you eat with everyone else?" I asked my cousin, sliding onto the wooden bench beside him.

He huffed, his attention fixed on the plate of roasted meat and potato in front of him. "I might ask you the same, Cousin. I haven't seen you around much lately."

I stared, watching him shovel overly large forkfuls into his mouth with gusto. "I've been busy."

"Busy?" he echoed, wiping his mouth with the back of his hand. "Doing what?"

"Preparing for the Royal Rites," I lied.

The flames wavered, as though someone had opened a window, but the cold chill that shivered down my spine had nothing to do with the wind. Every muscle in my body tensed as I turned.

"Father," I said, getting to my feet.

His dark gaze flitted between me and Odio, impassive and unwavering. "I've been looking for you."

"Me?" I clarified, glancing at where my cousin was still eating, seemingly unperturbed by the king's appearance.

"I wanted to talk to you about the Royal Rites. It's good to hear you're already preparing."

He stepped closer, his black robes catching the stone paving, and every instinct screamed at me to back away. The wooden bench dug into the backs of my thighs, my wings trapped against the tabletop.

"Sirain will have no problem with whatever the Fates throw at her," Odio said, pushing his plate away. He swung his legs over the bench to face his uncle. "Only Kwellen can beat her in a fight and even those wins are becoming less frequent."

I smiled gratefully at my cousin, beaming inside. It was true —there had been two instances recently where I'd bested my friend and guard. The conflicting surprise and pride on his face had been enough to make me laugh.

"Being a skilled fighter might not be enough," my father sneered. "Three of the four Rites change with each successor. You must train both mentally and physically. At least if you fail, Fin is up to the challenge of taking your place."

My heart stuttered. Failing the Rites meant death. It was something I was used to—my father speaking casually of my demise—but it didn't make it any easier to hear.

"Like I said," Odio stood, placing a hand on my shoulder, his long slim fingers gripping gently, "Sirain can handle whatever the Fates decide."

"Your opinion is irrelevant," my father said, his wings flaring as he stepped in front of my cousin. "Leave us."

Odio stared at the king, eye-to-eye and unfaltering. I watched, barely breathing and in awe of my cousin's fearlessness—a fearlessness that stemmed from the fact that his own father was the greater monster.

"Good night, Your Majesty," he said, dipping his head slightly. "Good night, Cousin."

He squeezed my shoulder once more then stepped around

my father and strode from the kitchen. I tried not to let my wings sag at the absence of his comforting presence.

"You weren't at the evening meal."

My attention snapped from the empty doorway to my father. I hadn't been at an evening meal for days. I'd been at the cliff with Rose.

"No, Father," I said. "The training grounds are quietest at that time, so I choose to practise then and eat afterwards."

His nostrils flared slightly as though scenting the lie that rolled from my tongue with ease. "Ruling Helle requires strength. Not just physical, but moral."

I raised my eyebrows in question.

"There can be no sympathy, not exceptions to rules," he continued, his garnet-flecked eyes flickering over my face as his lip curled. "We obey the Fates. Anyone who deviates from this path must be punished without hesitation. I don't think you're strong enough."

I swallowed at the brazen admission. "I am strong enough."

His sneer grew. "I've seen you looking away when I deal with insubordinates. You may think you show no qualms when drawing blood on the training grounds, but taking a life is a different kind of strength."

Willing my body not to tremble, I lifted my chin. "I'm strong enough."

"We'll see."

He turned and strode from the room without a second glance, leaving me breathless, braced against the table. My fingers ached as I loosened my grip on the tabletop. When I became queen, I didn't plan on killing anyone. The way my father dealt with people was barbaric. Sinking down onto the bench, I tried to calm my shaking hands. I'd never tell him that, but I was certain it wasn't weakness. Talking with Rose had only served to confirm that a land could be ruled without spilling blood. I closed my eyes and took a deep breath. Only an hour ago, I'd been filled with light and hope as I flew away from the cliff. Now, the darkness of the castle had sunk, festering into my bones, smothering, and suffocating.

I left the kitchens and went to my rooms, my heart as cold and empty as my aching stomach.

15
Pace

A gasp tore from me as the male's fist collided with my ribs, forcing the air from my lungs. I shook my head, sweat spraying from the soaked strands, and adjusted my stance before swinging at him. We'd started with short swords, but we were evenly matched and had managed to disarm each other after a few minutes. Fights didn't often get to the point of fists and feet, and adrenaline pulsed through my veins as I circled him, relishing the throbbing across my knuckles. The evidence would be a pain to hide but as I landed a blow to his side, I found it hard to care. There was an unspoken rule to avoid faces at tournaments as, with Hehven being a place of peace and harmony, black eyes would be difficult to explain.

The small crowd shouted encouragement as I ducked, lifting my leg into a kick that sent my opponent sprawling. His wings flared, halting his fall and he turned on me, hazel eyes blazing. I grinned, welcoming the challenge. Sweat glistened on his ebony skin as he swung a muscled arm in a right hook, but I dodged the punch, sinking my own fist into his side before swiping his legs from under him. He fell to the ground with a thud and the crowd cheered. For a moment, I thought he might get up, but then he sank backwards, his large chest heaving as he held up a hand in defeat. I inclined my head, a grin lighting my face at the win. Two Cupids stepped forward to help him up and we clasped forearms before he hobbled off to rest. Someone handed me a cloth and I accepted it gratefully, wiping the sweat from my face and neck.

"I can do that for you, if you'd like."

Lowering the cloth, I smiled at the female before me. "I'm quite capable, but thank you."

She pulled a plump lip under her teeth as she brazenly dragged her gaze over my body, lingering on my bare chest and torso. I watched her with amusement. She was often at the tournaments, and I'd be lying if I said I hadn't noticed her. Tall and toned, her long white hair hung in loose waves down to her waist. Her chest was more than ample, accentuated by the fact that she'd unfastened the top few ties of her dress, revealing cleavage I was certain wasn't displayed outside of the dingy hall the tournament was held in.

"You were very impressive," she purred, stepping closer.

I held my ground, draping the cloth over my shoulder. "Thank you."

It was clear what she was offering, and my blood fizzed at the thought of slipping off to a side room, feeling her breath on my chest, the heat from her skin. She clearly wasn't shy, and she might even unfasten her—I coughed.

"I should be going."

"Are you sure I can't persuade you to stay just a little longer?" she said, leaning close enough that when she sighed, her breath caught the beads of sweat on my chest, causing my skin to pebble.

Hesitation caught in my throat. Since my engagement, I'd refrained from indulging, but this time something else niggled in the back of my head. The thought of being alone with this attractive female didn't quite hold the same allure it usually would. A teasing voice echoed in my head, and I found myself thinking of Thorn. I frowned. Surely the two things weren't connected.

A loud cough sounded beside us, and I turned to find Tiesa staring between me and the female, her eyebrow arched, and her arms folded. "Sorry to interrupt."

I smiled an apology to the female and strode over to the chair where I'd left my shirt, Tiesa stomping behind. "How did you find me?"

"Does it matter?" she asked.

"No. What's up?"

Tiesa stared at me, her green eyes hard. "What were you doing with that female?"

"We were talking," I said, pulling my shirt on over my head and shrugging my wings through the slits. "What did it look like?"

"It looked like she was about to lick you," Tiesa snapped, glowering over her shoulder at where the female stood watching us, amusement curling her lips.

I sighed, pushing my damp hair from my forehead. "She wasn't going to lick me. No one was going to lick anyone. Now, why are you here?"

Tiesa blinked as though she'd forgotten. "Oh. Your parents want you."

Any lingering remnants of adrenaline evaporated instantly, my heart sinking to my gut. "Why?"

"How would I know? I'm just the lucky messenger."

Chucking the sweat-soaked cloth into a bucket, I lifted my hand in farewell to the Cupid who ran the tournaments and headed to the door. The sunlight was blinding compared with the dim interior of the hall and I squinted as I adjusted.

"How do you know one of them isn't going to tell the king and queen?" Tiesa asked, looking over her shoulder at the door as it clicked shut behind us.

"They won't. No one should be there. We're all breaking the rules together."

Tiesa muttered under her breath but didn't question it further as she spread her wings and leapt into the sky. I followed, swooping over the pale rooftops of the sprawling city of Dragoste. The winding streets were busy, with bustling market stalls lining the cobblestones, the sound of chatter and laughter punctuating the air. It was a glorious spring day, but I couldn't shake the cold chill from my bones as I struggled to remember the last time a meeting with my parents had ended well. We dropped down over the water and I cast my house a longing glance as we passed.

I was still lost in my spiralling thoughts when the palace guards heaved open the doors to the throne room. Light poured in from the tall windows, casting channels of golden light across the polished floor.

"Good luck," Tiesa muttered.

Casting her a withering look, I straightened my shoulders and pasted a smile on my face as I strode into the room. The king and queen were seated on their slender marble thrones, which caused my chest to tighten further. I'd learned the signs years ago. If they were standing, they weren't angry. If they were on their thrones . . . I resisted the urge to clench my fingers into fists at my side, my smile faltering.

"Good afternoon, Mother. Father." I bowed. "You wanted to speak with me?"

"Where were you?" my father demanded.

I blinked. "I was training."

"You weren't at the training rooms."

"That's because it was flight training," I spooled the practised lie. "I was building endurance, flying between here and Caracy."

My mother's gaze dipped to my battered knuckles before returning to my face. When she smiled, it didn't reach her eyes.

"What did you want to discuss with me?" I pushed. "Surely it wasn't to ask about my fitness regime."

My father shifted in his throne, his brows knitted as he glanced at my mother. "There's no easy way to say this, Son. We've had a complaint."

"A complaint?" I echoed, my mind tumbling through possibilities. "About what?"

"About you."

I swallowed. "Can you elaborate?"

My father pulled his hand over his face, pinching the bridge of his nose. Beside him, my mother clasped her hands in her lap, her back straight as she stared at me.

"One of our most revered Hands came to us with a worrying tale," the queen said, her golden eyes unreadable. "He said that you compromised his daughter's purity."

My mouth ran dry, air refusing to fill my lungs. "Excuse me?"

"You heard," my father snapped. "Is it true?"

"No! Of course not!" I shook my head, my eyes wide. "I swear on the Fates, I've never touched anyone."

My mother raised her clasped hands, resting her elbows on the arms of the throne. "Why would he think you had?"

I threw my arms out to the side in exasperation. "How should I know?"

A deep groan rumbled from my father, and I stared between the two of them in disbelief.

"Pace," my mother said, taking a breath. "I hate that I have to ask this but, do you still have your purity?"

"Yes!" An incredulous laugh built in my chest as my cheeks heated with mortification. "I can't believe you're even asking the question. Of course, I do."

My parents shared a look.

"Why should we believe you, when you lie to us constantly?" my father asked.

I lifted my hands to my head, unable to believe what I was hearing. "When do I lie to you?"

"You lied just now about where you've been," my mother said. "You lied about why you were late to meet Caitland. More and more often we find it hard to find you when we need you."

I opened my mouth to dispute the fact, but my mother cut me off.

"A mother knows when her son is lying," she said.

Disbelief and embarrassment slowly morphed into anger at their accusations, despite the fact they were mostly true. My eyes narrowed as I stared at their disappointed faces.

"I'm not lying about my purity. I might be a little lax on timekeeping and I might be a far cry from perfect, reliable Dashuri, but I would never compromise my purity." I shook my head, rage rippling through my limbs. "How could you even think that?"

It would have been so easy to throw it all away—to give in to the role of disappointing son completely. The Fates only knew how many times I'd had the opportunity. There was every chance I'd spent time alone with the female in question, but the idea that I'd take someone's purity was abhorrent.

"You might find it hard to believe," I bit out, "but the last thing I want to do is embarrass this family. I might never sit on the throne but, I assure you, I do care about the Dragoste family name and what it stands for."

"If that's true," my father said wearily, "what is this female talking about?"

"I don't know."

My mother sighed. "You have spent time unchaperoned around females?"

I groaned, my skin heating. "Yes."

"Pace." She shook her head. "You know you can't allow that to happen. As an unmarried male it would be bad enough, but as a prince . . . Now there's no way of disproving this female."

A cold chill licked at my skin. "So, what? It's her word over mine?"

My mother stood and stepped down off the dais, her ivory robes swishing against the marble. She came to a stop in front of me and placed a hand on my chest. "I believe you, Pace. I believe you still have your purity. However—"

"Let me talk to the female," I interrupted. "Perhaps I can find out what she thinks happened and set her straight. With a chaperone, of course."

My father mumbled something, and my mother shot him a warning look over her shoulder.

"It's worth a try," she said, reaching up to stroke my cheek. "I forget sometimes."

I frowned. "Forget what?"

"That you're not a boy anymore."

"Sentimentality aside," the king said, "you must promise to stop spending time alone with females. You say you don't want to dishonour the Dragoste name, then prove it. We just have to hope Lord Rakkaus doesn't hear about this."

I nodded, resisting the urge to slump against the weight of his words.

"There is a chance, of course," my mother said, "that this female is claiming such because she wants to secure herself a place as your wife."

My eyes widened. "Please tell me that isn't an option."

"This is exactly why you have to be careful," my mother said, clasping my hand between hers. "You're a prince. A very handsome one at that, and even the purest beings can be tempted by lust and power. I know it doesn't feel like it, but we really do want what's best for you. We want you to be happy."

I stared down at where she was holding my hand, marvelling at how much larger mine was than hers. "I'm sorry," I said. "I'll do better."

"That's all we ask," she said, squeezing my fingers.

Stepping back, I bowed again before turning and walking back towards the doors, the distance seeming twice as long as usual. Tiesa was still waiting for me and as the doors opened, she turned, her eyes wide in question, but I shook my head.

"I'm not allowed to talk about it," I said, continuing my purposeful stride towards the entrance.

Tiesa jogged to keep up. "Are you okay?"

"I'm fine," I said. "Just tired. I'm going home to take a nap."

She slowed, falling behind, but I kept going until I reached the entrance to the palace, where my stride lengthened into a run. Spreading my wings, I caught the breeze, carrying up into the air and out over the sparkling water surrounding the palace. Although I wanted to keep flying until my wings gave out and all the anger had been wrung from my system, I dipped, heading for my house on the shore.

Thorn's words from the night before worked their way to the forefront of my mind. It seemed I was burning things to the ground without even trying. My head pounded as I tried to think which female might have gone to my parents. It was true, I'd indulged in spacing a few times, but not since my engagement was announced. The thought of doing it when I knew I was promised to someone else turned my stomach and I knew beyond a doubt that I'd never crossed that line.

Dropping down in front of my door, I rubbed at my temples. Perhaps I would actually try and sleep. Either way, I knew I would spend the rest of the day waiting for the sun to dip toward the horizon so that the best part of my day could begin.

16 Sirain

The sea looked different in the daytime. Instead of choppy waves of inky black, we flew over shimmering peaks of sapphire and turquoise, the sun warming our wings. In the distance, grey clouds piled on the horizon, their rolling edges tinged black. I tried to ignore the sense of foreboding the sight wrapped around my heart, instead focusing on the thrill of seeing the human world lit up in all its colourful glory.

It wasn't just the clouds that were casting a shadow on my mood, however. Last night at the cliffs, Rose had been different. Something had happened with their parents, and I hadn't been able to get them to talk about it. The frustration I'd felt had taken me by surprise. I'd never felt the urge to hug someone in my entire life, yet as I felt Rose's unhappiness seeping through the shimmering lights of The Crossing, all I'd wanted to do was hold them in my arms and reassure them it was going to be okay. I wasn't sure what to do with those feelings, so I tucked them away, alongside Pace's feather inside my mattress.

"You realise what an incredibly bad idea this is, right?" Kwellen grumbled.

I exhaled. "Yes. Of course. But if the Cupids are working with the humans against the Fates, we need to know. We need to tell my father."

"You could have told him already," he retorted. "He could have sent Hands to investigate."

"You know as well as I do, my father would not entertain a hunch or a half-formed suspicion."

Kwellen huffed in response.

"Besides," I continued, "if we're right, the information will distract him from the fact that you've been accompanying the future queen through The Crossing for the past two years."

Odio cackled from where he was flying above us. "He'd behead you on the spot, Kwellen. Or perhaps hack off your wings first."

I shuddered because it was true. My father would have no qualms about executing my best friend, even if he was the son of the Lord of Devland. My father acted without reason or regret.

"You know the chances of them being here are slim, right?" Odio said.

I glanced up at him, the sun highlighting the hints of red in his wings and hair—the same royal red found on my father and brother's wings. "Yes. I do. It doesn't matter if the Cupids are here or not, though. We're simply listening."

That was why we'd ventured to the human lands during the day—a feat which had taken almost a week of persuasion—because there was a better chance of catching the Cupids conspiring with the humans. As heir to the throne, my duty was to make sure the orders given by the Fates were carried out. If the Cupids were interfering with that, we needed to know, and we needed to stop it. If that meant killing that Cupid—Pace—then so be it. Just like Rose had said, the night had passed, and the dawn had brought peace and determination. I swallowed, hoping Rose didn't know Pace. There was no way they'd forgive me for killing one of their own.

"There's Cove's ship," Kwellen called, tearing me from my thoughts. "Looks like they're not on the islands."

The frigate sat on the horizon, another similarly sized ship anchored not far away.

"Do you think they're meeting with someone?" I asked.

Odio dipped lower, flying beside me. "Looks like it."

We continued onwards, and I eyed the creeping clouds on the horizon wishing they were closer. Approaching in broad daylight was going to make it difficult to hide. Humans usually felt our presence as a shiver or sense of foreboding, catching sight of us as little more than a shadow. Even still, I couldn't help feeling exposed as we neared the ship.

The sails were gathered, a few humans moving around on deck, securing ropes. Swooping in, we landed amongst the rigging, assessing our next move.

"They'll be in the cabin," Odio said, his eyes narrowed as his hand moved to the dagger at his hip. As this wasn't a mission, he'd left his bow and arrows in Helle, a long sword between his wings instead.

I squinted down at the deck, wondering how we could discover what was being said without being seen. The windows were open because of the warm weather, but not even a hint of a voice reached us up in the rigging.

"We need a distraction," I muttered, the scraps of a plan coming together in my mind. "There's no way all three of us can eavesdrop, but if you can distract the crew on deck, I can get down and hide by the window."

"You want to go down there alone?" Kwellen asked. "I think not."

"You'll be up here keeping watch," I said. "If there's any danger, you'll probably see it before I do."

A ripping sound caused me to turn and my mouth to fall open as I found Odio slicing through rope and sailcloth with his blade.

"Get ready," he said as the heavy chunk of sail plummeted to the deck below.

Kwellen cursed and I grinned as a shout went up from the crew. Spreading my wings, I dove down toward the deck, while Odio and Kwellen leapt to another mast, hiding amidst the gathered sails.

Tucking myself between the crates and barrels, I tried to calm the frantic beating of my heart enough to hear the voices drifting through the open window.

"As I have already promised," an unfamiliar male voice said. "I will tell no one of your existence. You have my word."

"You'll excuse us if we still have concerns. We have no idea how good your word is."

My breath halted in my throat. I would recognise that voice anywhere. *Pace.*

"That is entirely understandable," the man said. "And I will endeavour to prove my trustworthiness to you."

"That isn't necessary," another male voice said. "We only came here to explain to Marlowe that we cannot help him."

Before I could question the sanity of my choice, I rose enough to see through the window. I balked at the sight before me. The Cupids had revealed themselves to so many humans. My stomach churned, bile climbing in my throat as I took in the scene.

Despite the large table in the centre of the room, only one person was seated. The voice I hadn't recognised belonged to the tall slender ruler of Liridona who'd been meeting with the Midnight Queen. Although it was only the second time I'd seen the man, there was something unsettlingly familiar about him. And if he was at all fazed at being surrounded by Cupids, he certainly wasn't showing it. Leaning back in his chair, his ankle resting on his knee, he looked the picture of ease.

In contrast, Marlowe stood with his arms folded and mouth bracketed, the long-haired Cupid beside him wearing a matching expression, and with no signs of the wounds he'd had the last time I'd seen him. Cove had her back to me, another dark-haired woman at her side but from their postures I could guess their expressions were equally wary.

The female Cupid stood, surveying the scene with open curiosity, her hand on the hilt of her sword. I noted the pale scar across her forehead, realising it must be the reminder Odio said he had left her with. I was painfully aware I'd avoided looking at Pace for as long as I could and, with my heart in my mouth, I took a readying breath and let my gaze drift to the tall male at the female Cupid's side.

His expression was neutral in comparison to the others, a hand on the hilt of his sword and the other on his hip. My heartbeat quickened as I realised, it was the first time I'd seen him when we weren't actively trying to kill each other. My pulse was an itching beat beneath my skin as I allowed myself to really look at him—the person who wanted me dead and whom I might have to kill—knowing that if he turned his gaze to the window, he'd see me.

There was no denying he was incredibly handsome. Especially when his pale golden eyes weren't blazing with hatred. His ivory hair fell in thick locks across his forehead, curling around his ears, the colour serving only to contrast the richness of his golden-brown skin. A sharp jaw held the plump lips I remembered from our first encounter, and I wondered what he looked like when he smiled. I'd noted his toned physique the last time we'd fought, but now I allowed myself to drink in the honed lines of his body and the way his clothes clung to his upper arms and thighs. His white shirt was unbuttoned enough to show the definition of his chest and I swallowed, my mouth suddenly dry.

"Can't help, or won't help?" Cove asked.

The long-haired Cupid pulled a large hand over his face. "You're asking us to go against the Fates themselves."

"What would happen if you did?" Marlowe asked.

"I don't know."

Marlowe reached out and placed a hand on the Cupid's arm. "If it saved hundreds of thousands of lives, wouldn't it be worth the risk?"

Pace sighed. "I think what Dariel is trying to say, is that this is bigger than us. The Fates control everything. If we went against their orders, it might make things worse."

"Like those demons?" Cove asked.

Pace shook his head. "Those demons are called Chaos. We don't know for sure, but I suspect their arrows are the same as ours, but instead of instilling positive emotions, they do the opposite."

My eyes widened. They knew who we were. The long-haired Cupid—Dariel—looked at Marlowe, placing a hand protectively on his shoulder. I narrowed my eyes at the gesture and the look that passed between them, remembering the way the human had fought Kwellen on the rooftop. Before I could ponder further, the Liridonan leader clapped his hands together, pulling everyone's attention.

"Perhaps we don't need to come up with an answer today."

"You already have our answer, Lord Bickerstaff," Pace said. "We can't go against the Fates."

Marlowe hung his head. "You would leave us all to die."

"That's not what we're saying," Pace argued.

"But it is," Cove said. "War is coming. Even if Liridona joins forces with the Wendell Islands, we would be slaughtered."

"I'm afraid it's true," Bickerstaff agreed. "I've seen first-hand the armada the Midnight Queen is building. Lord Diarke is yet to agree to meet with me and I fear he won't."

"He suspects you're spying?" the dark-haired woman beside Cove said.

"Indeed. Newbold has always been excessively secretive, but I do think this time Lord Diarke is hiding something more."

Pace leaned forward, bracing his hands on the table. "What

if we're missing something? I've been thinking about The Crossing."

"What about it?" the female Cupid asked.

"Where did it come from? Was it always there? Why do we have stories of demons? There must be something linking Hehven and Helle somewhere. I'm going to go to the libraries and see if I can find anything that could help us."

"I believe some old texts are kept on the Isle of the Fates," Dariel offered.

A sound above drew my attention and I turned, looking up at the rigging. Odio pointed out to sea, but from where I was hidden, I couldn't tell what he was trying to tell me. I opened my mouth to communicate the fact, but before I could, a shout rang out from one of the crew members and I stilled.

"Batten down the hatches!"

It was only then I noticed that the heat of the sun had faded, replaced by a brisk, chilly breeze. Above me, the blue sky was swathed with grey, the clouds moving fast enough to speed my heart rate. Glancing up at Odio and Kwellen, their gestures left no room for misinterpretation. We needed to get out of there. Fast.

The voices had risen inside the cabin, growing closer amidst heavy footsteps. I didn't hesitate as I jumped up onto one of the crates, spreading my wings and launching up into the air where Kwellen and Odio were waiting.

"Let's go!" my cousin bellowed.

I nodded, my hair whipping in my face as I beat my wings against the growing wind. The sea had changed from an undulating blue to a churning pewter, the white peaked waves spiking ferociously beneath us. I bowed my head and concentrated on keeping steady as the wind buffeted me, not daring to look at the ship we were leaving behind. A deep boom rumbled through the rolling clouds causing both Odio and Kwellen to curse repeatedly. Flying in high winds was dangerous enough, but in a storm? We were making little to no progress, and it was starting to look like we might be forced to find shelter and wait it out. A gasp tore from my lips as a deafening crack sliced through the air, the flash of light illuminating the dark clouds above us in a deep purple. Shouts of terror carried on the wind, and I turned before I could stop myself.

The lightning had struck the mainmast of the ship, amber flames erupting amongst the folded sails. The air was so heavy, I knew rain was on its way. Perhaps there wouldn't be any need to put it out. It was only as I turned away that something caught my eye. The wind slammed into me as I tried to hold in place—tried to see what it was. *Wings*. White wings were tangled in the rigging. I frowned. Why?

Ignoring the shouts of my friends behind me, I turned back back toward the ship, the wind speeding me along as though relieved I was finally doing what it was telling me. As I drew closer, I realised it was the female Cupid. Pace and the other one were trying to get to her, but the wind and flames were beating them back. They must have been trying to leave just after us.

The female's right wing was tangled in the rigging, her face wracked with terror as she tried to wriggle free, the flames growing ever closer. They needed to put the fire out. I opened my mouth to shout as much but stopped. We weren't supposed to engage. Listening only. I faltered, my heart slamming against my chest.

"What do you think you're doing?" Kwellen roared, reaching my side.

"I don't know."

Odio almost flew right past me, the wind was so strong. He backbeat his wings, grabbing at my arm. "We need to go. Now."

Shrugging him off, I swallowed, making my decision. I dove down to the quarterdeck, hoisting an empty barrel over the side into the churning sea.

"Sirain!" Kwellen barked.

"Help me," I ordered, diving down towards the sea.

I couldn't look at my friend, feeling the anger rolling from him as I tried to haul the half-filled barrel back up while the wind attempted to toss me about like an autumn leaf. Still barking curses, Kwellen grabbed hold of the other side and together we lifted the barrel up into the air above the ship.

I didn't dare look further down the mast, where I knew Pace and his friend were trying to get to her. Instead, I focused on tipping the barrel over, letting the seawater douse the flames and the female Cupid in the process. She shouted out in surprise; her green eyes wide as she stared up at us. I wondered whether she thought we were going to kill her.

Leaving Kwellen with the barrel, I drew a dagger from my thigh and allowed the wind to blow me into the mast. Clinging to it, I tucked in my wings and shimmied down toward the tangled female. She shouted something to me, but her words were ripped away by the storm. It didn't matter. I wasn't there to talk. Hacking away at the crisscross of rope around her wing, trying my best to avoid her feathers, I cut her free. The wind tossed her away instantly and Dariel swept after her like an arrow, his wings tucked in tight. When I looked up, I found Odio and Kwellen clinging to the mainmast, their weapons drawn and their faces grim. Their murderous gazes weren't fixed on me however, they were looking past me. My stomach lurching, I looked down.

17
Pace

Hand over hand, I hauled myself up the mast, the storm screaming in my ears as it tried to tear me away. Someone was yelling my name, the sound more like a whisper on the roaring wind, but I couldn't stop. Couldn't think. She was here. Again. I thought I'd made my peace with what she'd done to me, but seeing her here, on Cove's ship . . . She shouldn't be here. Why was she taunting me? I needed to get to that demon and . . . I paused in my climbing, glaring up at her, breathing hard, as she watched me with something that looked a lot like pity. What would I do when I got to her? Kill her? Throw her to the wind?

"Come down," a voice demanded, closer than should have been possible. "It's not safe. You need to get below deck!"

Tearing my gaze from the dark-haired demon, I found Marlowe just below me, rope looped tightly around his forearm and thigh. I blinked, looking past him to find the others on the deck, Tiesa and Dariel included, clinging to whatever they could to stop themselves from being tossed into the sea. I would have to let the demon go. They wouldn't go below deck without me. Casting a final glower at the female clinging to the mast, I nodded to Marlowe and began to climb down.

"That means you too," he yelled up at the Chaos. "If you want a chance of surviving this storm, you and your friends should come below deck."

I balked at his words, a shout of protest on my lips, but Marlowe loosened his grip on the rope, gliding back down toward the deck with an agility gleaned from a life spent aboard ships. They wouldn't join us. There was no way.

The thunder boomed, deafeningly loud, punctuated with blinding forks of lightning that spread out across the sea, illuminating the towering waves. I had almost reached the deck when the first fat raindrop dashed my face, running down my neck. Then the dark, rolling clouds burst open, and sporadic drops became a downpour. My chest tightened, and I gripped at the now sodden rope, unable to bring myself to look up. If the Chaos were going to attempt to fly in this storm, they'd be killed. Although, perhaps it would be the same outcome if they took Marlowe up on his offer.

Cove, Shanti and Emeric were no longer anywhere to be seen, presumably already below deck, when my feet found the slippery wooden boards of the deck. Marlowe held open the cabin door, the storm trying to wrench it from his grasp.

"Inside," he yelled. "Now!"

Every muscle in my body was coiled and tensed as I stepped into the cabin, Tiesa and Dariel behind me. It was only when the door slammed shut moments later, rattling on its hinges that I turned to find the three Chaos standing, like vast shadows, dripping before it. They weren't wearing their masks and the sight was jarring. The lean one, the archer, had pointed features and unusual hair, shaved at the sides but tied into a long braid down the centre of his head. The large one-armed Chaos was exactly as I'd expected—a mass of broad features and a wide jaw, his long dark hair loose at his shoulders.

"Weapons," Marlowe demanded, pointing to an empty chest, the heavy lid propped open. "I'm not having you kill each other on my ship. You can have them back when the storm passes."

The archer reached for the blade between his black wings, his expression as cold as the winds rattling the windows. "If we kill you, we could just keep them."

To his credit, Marlowe didn't flinch. "I'm saving you from the storm, you could at least show a little gratitude."

"Raise a weapon against him and just see what happens," Dariel said, the low timbre of his voice as threatening as the rumbling thunder outside.

The female Chaos stepped forward and my hand flew to my sword, but she merely unsheathed her dagger and dropped it into the chest, followed by the onyx sword strapped between her soaking wings. Her companions followed; their reluctance palpable as their threatening glances flickered between us. I met their steely gazes head on as I drew my own blade and placed it into the chest, Dariel and Tiesa following suit. As Tiesa stepped past me, I realised she was trembling, her wings streaming trails of cold water into puddles on the floor. Guilt twisted my gut. I had been so focused on the Chaos I hadn't even asked if she was okay.

"Thank you," Marlowe said, slamming the lid shut. He heaved open a heavy door and gestured at the dark stairwell beyond. "Try not to kill each other."

Dariel huffed, motioning for me to go first. I opened my mouth to protest, but the warning glint in his eyes forced my lips together. The ship was rocking uncomfortably, and I had to hold on to the wall to stop myself from lurching forward down the stairs. Lamps were already lit at the bottom, and I was surprised to find a large room with wooden tables lashed down at its centre and bunks lining the walls. Shanti came forward and handed me a blanket, which I took gratefully, rubbing the rain from my hair and face. I sank down onto one of the bunks beside Tiesa, tucking in my dripping wings.

"How are you?" I whispered.

She gave a half-hearted shrug. "I almost got burned alive but got rescued by a demon. I'm great."

Cove approached and tried to place another blanket around Tiesa's trembling shoulders but faltered as she tried to navigate her wings. "How do you even—"

"Allow me," I said, taking the blanket from her and arranging it over as much of Tiesa's back and wings as I could. She smiled gratefully.

"We only have a skeleton crew," Marlowe explained, shucking off his dripping coat. "They'll stay above or below deck on the other side of the ship to make sure things run smoothly. They know not to come down here."

Even as he spoke, I could hear the occasional order being yelled above the wind, the words swallowed by the storm before I could make sense of them. I exhaled, finally allowing my attention to drift to where the Chaos had gathered, watching us like cornered, wild animals as they tensed against the swaying of the ship.

"Why are you here?" I demanded. "I thought demons only visited the human world at night."

The female lifted her chin, her eyes narrowing. "We came to see if what we overheard in the Wendell Islands was true."

Her cold tone frosted the air between us, and I scrambled to remember the conversation we'd had with Marlowe when we'd returned for Dariel's arrows. What did she think she'd overheard? The shiver that ran down my spine had little to do with the freezing rain soaking my skin. If they had told anyone we'd revealed ourselves to humans. If they'd told the Fated . . .

Pushing my spiralling concern down, I folded my arms across my chest. "And what's that?"

"That you're planning on forsaking the Fates."

I flinched at the accusation. Had they come here seeking us

out? Maybe it wasn't a coincidence. Perhaps the Fates themselves had told them where we would be.

"We haven't forsaken the Fates," Dariel said from where he'd taken a seat beside Marlowe. "That's why we're here. To tell the humans that it's not our place to interfere."

Cove snorted. "That's exactly what your place is."

"I heard you," the female insisted. "Before, in the cabin. You were considering it."

"No one has committed to anything," Emeric said from where he was sprawled on a bunk, his long legs hanging over the end, looking perfectly at home on the listing ship. "We were merely discussing possibilities."

The female Chaos turned to him. "Well, one of those options cannot be going against the Fates."

Although she was right, Marlowe's heartbroken words from earlier still lingered. Would we be leaving them to die? When we'd arrived early that morning, the leader of the Wendell Islands had sprung Emeric on us. He had claimed it was because he wanted us to see that it wasn't just the Wendell Islands that needed our help—that if we helped them, they could prevent the war. Emeric was right. We had been discussing possibilities. However, we were yet to find one that led to a feasible solution. I wanted to help the humans. Emeric and Marlowe were vastly outnumbered by the other human lands. If there was only another way . . .

"What if we asked?" I said, looking to Dariel. "What if we asked my—the queen? We could explain that our arrows could prevent the war. She could send a message to the Fates via the Fated to see whether they'd agree to it."

Dariel shook his head. "And what if she said no? What if all it did was tell her what we've been doing?"

The unspoken meaning behind his words tightened my chest. It would tell her what *I* had been doing. Taking a deep breath, I straightened my shoulders. "What if she said yes?

What if this is a solution that doesn't mean angering the Fates or going behind people's backs?"

"Do you really think your little band of misfits could convince the Fates?" The large Chaos chortled. "Why would the queen of Hehven listen to you?"

"Fated Fates," the female Chaos murmured, her dark eyes widening as she balanced, clinging to the edge of a bunk. "You're a prince."

My heart dropped like a boulder. "What?"

"It makes so much sense," she continued, her eyes burning into mine. "The way you talk. The way you hold yourself. The way your friends are always poised, ready to protect you."

"You're wrong."

An awed smile lit her face, and she shook her head, the two Chaos breaking into grins beside her. "I don't think I am."

"Why did you save me?" Tiesa asked, her quiet voice drawing the burning tension away from me. I would have to thank her later.

The female Chaos frowned. "Because I'm not a monster."

"The scar across her face would beg to differ," Dariel snarled.

"It's a good question," I admitted. "You came here to stop us from interfering with Fate. Letting her die would have made sense."

The female scowled. "I'm beginning to wish I had."

"So, why did you save her?" I pushed. "You've tried to kill me enough times."

"I think you'll find it's been you trying to kill me," she huffed. "And like I said, I'm not a monster, despite what you think about my kind."

My gaze flitted to the two Chaos beside her, trying to find compassion in the hard lines of their faces and the tense set of their jaws.

"Do you know what I think?" Emeric piped up. "I think there's a balance between you."

The upbeat tone caused my shoulders to tense, his lackadaisical manner suddenly irksome. "What are you talking about?"

"Cupids spread positive emotions, and Chaos spread negative. We need both. People can't be happy all the time, just as they can't always be sad. You both have an important place in this world. Just like night and day." One of the male Chaos snorted, but Emeric just shrugged before continuing. "Our world was devastated after the last war and, even though another war looms, there have been years speckled with happiness despite the aching loss. No matter how bad things seem, joy and love will always find a way to combat the darkness."

His words settled in my soul. "Fear not the night—"

"The sun will always rise."

My head snapped to the female Chaos as she muttered the words at the same time. Her dark eyes widened as they met mine, the blood draining from her face.

"Rose?" she mouthed, although no sound left her lips.

My skin was too tight for my body as I stared at her. At Thorn. I shook my head. It wasn't possible. Every conversation we'd had at the cliffs flashed through my mind. It had been her. All this time, sitting on the other side of The Crossing. My fingers slowly curled into fists, my breaths becoming increasingly shallow as my skin heated. I'd bared my soul to her. How could I have been so stupid? How could I have trusted a Chaos? I'd thought we'd been friends, when really it had been no more than an evil, vindictive trick. The edges of my vision burned red as I got to my feet, my body trembling.

"You knew," I snarled, barely recognising my own voice. "You used me. Admit it."

She shook her head, her eyes still wide. "I had no idea. I swear."

"Was it not enough the first time?" I spat, taking a step towards her. "Do you get a sick thrill out of humiliating me?"

"Can someone please explain what's going on?" Tiesa pleaded, grabbing at my arm.

"What was the purpose?" I seethed, shaking free of my friend's grasp. "Were you trying to get me to confess to you? Trying to lure secrets from me? I bet you had a good laugh with your friends about it, didn't you?"

She took a step towards me, her features hardening as she looked me up and down. "Have you ever stopped to consider that maybe everything isn't about you?"

"Whatever." I shook my head. "Your sick little game is over."

"Good," she snapped, dropping her gaze.

I raised my eyebrows. "Don't pretend like you're sorry."

"All clear!" a voice bellowed down the staircase.

My head snapped to the sound, realising the boat was indeed no longer rocking violently, instead rolling easily over the calmed waves. I didn't spare so much as a glance at the female Chaos as I half flew up the stairs, consumed by the desperate desire to be as far away from her as possible. I was such a fool.

Breathing hard, I heaved open the chest and grabbed my sword. The door slammed as I wrenched it open and stormed out of the cabin, immediately launching into the sky. Whether the sailors on deck saw me or not, I was past caring. Bitterness coated my mouth, my lungs, and I swallowed, my skin prickling as I thought of how much I'd confided in Thorn. The fact that I'd felt something—a connection between us—caused my stomach to heave. I'd spent so many hours looking forward to spending time with her. My jaw clenched so hard my teeth ached. It had been her. The whole time.

I was going to tear that cliff apart, rock by rock.

18
Sirain

It had been him. The whole time. I clutched the edge of the wooden bunk, my mind spiralling. How could Rose be Pace? My head ached as I ran through the conversations of the last few weeks for clues—for anything that might have told me who he was.

"What's going on?" Kwellen asked, his hand gripping my shoulder.

I wasn't sure myself. "Nothing."

"What was he talking about?" Odio asked. "What does he think you've done?"

The room was silent, leaving only the sound of the crew above deck filtering down through the floorboards. I couldn't bring myself to look at the humans, their curious gazes a burning heat from across the room. The other two Cupids had barrelled up the stairs after Pace and I knew they'd already be long gone. *Good.*

"Let's go," I said, moving to the stairs.

No one tried to stop us as we left, and I breathed a sigh of relief. Our weapons were still in the bottom of the chest and as I strapped on my dagger and sheathed my blade, I wondered whether the Cupids would be waiting to ambush us. *No*. I knew in my heart they wouldn't. It had been more than clear that Pace wanted to put as much distance between us as possible. I tried to match Rose's gentle words of encouragement, thoughtful prose and craving for adventure with the serious angry exterior of Pace, but the pieces just wouldn't fit. How could the person who I'd sliced with my blade, who had looked at me with such unbridled hatred, be the same person who'd comforted me and made me laugh until my face ached? My eyes burned.

As Odio cautiously opened the cabin door, I drew in a ragged breath, trying to quell the nausea swelling in my gut. The air was still damp, crackling with residual energy from the storm, but the dark clouds were already in the distance, a faint rumbling echoing in their wake. Stepping out onto the deck, I spread my wings, shaking them out. They were still a little damp, but they'd dry out on the way home. I shot up into the air, hoping that Odio and Kwellen wouldn't press what had happened, but I knew I was setting myself up for disappointment.

"You need to tell us what's going on, Sirain," Odio urged the second we were over open water. "What was he talking about?"

I kept my eyes focused ahead. "Nothing. He's still just really angry about the feather I took."

"What's the big deal?" Kwellen asked. "People pull feathers out all the time."

"No, they don't," I said, shooting him a look over my shoulder.

He snorted. "Well, it happens with the people I spend my time with."

"Could you leave whatever sordid stuff you're into out of this?" Odio extended his wings, gliding just above my shoulder. "There's something you're not telling us, Cousin."

I shook my head. "Cupids remain pure until marriage. Like, *pure*."

"I can think of a million gestures a lot more intimate than taking a feather." Kwellen chuckled.

Odio fell silent above me, his face set in a frown.

"Wait," Kwellen said. "Pure, like not even a kiss?"

"Yes," I replied. "That's what pure means."

A deep laugh rumbled from him. "I don't think that other male will be pure for much longer. He seemed very friendly with that Marlowe human."

I thought about what Rose had told me on the cliff about purity, and realised I'd never asked why Cupids thought purity was so important. Did they believe the Fates would be angered if they kissed before marriage? I should have asked Rose when I'd had the chance. The thought slammed against my heart, and I winced. Rose was gone. There had never been a Rose. Just Pace. Who wanted me dead.

"We could kill them," Odio said.

"What? Who?" I asked.

"The Cupids," he clarified. "Chaos arrows are lethal to us, so I'm sure they would be to Cupids too. I could make it look like an accident."

I stared at him, the calm, coldness of his voice sending a shiver down my spine. "How do you even know that?"

"Know what?"

"That a Chaos arrow is lethal to our kind."

He stared back at me before looking away with the faintest shadow of a shrug.

"No," I said, just in case he needed clarification. "I don't want you to kill them."

There was no mistaking the ultimatum in his answering look. "Then he needs to get over the whole feather thing."

We flew the rest of the way back to The Crossing in silence, but the inside of my head was deafening as I tried to reconcile the idea of Pace with Rose. They were so different. Rose was funny, poetic and calm. No. Not always calm. I recalled with a pang the yell of rage I'd heard through The Crossing. It had been right after our encounter in the human world with

Marlowe and Cove. He hadn't told me anything. It was almost laughable to think we'd been swinging blades at each other and then spent the evening chatting like friends. The dense lights of The Crossing muted my senses, bringing momentary calm as I allowed myself to be dragged back to Helle.

"Are you going to be okay?" Odio asked as we emerged over the forest.

"Yes." I nodded, forcing a smile. "I just need to clear my head."

My cousin and Kwellen shared a look but didn't press it as we rode the winds back to Hadeon.

As soon as we reached the castle, they veered off with a nod, leaving me to my thoughts. I flew in through my bedroom window, immediately drawn to the hidden slit inside my mattress. Fishing out the long, gold and white feather, I held it up, staring at it as though it might give me answers. More than my sense of disbelief, I was struck by a profound sense of loss. Going to the cliff had become a routine. It was the highlight of my day, and now it was gone—no more than a smouldering pile of ashes. So much more than an anonymous confidant, Rose had quickly become my closest friend and I'd shared more of myself with him than anyone. More fool me.

My eyes stung, and I clutched at the feather as a rumble of frustration built in my chest. Even when I'd felt like I might crumble to pieces, the knowledge that Rose was out there, feeling just as lost and overwhelmed as me, had given me peace. And now it was gone.

As our conversations played on a loop in my head, a particular piece of information forced its way to the front of my mind, causing my intake of breath to catch in my throat. Pace was betrothed. To a female he'd only met once. My stomach rolled. Now I was even more sure about him being a prince. It sounded exactly like something my father would pull. I stared at the feather, trying to ignore the still lingering scent of sunshine. What did I care that he was getting married? I hated him.

A knock sounded at my door, and I shoved the feather inside my pocket, my hand going to my dagger. Fates help him if it was Fin. I was in no mood. The door edged open before I could ask who it was and my jaw clenched, my blood simmering beneath my skin.

"Sirain? Are you in there?"

My hand dropped to my side at the sound of my mother's voice, and I watched with wide eyes as she swept into the room. Her raven hair was twisted into a complicated pattern of braids and her long dark gown of flowing purples and reds, swished on the rough stone floor as she approached. Every time I looked at her, I couldn't help but see the queen I knew I'd never be. Her serious expression faltered as her eyes found me, and I realised I hadn't seen my mother in weeks. The thought settled in a cumbersome weight on my chest. By avoiding Fin, I had also been avoiding her.

"There you are," she said, her eyes moving over my bedraggled appearance. "What's wrong?"

"Nothing."

"You're lying." Her blue-black eyes flashed. "I can't remember the last time I saw you, and the first words you say to me are a lie?"

Heaving a sigh, I unsheathed my sword and stowed it next to my other weapons before taking out my dagger and placing it on the nightstand. "It's nothing, Mother. What did you want me for?"

"What I wanted you for can wait. Tell me what's troubling you. Is it your brother?"

The flicker of concern in her voice squeezed something in my chest and I turned away. "No. It's nothing, really."

"Sirain." I heard the whoosh of material against stone as

she stepped closer, placing a slender hand on my shoulder. "Please. Is it a boy? A girl?"

A bitter laugh burst from my lips. "Mother. I'm almost twenty."

"You don't stop liking boys or girls as you age," she snipped. "If anything, it gets worse."

I half turned, a smile tugging at my lips at her imperious expression. "Men, mother. That's what I meant. I have no interest in boys."

"Oh, they're still boys underneath all that brawn and bravado," she huffed. "Tell me what's upsetting you, please."

"Fine." I groaned, pressing my fingers to my temples. "I had a friend, but I didn't know who they were. I just found out, and it's someone who hates me."

"How did you not know who they were?"

I turned to find her face creased with a mix of confusion and concern. "I never saw their face. I can't tell you more than that."

"Why do they hate you?"

My stomach clenched. "I did something to hurt them, before we were friends."

"But they liked you when you didn't know who the other was?"

"Yes." Hearing her explain it made my head ache.

She reached up and traced a long alabaster finger down my cheek. "Why don't you talk to them? If they liked you before, they might forgive you. If you still want to be friends with them, that is."

I stared at the ground, studying the space between my sodden boots and the lush hem of my mother's gown as I considered her question. We would never be friends again. There was no chance Pace would ever forgive me, but I didn't want the idea of Rose and Thorn to be tainted by him thinking it had all been a cruel joke. It had been real. Even if it was broken, crumbled into a million pieces, I needed him to know that.

"You look like you've made a decision," she said, tucking a lock of hair behind my ear.

I gave her a small smile. "I think so, yes."

She nodded, and I caught a glimpse of familiar longing, edged with pain, in her eyes. I always had the feeling my mother was holding back. Whether it was words or physical affection, I could never be sure. "I hope things work out. If you've found someone—even if it's just a friend—who you care enough about to risk being hurt, then it's worth trying to salvage."

Moving to the window, I placed a foot on the ledge. There was little to no chance Pace was at the cliff, but I needed to be sure. "Thank you, Mother."

She gave me a tight smile, glancing over her shoulder at the door. "Your father wants you, by the way. That's why I came looking for you."

A cold chill coated my bones as my fingers tightened their grip against the stone.

The queen turned and walked to my door, not stopping as she called over her shoulder, "I'll tell him I couldn't find you."

I exhaled in relief and leapt from the ledge.

All the way to the cliff, I told myself he wouldn't be there. He would probably never go there again. If he was, however, I found comfort in the knowledge we would be separated by The Crossing. My heart slammed against my chest as I sat down on the edge, my wings trembling. I balled my hands at my side, staring out at the sea as it sparkled under the midday sun. It would be easy to turn and fly back right now. I'd never know if he was there or not. I turned and looked up at the shimmering lights, currently a dozen shades of green. In all those times we'd talked, how close had he been, I wondered. Had we only been mere strides apart?

I drew a shaky breath and closed my eyes. "Rose?"

The answering silence was punctuated only by birds overhead and the gentle crashing of waves on the rocks below. I exhaled in relief. Of course, he wasn't there. I sank to the warm grass and lay back, my limbs trembling. Did Pace really think I was so cruel that I'd orchestrate such an elaborate charade? I knew the answer. I was nothing more than a demon in his eyes. It didn't matter what we'd shared, or even that I'd saved his friend's life. He would only ever see me as the monster he'd unmasked on that island. The monster who'd taunted him, drawn his blood, and plucked a precious feather from his wing.

"Are you there, demon?"

I sat up at the harsh shout rippling through The Crossing. "Pace?"

"Which other gullible Cupid do you think it might be?"

"I didn't know. I swear—"

"Just don't," he growled. "I don't want to hear it."

I blinked, anger rapidly evaporating my forming tears. "If you didn't want to hear it, why are you here?"

"I don't know. I—"

"Save your confusion for someone who cares," I snapped. "You might not want to hear what I have to say, but I'm going to say it regardless. I need to."

The volume of my ragged breathing rivalled the waves crashing far below as I waited, fists clenched, for a response I wasn't sure would come.

"Fine. But not here."

I stared, seething, at the ripples of light. "What do you mean?"

"Let's deal with this once and for all." His voice was as hard as stone. "Meet me on the island. The one where you stole my feather."

"What? Now?" After waiting several moments, I tried again. "Pace?"

He'd gone. I looked around, at a complete loss of what to do. He'd left me with no choice. After all, it had been me who'd insisted he needed to hear what I had to say. Shoving down thick layers of trepidation, I spread my wings and headed toward the entrance to The Crossing. It was only as the folds enveloped me in green light, pushing me toward the human world, that I realised, I had left all my weapons at home.

19
Pace

The air was still heavy with static left behind by the storm, the sky remaining a murky grey as it leaked a fine mist of raindrops onto the writhing ocean. I stood, blinking droplets of moisture from my eyelashes, glaring at the rolling clouds. Waiting. My pulse was a steady thrum in my veins as my hand gripped the pommel of my sword, fingers clenching and unclenching. I wasn't sure whether she'd come, and if she did, I wasn't sure what I'd say—what I would do.

My confidence in navigating The Crossing had vastly improved since my first solo attempt, mainly due to understanding that focusing on the destination, and letting the lights guide you, was key. Once I'd emerged over the ocean, the rocky island hadn't been difficult to find, but it was even more miserable than I remembered. Stones and pebbles of varying sizes made up the island, barely thirty strides across, the dark sand more like mud between them. A cluster of weather-worn grey rocks a little taller than me stood at its centre, as though someone had hammered them through the ocean.

My gaze dragged over the rain-soaked ground, and I thought of how we'd fought on these very stones. My scar, now no more than a pale line, tingled at the memory of her blade pressed to my heart, her dark eyes flickering with malice. Thorn had said she hadn't known it was me. Or at least, she'd tried to. How could I believe the word of a Chaos? My teeth gritted as I realised, I didn't even know her real name. I'd bared my soul to her. Told her my secrets. My shoulders drooped; there was no way she could have known it was me. I'd given no clues. I'd made sure of it. Lifting my hands to my pounding head, I pressed my fingers to my temples. Perhaps it was the Fates. How else would she have known where to find me? Too many times, our paths had crossed when they shouldn't have—when the odds were so unlikely. Drawing a deep breath, I turned a slow circle, ensuring she didn't sneak up on me from behind.

My skin burned as I thought of how many times I'd counted down the hours until sunset—the joy that would light in my chest at the sound of Thorn's voice through The Crossing. I wrinkled my nose, even though my heart strained. There was no Thorn. I hadn't realised just how much I'd cherished the time I'd spent with her until it became a lie. My grip tightened on my sword.

I didn't hear the beating of wings until it was close—too close—the sound swallowed by the lingering winds. I turned, half drawing my weapon to find her descending several strides away beside the large rocks, her black wings scattering the fine rain. Her gaze immediately went to my sword, and I waited for her to draw hers, but she didn't. Instead, her eyes widened, and she took a small step backwards. I frowned, searching for her dagger or a hilt between her wings, but there was nothing. My hand slipped from my blade. She was unarmed.

"Are you going to try and kill me?" she called out, the wind whipping at her voice.

"Tell me," I said. "Tell me you knew it was me. Tell me it was all a lie."

She shook her head. "I know it's what you want to hear—

what you want to believe—but it's not true. Maybe you think it would be easier that way, but I swear, I didn't know."

I stared at her, my thoughts in disarray. Why had I asked her to meet me? What had I hoped to achieve? My sword hung heavy at my hip.

"How could I possibly have known it was you?" she continued. "I wasn't even completely sure you were male. You know as well as I do, it was impossible to tell through The Crossing."

My hand had drifted back to my blade and her eyes tracked the movement as I took a step closer. "Why did you save Tiesa?"

She threw her hands out at her sides in frustration. "I already told you. Why should I have to justify saving someone's life? I know you think I'm a monster—a demon—but I'm not."

My jaw tightened and I drew my sword, the metal singing as I stepped closer still. "Your first impression would suggest otherwise."

"Did you think Thorn was a monster?" she asked.

Her question caught me off guard and I paused. I couldn't merge Thorn with the female in front of me. Thorn filled my heart with hope and memories of laughter. The female clad in black leather before me filled me only with anger and hurt. Lifting my blade, I angled it at her chest.

She looked up at me, determination flashing in her eyes. "What do you want? Do you want me to tell you that I'm scared? That I'm sorry? Do you want me to fall to my knees and beg for your forgiveness? What do you want, Pace?"

The sound of my name on her lips caused my grip to tighten and my eyes to narrow. The scales always seemed to be tipped in her favour; but not for long. I took another step closer, and she stepped back, her eyes widening as she found herself pressed up against the largest of the boulders at the island's centre. I rested the tip of my sword against the tight black leather covering her heart.

As she stared up at me through the drizzling rain, I realised her eyes weren't the black I'd always assumed. Instead, they were a dark shade of violet-flecked purple, like polished amethyst. It was different—to be this close when I wasn't fearing for my life. The world seemed to quieten as I allowed myself to study the person who made me feel so . . . so ferociously. The fine rain rested on her hair like a crown of crystals and although wet, I could see glimmers of indigo amongst the long dark strands. The first time she'd angled a sword at my chest, her beauty had stolen the words from my lips. I'd almost forgotten. My gaze tracked over her snowy skin, lingering on the pink gathering on her cheeks and at the tip of her nose from the cold, before moving to her mouth. How could something so beautiful have caused me so much pain?

Slowly, she extended a wing, snapping my attention, and I pressed the blade closer, indenting the thick leather.

"Take a feather," she offered. "If it will put an end to this."

Staring at the long ebony feathers, edged with the same rich purples as her hair, I swore I could feel the exact spot where my feather was missing, burning. "You know I would never take a female's feather. Do you really think taking your feather will make us even?"

"If it makes you feel any better, I regret it." She lifted her eyes to look at me once more. "Chaos aren't like Cupids. We see something we want, and we take it. I saw you and I wanted proof. I didn't consider the consequences."

Despite the disgust skittering over my skin, a slither of sympathy wound its way into my chest as I recalled our conversations from the cliff. Thorn lived in fear of her own brother. I tried and failed to imagine what it would be like to live somewhere where I never felt truly safe. What kind of person would it make me?

"I'm sorry," she whispered.

My chest tightened at her words, but I didn't step back, couldn't lower my sword. I'd harboured so much anger towards the female at its tip for so long, I wasn't sure I knew how to let it go. So many nights I'd imagined making her feel the pain and humiliation she'd inflicted on me. She'd stolen so much more than a feather from me—she'd tainted the only thing I'd managed to do right, and my friends had almost been killed in the aftermath. No amount of apologising was going to atone for that.

"Pace suits you more than Rose," she said.

The corner of my mouth twitched, and I pressed my lips together, trying not to think of how often Thorn had made me laugh—had lightened the weight on my shoulders. "I think Thorn suits you."

She raised her eyebrows. "Really?"

For a moment I considered lying, but exhaled, saying nothing.

"Do you want to know my real name?" she asked. "Or will knowing make it harder for you to push that blade home?"

I looked from her to the sword pressed against her heart. This was the moment I'd thought about for months. One swift push and it would be done. I swallowed.

"Sirain."

I blinked. "Excuse me?"

"My name. It's Sirain."

"I prefer Thorn," I lied.

She smiled and I frowned in return. I didn't want it to feel like the cliff. *Thorn was gone*. The thought reverberated through my bones. *Gone*. But she wasn't gone. She was here. Right in front of me. If I killed Sirain, I killed Thorn. My head spun.

"Talk to me," she said, the words soft and careful.

"What?" I barked a laugh. "You think you'll be able to help me decide whether it's a good idea to kill you? I think you'll find you're biased."

"Killing me won't bring your purity back."

My spine stiffened. "No. It won't."

"Was I right?" she asked.

"About what?"

"Are you a prince?"

My eyes narrowed. "What difference does it make?"

She shrugged. "None, I suppose. Although, if I'm going to be murdered, I'd prefer for it to be at the hands of a prince of Hehven than a mere Hand."

My sword was growing heavy, but I couldn't bring myself to pull it back. *Murder*. It would be murder if I killed her. I had imagined my blade piercing her in the heat of battle, but here, unarmed, would I be able to live with that choice?

"Tell me," I asked. "Who's real? Sirain or Thorn?"

Pain flashed across her features as she looked to the ground. "They're both real as each other."

I shook my head. "I don't believe it. Thorn wasn't real. Whatever happened between us on that cliff wasn't real."

"Yes, it was," she bit out. "What about you? Was Rose real? Because I can't imagine you're capable of being that nice."

Exhaustion settled over me, heavy and cold as I stared at her, dripping, and trembling against the rock. My decision came with a weary sigh. "I'm not going to kill you."

I sheathed my weapon and turned away, shaking the water from my wings. It was over.

"It was real," she called out. "Every second of it."

Halting my steps, I closed my eyes. It didn't matter.

"I looked forward to it," she said. "Sunset was the best part of my day. Being there, with you, it was real. I need you to know that, Pace."

I exhaled, shaking my head. "Goodbye, Sirain."

"Wait. I have something for you."

Turning around, I watched as she reached into a pocket hidden in the side of her leather shirt. She pulled out a long white feather edged in gold and held it out to me.

"Take it."

I strode over and plucked it from her fingers, expecting to feel relief or satisfaction. I felt nothing.

"If your betrothed is any sort of decent female, she'll understand," Sirain said. "As I'm sure you're planning on telling her. I have a feeling honesty comes with the whole Cupid purity deal."

I stared down at her. "Don't."

"Well, if she doesn't understand, perhaps you deserve someone better."

Disbelief burst from me in a laugh. "Someone better? Who exactly did you have in mind?"

She lifted her chin, meeting my eyes, her fists curling at her sides. Her hair was soaked, the purple now vanished amongst the midnight strands. I hadn't noticed the rain growing heavier and as I reached up and shoved my hair off my forehead, the water sluiced through my fingers, running down my neck. Her leather suit seemed quite waterproof, I noted with annoyance, whereas my own white shirt and brown pants were soaked, clinging to me like a second skin. Sirain's gaze followed mine, tracking over my body, and my blood heated, my jaw clenching as I remembered how she'd looked at me the first time we had been on the island.

"What?" she asked.

I realised I'd reached for my sword once more. "I was just recalling our first meeting. The way you treated me."

Sirain leaned her head back against the rock with a groan, her long white neck stretching with movement. "Do I need to apologise again? That side of me . . ." She shook her head. "In Helle you can't show weakness. You can't show compassion."

"Maybe you just don't want to," I said. "Maybe it's easier to do whatever you want and not deal with the consequences."

She barked a laugh. "I'd say I'm dealing with a pretty big consequence right now."

"So, you're saying, if you hadn't had the others with you,

you'd have just let me go?" I scoffed. "It was all an act?"

A growl of frustration rippled from her throat. "You're infuriating, do you know that? How easy it must be in Hehven to prance around all high and mighty, always doing the right thing and being all pure."

"You think it's easy?" I snarled. "If you had paid any sort of attention on that cliff, you'd know that's not true."

Sirain stepped forward, her shoulders squared. "Oh, I'm sorry your parents are disappointed in you, and you have to marry a pretty female. Your difficult is a far cry from mine, Pace. Murderous younger brothers are just the tip of the iceberg. You have no idea what it's like for me."

"Likewise," I said, stepping close enough to force her to lean back.

Losing her footing on a rock, she stumbled back against the large boulder with a curse. "Oh, I'm sure it's really hard at the royal palace, Prince."

I growled, my hand moving to my sword, gripping the cold, wet metal.

She laughed as she tracked the movement. We were close enough I could feel the warmth of her breath on my soaking skin. "You might have your tournaments to make you feel like it's real, but when it comes down to it, I don't think you've got what it takes to kill—"

I'd drawn my sword, holding it across her throat, before she'd finished speaking. She stared up at me, wide eyed, droplets of water clinging to her lashes.

"You told me on the cliff that you'd never killed someone," I said, leaning closer. "So, either you lied, or you're all talk. Which is it?"

Her breathing was faster as she pressed herself back against the rock, but she still met my gaze, unflinching. "I don't remember. I was too busy being bored to death by crappy poetry."

A smile curled my lips despite myself. "I seem to remember

you thanking me for my crappy poetry."

I waited for her hurtful comeback, but it didn't come. Instead, her eyes dipped to my mouth. It was only then I realised just how close we were. My sword shifted with each intake of her breath and when she raised her eyes to mine, I blinked in confusion. Did she think I was going to . . .? My own pulse skipped at the thought. Beads of rain coated her face and my gaze tracked one as it slid down the slope of her nose. For a fleeting second, I imagined catching it with my mouth. The thought of her skin against my lips heated my blood and I inhaled sharply. Even though my mind screamed at me to do so, I couldn't step back. It was different. Different to the times I'd teetered on the line of touch, experimenting with the heady rush of restraint. The air was electric around us, every inch of my skin lit with longing.

As though pulled by an invisible force, I leaned closer. Close enough that if either of us swayed, or inhaled too deeply, our chests would touch. I blinked the raindrops from my lashes and her attention darted to my lips again. My gaze slid to her mouth, her pale pink lips slightly parted. Blood pounded in my ears as I leaned closer still, bracing a hand against the rock by her head. I thought she'd push me away, but instead, she stared up at me, confusion and wonder in her amethyst-flecked eyes. *What was I doing?*

I almost pushed off the rock, my wings already tensing to take to the skies. But I didn't. There had been times I'd allowed myself to hope that Thorn was female. Times I'd lain awake imagining what it would be like to meet her. Part of me had longed for her, had wanted her, for a long time. I flexed my fingers against the rain slicked stone, my heart racing. I shouldn't be doing this. My breathing was ragged as I studied the trickles of water tracing the graceful slopes of her face. It wasn't too late. I could step back. I *should* step back.

My fingers clenched into a fist against the rock.

20
Sirain

Every one of my senses was on fire. I could scarcely draw a breath, knowing if I did, it might close the gap between us. My fingers clenched at my sides, my limbs trembling in a way that had little to do with the icy rain, and everything to do with the summer-scented male so close I could almost taste him. He probably had no idea what he looked like, broad shoulders caging me in against the rock, his white shirt all but see-through, clinging to the hard lines of his chest and torso. His snow-white hair was falling in his eyes, the rain only serving to highlight the jaw that could cut glass. And his lips . . . Fated Fates, those soft, plump lips . . . I was grateful for the sword he still held across my throat because it took every ounce of self-restraint I had not to rise up on my toes and claim his mouth.

My pulse thrummed, a steady beat under my skin as I stared up at him. It wasn't until I'd got close—so close—that I'd realised how much I wanted him. I'd found him attractive from the first time we'd crossed blades, but when we'd talked, I'd heard it. *Rose*. Even without the distortion of The Crossing, it was the voice that had made life bearable, that had given me something to look forward to, even on the hardest days. The connection we had was special, and what we'd built together on the cliff was stronger than what we'd broken in person.

I wanted to reach for him—to wrap my arms around his neck and wind my fingers in his rain-soaked hair—but I knew I couldn't. And as the faint shimmer of gold glinting on his feathers caught my eye, I was reminded that I'd already taken from him once. I couldn't let this go any further. He'd never forgive himself. Forgive me.

Reaching up, I carefully pushed the blade away from my neck. He blinked, as though remembering where he was, and stepped back, the moment evaporating like morning mist.

"I'm sorry," he murmured.

"What for? Putting a blade to my throat?"

His lips parted. "No. For . . . that. I shouldn't have—"

"Nothing happened. There's nothing to apologise for," I said.

His eyes met mine and, to my frustration, my heart skipped. I watched, frozen in place, as he took another step back, the small space between us feeling as vast and cold as an ocean. At some point the rain had thinned to a fine mist and although my leathers were soaked, at least I was warm. I was surprised Pace wasn't shivering. He sheathed his blade, taking yet another step back and I wondered whether he would just spread his wings and disappear. Part of me would have preferred him to come at me with a sword again, and the thought irked me.

"What are you going to do about the humans?" I asked, grasping at something, anything, to prolong his inevitable departure.

He frowned. "What do you mean?"

"You were meeting with them to discuss messing with Fate, weren't you?"

"Like I said on the boat, we were telling them that it wasn't an option."

I narrowed my eyes. "You wish it was an option though, don't you?"

"Of course, I do. If there was a chance to spare the lives that would be lost through war, I'd take it."

I considered his words as I pulled my hair over my shoulder, squeezing the rainwater from it. "Do you think the humans are telling the truth? That the war will be as bad as they say."

"I do. Don't you?"

"I was in Dalibor not long ago and all the harbours I could see had been turned into shipyards. I didn't get a good look, though. We Chaos do our jobs and get out," I said pointedly.

If Pace was irked by my comment, he didn't show it, his expression pensive as he considered my words. "Would you be able to show me?"

"Excuse me?"

"I've only travelled through The Crossing alone twice and I've never been to Dalibor." He gave me a small smile as he pushed his soaking hair from his forehead. "Would you consider taking me there?"

Could I? I pressed my fingers to my temples and closed my eyes as I considered his request. It wouldn't be safe for him to travel at night, and I didn't want to risk any other Chaos seeing him, which would mean me visiting the human world during the day. There was no way I'd be able to tell Kwellen and Odio. Not yet. I'd taken a huge risk meeting him alone—and stupidly unarmed—but to do it again . . .

"It's okay if you don't want to," Pace said, interrupting my spiralling thoughts. "I'll figure something out."

"No," I said. "I'll take you. It's fine."

He raised an eyebrow. "Are you sure?"

"Yes." I nodded, then frowned. "How many times have you been through The Crossing?"

"This is my fifth time," he admitted. "You?"

"Hundreds," I muttered. "The day after tomorrow. As soon as the sun is fully over the horizon. I'll meet you here and we'll go to Dalibor.

A smile lit his face, and my stomach did a pathetic tumble at the sight.

"Thank you," he said. "I should be getting back before Dariel and Tiesa come looking for me."

"Sure," I said. "See you then."

He opened his mouth to say something, but shut it, a storm of emotions flashing through his gilded eyes. Giving him a tight smile, I stepped away from the rock and strode across the dark pebbles, shaking out my wings. When I reached the edge of the island, I launched myself into the air and headed for The Crossing. I didn't look back.

Forty-two hours. Almost two days since I'd last seen Pace. Forty-two hours of trying to figure out what we were now. Were we friends? Acquaintances? Had he forgiven me? Barely a minute went by when I didn't relive the memory of his body so close to mine—his lips dangerously near. My breath hitched and I realised with a frustrated groan that I now understood what he'd meant about nearness and restraint. Although I wasn't sure I would be able to hold myself back a second time. I shook my head. There wasn't going to be a second time. Meeting him today would be completely normal and uneventful.

My stomach churned as I made my way through The Crossing, the disorientating lights barely registering as I allowed myself to be pulled towards my destination. What if he'd forgotten our tentative truce? Would he be waiting for me on the island, sword drawn and burning hatred in his honey-gold eyes? I swallowed. Maybe he'd changed his mind. Maybe he wouldn't be there. The weight of my sword between my wings was comforting. If nothing else, this time, I was prepared.

Despite the blue skies and warm buttery glow of the morning sun, the small rocky island was just as ugly. Pace was already there, perched on top of one of the large boulders in the middle, staring out to sea. My heart skittered at the sight, and I scowled. This was a favour and nothing more. He looked up as he heard me approach, but remained seated, knees drawn, as I landed.

"You're late," he said.

"No. You're early."

I didn't wait for his response as I leapt back up into the air leading the way to Dalibor. The Crossing would have spat me out a little closer if I'd had it in my mind as my destination, but meeting Pace first meant an extra hour's flying time. Fortunately, the sky was clear, the temperature pleasant, and it looked as though we wouldn't be getting soaked to our skins again. My stomach tightened at the thought of soaked white cotton clinging to Pace's broad, heaving chest and I groaned inwardly. I should have said no. This was a terrible idea.

Sneaking back to the palace that night soaking wet, had been nerve wracking. I had been certain I would run into Fin or my father. If I'd bumped into Kwellen or Odio, I might have been able to explain it away, but luckily, I hadn't had to. Yesterday, my father had insisted I join him to meet with the Fated and the Captains, and I had to admit that I paid a little more attention than I would have previously. My interest was now far beyond the fact that the Fated were the only ones to interact with the Fates. The Fates were giving orders to Fated on both sides of The Crossing and my head ached at the thought.

"What's she like?" Pace asked, breaking the silence.

"Who?"

"The Midnight Queen."

I frowned. "I've only seen her a couple of times. Of course, you won't get to see her today."

"Why not?"

"Because she sleeps during the day. That's why she's called the Midnight Queen."

Pace wrinkled his nose. "That's a bit strange. Does the whole country do that?"

"No. Just her and her court." A smile crept onto my lips. "My cousin has a ridiculous crush on her."

"Cousin?"

"The Hand that was with me. Huge black bow and arrow?"

Pace's eyebrows raised in recognition. "What's the deal with the other one?"

"What do you mean, 'deal'?"

"Is he also your cousin? Friend? Husband?"

A snort burst from me before I could stop it. "He's my best friend. Has been since we were smallwings."

Pace frowned, his lips pressing together, before turning to me again. "Well, that's rather odd."

"What is?"

He shook his head, his ivory wings spreading wide as he rode the breeze. "You travelling to the human world with your cousin and your best friend."

"Why?"

"Dariel is my cousin," Pace explained. "Tiesa is my best friend."

My mouth formed a small 'o' in understanding. "Okay. That is a little coincidental. I'm assuming at least one of you is a Hand."

"They both are."

I tucked the information away for later, alongside the fact that he'd admitted he wasn't. As we flew over the endless expanse of ocean, I sneaked the occasional glance at him, hoping to the Fates he wouldn't catch me. He didn't seem angry with me. Perhaps our truce was holding. A flame of hope kindled in my chest. Perhaps I could get Rose back after all. At least, until he got married. My stomach somersaulted and I frowned, my shoulders tensing at my reaction. I didn't give two feathers about his future wife.

On the horizon, the dark green jungle of Dalibor rose from the waters and I couldn't help but feel a thrill at the thought of venturing there without Kwellen and Odio. We'd never strayed on a mission before, even though I longed to explore the human lands. A wry grin twisted my lips. Kwellen thought I was locked in my room with 'female problems', which would be enough to keep him away for the day. If he found out I'd travelled to the human world without him, he'd be beyond furious. I pushed away the thought of what my father would do to my best friend if he ever found out. *No.* He couldn't find out.

"It's enormous," Pace said as the land continued to spread out before us.

"Newbold is actually bigger," I said. "But I hear it's nowhere near as pretty."

"You haven't been?"

I shook my head. "No. In fact, I don't know anyone who has."

Even as I said the words, I realised how unusual it was. I resolved to ask Odio about it the next time I saw him. Dipping my wing, I turned, circling toward the tall coastal mountains that seated the Midnight Queen's palace. The first set of docks were not far from the road leading up the winding mountain path, so it was as good a place to start as any. I set down on a rocky outcrop just above the palace, the sprawling coast visible as far as the eye could see in both directions. Pace landed beside me, his gaze already fixed on the harbour below.

"That's a lot of ships."

I nodded, trying to ignore the brush of his wing against mine. "I thought it was strange. We flew back along the coast, and I saw at least two more harbours the same."

"Even from here, I can tell they're not cargo ships," he said. "They're preparing for war."

The dark metal of weapons glinted on the decks and in wagons and crates in the harbour. They weren't even trying to hide it. I hadn't seen how many warships the Wendell Islands had, and I'd only been to Liridona a couple of times, but I was fairly certain they didn't have enough vessels to withstand the ones before us.

"You know what I've always wanted to do?" I said, clapping my hands together. "Explore the jungle."

Pace turned to me, confusion splashed across his stupidly handsome face. "Excuse me?"

"The jungle." I pointed to the dense trees behind us. "Explore."

He glanced between where I was pointing and the harbour. "We came to—"

"See the ships," I said. "And we did. There are a lot of them. I can show you more harbours, but my wings are tired so I'm going to go and take a look around first. You're welcome to stay here, though."

Climbing down the rocky ledge, my fingers slipping on the dense moss, I tucked my wings in tight as I edged my way through the undergrowth towards the line of densely packed trees. A rustling sounded behind me, and I smiled. Once through the first line of trees, darkness swept in, the sun picking at spots on the floor through scattered beams of light. The towering trees were every possible shade of green, the thick russet trunks wrapped with twisting emerald vines. Sweeping against my knees and thighs, the large thick leaves of plants covering the jungle floor were interspersed with brightly coloured flowers, their sweet scent filling the air and soft petals leaning toward the light.

"Okay," Pace said, craning his neck to view the canopy. "This is incredible."

I grinned. "Right? This is my favourite of the human lands. If you travel further north, there are identical mountains, but the jungle stops about a third of the way up and the rest is thick snow."

We wound our way through the trees, the leaves dripping cool water on our heads and shoulders upon being disturbed. Creatures hummed and clicked, hidden amongst the shadows, but it still felt more tranquil than anywhere I'd ever experienced. The further in we trekked, the more the light dimmed, until the dappled sunbeams peppering the floor faded to a murky glow.

"I've seen these before," Pace said, reaching for an unusual green fruit. "I saw Cove eating one once."

He plucked it from the branch and tossed it to me before picking another for himself. It was round, with a thin, smooth, pale green skin. I gave it a gentle squeeze, feeling the flesh give way beneath my fingertips.

"It's delicious," Pace said, swiping his mouth with the back of his hand. "Like an apple but sweeter and juicier."

My eyes snagged on his tongue as he licked his lips, and my skin heated. I looked away, frowning at the small fruit. What was wrong with me?

"Please tell me you have apples in Helle."

"Of course, we do."

He gave me a half smile. "What then? Do you think I'm trying to poison you?"

I rolled my eyes and took a tentative bite of the fruit, annoyed to find his description couldn't have been more accurate. Looking up, I found his smile had faded, his jaw taut and his gaze fixed on my mouth.

A low rippling growl rumbled around us, and I dropped the fruit on the floor, reaching for my weapon. Glancing at Pace, I found he'd done the same, his eyes the only thing moving as he surveyed our surroundings.

"I don't like the sound of that," I whispered.

Pace shot me a warning look as another growl reverberated nearby. Either the beast had moved, or there was more than one. I had no idea whether whatever it was could climb trees, but opening my wings with a snap, I jumped into the air, alighting on a branch several feet above the ground.

"Hey!" Pace called.

I opened my mouth to tell him to come up, but before I could, three large black creatures burst from the dense green undergrowth. A silent scream left my mouth as they leapt at Pace, a mess of jagged teeth, strings of saliva and claws. He sliced his sword through the first creature and raised a knee to kick the second away. Before the third could pounce, Pace sprang into the air, only spreading his wings once he was above the snapping teeth of the creatures. He landed beside me, his jaw clenched as he stared down at the beasts. I exhaled in relief, sheathing my weapon.

"What are they?" he asked, watching as the remaining two began circling the tree.

I'd never seen anything like them before. Their black fur was thin and slick, and they were the size of pigs, but slimmer, with long snouts and no tail. Despite travelling in packs, they seemed to have no remorse for the fallen beast. "I have no idea. Some sort of wolf-pig?"

Pace sat down beside me, wiping his blade on a leaf before sheathing his weapon. "At least they can't climb trees."

As if it understood us, one of the creatures huffed, resting its front paws against the tree trunk. After a moment, it tore its long claws through the bark before resuming its circling.

"Want another?"

I looked up to find Pace holding out another of the sweet fruits. "Thanks."

Our fingers brushed as I took the fruit, and I watched the bob of his throat as he swallowed before turning away. We ate in silence, watching the creatures snorting and snuffling as they patrolled below, but I could feel Pace's occasional glances searing into my skin. Several times, I thought I heard a small intake of breath as though he wanted to say something, but words never came. I tossed the core of my fruit down to the beasts and they sniffed at it before glaring up at me with dark eyes.

"I think they'd prefer it if you threw down a limb," Pace observed.

I leaned back against the trunk and folded my arms. "Are you offering one?"

Shooting me a withering look, he pitched the remainder of his fruit into the bushes. It was still hard to fuse the idea of the Cupid sitting beside me with the voice from The Crossing. Even after all the time we'd spent together, things felt different in person. I wasn't sure how I felt about it.

"So," I said. "Do you really think you'll be able to persuade your mother to help the humans avoid war?"

Pace sighed. "I don't know. Possibly. There's just so many things I don't—wait. Why are you smiling?"

"I knew you were a prince." I grinned as Pace's face fell. "That's the gold in your wings and hair, right? Your cousin has it too, but your friend doesn't."

He rubbed a hand over his face before taking a deep breath. "Fine. You got me. My mother is Queen of Hehven. Her brother is Dariel's father."

"You said something about a brother on the cliff," I probed. "Older or younger?"

He turned to look at me, his expression guarded. "Are you seriously expecting me to tell you all the inner workings of Hehven?"

I stared back, my heart feeling a little heavier. "No. I suppose not. What if I told you, I swear not to tell anyone?"

He looked away. "It's going to take a little more than a trip to Dalibor and some fruit to build trust between us."

Swallowing a sigh, I studied the bark of the tree, plucking leaves from the branch and rolling them between my fingers.

Below us, one of the beasts had wandered off, with the other curled up, snoring softly amongst the roots.

Pace got to his feet, reaching to the branch above to steady himself. "Are you ready to get out of here?"

"Up or down?"

He wrinkled his nose at the slumbering beast before peering upwards through the thick canopy. "Shall we try up?"

I nodded and stood, hoisting myself up to the branch above. It was tough going, with our wings snagging on twigs and branches, but after several minutes, the light grew brighter, and flashes of blue sky could be seen between the leaves. As we burst free, several clusters of small colourful birds squawked in annoyance, scattering into the air, and I laughed as I followed, lifting my face to the sun. When I opened my eyes, I found Pace watching me, a small crease between his brows.

"What?" I asked.

He shook his head and pointed toward the shoreline. "Will you show me those other harbours?"

In answer, I dove, skimming the emerald canopy toward the sparkling blue expanse of water. As we flew along the coast, keeping to the tree line, Pace's expression darkened with each repurposed harbour we came across. The sun had moved past midday, starting its descent when I slowed, my wings beginning to throb.

"I need to head back," I said. "Did you see everything you needed to?"

He nodded, his attention focused on the ships being constructed further down the coast. "Yes. Thank you."

I turned, ready to lead the way back toward The Crossing, when a hand wrapped around my wrist, tugging me back. Turning in surprise, I shook him off. "What?"

"Can we talk for a second?"

I studied him, trying to read his expression, and finding nothing. "We've had all morning to talk."

"I'm only asking for a minute or two. Please?"

"Fine."

We headed down to a small cove along the coastline, where the jungle seeped into the golden sand and the sea lapped at the shore in gentle crystalline waves. As soon as we landed, I took a step back, distancing myself. Pace stared down at me; his eyes slightly narrowed. I wilted a little under his gaze and forced my shoulders back, lifting my chin.

"What is it?" I prompted.

He shook his head. "I thought maybe we could talk about us."

"Us?" I repeated. "Is there an 'us'?"

"I don't know. That's what I wanted to talk about." He turned to face the sea with a sigh, the warm breeze fluttering through his feathers.

"Are you done trying to kill me, then?"

The second the words were out of my mouth, I regretted them. We'd been getting on quite well and I'd begun to hope that maybe what we'd had on the cliff hadn't been completely destroyed. He shoved his hands in his pockets and stared down at the ground, causing locks of white hair to fall across his forehead.

"I'm sorry," he said quietly. "It was never about you. All that anger . . . I shouldn't have come to the human world on my own. I put myself in danger, and you taking a feather could have been something so much worse. It could have been someone ending my life. It could have been *you* ending my life. Almost all of my rage was at my own stupidity."

I pressed my lips together until they ached, trapping in the question I so badly wanted to ask. Did that mean he'd forgiven me? Could we salvage our friendship, or was this excursion merely the full stop at the end of our story?

Pace sank down to the sand with a sigh, wrapping an arm around his bent knee. "It took me too long to realise that nothing happened after you took my feather. The world didn't end. The Fates haven't punished me. My friends and family couldn't even tell." He glanced at me before returning his gaze to the waves, rhythmically soaking the sand just beyond our feet. "The fact that Helle exists, and you have Hands carrying out the exact opposite of our orders from the Fates to the same humans . . . I can't pretend it hasn't shaken my faith."

Sitting down beside him, I pulled the warm sand through my fingers. "So, what now?"

He glanced at me briefly, before returning his gaze to the lapping waves. "I don't know."

I sighed.

"I miss Thorn."

My heart skipped as I turned to look at him. "Pardon?"

"What you said on the island, it's the same for me. Sunset has been the best part of my day for weeks. I miss it."

I stared at him, drinking in the awkward set of his shoulders. Taking a breath, I tried to hide the fragile hope in my voice. "It doesn't have to end."

Pace ran a hand through his hair. "I'm still trying to make sense of everything. There's just so much . . ."

"So much what?"

He groaned. "Stuff. I don't know. Everything. I'm still trying to get my brain to understand that you and Thorn are the same person."

"I know that feeling," I muttered.

Pace laughed softly. "Yeah. I can see how you'd have trouble believing I'm Rose after the number of times I've tried to kill you."

"I think," I said carefully, "if you'd really wanted to kill me, you would have."

He nodded, his lips pressed together so tightly, the colour faded.

Silence settled over us once more and I wondered whether

his head was a whirlwind of half formed questions and awkward truths like mine. After a painful number of minutes, I pushed down the heavy feeling in my gut and got to my feet.

"I should go," I said. "Maybe I'll see you at the cliffs someday."

Pace looked up at me, his brow creased. "What?"

"This," I gestured between the two of us, "only seems to work when we're separated by The Crossing. So perhaps it's best if that's where we keep it."

"It worked today," he said, pushing to his feet. "Didn't it?"

My eyes burned and I dug my nails into my palms, hating the effect he had on me. This was why Chaos didn't get too attached. Caring made you weak.

Pace stepped forward, his eyes flitting over my face. "What's wrong?"

"We can't do this," I said. "Rose and Thorn worked. It was real, but it wasn't *real.* Do you know what I mean?"

"I think so. But what does that have to do with now?"

I opened and closed my mouth, trying to find the words, but I couldn't bring myself to utter them. How could I explain to the Cupid before me that I couldn't stop thinking about him? What kind of female did it make me that I felt as I did, even after he'd held a sword to my throat? Maybe it was because I was a Chaos. Perhaps I wasn't capable of 'normal' feelings.

"Hey." Pace stepped closer, his words gentle as the breeze as his shadow swallowed me whole. "Tell me."

I shook my head. My wings tensing, ready to escape.

"Would it make it easier if I hid behind a tree?" he suggested, giving me a lopsided grin.

A laugh burst from my lips. "Excuse me?"

"Well, you spoke freely enough through The Crossing," he explained. "We don't have that option, so a tree will have to suffice."

"You're not hiding behind a tree." I snorted.

He shrugged. "Back-to-back, then."

Before I could protest, he turned around, leaving me staring in bemusement.

"You have to turn around too," he said. "And don't fly off. I'd have to chase you, and that would be extremely annoying."

Huffing a sigh, I turned around. "This is ridiculous. Now what?"

"Now, we talk."

"I'm confused as to what we've been doing so far."

There was a rustle of feathers, and I jolted as he reached back, taking my hand in his. I stared in surprise as he laced his fingers with mine, his touch warm. Such a simple gesture, but I couldn't recall the last time someone had held my hand. His grip was firm, his thumb rubbing slow circles against my skin.

"I imagined meeting you so many times," he said. "It seemed pointless, but I still hoped."

My eyes closed as I tried to steady the pounding rhythm of my heart. "I hoped too."

"On the island," he said, his words barely more than a whisper. "I wanted . . ."

A tear escaped, dragging a warm trail down my cheek. "I know."

His slow circles stopped. "What?"

"I know you wanted to kiss me," I said, my heart contracting at what needed to be said. "That's why I pushed you away. I couldn't let you."

"Couldn't let me?" he repeated.

Another tear chased the first and I squeezed my eyes shut, trying to prevent more from following. "We can never work. You're a Cupid. I'm a Chaos. What kind of friend would I be if I let you throw away your purity on something that's already broken?"

His wings brushed mine as he turned to face me. For a second, I considered running. It would be easier. The air seeming far too thin, I turned around, trembling as I raised my gaze to look at him. How had I ever dared to steal a feather from this creature? He was breathtakingly handsome, and I hated how much I wanted him. A large spiteful, protective part of me was already searching out hurtful things to say—daggers crafted from words that might spark hatred back to life in his eyes. Somehow, this Pace, looking at me the way he was, seemed more dangerous than the one who had come at me with a sword in his hand.

Before I could select my verbal weapon, he reached out and wiped a tear from my cheek. I trembled at the gesture—the gentle affection so unfamiliar.

"Who says this is broken?"

I laughed, cold and bitter. "How is it not?"

"It doesn't feel broken to me," he said, reaching out and trailing his fingers through a loose strand of my hair.

I drew a shaky breath. "You have serious issues."

He chuckled, his golden eyes sparkling. "Yes. I suppose I do."

"Pace," I said. "I'm serious. You don't want to do this."

"How do you know what I want to do?"

I looked up at him, my heart somersaulting in my chest at the burning intensity of his gaze. "You told me, on the cliff, how your parents were disappointed in you. I can't imagine they'd approve of this."

"I remember you telling me I was overthinking it," he said, stepping close enough that I could feel the heat of him. "You told me I had two choices: follow the rules or burn it all down."

"I did. So?"

He lifted a hand to my face, cupping my cheek, and I inhaled sharply. "So, the day I met you was the day I lit the match."

Before I could find the words to respond, he dipped his head, plump lips parted. I berated my heart for its relentless pounding but couldn't—wouldn't—stop myself from lifting my face to meet him. His lips were even softer than I'd imagined, and there was something intoxicating about the gentle reverence Pace showed; the barely there touch so different to the arrogance and snatching I was accustomed to in Helle. I wanted to wrap my arms around his neck and wind my fingers in his hair, but part of me was still waiting for him to back away in horror—to realise what a monumental mistake he'd made.

After only a few seconds, he pulled away, just a little, eyes still closed as though trying to decide what to do next. My pulse thrummed, a steady beat under my skin, as I stared up at him. It took every ounce of self-restraint I had not to rise up on my toes and reclaim his mouth—to kiss him properly. Thoroughly. A silent whimper built in my chest at the thought. This was on him. Even if it physically pained me to hold back.

Pace rested his forehead against mine and opened his eyes. I stared up at him, marvelling at their pale golden colour, somewhere between honey and the soft light of dawn. Carefully, slowly, I reached up a hand and placed it against his cheek. With a sigh, he leaned into it, his eyes fluttering shut again. Was it a sigh of regret? I started to lower my hand, but he took hold of it, bringing my fingers to his lips.

Reaching for him, I let my fingers trail his strong jaw and ran them through his soft ivory hair. My toes curled as he dipped his head and pressed his lips to mine once more. It was tender and sweet, and with an aching heart, I sank into it, my hands sliding around his waist. Perhaps I shouldn't have—perhaps later, back in my rooms, I would blame it on the fact I was a Chaos—but I pulled him closer, my fingers gripping the firm skin of his back as I dipped my tongue between his lips. He tensed against me, and I bit back my smile, kissing him deeper. The soft groan that rumbled from his chest when I brushed his tongue with mine melted any self-control I had left. He pulled me closer, and I allowed my hands to explore the hard slopes of his shoulders and chest. I kissed Pace utterly and thoroughly until we were both dizzy and breathless, our lips swollen, and our cheeks flushed.

His chest rising and falling hard, Pace pulled back, trailing his fingers through my hair, his mouth still tantalisingly close.

"Are you okay?" I whispered.

He nodded, opening his eyes. A smile curled his lips as he looked up at the sky. "The world hasn't ended. I'm a little disappointed."

I smiled back, my blood singing in my veins. "Not regretting your choice, then?"

"No," he murmured. Leaning forward, he ghosted slow kisses along my jaw. "Let it burn."

Do not be afraid; our fate cannot be taken from us; it is a gift.

~ Dante

21 Pace

It had been three days since Dalibor. Three days since we'd sunk to the sand and I'd held myself over Sirain, night-kissed tendrils of hair stark against the silver sand. My heart quickened, my lips curving into a smile at the thought of her pink cheeks and swollen lips, her amethyst eyes bright as she reached for me. Tomorrow, I'd sneak through The Crossing and travel with her to Newbold to see what Lord Diarke was up to. Tomorrow. *One more day*.

Every sunset we met at the cliff, but it was different now, sitting beside the lights knowing exactly who I was talking to. Thorn was Sirain—Sirain who I'd kissed. A lot. My skin heated at the memory of her lips, her tongue, of her hands as they sneaked their way under my shirt. I coughed, pushing the thought away. Talking on the cliff wasn't enough anymore. I still wanted to talk, but I wanted to see her; touch her. *One more day*.

"You seem happier, my love."

I turned to my mother, hoping she couldn't read the guilt in my eyes. "Yes. I am."

"I'm so glad."

She stopped in front of a bush covered in small white flowers, stooping to smell one. The scent hit me, and my chest tightened.

"When did we get jasmine in the royal gardens?" I asked.

"Your sister requested it only yesterday." My mother turned to me with a teasing light in her eyes. "She said she asked you which flower had the prettiest smell, and this was your choice. She was quite insistent."

I had told Amani that. I turned away, pretending to inspect a rose on another bush as I silently berated myself. After our afternoon on the beach, I'd realised that Sirain's hair smelled like jasmine. The plant only grew in the far north of Hehven and I tried not to think about the effort someone had gone to, to fulfil my sister's whim after my careless words.

"May I ask what has caused you to appear so happy?" my mother asked, continuing down the path.

I linked my arm with hers and smiled. "Do I need a reason?"

"No. You don't. I'm glad you are, though."

The palace gardens were sprawling, weaving circles and loops between two of the courtyards. Large shrubs shaped into twisting figures dotted the pathways and the sound of fountains filled the air. It was the queen's sanctuary. I watched her slender brown fingers as they carefully twisted dead buds from stalks, checking leaves.

There was a reason I'd accompanied my mother on her walk through the gardens and, taking a deep breath, I forced out the question I'd been planning for days. "Have you ever been to the human world?"

Her fingers stilled. "Why would you ask that?"

"I was curious."

"No," she said, glancing over her shoulder in the direction of The Crossing. "The royal family could never take such a risk."

"Dariel is part of the royal family."

She turned to me fully, then. "What's this about? Please don't tell me you're going to try and convince me that you should become a Hand. I thought we finished with that when you were a boy."

"No, of course not." I straightened my wings as I cringed inwardly at memories of arguments I'd had with my parents at fifteen, when Dariel had been allowed to start training with the Hands, and I hadn't.

"Then why would you ask?"

It was hard not to feel like a child under her suspicious gaze, but I forced myself to stand tall. "I only wanted to know how much you knew about the human world."

"I know enough. Why?"

"I heard some Hands talking," I said, relieved as she began walking again. "They said there was another human war coming,"

"The humans are always warring. It's in their nature. That's exactly why the Fates must intervene."

It was the same reasoning I'd heard my entire life. "Why don't the Fates intervene more?" I pressed. "Why not prevent war?"

My mother stopped walking, and the look she gave me set my stomach rolling. Queen Maluhia Kärlek Amani Dragoste, ruler of Hehven and all Cupids stared up at me, her gilded eyes burning. "Are you questioning the Fates, Pace?"

"No," I hastened. "Not at all. I was merely reasoning that if Cupids are the guardians of love, peace and hope, why wouldn't we use that position to ensure peace in the human world?"

"It's not that simple, Pace. It's all about balance."

My shoulders stiffened. *Balance*. I knew she was talking about the Chaos. I itched to ask, but there was no way I could without giving away what I'd done. What I'd dragged Dariel and Tiesa into.

She placed a hand on my arm. "Don't worry about the

humans, my love. They'll war, they'll survive, and they'll fight again. Just be thankful you'll never know the tragedy of war."

We reached one of the marble fountains in the centre of the courtyard, a mass of twisting white wings, their tips towards the sky as water cascaded down between the feathers. I trailed my fingers through the rippling surface. I'd visited the libraries yesterday, requesting that all the oldest books and scrolls pertaining to Hehven's history be delivered to my home. There had been far fewer than I'd expected, and already I'd made my way through half the stack with nothing to show for it. Lifting my hand from the water, I watched the droplets fall from my fingers.

"We managed to get the truth from the young female," the queen said, her golden eyes meeting mine.

I froze, my blood ice in my veins. "What?"

"Manners, Pace." The queen frowned. "The young female who accused you of tainting her purity. I spoke with her."

"What did she say?" My chest was so tight, I could barely take in enough breath to form the words.

"She confessed fairly quickly that she had fabricated the lie," my mother said with a sigh. "I don't think she'd properly considered the severity of her words. Once she found herself with me and the threat of dishonouring the Fates with lies, she admitted that you had spent time alone together but never actually touched."

I waited for relief to flood through me, but it didn't. "That's great news."

"Yes. It is." She turned to me, her eyes searching. "I hope you understand now that you must think carefully about the choices you make."

"Of course." I nodded, attempting not to wilt under her appraising stare. "Thank you."

"Now that we've fixed that problem, your father and I need to talk to you about your role," she continued, her arm linking with mine again. "Once you turn twenty, you have some important decisions to make."

My stomach turned to lead at the mention of my birthday. "Oh?"

"There are a lot more royal responsibilities you'll need to take on. You also need to decide whether you and Caitland will live here at the palace, or whether you'd prefer to live in Rakkaus near her family. You certainly can't live in your little hut."

My chest tightened, my breathing shallow. *Caitland*. I hadn't spared her a moment's thought since discovering Thorn was Sirain. When I'd met Sirain to visit the lands of the Midnight Queen, I'd still been unsure of what was between us. I hadn't planned on kissing her. I certainly hadn't planned on kissing her a second time. Or a third. Or a fourth . . . Guilt dragged icy fingers through my gut. I'd told Sirain that I'd made my choice —to burn it all down. Yet, here I was, still trying to follow the rules. Trying to pretend I was something I wasn't.

My mother reached out and touched her fingers to my cheek, her eyes searching with such intensity, I started to wonder if she knew what I was thinking; what I'd done. "Your birth rite means that your actions will never affect just you alone, Pace. As a prince, your choices will always ripple out to affect the people around you. If you truly care about your friends—about your family—you must remember that."

I stared down at her, her touch searing against my skin. "I know."

"Do you?" she pressed. "We are all part of a greater plan, Pace. I know you didn't ask to be a prince and you've warred with that fact for most of your life, but it doesn't change the fact that it's true. You will always have responsibilities, and you must start putting them first. Even if it means making sacrifices. The right path is rarely the easiest."

She let her fingers drop and I exhaled. My mother had said

she could tell when I was lying, and I believed her. Now, standing in front of her with my purity in tatters, I wondered whether she could tell. Did the Fates know? Would they tell her? Did they even care? My heart shoulder-barged against my ribs as I swallowed. She was right; my actions affected so much more than just myself.

"I'll think about it, Mother," I said, carefully sliding her arm from mine and dipping into a shallow bow. "I'm late to meet Dariel, but I promise I'll think hard about what you've said."

Her answering smile told me she didn't believe a word I was saying, but I couldn't dwell on it. I took a few steps away before spreading my wings and launching into the air, the smell of jasmine taunting me on the breeze.

Guilt was bitter on my tongue. There were just under eight months until I saw Caitland again. I couldn't marry her. Besides the fact that I'd never wanted to in the first place, it wasn't fair on her. She deserved a pure Cupid who could love her wholly. I swallowed the nausea building in my throat as I realised, I would have to tell my parents. My blood ran cold at the thought. Standing on the beach, face-to-face with Sirain, it had been easy to make my choice. But now, faced with the consequences, I didn't even know how to begin letting go of the role I'd been playing my whole life.

The spring breeze felt unseasonably cold against my skin as I headed to the forest clearing where I was to meet Tiesa and Dariel. My mother's words lay, unbearably heavy, on my mind. I'd made a choice. I'd chosen Sirain. But when I'd lit the match, I hadn't considered it might burn anyone other than me. If I told my parents the truth, Dariel and Tiesa would be stripped of their titles for accompanying me to the human world. And poor, sweet, flightless Caitland . . . The embarrassment it would cause her family when they discovered her betrothed had sullied himself before their wedding—with a Chaos, no less. I swallowed painfully as I pictured the hurt in her eyes and the disgust and disappointment on my parents' faces. Was my happiness worth hurting so many people?

Swooping upwards, I closed my eyes, as though the wind might carry answers. There was an answer, and it blazed, burning like a brand against my heart. My mother had said the right path was rarely the easiest. I knew what the right thing to do was, and it was going to make me miserable. I tried not to think of how happy I felt when I was with Sirain—of the comfort her friendship gave me. I pushed the taste of her from my mind. She'd told me on the beach. She'd tried to stop me, told me that it wouldn't work. That we were broken. I hadn't wanted to hear it, but perhaps I should have listened. After all, what future did we have with The Crossing between us?

My throat was thick as I dived down toward the sprawling emerald forest. It was time to face up to my responsibilities. Time to follow the rules. I'd live with guilt to protect my family, my friends, Caitland. It would get easier. Feelings faded. Years from now, happily married to Caitland, this would all be a fond memory. Resolve settled like a jagged boulder in my gut. When I saw Sirain tomorrow, I would end it.

Tiesa and Dariel were already standing in the clearing when I arrived. Both wore their quivers, but they were empty of arrows—purely an attempt at an excuse for being in the human world if we were seen by other Hands. As Captain, it was doubtful anyone would dare to ask to see Dariel's orders from the Fates. As for me, we would cross that bridge when it came to it.

"Nice of you to show up, Cousin," Dariel called as I landed.

I folded my wings, staring up at The Crossing shimmering behind them. The sheer size of it never ceased to amaze me. "I was talking to my mother."

"Oh?"

"I asked her about the humans."

Tiesa gasped.

"Why would you do that?" Dariel demanded.

"I wanted to know whether the Fates had ever intervened during previous human wars," I said. "I also wanted to see how she'd react."

Tiesa watched me through her fingers. "And?"

"She was appalled and suggested I was questioning the sanctity of the Fates."

"Of course, she did!" Dariel lifted a hand to his brow, pulling his golden tattoos taut across his dark skin. "It's like you're actively trying to get us in trouble."

Shooting him a withering look, I turned my attention to the rippling lights beyond the clearing. If they knew that I'd been back to the human world without them twice . . . If they knew what I'd done . . . I swallowed the thought. After tomorrow, it wouldn't matter.

"Come on," I said. "Let's not keep Marlowe waiting."

Allowing The Crossing to pull me towards my destination had become easier. Trust was key but submitting yourself to the lights as it stole your senses still went against my every instinct. We were thrust out over the ocean, the midday sun dappling the waves beneath us. It had been Dariel's suggestion to visit the Wendell Islands and although surprised at the request, I had to agree it was necessary. The last time we'd seen the young leader, he'd sheltered us from the storm, and thanks to me, we'd flown off with little more than a goodbye.

Before long, the smaller of the Wendell Islands began to pepper the ocean. Most on the outskirts were uninhabited and I couldn't help but think how the splotches of golden sand and clusters of palms were infinitely nicer than the rocky sandbank I would meet Sirain on tomorrow. I pushed the thought of her away. It would do no good. Not when I was planning to see her for the last time tomorrow. The thought twisted in my chest, but I shook it off. I was doing the right thing.

It took me a moment to realise we were approaching the main island from a different direction than the last time, and I frowned as I tried to gather my bearings. From this angle, the city was hidden from view by the tree-covered peaks at its centre. My attention snagged on a small waterfall between the rocks, and I let myself drop lower, following the flow of water as it wound its way down the steep mountainside. Tiesa called my name, but before I could angle my wings to rise, I spotted something that pulled me further away. Almost at the base of the craggy mountain, the waterfall met with two streams, merging to create a shimmering curtain almost hidden from view behind the trees. The crystalline waters fed into a small pool which then trickled off into smaller tributaries, disappearing into the forest. It was stunning.

"Pace? Come on!"

Glancing up, I realised just how far off course I'd strayed and, lifting a hand in apology, I beat my wings and shot upwards to re-join them. Tiesa threw me a questioning look but didn't press the matter as we rounded the side of the mountain, and the city came into view. Without waiting, we headed straight to the highest balcony. There was a chance Marlowe would be at sea, but it made sense to try the island first.

The doors were open, allowing the breeze to sweep the room and Dariel stepped forward, gesturing for us to stay back until he could be sure it was safe. My hand rested on the sword at my hip, and I knew at my side, Tiesa was doing the same.

"Dariel!" Cove's voice rang out onto the balcony. "Are the others with you?"

As we followed him into the room, my gaze fell on the heavy wooden table, and I tried not to think of how my cousin had lain injured on it not so long ago. Instead, I turned my attention to where Cove was standing, a bemused smile on her face. Shanti stood beside her, the small dragon curled around her shoulders, watching us with narrowed yellow eyes.

"We didn't think we'd see you again," Cove admitted, gesturing for us to sit. "I'll go and fetch my brother."

Without waiting for a response, she strode from the room. Shanti gave us a small smile, the dragon huffing at us as she returned to her seat.

"He's not good with other winged crea—" she stumbled over the word, her face paling. "He doesn't like wings."

I pressed my lips together. At least she hadn't called us birds.

"What's its name?" Tiesa asked.

"Cuthbert," Shanti replied, and the dragon's nostrils sent small plumes of smoke into the air in response. "Although, he gets called Bertie more often than not."

"Bertie," I repeated slowly.

Locking eyes with me, the beast opened its mouth just enough to reveal a host of razor-sharp teeth, as though daring me to comment further. Before I could lose myself to a staring competition, the door opened and Marlowe strode in, his face lit by a beaming smile.

"How wonderful," he said, his arms spread wide as we got to our feet. "I wasn't sure if we'd see you again."

"That's what I said." Cove laughed as she shut the door behind them.

"I'm not sure what the customary greeting is in Heaven," Marlowe said. "But in the Wendell Islands, we do this." He held out his arm and I mirrored the action. Gripping my forearm, just below the elbow, he nodded for me to do the same.

"Hehven," I gently corrected his pronunciation.

"Fascinating." His smile brightened further as he turned to greet Tiesa and Dariel.

"Apologies for arriving without warning," Dariel said. "I—we—felt an explanation was due for the way we left your ship."

Marlowe's grip lingered on Dariel's arm. "Never apologise for coming to visit us. It's always the highest of honours."

"I have to admit," Cove said, taking a seat beside Shanti. "I have many, many questions about what happened on the ship."

My fingers tensed against the arm of the chair. It had taken a lot of denial and avoidance to convince my friends that they'd misunderstood what had happened between Sirain and I that day. That my anger had been due to something she'd whispered to me about my feather—taunting me. Tiesa had been the hardest to convince, but Fates be praised, they'd eventually let the matter drop.

"Indeed," Marlowe agreed, sinking down onto a chair. "The demons were the same ones who attacked you on the roof?"

"Chaos," I corrected. "Yes. The same. Although it was my fault. I attacked them."

"Why?" Cove asked.

I felt Tiesa's gaze burning into me. "It's a long story and an irrelevant one. Any grudge we had was rectified when the female Chaos saved Tiesa."

"The grudge felt pretty real on the ship," Shanti muttered.

"I spoke to the queen today," I said, attempting to steer the conversation toward safer ground. "I asked her whether the Fates had intervened in previous human wars."

"And?" Marlowe asked.

"She was appalled that I would even suggest such a thing."

"So, there's no way the Fates would help us?"

I shook my head. "No. I don't think there is."

His face fell and Dariel tensed beside me.

"Thank you for trying," Marlowe said, his smile crumpling. "I'm grateful for that alone."

He excused himself, stepping out onto the balcony for fresh air, and leaving the room heavy with disappointment. I tried to ignore the guilt curling in my gut. Humans had warred for centuries before I was born and would continue to do so for centuries after I was gone. It wasn't on me or the Cupids to prevent their wars. They should be able to do so themselves. My reasoning did nothing to ease my discomfort.

"Perhaps there's a way around the Fates," Shanti suggested.

"There is no sidestepping Fate." Dariel got to his feet. "If you'll excuse me."

I watched, eyebrows raised, as he followed Marlowe out onto the balcony. It hadn't escaped my attention that my cousin was dressed in his finest Hand uniform—the only finer clothes he owned were his Captain's robes, worn only for formal events. His long hair was carefully braided, and he seemed even more tense than usual. It was hard not to wonder whether there was another reason Dariel had suggested the visit.

"Would you like something to drink? Eat?" Shanti offered. "Please stay and have lunch with us."

I smiled in thanks. "That would be lovely. Thank you."

Shanti stood and I was surprised when Cove joined her. Although, as they reached the door, already talking in hushed voices, I suspected they wanted the chance to talk alone.

"What do you think is going on with those two?" Tiesa asked, her arm slung over the back of the chair as she watched Dariel and Marlowe on the balcony through narrowed eyes.

Someone had closed the doors, keeping whatever conversation was happening between them private.

"I'm not sure," I admitted. "He seems very attached to the human, though."

Tiesa turned to look at me, the bright light filtering through the windows causing her gold Hand markings to shimmer against her brown skin. "You should have a talk with him."

I raised my eyebrows. "Excuse me?"

"If he's developing feelings—even ones of friendship—it can't happen. We shouldn't even be here today, should we?" She shook her head as she returned her attention to the balcony. "It's clouding his judgement, and he's the sensible one."

Swallowing, I watched as Dariel laid a hand on Marlowe's shoulder, the human leaning into him. He was just comforting him. That was all. The thought echoed hollow in my mind, an empty lie.

"Why, though?" I asked.

"Why what?"

"Why can't we let them be? If they're happy they—"

"Are you serious?" Tiesa whirled on me, her green eyes wide. "He can't compromise his purity with a human. His parents—your parents—would be furious! What self-respecting Cupid would marry him knowing he'd given away his purity?"

My face burned and my pulse raced but I forced myself to hold her incredulous gaze. "What's so wrong with humans? Just because they're different to us—"

"That's not the point," she said. "It's the rules. If there really is something between them it shows that he's abused his position as Captain. He's broken the laws of Hehven and defied the Fates."

Tiesa's harsh words were the cold hard truth. Dariel's title would be taken, and he'd be broken by the humiliation. It would destroy him. Even if he chose the human, where would they live? Dariel couldn't live in the human world. Not with wings. A painful and abhorrent solution crept into my mind, and I pushed it away, the thought sending waves of nausea rolling through me. If I could come to see that making the right choice, no matter how miserable it made us, was the only way, surely my straitlaced cousin would arrive at the same realisation.

"I'll speak to him," I said.

Tiesa nodded. "Thank you. It's for the best."

It was. Yet another right path edged with heartache. My decision to put a stop to whatever was happening between me and Sirain was slowly, achingly, solidifying. We had no future.

If we continued, the only thing it would serve to do was hurt the people I cared about.

"What if he's already lost his purity?" I asked.

Tiesa raised her eyebrows. On the balcony, my cousin and Marlowe were still deep in conversation. Their heads close together, Dariel's hand rested on the human's shoulder.

"He couldn't have," she said. "They've never been alone."

"Hypothetically, then."

"Why?" Tiesa's eyes narrowed.

"Do I need a reason for a hypothetical question?"

She sighed. "I suppose, as it's only us that know, he could hope the Fates don't out him. I think the lie would be too much to bear though. It's not in our nature."

Cove and Shanti's laughter reached us just before the door opened, and I smiled, trying to imagine having someone—loving someone—so effortlessly. Perhaps that was what Caitland and I would have one day. The feeling that stirred inside me was not one of hope.

Things were strained as we flew back toward The Crossing. During the meal, the laughter and conversation had flowed easily, and I'd enjoyed getting to know the humans and finding out about their world and their customs. Every so often, however, my attention would be drawn to the lingering looks and small touches between my cousin and Marlowe, and tension would clench my wings.

"I want to help them," Dariel said, pulling me from my thoughts.

Tiesa gave me a meaningful look, but I ignored it.

"What can we do?" I asked. "We can't go against the Fates."

Dariel frowned. "I'm not sure yet, but I'm not going to leave them to be slaughtered."

"What has got into you?" Tiesa asked. "It's not our purpose to protect the humans. Our purpose is—"

"Don't lecture me on our purpose," Dariel snapped. "It will serve you well to remember that I'm your captain."

Tiesa barked a laugh. "I think it would serve *you* well to remember that."

I opened my mouth to intervene, but Dariel didn't respond. Instead, he flew a little ahead, distancing himself.

"Tiesa," I warned, as she eyed him. "Leave him be."

She shook her head, lifting her gaze to me. "Talk to him. Before it's too late."

The weight of her words threatened to drag me beneath the waves.

22
Sirain

Newbold was not what I had expected. The largest of the human lands, it sprawled as far as the eye could see, but very little was visible. Even before we'd reached the rocky cliffs that rose from the ocean like a monster's maw, curling fog obscured our vision as though trying to keep the land from prying eyes.

"It's so dreary," Pace muttered. "Why would anyone choose to live here?"

I shot him a glance as we edged along the coast, searching for signs of life. "You think they have a choice?"

It was the first time he'd spoken since we'd set off. He hadn't come to the cliff last night and when I'd asked him about it, he'd shrugged it off, saying he'd been busy. His indifference had stung and the long flight to Newbold had provided plenty of time for me to feel like a fool, my insides tying themselves in knots as I wondered what had happened—why things felt off. I didn't want to push him, though. If he didn't want to talk about it, fine.

"Look." He pointed.

A dark stone tower was visible on the clifftop, the grey-green grass overgrown against its sides. At the top of the tower, a large flame burned, bright against the mist. In the distance, similar flames could be seen dotted along the coastline.

"What do you think they're for?" I asked.

Pace turned to me, a frown on his face. "I'm not sure, but I don't like it."

A faint whistling cut through the eerie silence. My heart leapt into my mouth as I realised what it was and I dove for Pace, shoving him out of the way. The arrow sliced through the air, arching back down into the fog below. My heart pounded in my throat as I clung to him, staring at the small tower.

Pace stared at me, his eyes wide. "They shot at us?"

"We need to get higher."

I let go of his arm and we climbed into the thick cloud. It was a little like being inside The Crossing, but wet and nowhere near as pretty. "I think they're watchtowers," I said. "Whatever Lord Diarke is doing in Newbold, he doesn't want anyone seeing."

"What if the human that fired the arrow tells someone what they saw?"

"And what would they say?" I gave him a pointed look. "They saw two winged beings and shot at them?"

Pace shook his head. "This doesn't feel right."

We flew inland, keeping a slow pace well within the clouds, and hoping a mountain didn't emerge suddenly in front of us. After a few minutes, I extended my wings, letting myself glide downwards just a little, to where the cloud thinned. I could sense Pace behind me, his wingbeats near silent.

Below us, a sprawling city of dark stone stretched as far as the eye could see in all directions. Curling smoke rose from chimneys and humans in dark clothing moved along the narrow cobblestone streets. I tried and failed to find any greenery. As we flew on, merging with the clouds, I realised Pace was much better suited for camouflage with his white wings, but hopefully from such a height, we'd both be passed off as large birds.

"What's that?" Pace asked, flying level with me.

I followed his gaze to find an enormous, muddied field filled with lines of black moving in waves and it took me a moment to realise that the lines were humans. As we grew closer, the sound of shouting filled the air and my breath caught in my throat. *Soldiers*. The further we flew, the more the lines stretched on. There must have been tens of thousands of them. Maybe more. Unease settled in my gut.

"I think we've seen enough," I said.

Whether Pace agreed or not, I didn't wait to find out as I rose into the cover of clouds and headed back the way we'd came. My hair and wings grew soaked, my leathers darkening with moisture, but I didn't allow myself to slow until the clouds thinned, and the warmth of the sun could be felt once more. A glance over my shoulder told me that Newbold was out of sight, and I shuddered. I never wanted to see that miserable place again.

"I need to tell Marlowe," Pace said.

"Excuse me?"

He flew level with me, his eyes fixed ahead. "You don't have to come. I'm pretty sure I can find my own way, but I'm going to go to the Wendell Islands and tell him what we've just seen."

I stared at him, his white hair silver from the moisture. "Why?"

"Because it's the right thing to do."

It took everything I had not to roll my eyes. "Seriously? Is that the Cupid motto?"

"Like I said. You don't have to come."

He angled his wings to catch an updraft and I watched as he took off in the direction of the tropical islands. It looked like he did know exactly where he was going, which made me wonder how many times he'd been there with his friends.

Gritting my teeth, I beat my wings, catching up with him. "Fine. I'll come."

Pace gave me a smile that bordered on a grimace. "Don't

take this the wrong way," he said, "but I'd rather Marlowe didn't see us together. If he mentioned it in front of Dariel or Tiesa—"

"Oh, I get it," I said. "You're embarrassed to be seen with a Chaos."

"No," Pace said, eyes wide. "It's just—"

"I'm joking. Calm your feathers."

I didn't have to look at him to sense the glare he sent my way. His words hadn't been lost on me, though. They were obviously meeting with Marlowe frequently if he was worried about the human saying something.

After a few minutes, I chanced a glance at the Cupid prince. Things were definitely different. He hadn't looked at me for more than a second, and I hated the disappointment that wrapped itself around my throat. Despite numerous training sessions with Kwellen and throwing myself into meetings at the castle—to my father's begrudging approval—I hadn't been able to shake the memory of Dalibor. Often I would be listening to some lord or lady whining about stray goats or teenagers vandalising buildings, when the image of Pace, his face haloed by the sun as he held himself over me, would fill my mind, causing my stomach to flip and my breath to catch. It was seared into my brain along with the taste of his lips and the feel of his warm skin under my fingers. I shook my head. Now that I'd taken him where he needed to go, perhaps things had come to an end. He'd got everything he'd needed out of our relationship. Perhaps that was why he hadn't come to the cliff last night. I ignored the way my heart clenched painfully at the thought.

"Wait for me?" he asked.

It took me a second to realise what he meant. I'd been so lost in thought, the Wendell Islands had already begun to speckle the ocean below. In answer, I descended to one of the small islands, barely more than a sandbank, with a cluster of bushes and palm trees at its centre. Standing on the sand, I watched Pace's white wings disappear into the distance and considered leaving. Every modicum of common sense screamed at me to spread my wings and head back to The Crossing—to never see the white-haired prince again.

I peeled off my damp boots and sank my toes into the warm sand.

The sunshine was glorious, and I plunged my hands into the fine sand, letting the grains run between my fingertips. I had no idea how long I'd been lying on the beach, eyes closed as the sun dried the remnants of Newbold from my body and clothes. After shedding my boots and leather top, I'd stretched out my wings and embraced the warmth of the sand, trying to think of anything other than what I should say to Pace when he returned.

I heard his wingbeats a moment before his shadow blocked the sun from my face. "Do you mind?" I said.

He moved but didn't sit. Had something happened? Dread weighted my chest as I reluctantly opened my eyes. Pace stood, arms at his side before me and I looked him over, scanning for injuries—for any sign of blood—but there was nothing. Pushing up onto my elbows, I let my gaze travel to his face and my breath caught. Pace stared down at me, the fierceness in his eyes reminiscent of the way he'd looked at me before he tried to kill me. I watched his golden gaze flicker between my face and my chest.

Realisation settled over me and I grinned. "Have you never seen a female in her undergarments before?"

Pace clenched his jaw and sat down beside me, his attention focused on the water as it lapped at the edges of the island. I pressed my lips together, fighting a smile. My white camisole with its thin straps wouldn't be out of place in a training ring in the midst of summer. It hadn't even occurred to me the effect it might have on Pace. Fates and feathers, if I'd taken my trousers off too . . .

"Would you prefer me to put my leathers back on?" I asked. "I'm sure they're dry now."

"It's fine."

"Are you going to be able to look at me?" I asked, wrapping my arms around my knees.

His wings folded tighter against his back, the feathers dragging through the sand. "Not without forgetting what I need to say."

My heart dipped painfully. I'd known it was coming. It was fine. After all, hadn't I been planning to end things myself? If that was true though, why was I finding it hard to breathe?

"Thank you," he said. "For taking me to Dalibor and to Newbold. I can never repay you for putting yourself at risk like that."

"It's fine," I said. "I wanted to go anyway."

My words sounded churlish, and I cringed.

"We can't see each other again."

Each syllable burned against my chest, and I fisted the sand, trying to take a breath that wouldn't betray my emotion. "Fine."

"It's the right thing to do," Pace muttered, his gaze dropping to the sand.

"Of course."

"I don't think we should meet at the cliffs anymore either."

My eyes burned and I dug my fingers into my palms. Perhaps I was overtired. I blinked, staring at his hand half covered in sand, a hair's breadth from my own. His golden skin was luminous beside my moon-white fingers. He sighed, shifting slightly. The side of his hand brushed mine and I watched as he stilled but didn't move away. I didn't want it to be over. As much as I tried to convince myself, I knew I didn't. The sliver of skin against mine burned and I couldn't tear my gaze away. Pace was right. It was the sensible thing to do. There was no way this would end well. It made sense to stop now before it got out of hand.

His little finger lifted, looping over mine. "I'm sorry," he said. "This is my fault. I shouldn't have kissed you."

"If I hadn't wanted you to kiss me, you wouldn't have got the chance," I snapped.

He huffed a laugh and lifted his hand to cover mine, linking our fingers. I watched, mesmerised as fine rivers of sand trickled between the gaps.

"I don't want to end this," he whispered.

My heart pounded with such ferocity, I felt nauseous as I stared at our hands, the way his long, strong fingers eclipsed my own. The selfishness of my words stung, even before I said them. "Don't, then."

I felt him look at me then, and I forced my gaze from our hands to his face. His golden eyes were dark with warring emotion, the sea breeze whipping through his white locks. Pace had the kind of face that made me wish I could paint.

"I have to," he said, a furrow appearing between his brows. "There's no future for us. Mine is already laid out and—"

"Says who?" I interrupted. "Do you have word from the Fates?"

The furrow deepened. "You know what I mean."

I did. I also hadn't planned on trying to persuade him not to end things. My head spun and I tried to still my thoughts—to get a hold of myself. My gaze returned to our clasped hands. Pace followed the movement, starting to let go of my fingers.

"Don't." I tightened my grip, holding him still. "Not yet."

He gave me a sad smile. "It feels nice, doesn't it?"

I nodded, hoping he couldn't see the colour staining my cheeks. If my father saw me acting this weak in front of another, he would give me a beating to remember. "I think my mother held my hand sometimes as a child."

Pace squeezed my fingers, his thumb rubbing slow circles like he had during our first kiss. My eyes started to burn again, and I looked away.

"Perhaps the Chaos and Cupids are more similar than we think," Pace said. "I don't think I've held someone's hand since I was a child either."

I sniffed, but there was a sad truth to his words. Although physical intimacy was commonplace in Helle, affection was not. I wasn't even sure my parents liked each other. I tried to remember whether I'd ever seen them kiss.

"My mother used to hold me in secret," I admitted. "She would stroke my hair and let me lay my head in her lap. My father almost found us once and I was terrified she'd stop."

"Did she?"

"For a while. As I grew older, I craved it less anyway."

"Was she like that with your brother?"

I snorted. "Fin would never let anyone close enough for that. I don't think he'd be capable of kissing someone without drawing blood."

"Do you have just the one brother?" Pace asked.

"I have a younger sister. She's sixteen. She doesn't seem as cold as Fin, but I don't see enough of her to be sure." Even as I said the words, I swore a silent promise to spend more time with Malin, if only to ensure she didn't end up like our brother. A memory from the cliff flitted to mind and I turned to Pace. "You have a sister too. She likes flowers."

Pace looked at me in surprise. "How did you know that?"

"You told me. On the cliff."

Recollection sparked in his eyes. "I did. Yes. Amari. She's ten."

"You love her."

"Of course, I do. And even though Dash is a pain in the wings, I love him too." He raised his eyebrows as realisation sank in. "You don't love your siblings."

It wasn't a question, so I didn't answer.

"What about your friends?" Pace asked.

"I don't know," I admitted. "I've never thought about it."

His grip tightened on my hand. "I'm sorry."

I pulled away, instantly regretting it. "I didn't ask for your pity."

We were done, I realised. What else could be said? Sitting there, holding hands, we were just prolonging the inevitable. Reaching for my boots, I started pulling them on. I could feel Pace watching me, but I refused to look at him. With a shaky exhale, I stood, stooping to pick up my top.

When I turned to bid Pace goodbye, I found him standing right behind me. I staggered back a step, staring up at him. "What are you doing?" I asked, pressing my hand to my heart. "Trying to startle the feathers off me?"

He reached for my hand, linking our fingers as he regained the space I'd put between us. "You understand that I don't want to let you go, right?"

"Is that supposed to make this easier? To make me feel better?"

He shook his head. "Nothing could make this easier. This is the hardest thing I've ever had to do."

"But you do have to," I said. "Like you said, there's no future for us."

He nodded, his gaze flickering over my face as though memorising every detail. "No future."

"It was fun while it lasted," I said, the hitch in my voice betraying my attempt at nonchalance.

"Do you remember I told you on the cliff that I fought in tournaments to feel alive?" Raising a hand, he traced his fingers down my cheek. "The time I've spent with you has made me feel more alive than any tournament ever could. When I'm with you, I can breathe."

A sob lodged in my throat. "Stop it."

Dropping my hand, he stepped back. "I'm sorry. I just—"

"I know."

The air felt too thick, the sun too hot—too bright. I turned. "Goodbye, Pace."

"No."

I paused; my wings already outstretched.

"No," he said, his voice hard and firm enough to cause me to turn. "I know why I'm doing this. I understand that by not letting you go, I risk hurting the people around me. But what if I don't?"

My wings drooped as I stared up at him. The pain was almost too much to bear. I wondered whether I should have left when I had the chance. "What are you talking about?"

"If I choose you. If I choose myself—my own happiness. The people around me might get hurt, but people get hurt all the time. If they cared one iota about me, they'd want me to be happy. Right?"

"What do you want, Pace?" I asked, my sigh weighting my shoulders.

He stepped closer, his golden eyes like rays of sunshine as they seared into mine. "You, Sirain. I want you. I know I shouldn't. I know we need to end this, but I don't know how to let you go. I don't want to let you go."

I swallowed, letting him tug me closer until there was no space between us at all. The warmth of his skin was enough to steal my breath as he pressed against me.

"What do you want, Sirain?"

My toes curled at the sound of my name on his lips, and I reached for him, cupping his face, and running my thumb across his plump bottom lip. I shouldn't. There really was no future for us. Pace was willing to risk his family, his friends, to be with me. He'd bared his soul to me, but mine was still half in shadow. He might not be destined for the throne, but I was. At some point in the future, I would have to face my responsibilities.

Staring up at him, a vision of warm gold and pure white, I pushed reason into the dark, desperate corner where it belonged. When I was with Pace I felt, *more*. I was more than a Chaos. More than my ruthless father's reluctant choice to succeed him. More than how Fin made me feel when his glare stripped the flesh from my bones. With Pace, I was worth something. I felt like there was hope.

As much as Pace made me feel I could do anything—be anyone—I was still a Chaos. I knew in my blackened heart I should let him go and make the decision easier for him. Maybe that was why I didn't. Perhaps my selfish Chaos nature was the reason I pushed common sense over the edge of the cliff, letting it shatter on the rocks below.

"You, Pace," I breathed. "I want you."

He sighed, his eyes closing briefly, and when he opened them again, they flashed with a familiar fierceness. Taking my face in his hands, he kissed me. This time, there was nothing gentle about it.

23
Pace

The currents filtering through my wings were warmer than they had been. Summer was just around the corner, only two weeks away, and the air was fizzing with the excitement only a Festival could bring. Not a day had passed without speaking to Sirain since making possibly the most dangerous decision of my life. We not only continued to meet at the cliff to talk every sunset, but in person most days too, either on the rocky island or the outskirts of the Wendell Islands, depending on how much time we had to slip away. Every time I saw her, I marvelled at how I ever thought I could walk away.

My heartbeat strummed in my throat as I waited at the door of the sprawling farmhouse, more understated than I'd expected for the home of a Lord. It hadn't been hard to find the Rakkaus family home amongst the homesteads scattered across endless fields of greens and golds. The lord and lady's house was built at the foot of a large hill, a little higher than the rest of the farmlands, as though watching protectively over the province. I exhaled, shaking out my hands at my sides. I would tell my parents at the Festival that I wouldn't be marrying Caitland, but today I would tell her, and her father.

I stood tall, wings and shoulders back as the door creaked open. A male smallwing stared up at me, his silvered eyes wide. He couldn't have been older than five or six.

"Good morning," I said, relaxing my stance a little. "I'm looking for Lord Rakkaus or Caitland. Are they here?"

The smallwing gawked for a second more before shouting for his mother, and I grinned as he ran back into the house out of sight. Blowing out another breath, I tried not to fidget. It was time to face up to the consequences of my decision. Sirain and I had arranged to meet just after midday on our desolate isle, but every second we spent together was accompanied by a small hard knot of guilt that lingered between my shoulder blades—an uncomfortable reminder of my obligations. My smile faded as my heart rate resumed its frenetic rhythm. I'd lit the match, and now I'd see just how flammable the people around me really were.

The woman that appeared in the doorway was unmistakably Caitland's mother, sharing the same delicate features and silver eyes. Those eyes widened in recognition as she took in the golden hues amidst my feathers and dipped into a curtsey.

"Your Majesty. To what do we owe this honour?"

I'm here to potentially break your daughter's heart. I bowed, then took a deep breath. "Apologies Lady Rakkaus, I know I'm not supposed to see Caitland until the wedding, but I really need to speak to her. Her father too, if he is available."

She glanced over her shoulder. "Caitland is helping in the kitchens, but Lord Rakkaus is still out working in the fields. He should be returning for lunch within the hour, though. Please, come in."

Lady Rakkaus stepped to the side, and I tucked my wings in tight as I entered their home. The rooms were large, but the way things were positioned felt odd. Despite being folded, I found my wings knocking into things as I turned, which only served to exacerbate my nerves. Following Caitland's mother through the sprawling farmhouse, I noticed that like her daughter, her wings were slim and weak. I frowned, trying to reason why anyone would have wings and not use them.

Lady Rakkaus slowed as we reached a living room. "Please, have a seat, Your Majesty. I'll go and fetch Caitland."

Settling into a wide chair, I let my wings hang through the dipped back as I ran through the twenty versions of what I had planned to say. I'd thought long and hard, but it turned out there was no gentle way to break off an engagement. I straightened at the rustling of wings, standing as Caitland and her mother entered the room.

"May I fetch you some refreshment, Your Majesty?" Lady Rakkaus asked, dipping into another curtsey.

"No, thank you." I smiled. "I'm fine."

She nodded, shooting a glance at her daughter's bowed head. "I'll be in the kitchen if you need me."

"Please," I said to Caitland, my tone soft so as not to startle her. "Will you sit with me?"

She nodded; her gaze fixed on her feet as she selected a chair a little further away from me than I would have liked. I swallowed a sigh.

"Thank you for meeting with me," I began. "I know our parents had planned for us to wait until the wedding to see each other again, but I need to talk to you."

Caitland looked up, and I expected to see worry in her expression but there was something else I couldn't quite put my finger on. "What did you want to talk about, Your Majesty?"

"Pace. Please." I took a deep breath, exhaling as I ran a hand through my hair. "There's no easy way to say this, but—"

"You want to break off the engagement."

I blinked, the words I'd been dreading saying for days still half formed on my tongue.

"It's okay," she said, meeting my bewildered gaze with a

shrewd intensity that only served to confuse me further. "You don't have to feel bad about it."

"It's not you," I said, leaning forward. "There's . . . There's somebody else."

Caitland nodded. "I would expect so."

"Pardon?" I frowned, wondering what had happened to the painfully shy female from the Festival. "I'm not sure what you're implying, but this happened after we met. Sort of."

"I assure you I meant no offence." She returned her gaze to her lap, smoothing her long brown skirts. "What do the king and queen say?"

My chest tightened. "They don't know. I wanted to tell you first."

"Thank you." She nodded, a slight frown creasing her forehead.

I stared at Caitland, my wings prickling with curiosity. She was still softly spoken, and I felt like if I made any sudden movements she might faint, but she no longer seemed terrified of me. "You're not angry?"

She looked up at me, a small smile at the corner of her lips. "No. I knew you didn't want the marriage. When you were late to meet me, I knew."

I winced. "I'm so sorry, Caitland. That was beyond rude of me."

"It's okay." She clasped her hands together, casting a furtive glance over her shoulders as she dropped her voice. "I'm in love with someone else, too."

"Oh." I sat back; my eyebrows raised. "So, we would have been *really* miserable if this wedding went ahead."

Caitland's shoulders drooped. "I appreciate you coming to tell me the truth, but our parents have agreed to this wedding. Will they let you call it off? Are you going to tell them that you want someone else?"

I swallowed. "No. I can't tell them about her. I'm hoping I can reason with them."

"May I ask you a question?" Caitland looked up at me, the delicate furrow between her brows returning.

"Of course. Anything."

"Why did your parents want you to marry me?"

I leaned forward, a wry smile curving my lips. "They think I'm reckless and irresponsible. They thought a nice, sensible girl like you would sort me out."

Her eyes widened into two silver moons. "Reckless and irresponsible?"

"No? I must say I'm relieved the rumours don't appear to have reached this far north," I said, huffing a wry laugh. "My parents are concerned that the good Cupids of Hehven have little to talk about besides who I've spent time with and what we might have got up to."

"Oh." Caitland's brows fell, the thoughtful furrow returning.

"You've had a lucky escape," I continued. "I'm sure the Cupid who has your heart is a much better choice than me."

"It would seem so." A smile ghosted her pale pink lips. "He's quiet and sensible."

I laughed, the tension that had nested in my shoulders beginning to dissipate. "Your mother told me your father would be back soon. I'll inform him of our decision."

"No." Caitland's eyes widened once more as she shook her head. "He won't understand. He won't allow it."

"Then what do you suggest we do?"

"Let me speak to him. I think I can get him to call it off."

I frowned. There was no rule book for a situation like this and I didn't want to risk offending Lord Rakkaus further by leaving.

"Please. Trust me." Caitland stood, glancing again over her

shoulder at the door. "You should leave before he returns from the fields."

"Are you sure you'll be able to convince him?" I stood, making to stretch my wings, but pulling them back at the last second as they brushed the table.

"Yes. Now go."

Reluctantly, I let her lead me back to the front door. She seemed confident, and she knew her father better than I did, but it still felt cowardly to leave things this way. We reached the door and I turned, dipping a bow at my soon to be ex-fiancée.

"Thank you for being so understanding, Caitland," I said. "I hope things work out between you and your love."

She smiled, her eyes lighting in a way I hadn't seen before. "May the Fates favour your love also. Thank you for being strong enough to try and stop this, Pace. If you hadn't, we'd soon have been married and miserable."

"May I ask a question?" My curiosity won out as I stepped back out into the late morning sunshine. "Why don't you and your family like flying?"

Caitland's eyebrows shot up. "Our work is on the ground. We only need to fly as high as the tops of the fruit trees. Why would anyone need to touch the clouds?"

Another laugh rippled in my chest at her incredulous tone. "Why, indeed. Thank you, Caitland."

With another bow, I spread my wings and leapt into the air towards the clouds. With each beat of my wings, the knot of guilt between my shoulder blades loosened, and by the time I reached The Crossing, I felt lighter than I had in a long time.

Sirain was waiting on the boulders when I arrived, the wind tossing her hair in long dark ribbons. I alighted before her and held up my hands. Her answering smile tightened my chest and, as I lifted her down from the rock, I wasted no time in pulling her to me.

"Hey," I murmured against her lips.

"Hey."

"I've had an idea." Setting her on the ground, I linked my fingers with hers.

"Dangerous."

I winked and tugged at her hand. "Come on."

We flew until the ocean turned from grey to sapphire blue, and the Wendell Islands drifted into view. There had been a few times we'd spent our time on the deserted outer islands, but when we continued toward the main island, Sirain glanced over at me.

"Where are we going?"

I said nothing, smiling as I dipped toward the tree-covered mountain at the centre of the isle. On the way through The Crossing, I'd decided not to tell Sirain about Caitland. I wasn't sure how she felt about my betrothal. It wasn't something we'd talked about since we'd chosen each other. Even so, I scarcely wanted to get my own hopes up. Whatever Caitland was planning, I hoped to the Fates it worked.

Searching the side of the mountain, I grinned as I found the small waterfall I'd been looking for, following its flow downwards. It was just as I remembered, and I dropped down into the clearing, spreading my wings and alighting at the side of the crystal-clear pool.

"This is . . ." Sirain's words trailed off as she landed beside me, staring up at the sheet of water cascading over the rocks.

It was louder than I'd expected; the water churning into a fine mist where it hit the pool, ghosts of rainbows playing in the spray. I wiped the fine sheen of sweat from my brow as I squinted up at the sun. With only two weeks until the summer solstice, the heat in the Wendell Islands was already stifling.

Movement caught my eye and I looked down to find Sirain tugging off her boots. "What are you doing?"

She looked up at me like I'd asked her what colour the sky was. "What does it look like?"

I watched, frozen, as she unfastened the clasps at her side and slid the top half of her leathers from her arms, dropping them on the floor. Swallowing hard, I tried to tear my eyes away from the delicate silken straps of her slip against her snowy skin. My blood roared in my ears as loud as the waterfall, and when her fingers went to the fastenings at the top of her trousers I turned away, my skin hotter than the Wendell sun.

Sirain's resulting laughter filled the air, but I kept my eyes on the tree line as her remaining leathers fell to the floor with a soft thud. Seconds later, a splash echoed around the clearing.

"Are you coming in or not?"

My blood thrumming, I turned to find Sirain in the centre of the pool, her dark hair fanning out around her in the water. "Fine."

She grinned at me then ducked under the water out of sight. I'd pulled off my boots and had started unfastening my shirt by the time Sirain resurfaced, water cascading from her dark wings and clinging to the feathers like diamonds. My fingers stilled as I met her gaze, and as I continued undressing, she followed the movement, her eyes twin pools of dark flame. Watching me pull the shirt from my shoulders, placing it beside my boots, my skin burned under her stare. I couldn't bring myself to remove my trousers, telling myself it was warm enough, that they'd dry quickly. I held Sirain's searing gaze as I slipped down into the cool water and swam towards her. It was colder than I'd expected, but more than a welcome relief against the burning sun. I reached for her, but she swam backwards out of my reach.

"How's your brother?" she asked.

I frowned. My parents had called a meeting earlier in the

week and outlined my choices: either move to the north and set up a North Hehven council, to save the lords and ladies there from having to travel to Dragoste each week, or stay in the south and take on Dash's current role overseeing the Captains of Fate. Whether Caitland managed to persuade her father to call off the engagement or not, it was likely to be a choice I would still have to make, and ever since the meeting, my brother had been hounding me to decide.

The choice was easy. I didn't want either job but staying in Dragoste was the preferable choice. Dash's job consisted of receiving reports from the Hands, following their missions, and keeping records. As he'd tried to persuade me what an interesting job it was, I'd struggled to breathe, wondering what the likelihood of him finding out via one of these reports that Dariel, Tiesa and I had been travelling through The Crossing without orders from the Fates.

"Dash was knocking on my door first thing this morning," I admitted. "I'll tell him tomorrow. I know that as soon as I do, he'll insist I shadow him day in and day out."

Sirain wrinkled her nose. "That's intense."

"It means I won't be able to come and see you," I said, reaching for her. My fingers grazed her cheek before she kicked away again. "How's Fin?" I asked. Two could play at this game.

She shuddered. "He's the same sadistic prick."

"He hasn't tried to hurt you again, has he?" I asked. Every muscle in my body tensed at the thought.

A few days ago, he'd 'accidentally' knocked Sirain down some stairs. She'd only stumbled a step or two before her wings caught her, but she'd twisted her ankle. If I ever met Fin, I wasn't sure I'd be able to stop myself from tearing his head from his body.

"I've managed to avoid him," she said. "I only wish I could avoid my father."

It was hard to feel anything other than tense when Sirain

talked about her family. Sometimes I lay awake at night trying to think of ways I could whisk her away from Helle—from them. It was a daydream that could never be, though. I'd tried to bring her through The Crossing to Hehven once, if only to see if it was possible, but whatever forces were at work inside the dense lights, ripped us apart to our separate sides before we could blink.

"Want to see what's behind the waterfall?" she asked.

I glanced up at the thundering curtain of water. The mountain was sheer on either side, which meant climbing up behind it would be difficult. Perhaps we could fly around. Before I could suggest it, Sirain swam close to the spray and ducked underneath. A shout left my throat before I could stop it. Although capable enough, a Cupid's wings aren't designed for swimming. I moved toward the rainbow dusted mist, my breath halted. Had she come up on the other side or was she being pushed down beneath the pummelling cascade?

"Sirain?" I called, swimming closer.

"Hurry up!"

I exhaled in relief at the sound of her voice and, taking a deep breath, ducked down as far under the waterfall as I could before my wings started to resist. The force churned the water white and the currents pushed and pulled at me as I made my way underneath. Bursting to the surface, I gulped at the air, shaking the water from my hair.

"Took you long enough," Sirain teased.

It was darker on this side of the waterfall, the sun filtering through the wall of water in shimmering trickles, dancing on the dark cavern walls. It was only a shallow indent into the mountain, the pool of dark water a quarter of the size of the one on the other side.

"Are you happy now?" I asked, swimming to where Sirain was treading water. "Is your curiosity sated?"

"Almost," she said. "I want to see if the cavern leads anywhere."

I frowned, eyeing the ledge of rock she was heading towards. Beyond it, the cavern was dark enough that I'd assumed it was pure rock. "Even if it does," I said. "You're hardly dressed for exploring."

Sirain rolled her eyes at me over her shoulder and heaved herself onto the rocky ledge. Water cascaded from her wings, and she extended them, shaking off the excess.

She turned to me, pulling her long dark hair over her shoulder. "Coming?"

My reply lodged in my throat as my gaze travelled the length of her soaking figure. Her white slip and undergarments were almost completely see-through and, remembering myself, I looked away. It was too late, though, the image of her standing there, dark wings outstretched and water cascading over her body was seared into my brain for all eternity.

At the sound of footsteps, I allowed myself to look again. Sirain had moved to the back of the cave, her wings folded as she moved her hands along the rock wall. Swimming to the edge, I pulled myself out of the water, immediately regretting it as I shivered, my skin pebbling.

"Did you find a secret passageway yet?" I asked.

"No."

The disappointment crammed into that single word curved my lips into a grin. When she turned, I tugged her to me, sliding my arms around her waist. "I'm sorry."

"Perhaps you can distract me from my disappointment." She pouted.

I dipped my head, pressing a kiss to her neck. "I can certainly try."

Sirain's hands stroked up my stomach to my chest and I captured her mouth with mine as I pressed her gently back against the cool rock. The feel of her scantily clad body against mine was torture and after a minute, I stepped back.

"What's wrong?" she asked, reaching for me.

"You—"

"Me?"

"Not, you." I groaned. "It's just . . . You're practically naked."

"And?"

I didn't have to look at her to know the teasing grin she would be wearing. "And I want . . ."

Her hands slid up my body again and she gripped my chin, forcing me to look at her. "What do you want, Pace?"

"I want to touch you." I barely recognised my own voice, the words rough and uneven.

Sirain rose on her toes and tipped my mouth to hers. "Touch me, then."

I stared at her, the purple in her eyes like twilight in the dim light of the cavern. My blood roared in my veins, my heartbeat louder than thunder as I kissed her again. I could barely form a thought as I moved my hand from her shoulder, my fingers seeking the places I'd tried so hard not to let myself think about. Her answering moan trembled against my lips, and I groaned in response, pulling her closer.

I marked every arch of her back, every intake of breath, every sigh and whimper—memorising each sound and movement like notes to a song I was learning by heart. When her hands balled into fists in my hair and her breath caught at my ear, my name on her lips, I knew I would never tire of the melody.

As her breathing slowed, Sirain rested her head against my chest, and I stroked my fingers along the arcs of her wings, pressing kisses to her temple. Her fingers moved to the button of my trousers, and I stilled.

"Do you trust me?" she asked, staring up at me.

I considered her question, aware of every fibre of my being waiting silently, as though unsure what my answer might be.

"Yes," I said. "I do."

Her eyes widened a fraction, but then she smiled and pulled me to her for a kiss that set my blood roaring once more. When she pulled back, her fingers found my buttons and with a smile on her lips, she began a blazing trail of kisses down my chest.

24
Sirain

Watching Second Prince Pace Maluhia Kärlek Dragoste of Hehven, come completely and utterly undone at my touch, was the most breathtakingly beautiful thing I had ever seen, and I knew I would gladly walk through fire if it only meant I had the chance to witness it again.

25

Pace

"Pace? Pace!"

Lost in thought, it took me a second to realise that Dariel was calling my name and another to realise that we'd reached land. Below, the cities of Liridona sprawled out in clusters of winding streets and peaked roofs. The buildings were tall and thin, many painted in bright colours, with carved wooden shutters open to allow in the warm spring breeze. Between the sporadic cities and villages, the land was flat and interspersed with lush green fields, giving a homely feel. Looking at the tightly bundled towns and farming villages, I could see why Lord Bickerstaff was so desperately trying to avoid war. Liridona and the Wendell Islands were different to Dalibor and Newbold. When war came, they would pay a far heavier price.

As we reached the largest of the cities, the boroughs dotted with parks and ponds, Dariel pointed to a large manor on the leafy outskirts. A long path led to the front where an enormous fountain took up much of the white gravelled courtyard. I nodded and followed my cousin as he swooped down towards the building.

I'd been surprised when my cousin had informed me he

was going to visit Lord Bickerstaff and would like me to join him. Of course, I hadn't hesitated to accept. Liridona was the last of the human lands I was yet to see, and Emeric was an intriguing man. What had struck me as strange, however, was that not only was this not a mission from the Fates, but Dariel had requested that we keep the trip from Tiesa.

Ever since our last trip to the Wendell Islands, she'd been extremely vocal regarding her opinion on helping the humans. I could understand why he would want to keep this visit a secret, but the omission sat heavy on my chest. Tiesa had also taken every opportunity since our last visit to pester me to speak to Dariel about Marlowe. I hadn't, and I wasn't planning on doing so any time soon. I was in no position to lecture my cousin on impossible relationships.

Dariel led the way to a balcony at the back of the house and landed, his wings barely folded before he knocked confidently on the thin glass. I narrowed my eyes, about to ask whether he'd been here before, when the doors swung open.

Emeric Bickerstaff's tall, lean frame appeared, a smile on his narrow face. "Come in, friends. Come in."

I followed Dariel into the room, completely unsurprised to find Marlowe waiting for us. As Emeric welcomed me, I watched my cousin greet the Wendell Islands' leader, their faces lit with bright smiles as they gripped each other's arms. My stomach sank. There was definitely something going on between them and I was beginning to realise it went deeper than I'd first thought.

Emeric ushered us forward and I took in the large room, noting how different in style it was to the last human room I'd entered. Instead of the low, dark wooden beams and bare stone walls of the Wendell Islands, this room was almost tall enough to fly in. Large, jewelled chandeliers hung sparkling from the white ceiling and the walls were covered in pastel stripes that glimmered slightly in the sunlight, with wide paintings in gilded frames taking up most of the wall space.

"Thank you for meeting with us," Emeric said, gesturing for us to take a seat on one of the many pale blue and green upholstered chairs.

There was a table laid out with tea and as Marlowe set about pouring cups, as though it was something he did regularly, I took a seat. It was the first time I'd seen Emeric on solid ground. Dressed in a simple shirt and trousers, there was a keenness to his eyes—the intelligence clear in the dark depths that looked almost purple when they caught the light. Sitting so close to him, I could see the grey at his temples and the weathered lines around his eyes and mouth. He was older than I'd first realised, although he carried himself like a man half his age. He was probably a similar age to my parents.

I gestured to my cousin, who was focused on Marlowe as he set the steaming cups on saucers. "I must admit, I'm curious to know why we're meeting. My cousin has kept the reasons quite guarded."

Emeric gave me an apologetic smile. "Then please allow me to explain. I understand you spoke to the queen regarding the Fates' involvement in previous wars?"

My attention snapped to Marlowe, who had the good sense to look guilty, as Dariel shifted protectively beside him.

"Yes," I admitted. "She was abhorred. The Fates only involve themselves as they see fit."

Emeric nodded. "I understand that although it would be the easiest route to preventing the war, it's too much to ask for you to go against your family and the Fates. I'm wondering whether we could utilise the Cupids in a less intrusive way."

"Less intrusive?"

Emeric inclined his head. "What if you could gather information for us?"

The realisation of what he was asking settled over me like the uncomfortable itch before a sneeze. "You want us to spy?"

"Yes."

Although common sense screamed that spying was a bad idea, it was exactly what I had already been doing with Sirain. I turned to my cousin and found him watching me, his eyebrows slightly raised. Had this been his suggestion? Had he promised Marlowe our help, knowing he needed me to back him?

"I've already informed Marlowe that Newbold are training troops," I said, ignoring Dariel. "They have tens, possibly hundreds of thousands of soldiers training in combat. They have watchtowers armed with archers along the coast designed to keep prying eyes out."

Emeric paled. "How do you know this?"

Dariel's questioning glare seared into the side of my face, but I kept my attention on Bickerstaff. "I went. I wanted to see what they were up to. Luckily there was heavy cloud, so I managed to keep hidden."

"This is not good," Emeric said, scratching his chin. "Not good at all."

"I planned on telling you today," Marlowe said. "Pace only told me less than a week ago."

Emeric lifted a hand in a dismissive gesture, his eyes still fixed on me. "Did you find anything out in your libraries?"

"No. I've been through every book, scroll, and text old enough to warrant importance. There's nothing."

"You mentioned there might be some somewhere else?" Marlowe said, placing a hand on Dariel's arm.

"The Isle of the Fates," I muttered. "Only the Fated can visit the island."

Emeric leaned forward, his eyes bright. "The Fated?"

"Those who have sworn their lives to serve the Fates," Dariel explained. "They are the only ones who see the Fates in person. They take the orders from the Fates and give them to the captains."

Emeric nodded slowly. "And you are a captain, Dariel?"

"Yes." Dariel looked at me, his mouth pressed into a tight line. "My sister, Amare, is a Fated."

Silence settled in the room, questions hanging in the air like autumn leaves not quite ready to fall.

"I'll ask her," Dariel said quietly. "I'll see what I can find out."

Emeric sat back with a sigh. "There's still hope for peace then, it seems."

Dariel huffed. "Unless a Chaos sneaks into your room and uses an arrow to turn you against each other."

Marlowe and Emeric shifted in their chairs.

"That doesn't make any sense," I argued. "Emeric is only in league with Marlowe. If the Fates decided to send Chaos after either of them, it would only serve to drive apart the peace between them, which would ensure war."

Even as I said the words, I knew it was a possibility. The Fates didn't concern themselves with the survival of the humans. How they decided where the Cupids and the Chaos went, I had no idea. It was something that wasn't questioned, just carried out.

"You should go into hiding," Dariel suggested. "Cupid arrows can't be shot through glass or walls, so I'm assuming Chaos arrows are the same."

Marlowe reached out his hand and rested it on my cousin's knee. "You can't expect us to hide indoors until the war is over."

"Perhaps a sort of armour could be developed?" Emeric suggested.

Dariel shook his head. "The arrows can pierce anything the target is wearing."

My gaze lingered on where Marlowe's hand still rested on my cousin's knee.

"I have to admit," Emeric said, pulling my attention. "I'm curious why you took it upon yourself to travel to Newbold by yourself. Was it purely curiosity?"

"I want to help you," I said. "I don't want war and the thought of so many avoidable deaths is appalling. I went to Newbold to be sure that war was coming—to Dalibor to see the ships too. I needed to know."

"How many times?" Dariel asked. There was an uneven edge to his voice that made my wings tense. "How many times have you travelled to the human lands alone?"

I couldn't help myself. I looked pointedly at where Marlowe's hand still rested on his knee before returning my gaze to his. "I wasn't alone."

Dariel stiffened and Marlowe moved his hand, reaching for his cup of tea. "Who were you with?"

"How many times have you been to the human lands—to the Wendell Islands—without orders from the Fates, Cousin?" I countered.

"That is entirely different," he said, gripping the arms of the chair.

I tilted my head, taking a leisurely sip of my tea. "And why is that, Dariel? You're not my personal guard."

"And yet," he bit out, "it would be my head the king and queen would have if anything happened to you."

I was vaguely aware of Emeric and Marlowe watching us, but I didn't care. I took another sip of tea, biding my time as I tried to decide whether to tell Dariel the truth. Perhaps if I did, he would admit his own transgressions. My chest tightened as I realised, I needed him to confess. I needed to know I wasn't the only one tempting the wrath of the Fates.

"Who's been bringing you through The Crossing, Pace?" he pressed. "I know it's not Tiesa. If you've involved someone else in this . . . you have no idea how much trouble it could cause."

I set my cup down on the table. "No one's been bringing me through the Crossing. I've been meeting someone here."

Dariel leapt to his feet, his eyes blazing and his wings flaring. "Fated Fates, Pace. Stop playing games! Who is it? Liebe? Jacayal? Milovat?"

"It's not a Cupid."

"What do—" His words halted as his eyes widened in realisation. "A Chaos?"

"Why would you be meeting a Chaos?" Marlowe asked, suspicion heavy in his voice. "I thought you were enemies."

I slid my gaze to him. "Cupids have no enemies. We didn't know the Chaos existed until recently. We had a bit of a misunderstanding."

"A misunderstanding?" Dariel spluttered. "I've never seen you so angry, Pace. I honestly thought you were going to kill that female."

My gut twisted at the thought, my skin suddenly cold. What if I had? What if I'd driven my sword through Sirain's heart? I would have never heard her laugh or seen the way the sun turns her eyes the colour of amethysts. I would never have known what it's like to be truly comfortable with someone—to listen and be listened to without judgement. I would never have lain, content on the beach, pressing feather-light kisses to her neck as I breathed her jasmine-laced scent.

"I think perhaps you two need to talk," Emeric said, getting to his feet and stretching. "Allow me to give you a tour of the gardens, Marlowe. Preparations have already begun for the Summer Festival of Fates."

Marlowe darted a look at Dariel, but my cousin's heated stare was fixed wholly on me.

"Thank you," I muttered as they left the room, closing the door behind them.

"Who is it?" Dariel demanded. "Is it her? The female?"

I sighed, rearranging my wings in an attempt to get

comfortable on the human chair. "How about a trade in information?"

Dariel stared. "Excuse me?"

"Tell me the truth and I'll tell you the truth. You've been coming to the human lands by yourself, without orders from the Fates, haven't you?"

The muscle in his jaw tensed. "Yes."

I almost smiled. My Fate-abiding, straitlaced cousin, breaking the rules. I wondered whether his secret had also been eating him alive.

"Her name is Sirain," I said, a thrill running through me at saying her name to someone else. "You were correct. She's the female who took my feather."

Dariel pulled a hand over his face. "And now you're, what? Friends?"

"She gave me the feather back," I said carefully. "We talked."

"Oh, Pace." Dariel's eyes were wide enough for me to see the whites around his blue irises. "Please tell me that's all you've done."

My skin warmed as my mind conjured images of things that were definitely more than talking. It had been almost a week since the waterfall, and we'd already met there two further times. With preparations underway for the Festival of Fates, it seemed neither of us were able to get away as much as we would have liked. We'd talked at the cliff last night and met briefly on our rocky island the day before, but it wasn't enough. It never felt like enough.

Something must have shown on my face, as Dariel's groan tore me from my thoughts.

"What have you done, Pace?"

"What have *you* done, cousin?" I barked, my patience slipping. "You promised the truth. So, tell me. What's going on between you and the human?"

Dariel flinched. "His name is Marlowe, as you well know."

"Fine. What's going on between you and Marlowe? Are you just friends?"

Something changed in Dariel as he exhaled, slumping in his chair. When he lifted his head, his brows were pinched but his lips were curled in a smile. "I love him, Pace."

"What?" I choked out.

"I love him."

"I heard you the first time," I muttered, my mind reeling. "How? When?"

"I felt it the very first time we met—"

"When his sister put a knife in your shoulder?"

"When he tended to the wound afterwards," Dariel said, giving me a warning look. "I couldn't fight it—the connection. I came back and couldn't stop."

I ran a hand through my hair, my mind still spiralling. I'd suspected something . . . but love? "Does he feel the same way?"

Dariel nodded, his smile tugging at the corner of his mouth. I wanted to hug him and punch him at the same time. I wanted to ask him how he pictured this ending. He couldn't live in the human world and there was no way Marlowe could come to Hehven.

My head snapped up as a thought occurred. "Did you . . .? Your purity?"

"No!" Dariel's vehement response pushed me back in my chair. "How could you think that?"

How could I, indeed. My skin heated as I realised, disobeying the Fates and foregoing the sanctity of being a Cupid appeared to be two entirely different things for my morally skewed cousin.

"And you, Pace?" Dariel asked, his expression wary. "Please tell me you haven't sullied yourself with that Chaos."

I was on my feet, my fists clenched, before I'd formed the response. "Don't."

"All of it?" He shook his head, pulling his hand over his mouth. "Is it all gone?"

My breathing was heavy, my fingers aching from squeezing into my palms so tightly. "Not that it's any of your business, but no."

I could tell he wanted to press the matter, to find out just how far I'd strayed from the path, but he relented.

"You have to end it, Pace," he said gently. "You know that, right?"

A burst of laughter ripped from my throat. "Please tell me you're joking. You're hardly one to talk!"

Dariel's eyebrow arched. "I haven't acted on my feelings physically."

"What does that matter?" I asked. "Do you think your parents are going to allow you to marry a human because you waited until your wedding night to be intimate? You're delusional, Dariel."

It was my cousin's turn to return my bitter laugh. "I don't know who you are anymore."

Trying to calm the erratic pounding in my chest, I stalked over to the window, my fingers gripping the white painted sill. I wasn't sure I knew who I was anymore, either. Closing my eyes, I took a shaky breath. Sirain would know exactly what to say. I could hear her calming tones, her fingers stroking the tension from my shoulders and wings as she put everything into perspective.

"What about Caitland?"

My fingers gripped the windowsill tight enough the wood groaned. "What about her?"

"Have you considered your fiancée's feelings at all while you've been gallivanting with . . ."

"Sirain," I growled. "Her name is Sirain. And of course, I've thought about Caitland."

Dariel shifted in his chair, his feathers rustling. "And?"

I lowered my head, resting it against the cool glass. "I'm going to tell my parents at the Festival next week that I can't marry her."

"What possible reason are you going to give that would allow you to break the engagement?

"I plan on asking them to give me a few more years." The glass fogged as I exhaled. It was only a half lie. "I'm going to tell them I want to focus on training with Dashuri before settling down."

"And what happens in a few years?"

Red tinged the edges of my vision, the muscles in my shoulders coiling. "I could ask the same of you, Dariel. Are you moving to the Wendell Islands or is Marlowe growing a pair of wings?"

The silence that filled the room was as thick as cream, and I struggled to fill my lungs. I knew my words had hurt him, but they were still the truth. Pain was an inevitable side effect of the paths we'd both chosen.

"Do you love her?"

Dariel's cautious question settled around me, stealing what little air I'd managed to take in. Before I could gather my thoughts, a tentative knock sounded at the door.

"Dariel?" Marlowe's voice called from the other side.

I continued to stare out of the window as the humans returned, taking their seats. My cousin's question sat on my chest like a boulder, and I wondered whether I'd made a mistake confiding in him.

"Did you sort out whatever was between you?" Emeric asked.

Dariel sighed. "We're getting there."

I turned around; my attention instantly snagged by Marlowe holding Dariel's hand. Whatever I had been going to say was ripped from my mind, as I shook my head in disbelief. "So, everyone knows about you two?"

"Emeric is hardly everyone," Dariel countered.

"I'll try not to be offended by that," Emeric said, a smile twisting his lips. "I'll admit, I haven't known for very long."

I stared at my cousin. "Longer than me. His flesh and blood."

Dariel barked a laugh. "And when were you going to tell me about Sirain?"

Ignoring him, I found my eyes wandering to their clasped hands once more. What would it be like to sit in a room with my family and friends, Sirain at my side, her hand clasped in mine? I shook the thought from my head.

"I know now might not be the best time," Emeric said, folding a long leg over the other. "But I want you to know that you and your kind are safe here. I promise you. I would be honoured if you and Sirain would pay me a visit one day soon."

I gave him a tight smile, wanting nothing more than to get out of the room. The urge to leap from the window, spread my wings, and let the wind sooth my too-tense muscles was almost too much to bear.

"Will you consider our proposal?" Marlowe asked.

Turning to him, I realised my cousin would spy for the humans whether I consented or not. "I need to think about it."

Marlowe inclined his head. "Of course."

"If you want to stay, Cousin," I said, backing towards the balcony doors, "I understand. But I need to go. I can make my own way back."

The look of disappointment on both my cousin and Marlowe's faces added to the weight on my shoulders.

"No, I'll come," Dariel said. He stood and took both of Marlowe's hands in his. "I'll see you soon."

I nodded at Lord Bickerstaff. "Thank you for your hospitality."

"Any time," he said. "And I meant what I said. You're welcome here any time. The balcony doors are always kept open, and this room is off limits to anyone besides the people in here right now. Don't tell the enemy."

I responded to his wink with a half-smile, wondering how many times my cousin and Marlowe had sought refuge there. Opening the balcony doors, I spread my wings and leapt.

Despite expecting an interrogation on the way back to The Crossing, Dariel didn't say a single word. As we swept through the clouds toward the ocean, I was glad. The arguing inside my head was loud enough for both of us.

26
Sirain

Pressing my lips together, grinning on the inside, it took all my self-control not to twirl in front of the mirror as I assessed my reflection. To the servant weaving the last few black diamond jewels into my long braid, I looked bored. On the rare occasions I was forced to forego my black leathers, I would don a long black dress of light, flowing material. Simple. Barely meeting requirements and irking my parents in the process. However, when the latest selection of servants yet to be dismissed for breathing too loud, or being too anything, brought dresses to my rooms for my approval, I didn't instantly reject them.

Comprising of the softest, lightest silk, two deep purple strands covered my breasts, crossing and tying at my neck. The skirt consisted of two panels, fading from deep purple at my hips to the dark pink of the sunrise before a storm where the hem brushed the floor. A fine, barely there layer of black chiffon drifted from my hips to my feet as though trying to hide the fact that the entire length of my legs was visible with every step. *Pace wouldn't be able to handle this dress*, I thought to myself, almost breaking my pretence at boredom.

"Will there be anything else, Your Majesty?"

I flicked a hand in the servant's general direction, and she backed out of the room, her black wings tucked so tightly they were nothing more than a shadow. The second the door clicked shut behind her, I strode to my dresser and grabbed a dagger from the drawer, strapping it to my thigh. There was no way I was going to attend the Festival of Fates dressed the way I was without visible protection.

Music and laughter were already floating up from the courtyard, the merriment increasing steadily with each passing hour, as wine had been flowing since breakfast for some. Judging from the state of my brother when I'd seen him a couple of hours ago, wine had been his only breakfast. Giving myself a final once over in the mirror, I gave my wings a shake, smiling at how the darker part of my dress matched them perfectly.

For just a moment, I allowed myself to indulge in the fantasy. Walking down into the Festival to where Pace would be waiting. He'd look up and see me and his mouth would fall open, his eyes lighting up in approval. We'd spend the day dancing and laughing, stealing touches and kisses in the shadows. Even as warmth spread, tingling through my body at the thought, my heart tugged, heavy in my chest, at the truth. It would never be more than a fantasy.

Lifting my chin, I straightened my wings. There was no point prolonging the inevitable, steeling myself, I began the long descent from my rooms to the Festival below.

Five minutes after stepping out into the main courtyard, I was ready to stab someone. Usually when I arrived somewhere, people would bow, averting their eyes and halting their conversations. Now, whispers followed me like snakes as I moved towards where my parents were seated on tall carved onyx thrones. Several pairs of eyes lingered in ways they would never normally have dared, causing my fingers to twitch at my thigh, brushing against the handle of my dagger.

"There you are." My mother raised her sharp chin at me, causing her spiked obsidian crown to glint amongst the blue-black hair hanging loose around her shoulders.

I dipped my head. "Mother. Father."

"You look beautiful," my mother said. Her face remained cold and distant, but her midnight blue eyes glinted with the smile she'd never show in public.

My father sniffed, his upper lip curling as he looked at me. "You should know better. You don't want any heirs snapping at your back before you're on the throne yourself."

Shoulders stiffening, a retort formed on my tongue, but my mother laid a slender hand on the king's black sleeve. "Nemir, leave her be. Go have fun, Sirain. Enjoy the Festival."

Dipping another small curtsey, I turned and walked away. It hadn't escaped my attention that Malin hadn't been sitting with them. I hoped she wasn't with Fin because that would lead to nothing good. Ignoring the stares and whispers, I searched the tables clustered with people for Kwellen or Odio. Truth be told, I was a little irked at Kwellen. As my personal guard, he should have been waiting to escort me from my rooms. There would certainly have been fewer whispers with him at my side. I knew why he hadn't been there, though. Ever since things had changed between me and Pace, I'd seen less and less of him. If I wasn't at the cliffs or in the human world, I was in meetings. The only time I saw him or Odio was on the rare occasions I would make it to training.

If Odio was bothered by the significant decrease in time I spent with him, I had no way of knowing. He was a law unto himself. Kwellen, however, had been my closest friend and confidant since I was old enough to fly. Unlike my cousin, he had made his annoyance perfectly clear during training, when he'd almost severed my arm from my body. He was sulking. The thought fanned the flames of annoyance building in my stomach. He should be with me. I shouldn't have to look for him.

Whooping and hollering at a nearby table caused me to stop and turn in time to see a young male launch into the air.

Climbing high, the rest of the table cheered and shouted, and I raised my eyebrows as the male stopped, his wings beating for a second before he dived downwards. It was then I noticed another young male had climbed onto the table, a piece of what looked like cake between his lips. My eyes widened. This was pure stupidity. The diving male approached at speed, back beating his wings to try and slow himself as he opened his mouth to take the cake. I winced as they collided, their companions sprawling as food tipped everywhere, the table in uproar.

"Idiots."

I looked up to find Kwellen standing beside me, his lip curled in a sneer as he surveyed the hysterical group of young males. "Where have you been?"

He turned to me, his dark eyebrow raised. "I could ask you the same question."

I rolled my eyes. "If you were doing your job, you'd know."

"That's not what I meant, and you know—" Kwellen stepped back, staring at me like I'd sprouted a second head. "What are you wearing?"

"It's called a dress."

"Wait," he said, squinting at me. "Have you done something to your face?"

My cheeks burned and I turned away, heading to a quiet table at the edge of the courtyard. When the servant had offered to add a little colour to my cheeks, lips and eyes, I'd let her. "Stop being a jerk."

Kwellen held up his hand, his long legs easily keeping pace with my hurried stride. "Why are you being so sensitive? You look incredible. It's just . . . different."

I slumped down on a bench. "Thanks."

"Can I ask why? Or will you stick that knife in my gut?"

All I could do was shrug. I couldn't give the truth. It had been two days since I'd spoken to Pace at the cliff. I hadn't been able to see him in person for four. It was the longest we'd gone without speaking and it was driving me to distraction. The worst part was, I was worried. We hadn't mentioned his betrothed since we'd started meeting up in the human world, but I certainly hadn't forgotten. As far as I knew, he was still planning on marrying her. My gut twisted at the thought. Sometimes when I was around Pace, I felt so exposed it halted the breath in my lungs. Did he know he held my beating heart in his hand?

My fingernails dug into my palms as I stared out at the crowds of Chaos, raucous laughter drifting on the warm breeze. I'd dressed up for Pace. Even though I knew he'd never see it. I hated myself for it. If there was a way to rip my heart from his hands and lock it back in my chest, I wondered whether I'd take it.

"I miss you."

My head snapped to the large, hairy man beside me. "Excuse me?"

It was his turn to shrug. "I do. Ever since that night on the human's boat, it feels like things have changed. Like you're avoiding me."

"Are you drunk?"

"Sirain." He leaned his arm on the table with a heavy sigh. "Talk to me. Is it because of what happened that night?"

Even sitting, he towered over me, and I stared up at him. The night on the boat when I'd saved Tiesa seemed like a lifetime ago. "What do you mean?"

"I was angry with you for going back. For saving that Cupid." He tucked his long dark hair behind his ear. "It wasn't that I wanted the Cupid to die, it was that I didn't want *you* to die."

"I'm not angry about what happened on the boat," I said carefully.

"What is it, then? Where are you? Sometimes Odio and I try to find you and it's like you've disappeared."

I felt the guilt as it flickered across my face. Too late, I looked away, but not before I saw Kwellen's eyes widen.

"No," he breathed. "Please tell me you haven't been going through The Crossing alone."

"I'm more than capable of looking after myself."

Kwellen leapt to his feet, his dark eyes flashing. "Why would you do that? Do you have any idea how much trouble you'd get in if anyone found out?"

"Do you mean how much trouble *you*'d get in?"

Kwellen snorted. "Sure, the king would put my head on a spike, but if you think he'd let you walk away unpunished, then you're more stupid than I thought."

He was right, of course. My eyes burned at the thought of the pain my father would inflict, both on me and to the people around me, if anyone found out what I had been doing—at the thought of never seeing Pace again.

"Why?" Kwellen asked, sinking back down beside me. "Why have you been going back? Why risk it? If that Cupid saw you—"

"That's not a problem," I interrupted. "The Cupids aren't a threat anymore."

"How could you know that? What did you do?"

The warm air was too hot in my lungs. I needed to get out of there. "Just drop it, Kwellen."

"I swear, if that Cupid lays a finger on you, I'll rip his wings—"

My hand went to my dagger. "Drop. It."

Kwellen's gaze moved from my bared teeth to my fingers clenched around the hilt of my dagger. With the slightest shake of his head, he stood and walked away. I watched until his broad frame was swallowed up by the crowd before I let myself sag against the table.

Perhaps I should have told him. His concern had taken me by surprise, and I wasn't sure what to do with it. Around me, the noise of the Festival seemed to grow, curling in around me until I could feel the mirth like iron manacles around my wrists and ankles. I was fairly certain he wouldn't tell my parents. Closing my eyes, I exhaled slowly, trying to calm my frantic heart as it slammed against my chest. With a final look at the frivolity surrounding me, I stood and spread my wings, heading to the only place I knew I'd be able to breathe.

27
Pace

Wiping my hands on my trousers, I gritted my teeth and stepped through the open doors into the throne room. Outside the palace, the Summer Festival of Fates was in full swing, the heady scent of flowers thick in the air. After my journey to Rakkaus, I couldn't decide if the flicker in my heart was one of hope or fear, and it took all my strength to hold my wings and shoulders up as I approached my parents. The Fates only knew what the repercussions of that visit were and whether it was the cause of the matching pained expressions they wore.

"Pace," my mother said as I stopped in front of the dais, bowing low.

I looked between them, the anger rippling from my father almost palpable. "I assume something of great importance has happened for you to summon me during the Festival? Is everything all right?"

"Lord Rakkaus visited us this morning," the queen said, her hand on my father's as he gripped the arm of his throne with white knuckles.

My stomach dropped into my boots. "Oh?"

"He wishes to call off the engagement."

My heart stopped. "He what?"

A low growl sounded from my father, and he got to his feet, striding to the window. I watched him, my mind working a million miles an hour to figure out what was going on. What had Caitland done? Did they know I'd visited her? I turned to my mother, trying not to wilt under her disappointed gaze.

"He heard the rumours, Pace," she said softly. "He said he was honoured that we considered his family worthy of royal marriage, but he couldn't willingly give his daughter to a Cupid with such questionable morals."

"But I didn't do anything," I croaked, unsure why I was fighting against the result I wanted. "The female confessed."

My mother shook her head, her golden earrings brushing her shoulders at the movement. "Some say there's no smoke without fire, Pace. Lord Rakkaus was not willing to risk it."

"So, what now?" I could hardly breathe, my fingers grasped in a tight knot at my back. My gaze flitted to where my father remained, seething, at the window.

"Your efforts shadowing Dashuri and learning his role have been noted." The queen sighed as she glanced at the king. "With that in mind, your father and I have agreed to give you until your twenty-first birthday to prove that you are responsible enough to choose your own partner."

It was all I could do not to collapse to the floor in relief. Laughter bubbled in my chest, but I coughed it down, dipping into a bow instead. "I won't let you down, Mother. Father."

When I lifted my head, my mother's smile was tight, as though she knew I'd already let them down more than they could ever know.

"Your reputation is in tatters." My father said, looking over his shoulder. "Try not to sound so relieved."

"All rumours, Father," I said, willing a calm I wasn't feeling into my voice. "In time, they will be forgotten."

He huffed in response. "Let us hope so."

I looked to my mother, and she raised a hand, signalling that I was dismissed. Halfway across the throne room, I turned back.

"I truly am sorry for any pain I've caused you," I said. "It was never my intention."

My mother's shoulders dropped slightly. "I know, Pace. We both do."

Casting one final glance at my father, silhouetted against the tall window, I turned and walked away. I made it around two corners before sagging against the wall, sucking in a breath of relief. Caitland must have told her father. She'd known the dishonour would force him to break the engagement. It was a risky move, but it had worked. I leaned my head back, closing my eyes. All I had to do was play my part and perhaps things would be okay. Maybe no one needed to get hurt after all.

At the sound of approaching footsteps I straightened, arranging my clothes and wings, and headed outside into the courtyard. The gathered crowd parted gently before me, and I moved through the tables in a daze, barely seeing the smiling faces and colourful decorations. When I arrived at the outer edges of the gardens, I stopped. The water surrounding the palace was glowing with the golden shimmer brought only by the late afternoon sun.

Shoving my hands in my pockets, I stared at The Crossing in the distance, the lights more purple than usual. Just play my part. I blew out a slow breath, extending my wings and letting the warm breeze ripple between my feathers. The question Dariel had posed at Emeric's manor echoed in my ears. My parents had given me until my twenty-first birthday, but what would happen then? I'd promised not to let them down. That's all I'd been doing for the past few months.

My pulse quickened at the thought of the cause. It had only been a couple of days, but it felt like I hadn't spoken to Sirain in weeks, and the idea of her was all consuming. Every waking hour was spent reliving the moments we'd spent together and the conversations we'd had. My dreams were filled with dark wings and moonlit skin.

Above the steady hum of the Festival, my ears pricked at the sound of wings, and I scanned the skies. A familiar figure headed over the water towards the forests and, casting a quick glance around, I leapt into the air and followed. Whether he heard me coming or just wasn't bothered by being caught, I couldn't be sure, but my cousin didn't show a lick of surprise when I glided to his side.

"Where are you off to?" I asked.

The gold markings on his brow creased as he turned to me. "Don't ask questions you don't want the answers to, Pace."

"Oh, but I do want the answers, Dariel." I took in his smart navy-blue jacket and polished boots. "You're going to see Marlowe, aren't you?"

Dariel's eyes widened.

"There's no one around," I chided. "Answer me."

"Yes. I'm going to see Marlowe. He was telling me how they celebrate the Festival in his lands, and I was curious. So he invited me to see for myself."

"How though?" I huffed in disbelief. "You can't just walk around with your wings."

"Marlowe said he'd organised something."

"Oh, did he?" I shook my head, barely recognising the male flying beside me.

Jealousy coated my tongue and I winced at its bitter taste. Dariel was going to spend the Festival with the person he loved, while I sat around and pretended, living the way others thought my life should look like. It hit me hard—the ache of missing Sirain. Two days was two days too long. What was she doing? Was she enjoying the Festival? I pictured her laughing and dancing and my chest tightened.

Slowing the beating of my wings, I fell behind as I watched

Dariel continue onwards to The Crossing. On the horizon, the sun was lowering between stripes of peach and gold, the soft light gilding everything it touched. It was the slimmest of chances, but I had to take it. Trying not to get my hopes up, I turned and flew to the cliffs.

By the time I landed, the sun was hovering above the horizon, the brightest stars beginning to flicker into existence. I barely took time to catch my breath before I called out, "Thorn?"

"Don't you have somewhere more important to be?"

Relief rippled from me in a chuckle. "You're here."

"I needed some space."

The smile on my face widened. "How about a different space?"

"What do you mean?"

"Can you get away? Will you be missed?"

The silence as she considered her answer seemed to last an eternity, and I pressed my lips together, scuffing at the blue-green grass, to stop myself from hurrying her.

"When?"

"Now."

"Okay."

I exhaled with a smile, lifting my fingers to the ripples of light. "See you soon."

My relief shifted into something else as the glowing curtains of The Crossing swept around me. I tugged at my white tunic, feeling overdressed. At least I wasn't wearing my crown. Fidgeting with the neck of my shirt as I emerged over the darkened waves, I tried to calm my nerves. I wasn't even sure what I was nervous about.

When the fateforsaken pile of rocks came into view, a thrill shot through my chest as I saw that Sirain was already waiting, her wings to me. The sun had dipped below the horizon, leaving the sky a deep sapphire blue, highlighted only by the silver disc of the moon, and as I slowed the beating of my wings to land, she turned.

I wasn't sure what happened first. Whether it was the pang in my chest as my heart faltered, or the stumbling flip of my stomach. Perhaps it was my breath leaving my body entirely or the feeling of floating, even when my feet were firmly on the ground. Either way, I was unable to form words as I stared at her. Her long dark hair was woven with jewels that caught the moonlight, her eyes darker and more striking than usual. Her dress . . . I swallowed, my mouth as dry as a sandbank. Her dress was a masterpiece in temptation. I allowed my gaze to roam over the thin, floaty material, snagging on the soft white curve of her waist and the long length of leg between the splits in the skirt.

"Pace?"

I blinked, my senses swirling as I returned my gaze to hers.

"Are you all right?" she said, taking a step closer, her expression lingering between amusement and concern.

"You look . . ." I shook my head. "There are no words, Sirain."

She smiled, her cheeks colouring. "You don't look so bad yourself."

It was then I realised, I was far too many strides away from her. Folding in my wings, I closed the distance between us, scooping her up into my arms and claiming her lips.

"I've missed you," I said, resting my forehead against hers.

"I missed you too."

She sighed, her breath warm against my skin, and I held her to me, savouring the feeling of having her in my arms. As we stood, neither of us wanting to let go, an idea started to take shape in my head. "I want to take you somewhere."

"Where?"

I entwined her fingers with mine. "How would you like to see how the humans celebrate the Festival of Fates?"

Her dark eyes widened. "Really?"

"You can't expect me to allow you to waste a dress like that on this miserable pile of pebbles," I said, dipping to press a kiss to her bare shoulder. "Do you want to?"

She nodded, her eyes sparkling, and I lifted her hand to my lips.

As we spread our wings and headed into the darkening evening sky, I was more than aware that my plan was barely half an idea, but if it was safe for Dariel to visit Marlowe, surely it would be safe for us too. Either way, I had no plans to engage with the humans. All I wanted was to spend time with Sirain. She dipped a wing, riding an updraft that took her soaring up towards the clouds before swooping back down to the water. I beat my own wings faster to catch up and as she turned to me, her face bright with laughter, I knew the answer to the question Dariel had asked me in Liridona. The truth was, I'd known for a long time.

28
Sirain

I had never seen so many lights. Every window of every house in the Wendell Islands was lit by candles. The main island glowed like fire amidst the archipelago, the cities and villages a burning crown around the dark mountain rising from its centre. Streets were decked with strips of coloured material fluttering like butterflies in the breeze, and tables lined the paths between houses, laden with food and drink as people laughed and danced. The sounds of merriment filled the air, sweeter than honey. A large bonfire lit the centre of the square, and I watched the musicians playing and dancing as revellers in brightly coloured clothes drifted around them. Following Pace towards Marlowe's mansion, the joy was palpable, filling me with every breath.

Pace alighted on the rooftop, holding his hand out to me as I landed beside him. He looked every bit the prince in his fitted white tunic, the gold embroidery at the sleeves and edges matching the shimmer in his hair and wings. My stomach twisted a little at the thought of what had happened the last time we had been on Marlowe's roof. When we'd last stood where we were, Pace's golden eyes had burned with hatred. Looking up at him now, I found they burned with something entirely different.

Pace laced his fingers with mine, lifting his other hand to

my cheek. "I still can't find words that do justice to how you look tonight," he said. "I've never seen anyone more beautiful."

My skin heated at the compliment, and I closed my eyes, turning my head to press a kiss against his palm. How things had changed since we'd met on the cliffs at the Spring Festival. A familiar unease wrapped itself around me as I thought of the Festivals yet to come. Pace would marry his betrothed at the Winter Festival. I should ask. I wanted to ask.

Pace's brow creased as he reached out and tucked wisps of hair that had blown free from my braid behind my ear. "You're frowning. What's wrong?"

Shaking my head, I turned my attention to the bonfire in the square below, watching the amber embers flicker and twist in the pale smoke as it danced into the sky. In a fight, with a sword or dagger—or even my bare hands—I was fearless. I would face down any opponent, male or female, secure in the knowledge the odds of winning were in my favour. When it came to Pace, however, the odds were always stacked against me. He made me weak.

"Tell me," Pace said softly at my ear, his lips brushing my cheek. "You know you can tell me anything, right?"

Before I could change my mind, I turned to him. "Are you getting married?"

Pace's eyebrows shot up, his eyes widening. "Pardon?"

"The female your parents chose for you," I said, forcing strength I didn't feel into the words. "Are you marrying her at the Winter Festival?"

He stared at me, his eyes moving over my face until, finally, he gathered up my hands and pressed them to his chest, over his heart. "What do you think?"

"I think you're the second prince," I said carefully, trying to ignore the steady pounding of his heart beneath my fingers. "And you're duty bound to do what the crown asks of you."

Pace gently squeezed my hands. "The engagement has been called off."

"Oh." My heart stumbled in my chest. "Why?"

A wry smile twisted his lips. "Her father heard rumours that I had questionable morals."

"Oh? And your parents were okay with that?"

"Not really." He shook his head. "But I've been working hard with Dash, so they've said they'll give me until my twenty-first birthday to prove that I'm sensible enough to choose my own partner."

"What happens if they try to force you again?"

"They can try." His expression darkened. "I'll renounce my title. Run away. Something. Anything."

I looked away. "You make it sound so easy."

"What?"

"Escaping duty." The words slipped from my lips before I could think.

"What do you mean?"

"Nothing," I hastened, pasting a smile on my face.

I still hadn't told Pace my title. He hadn't asked, and the longer we spent together, the bigger the omission felt. Every now and again the guilt constricted my lungs. It was selfish of me to keep him when I knew we had an expiration date. My father was healthy, and I couldn't imagine him passing on the throne any time soon, but perhaps that would make it worse. What if we had years together and then had to end things. I winced at the sharpness in my chest. Could I do this for years? Meeting in the human lands? What would happen when the war started? What we had was already so impossible. I stared out at the clusters of humans dancing around the fire below, their carefree laughter carrying on the breeze.

Pace reached out and touched his fingers to my cheek. "What's wrong?"

"How was the Festival in Hehven? Clearly riveting."

His frown wavered at the change of subject before melting into a smile. "Oh, most certainly. I could hardly tear myself away. But then, I pictured you dancing and having fun at your Festival and got rather envious. Although, when I was imagining you, you weren't wearing this, so now I'm even more jealous."

I smiled. "You needn't have worried. I haven't danced at a Festival in a long time."

"In that case." He bowed low, his wings rustling as he extended a hand. "May I have this dance?"

Laughter built in my chest as I dipped a curtsey.

As would be expected from a prince, Pace was an excellent dancer, and as music drifted up from the square below, we made the rooftop our own personal ballroom. We moved around the space, dipping, and spinning, the thin fabric of my skirts wrapping around my legs until I laughed, my body glowing with warmth. Every few minutes, Pace would pull me to him, kissing me deeply. The way he looked at me, his golden eyes gleaming, made my heart feel too large for my body, swelling to the point of pain. There, dancing on a human rooftop, I had never felt so complete—so happy.

Eventually we slowed, sinking down on the edge of the roof to catch our breath and watch the humans as they celebrated. The bonfire was still burning strong, casting an orange glow on everyone and everything around it.

Pace shrugged off his jacket, placing his hand over mine. "Were you honestly worried?"

I kept my eyes on the humans below, watching as they spun each other around in giddy circles. "About what?"

"My betrothal."

I glanced at him out of the corner of my eye. "What do you think?"

"I don't know," he said. "You seemed bothered, but . . ."

"But what?"

He sighed, pushing a fallen lock of snow-white hair from his forehead. "It's hard to read you sometimes."

"I was bothered," I admitted, turning my gaze elsewhere. "Of course, I was. The thought of you with someone else? It made me want to rip the world to shreds with my bare hands."

Pace said nothing, and after a minute, curiosity got the better of me and I turned to find him watching me with a smile on his lips. "What?"

His lips parted with an intake of breath as though about to say something, but then he leaned forward and took my face in his hands, pressing his lips to mine. I reached up and slid my hand across his jaw, sinking my fingers into his hair as he held me. My heart swelled as I ran my hands over him, reacquainting myself with every beautifully perfect inch of his broad chest and shoulders.

Whenever we were apart, I managed to convince myself that it was perfectly fine that there was no feasible future for us. What we had was enough, and when it was over, I'd be okay. Every time I laid eyes on him, however, my heart would cackle at my naivety. I cared about Pace more than I had ever cared about anyone in my entire life and the thought both thrilled and terrified me.

Breaking our kiss too soon, Pace took my hand, his thumb rubbing the small, gentle circles I sometimes retraced when we weren't together. He stared at me with an intensity that caused my toes to curl and my heart to race, and I swallowed, fighting the urge to look away.

"What?" he asked, his words still breathless from our kiss.

I watched the way the firelight lit the flecks of bronze and copper in his eyes for a moment before dropping my gaze to our intertwined fingers. "You shouldn't look at me like that."

"Like what?"

"Like you're not sure whether you want to kiss me or bite me."

Pace laughed, the deep sound vibrating deep in my belly. "Can't it be both?"

I smiled, even though my stomach was turning over on itself. He really shouldn't look at me like that. I didn't deserve it.

"Do you want to know what I'm really thinking when I look at you?" he asked, lifting my hand to his lips. "I'm thinking that you're the first thing I think about in the morning and the last thing I think about before I go to sleep. It physically hurts when I can't see you or hear your voice—when I don't know when I'll see you next. You've seeped into my blood and wrapped yourself around my heart. It beats for you, Sirain. Only you."

"Oh," I breathed.

"Sirain," he rumbled, his thumb brushing my cheek. "I love you."

I stared, unable to take a breath. My heartbeat echoed in my ears. At some point, I realised my mouth was open and I closed it, turning back to the Festival as my cheeks burned.

Pace gently turned my face back to him, pressing a soft kiss to my forehead, then my nose, then my lips. "I'm sorry if that scares you, but it's the truth. And whether you love me too or not, it won't change how I feel about you."

My mouth dry, all I could do was nod as he wrapped an arm around my shoulders and pulled me to him. I wanted to tell him. I wanted to tell him that I'd never cared about anyone as much as I cared about him—that when I was with him, it was the only time I felt like who I was supposed to be. I'd never loved anything or anyone before, but when I was with him, it felt like my heart would burst. I wanted what we had, always, and it scared me to death.

"I think I do love you," I whispered against his chest. He stiffened at my words, his fingers gripping a little tighter. "I just wasn't expecting it to hurt so much."

Pace huffed a laugh as he pressed a kiss to my hair. "Yeah. Me either."

I lifted my head to look at him, and he closed what little space remained between us. It was a gentle kiss—smiling lips, and soft caresses—until it wasn't. My fingers made quick work of his buttoned tunic, sliding across the smooth skin and muscle beneath, as his hands ran the length of my bare legs, gripping my thighs. I wasn't sure I had ever wanted anything more than I wanted Pace in that moment.

Breathless, he pulled back, his eyes searching. "You're cold."

"I'm not."

"Sirain, you're shivering."

It was only then, as the evening breeze tossed at the tangled layers of my dress, I realised how much the temperature had dropped.

"Do you trust me?" Pace asked.

I raised my eyebrows, remembering when I had asked him the same, and didn't hesitate in my response. "Yes."

"Wait here."

Pace got to his feet and after a quick glance around, he spread his wings and flew over the back of the mansion, out of sight. I exhaled. *He loved me.* The sharpest blade in Helle wouldn't have been able to scrape the grin from my face. After barely a minute, I turned at the sound of wings to find Pace landing beside me, mischief flashing in his pale eyes. He held out his hand to me and I took it.

"Where are we going?" I asked.

He threw a smile over his shoulder, leading me toward the back of the mansion, and we dipped, following the row of windows along the top floor. Just as the rest of the city, every window was lit with a candle and Pace came to a stop at one of them, prising the shutters open. I watched as he lifted the candle with one hand, using the other to steady himself as he climbed in through the narrow frame, tucking his wings in tight. Once he was in, he held his hand out to me and I climbed down into the room.

As Pace placed the candle back on the window ledge, pulling the window closed, I turned a slow circle, taking in my surroundings. There wasn't much inside the room. A mahogany dresser, an oversized mirror with a gold frame, and a large bed made from ornately carved dark wood.

"What are we doing?" I whispered. "We don't know whose room this is."

Pace picked up a chair by the dresser and carried it to the door, wedging it under the handle. "It's a guest room," he explained. "This place is enormous; I knew not all the rooms would be used."

"What if someone comes?"

"That's what the chair is for."

"Oh."

I stood, suddenly unsure what to do with my limbs as Pace drank me in, his gaze travelling slowly over the length of my body. His shirt was still unfastened, half untucked, revealing the quickening rise and fall of his toned chest.

His eyes met mine. "Come here."

My stomach swapped places with my heart at the command, my pulse flickering across my skin as I walked toward him. As soon as I was within reach, he took hold of my hand and pulled me against his chest, crashing his mouth against mine. I breathed him in, his heady mix of sunshine and sea salt coaxing a moan from me as I wrenched the shirt from his shoulders. My fingers marvelled as they traced his dips and grooves, my own skin burning under his feather-light caress.

"Sirain," he ground out, his lips tracing my jaw. "I want you."

"You have me."

"I want all of you." Pace swallowed, and I tracked the movement, watching as his throat bobbed.

When I raised my gaze to his, my mouth ran dry at the

desire blazing in his golden eyes. "I want you too, but if we cross that line . . . Your purity . . ."

He took my face in his hands. "Sirain, I love you. There isn't a line that exists that I wouldn't cross for you. For us."

"Are you sure?" I whispered.

In answer, he kissed me again. Every tug of his lips, every touch of his tongue conveyed a message, louder than if he'd shouted it from the rooftop. *I love you*. Pace's fingers found the clasp at my neck and my dress fell away, pooling at my feet. A soft sound fell from his lips, and I rose on my toes to catch it with my mouth as my fingers made short work of shedding the remaining barriers between us. My head spun as we stumbled backwards to the bed, my blood roaring with desire. It was loud enough to drown out the tiny voice in the back of my head. Pace was giving everything to me. Everything. And I hadn't told him who I was. If I was a better female, I might have stopped, but the feel of him against me was too much. By choosing me, Pace had set fire to his life, and now I was burning in the flames. It would be fine. We would be fine. He loved me. And I loved him.

We melted into each other, a glorious symphony of skin, until there was nothing between us but promises and wishes and hope. Shattering into a million diamond shards under Pace's gentle reverence, I marvelled at the beautiful agony that swelled in my heart at feeling something so deeply and thoroughly. Pace pulled me to him, his strong arms wrapping around my waist, under my wings, as though he never planned to let go. And as I lay there against him, pressing kisses to his heaving chest and cocooned between soft white and black feathers, I hoped he never did.

29
Pace

I imagined it was the closest feeling to drowning. When we were apart it was harder to breathe—the desire to see her, touch her, pressing heavy and suffocating on my chest. When we were together, it was a different type of drowning. Then, I gave myself willingly, letting her presence fill my lungs, pulling me under into blissful oblivion.

Water cascaded over Sirain's creamy skin like precious jewels in the dim light of the cavern as she cried out my name, the echoes lingering amidst the dark rocks. Pulling her to me, I buried my face in her neck, my brain scrambling for ways to have this always—to have *her* always.

At Marlowe's mansion, we'd fallen asleep in each other's arms, and I would have gladly given a wing to wake up with her again. I'd thanked the Fates that no one had tried to come into the room, and we'd left through the window as soon as we could bring ourselves to untangle.

In the month since the Festival, I'd only managed to visit the human world a handful of times, and it wasn't enough. Not by a long shot. Dashuri was taking his role as my mentor as seriously as one would expect, which meant I barely had a second to myself.

"I've missed you so much," I groaned against her skin.

Sirain ran her fingers through my soaking wet hair, sending trickles of water down my neck as she tugged at my earlobe with her teeth. "I thought it would get easier," she murmured "but I swear it's getting harder."

I heaved a sigh and she wriggled out of my arms, floating in the dark waters of the pool. From the lack of light filtering through the deafening waterfall, I suspected that if the sun hadn't set, it would soon.

I hadn't mentioned the Festival to Dariel, and it was strange to think that he'd been there somewhere with Marlowe. Ever since we'd unearthed each other's secrets, things had been strained. Which was why it had been such a surprise when he'd cornered me at the training rooms.

I moved across the pool to where Sirain lay with her eyes closed, her hair merging with the dark water. "We've been invited to Liridona."

She opened an eye. "We?"

"Yes. We. Emeric extended an invitation to us both a while ago, but I forgot. Now, he's formally invited us to an event, via Dariel."

Sirain opened both eyes, fixing me with her dark stare. "Why? How does he know about me?"

I opened and closed my mouth as I realised I hadn't told her what had happened with Dariel the last time I'd visited.

"I'm sorry. I told Emeric what we'd seen at Dalibor and what had happened at Newbold. I didn't mention you, but Dariel kept pushing about me going by myself and I said I hadn't." Sirain had gone completely still, the water resting up to her chin as she watched me. I took a deep breath before continuing. "Emeric was there when Dariel figured out I'd been meeting with a Chaos."

Despite the roaring of the waterfall, the silence was deafening. Eventually Sirain turned and pulled herself out of the water. I watched, hardly daring to breathe as she wrung the water from her hair and pulled a towel from the leather satchel she'd brought.

"Sirain—"

"Do you trust him?"

"Yes. I do. With my life."

She towelled her hair, shaking the water from her wings. "You want me to come."

Frowning at the statement, I made my way to the edge of the pool and pulled myself out. I reached for Sirain, but she threw the towel at me instead. Accepting it with a sigh, I dried the water from my skin.

"I do want you to come. I want to spend time with you, and Dariel will be there." I paused, watching her carefully. "I'd really like you to meet him. Properly."

"What about your other friend? Tiesa?"

Guilt slammed into my stomach, and I winced. I'd barely seen Tiesa over the last couple of months. I couldn't remember a time before my fiercely opinionated friend—she'd always been a part of my life. Ever since that first trip to the human world however, a crack had formed in our friendship. Tiesa had always had strong opinions, quick to question Dariel and I even as smallwings. We'd always laughed her off with eye rolls. It was just the way she was. The crack was now a gaping ravine. I didn't want her opinions. I couldn't shrug off the way she held the word of the Fates above all else. Her righteousness was now a towering wall between us, and I couldn't see a way to tear it down.

"No," I admitted. "She won't be there."

Sirain raised an eyebrow, but I kept my face impassive. I didn't want to get into what was going on between Marlowe and Dariel. Discussing how completely hopeless whatever they had between them was would only serve to highlight the flaw in our own relationship.

"Fine." Sirain stepped to me, taking the towel and throwing it down on top of her bag. "I'll come. But if the humans try to capture us, don't expect me to save you. I'm using you as a distraction."

I was fairly certain she was joking, but I closed the distance between us, taking her face in my hands. "I would die before I let anything happen to you, Sirain."

"Let's hope it doesn't come to that, then," she said, rising onto her toes and pressing her lips against mine.

"Do you want to tell me what, in the name of all that's Fated, is going on?" Sirain asked, slowing the beating of her wings.

I shook my head, my eyes wide as I took in the sight below us. "I have no idea. No one said anything."

Music spilled through the open front doors of Emeric's manor, mixing with the steady roar of the enormous fountain, as we drew closer. The winding path was filled with people—humans—walking in groups, talking and laughing . . . with wings. Every human had a large pair of wings strapped to their back. Most were either black or white, but I could see some in almost every conceivable colour. They varied in size—some barely large enough to count, and others almost as large as my own.

As I passed high above the courtyard, circling around to the balcony Dariel had entered through last time, the courtyard fountain caught my eye. I hadn't noticed the last time, but the marble figures were winged, shooting spurts of water into tumbling arches from the arrows primed in their carved stone bows. I frowned.

The balcony doors were unlocked, just as Emeric had promised, the room beyond empty. Sirain followed me in, her hand lingering over the dagger at her thigh as she took in the space. She wasn't wearing her typical leathers. I knew she'd say it was because it was too hot, but there was a slight nervousness to her demeanour that told me the sleeveless, dark purple blouse and carefully braided hair were more to do with meeting Dariel than the temperature. A smile curved my lips as I watched her poke a delicate figurine.

"So, is your cousin here?" she asked.

"I don't know."

Sirain turned to look at me, a wry smile curling her lips. "Is there anything you *do* know?"

"Oh, there's a lot I know," I said, stalking towards her. "I know you look stunning. I know I love you. And I'm fairly certain there will be a lot of empty rooms around here somewhere."

"This one's empty," she murmured.

A rumble sounded in my throat as I crowded her against the wall, dipping my head to press a kiss to her neck. "What if someone comes in?"

Sirain reached up and unfastened the top button on my shirt. "Then they'll get an eye full."

I chuckled, and pressed against her, coaxing a whimper from her lips. A cackle of laughter sounded right outside the door, and we jumped apart, weapons half drawn. Whoever it was continued down the hall, oblivious to the presence of two, armed, winged beings on the other side of the door. Sirain slipped out from between my arms and crossed the room, her hand reaching for the ornate gold handle on the door.

"What are you doing?" I hissed.

She ignored me, pushing down the handle and opening the door a fraction. I cursed under my breath, edging towards her as she peered through the gap. Voices sounded outside, the music louder.

"They're everywhere," she whispered.

"Emeric should come at some point," I said. "He's expecting us."

"Why don't we go and find him?"

I reached out and pushed the door closed, my eyes wide. "Have you lost your mind?"

"Everyone is wearing wings," she said. "We'll blend right in."

"There's a pretty big difference between the chicken feathers and glue the humans have strapped to their backs and our wings," I said, extending my own in emphasis. "Do you really think they won't notice that ours are real?"

She shrugged, moving to open the door again. "Only one way to find out."

"Sirain," I hissed, grasping her hand in mine. "You were the one who was worried about the humans capturing us, and now you want to just walk freely into a crowd of them?"

In answer, Sirain rose on her toes and pressed a kiss to my lips. "You said you'd die before you let anything happen to me, so it looks like you're coming too."

Before I could reply, Sirain heaved the door open and stepped out into the hallway.

"Come on," she said, reaching for my hand.

My breath was a solid mass in my lungs as I followed her, pulling the door closed behind me. The brightly decorated corridor was a slap in the face after the pale pastels and golds of the room we'd entered. Dark blue and red striped wallpaper adorned the walls, contrasting with the thick gold carpet muffling our steps. If Sirain was nervous it didn't show, as she strode down the corridor, her dark wings tucked in tight.

Laughter rumbled towards us, and I reached out and placed a hand on Sirain's shoulder. "I think we should go back and wait for Emeric."

Sirain looked at me, her amethyst eyes glinting. "Scared?"

"No."

“Look. If they look like trouble, we kill them.”

My eyes widened. “What?”

“I’m joking.”

Before I could respond, two human men rounded the corner. They looked to be in their fifties or sixties, wearing large white wings covered in silver glitter. I froze, my fingers tensed, ready to draw my weapon should the need arise.

“Look. At. Your. Wings!” one of the humans exclaimed, clasping his hands together.

My hand closed around the pommel of my sword.

“They’re stunning,” the other human agreed. “Who made them for you? That has to be Emilo’s work.”

“Oh, definitely. He’s always booked up a year in advance though.” He stepped forward, his hand lifting. “May I—”

I turned slightly, angling my wings away from him. “I’d rather you didn’t.”

“Of course,” the human dipped his head in apology. “They must have cost a small fortune. Enjoy Plumataria!”

Their gazes lingered as they continued down the corridor, and I tried not to move my wings until they were out of sight.

“Plumataria?” I muttered.

“Do you see?” Sirain grinned. “The idea of us having actual wings is too much to cope with. It’s easier to believe they’re some fancy expensive ones.”

I blew out a slow breath. “A couple of humans up here is very different to a room filled with them.”

“What are you scared of?” Sirain asked, taking my hand in hers.

“I’m scared of something bad happening. You should be too.”

Sirain brought my hand to her lips, kissing my fingers. “Something could always happen, but if Emeric is as trustworthy as you believe, he won’t let it.”

I rolled my neck, trying to ease some of the tension that had built there. "I just have a bad feeling."

"Imagine, Pace. We can be us. You and me. In a room filled with people." She squeezed my hands. "When will we ever get this chance again?"

Her words caused a myriad of emotions to rise and fall in my chest. The thought of being able to spend time with Sirain like an ordinary couple at a party was undeniably tempting. At the same time, however, her words of hope only served to remind me that we would never be a normal couple. Try as I might, I couldn't see a way in which our lives wouldn't consist of stolen moments and neutral territory.

Pushing the thought away, I smiled down at Sirain. "Okay."

Fate will find a way.

~Virgil

30
Sirain

A sweeping staircase led to the party below. The bannister was shining gold, as seemed to be Emeric's preference, but what snagged my attention were the delicately carved feathers that formed the balusters beneath. What was it with the leader of Dalibor and feathers? I'd noticed the elaborate fountain in the courtyard too. Pace squeezed my hand and I looked up at him in question, but his attention was fixed on the heaving crowd at the bottom of the stairs. Staring at the strong lines of his jaw and the plump curve of his lips, my heart fluttered. It always did. I let my gaze take in the way his hair curled around his ears, so white against the rich copper of his skin and realised I'd expected my reaction to fade with time. It hadn't. Perhaps if we were able to see each other every day, my heart wouldn't react with such aching severity. That would never be the case, though. No such future existed.

There were six days remaining until my twentieth birthday, and my father had informed me yesterday that the Fates had deemed my Royal Rites begin four days before. My shoulders tensed, my spine straightening as my father's words crashed in around me. Four days, four Rites. The Rites would demonstrate my ability to rule Helle and prove my faithfulness to the Fates, who would decide each task. I'd asked my father what his Rites had consisted of, but he'd sneered down his nose at me and ordered me to go and train with Kwellen. I wasn't worried about the Royal Rites. I was worried that once complete, it would be nearly impossible to sneak through The Crossing. My chest ached as though ten warriors rested on it.

"Do you want to dance?" Pace asked.

I blinked, completely unaware that we'd reached the bottom of the staircase and were now standing amidst the heaving throng of winged humans. Although it was clear they didn't suspect our wings were real, their eyes and attention lingered in the way the two humans upstairs had.

"Perhaps a drink first?" I suggested, nodding towards the heavily laden tables set up around the outside of the room.

Never letting go of my hand, Pace led me through the crowd. The large entry hall was packed with people, a band of musicians playing on a raised platform beside the stairs. It seemed there was a ballroom through a large open doorway to my left, the flow of people between the two rooms a steady river of laughter and feathers. Tables dressed in white cloth and adorned with bunches of black and white silk lined the edge of the room, with towers of delicate glasses at their centre and overflowing bowls of fruit and food that looked different to any I'd ever seen before covering the surface.

It was a peculiar sensation being in a crowd with Pace. As we moved through the throng, I tried not to think about what Kwellen or Odio would say if they knew I was in a room filled with humans, with only a dagger at my thigh. I definitely didn't allow myself to think about what my father or Fin would say. A shudder snaked its way down my spine.

"Are you okay?" Pace asked, handing me a glass of what looked like sparkling wine.

I sniffed at it, the bubbles tickling my nose. "Yes. It just feels strange."

Pace slid his arm around my waist, pulling me to his chest, and kissed me deeply. My head spun as I melted against him, intoxicated by his warmth and the scent of summer. That's what Pace smelled like. Beaches, sunshine, and blue skies. He smelled of freedom.

"What was that for?" I asked when he finally pulled back.

He smiled. "Do I need a reason to kiss you?"

I leaned against him, the happiness in my heart almost eclipsing the shadow of hopelessness that lingered there.

"Pace!"

Our hands flew to our weapons as the crowd parted, allowing a tall, loping figure through. Dressed in an elaborate black frock coat adorned with gold brocade, his black wings were almost as large as mine. Stopping in front of us, his eyes bright as he smiled, he dipped into a bow.

"I'm honoured you chose to grace us with your presence." He lifted his head, a strange look flickering across his face as he turned to me. "Sirain, I presume? Emeric Bickerstaff at your service. It's an honour to meet you properly."

I gave him a tight smile in return. "Thank you for the invitation."

He turned, standing beside me as he gazed out at the festivities. "I hoped you'd sense my intentions. Today you are free to wander as anyone else."

"Why, though?" I asked. "What is this?"

Emeric glanced at me, a crease appearing between his brows. "I started Plumataria almost twenty-five years ago. One month after the Summer Festival of Fates, Liridona celebrates angels and demons alike, with no purpose other than joy and frivolity. No sacrifices, no offerings. Just fun."

"Sounds like something Helle would enjoy." I turned to Pace. "I can only imagine how appalled you are by the idea."

He raised his eyebrows, attempting a stern look, although his mouth twitched at the corners. "There's nothing wrong with requiring a purpose for celebration."

Emeric reached for a glass from the table and gestured to the room. "Ah, but there is a purpose. Fun!"

I couldn't help but smile as the music changed to a livelier tune, and the humans whooped and hollered in delight. The Liridonan leader's laid back attitude was infectious, and I was struck by the same strange sense of familiarity I'd had when I'd seen him on Marlowe's ship. I wasn't sure why, but I couldn't shake the unease at the tip of my spine.

"Is my cousin here?" Pace asked.

Emeric shook his head. "He's travelling by boat from the Wendell Islands, so won't be here until later. I told them to come yesterday and stay the night, but they declined my offer."

I frowned, looking between Emeric and Pace. Why would a Cupid be travelling by boat? I opened my mouth to ask, but Emeric turned, taking my hands in his.

"I'm so glad you came, Sirain," he said. "I would very much like to talk to you later, if you would allow it?"

"Sure," I said, unable to think of a reason to refuse.

He gave my hands a gentle squeeze before stepping back and dipping a small bow. "I must go and circulate with my guests, but I will find you later."

I watched him disappear into the heaving mass of bodies and wings, an anxious feeling prickling my stomach.

"I told you he was nice," Pace said.

I hummed my answer, the niggling feeling causing my feathers to twitch as I sipped my drink. Growing up in a land where people hid their true intentions had enabled me to spot a lie a mile away. Emeric was hiding something—I was sure of it—and there was no way I was going to be able to relax and enjoy myself until I had some answers.

Handing my almost empty glass to Pace, I kissed his cheek. "I'll be back in a minute."

"What? Where are you going?"

I raised my eyebrows. "Where do you think?"

Understanding flickered in his eyes and he coughed. "Oh. Will you be okay?"

"I'm going to the bathroom, not slaying a dragon. I think I'll be fine."

Pace rolled his eyes, giving my hand a gentle squeeze. "I'll wait here, so you can find me."

I laughed. "I think I'll be able to spot the only tall handsome male with white hair. And even if you were sitting down, I'd just have to follow the trail of whispering women."

He frowned. "Don't think I haven't been giving warning looks to every man who's looked at you for more than a second."

"Oh?"

"This is the downside of having to share you with other people," he said, pulling me to him and sliding a hand into my hair. "It's bringing out a very dangerous side of me."

Warmth coiled in my stomach at his rumbling tone. "Oh, really?"

Pace trailed kisses along my jaw, his teeth tugging on my earlobe. "When you get back, why don't we explore and find somewhere quiet?"

My blood pulsed, my limbs tingling in anticipation. "Sounds like a plan."

It took more willpower than expected to walk away from him, but I did. Something about Emeric was off. I couldn't place the flicker of emotion that had crossed his face when he spoke to me. I'd thought at first it might have been fear, seeing as how the first time we'd met had been during the storm. It wasn't, though. It looked like sadness—regret. What would the leader of Liridona have to regret? My blood roared in my ears as I turned down a quiet hallway. Regret looked a lot like guilt. Guilt was worrying. What if this was a trap after all? My steps slowed as I wondered for a second whether I should have confided in Pace. I didn't like leaving him out there alone, but I knew he would have tried to deter me. He was blind when it came to the humans—his Cupid innocence painting them in a rosy glow.

I tried fifteen doors before I found one that was locked. The manor was enormous, and I knew Pace would be getting worried and coming to look for me at any second. Stepping back, I sneered at the gold feathers decorating the painted double doors. I knew in my gut this was an important room, and sliding my dagger from its sheath, I angled it between the crack. Wedging the blade against the bolt, I levered my weight against it until it slid back, the door creaking slightly. I moved quickly, angling the knife, and manoeuvring the lock free.

Slipping inside, I closed the doors as much as I could, the protruding bolt stopping them from closing completely. I didn't care. It could be any one of the hundreds of guests Emeric had invited into his home that had broken in. I had to move fast; I was already on borrowed time. The room was almost certainly Emeric's office and I sighed in relief. I had wondered whether he might have chosen a room on an upper floor, but had hoped that for the sake of meetings, it would be downstairs.

A large pair of gilded wings hung over a large white fireplace, and I blew out a slow breath. The obsession the human had with wings was worrying. I turned to the sprawling wooden desk beside the window and started opening drawers. What I was looking for, I had no idea. There were papers, filled with human scribble I couldn't decipher, but nothing that called to me. My blood hummed in my veins. It was as though something in the room was reaching out to me—taunting me. I turned in a slow circle, taking in the paintings on the walls for the first time. Each and every one depicted winged beings. I stepped closer to one, the uneasy feeling in my gut intensifying. The beings had black wings. *Chaos wings*. Their faces weren't those of the demons the humans believed us to be. They were dark haired and beautiful. I swallowed.

Moving to the fireplace, my attention snagged on an unusually shaped frame. Long and slender, it rested beneath the giant golden wings that had accosted me upon entering. The frame was gold, as all the others, but slimmer and more delicate. The pounding of my heart was booming thunder as I moved close enough to see what was encased within it. It wasn't a painting. It was a feather. A single, long, black feather. It wasn't entirely black though. A vein of cerulean ran through the vane. Nausea rose in my throat, and I stumbled backwards. I knew that feather. I'd stared at feathers identical to it my entire life. I reached for the frame with trembling fingers.

"Sirain?"

I whirled to find Emeric standing by the doors, a pained expression on his face. "What is this?" I demanded, holding out the framed feather.

"This is what I wanted to talk to you about," he said, heaving a heavy sigh. "Perhaps you would like to sit?"

Even though my legs felt as though they might give way at any moment, I straightened my spine and shook my head. "Tell me. Why do you have a Chaos feather? Why do you have *my mother's* feather?"

Emeric pushed a hand through his greying hair, stepping further into the room. "I met your mother twenty-six years ago."

"Impossible."

He arched an eyebrow. "How so?"

"My mother hasn't travelled to the human world."

"Did she tell you that?"

I faltered. She'd hadn't. "She wouldn't . . ."

Emeric stepped closer, a sad smile on his lips. "Just as you wouldn't? Your parents don't know you come to our world, do they? She was curious, just like you. Rebellious."

"It's not possible," I mumbled; the human's words reaching me as if through a thickening fog.

"I suspected you were her daughter as soon as I saw you. You look just like her." He moved closer until he was right in front of me. "I always wondered . . ."

My hand reached for the fireplace, steadying myself. This wasn't possible. "Why do you have her feather?"

"Are you sure you don't want to sit down? No? Okay." He sighed. "Your mother gave me the feather."

A cold, cruel laugh burst from my lips. "Why would she do that?"

"Because we were in love."

The world dropped away at my feet, and I clutched at the mantelpiece. "No."

"It's true. We were friends at first, but then we fell in love. It was for her that I created Plumataria. It was one day a year where we could be together like any other couple."

I clutched at my stomach, his words bearing down on me like boulders.

"When the queen of Helle arranged her betrothal to Crown Prince Nemir. Briga was devastated." Emeric sighed; his face etched with pain. "The night she told me was the last time I saw her."

I shook my aching head. "This doesn't make any sense."

"Let me show you something."

Emeric strode across the room to a pair of black velvet curtains. He pulled on a thick golden rope at the side, and they drew back to reveal a painting. Thoughts swirled like mist in my mind, just out of grasp, as I stumbled toward the lifelike portrait. It showed a young couple, clearly very much in love. There was no denying that one of them was my mother. Her blue-black hair hung loose down her back, her wings painted to perfection behind her as she gazed up at the man holding her hands to his chest. The man was handsome, with thick hair that hung to his shoulders, a violet tint to the dark waves. It must have been at Plumataria, as he also sported a pair of black wings—wings I recognised as the very ones Emeric wore beside me. It was true. My mother and this human . . . I stared up at the painting, marvelling at how young they both looked. Emeric's eyes were bright in the painting, almost purple in colour.

I turned to him, noticing for the first time the amethyst colour of his irises. My feet staggered backwards, my head shaking. "No."

That look of sadness I had glimpsed before flashed across his face. "Sirain—"

"No," I said. "Don't say it."

"I think I might be your father."

I half ran, half flew from the room, the endless hallways causing my head to spin. A large window called to me, and I sprinted towards it. I couldn't hear myself think. The world was closing in on me, crushing against my chest. My eyes burning, I heaved the window open and climbed out, soaring up into the air. The wind filled my lungs, and I closed my eyes as I climbed higher.

It was only when I was over the vast expanse of heaving sea, that I realised I still had the framed feather clutched in my hand. *Pace.* I shook my head, tears streaming down my face. Emeric would tell him I'd left, but without making plans, I had no idea when I would see him again. A sob of anger ripped from my throat. I wasn't sure who I was angrier with, the human, or my mother. He couldn't be my father. It was impossible. Trembling with rage, I flew faster, desperate to reach The Crossing. I needed to speak to the queen.

31
Pace

A growl tore from my throat as I slammed my hand against the wall. Turning on my heel, I resumed my pacing, clenching and unclenching my fists—my house feeling too small to contain my frustration. Emeric had refused to tell me what he'd said to make Sirain leave without saying goodbye—told me it wasn't his secret to share. *What did that even mean?* I'd left immediately, trying to catch up to her, but there was no sign. I had tried the cliffs, but she wasn't there either.

A tentative knock sounded at my door, and I scowled. "Who is it?"

"Tiesa."

My anger quelled as though doused with water, and an all too familiar guilt spiralled like smoke from the extinguished flames. "Come in."

She looked different. How long had it been since I'd seen her? Tentatively, she stepped into the room, closing the door behind her. "Are you okay?"

I shrugged. "Sure."

"Pace." She shook her head. "I miss you. I don't know if it's something I did, or something I said . . . I know I wasn't as understanding as I could have been about Caitland, but I'm sorry. I . . ."

I stared at her, wondering how I could explain the void that was steadily increasing between us without upsetting her. "You didn't do anything," I lied, sinking down onto a chair, my wings like lead weights at my back. "I'm sorry I haven't been around. I've been a terrible friend."

"I'm not going to argue with that."

I snorted, giving her a sideways look. "You look different."

"I cut my hair."

Sitting up, I looked at her properly. She had. Her snow-white hair had trailed in braids almost down to her waist, but now it rested against her shoulders. "It looks nice."

"Pace, where have you been?"

I gestured for her to take a seat, my jaw clenched as I wondered whether I should tell her. I owed her the truth. Almost twenty years of friendship deserved honesty. A deep sigh built in my chest. There was just so much.

"Do you remember what happened on the ship?" I asked.

"Yes," she said, settling into a chair opposite. "That Chaos female said something about roses, and you flipped."

I huffed a laugh. "Yeah, well. It's a long story, but I'd been talking to a Chaos through The Crossing. Don't ask me how. I have no idea. I didn't realise it was her. The chances . . ." I shook my head. "I thought she'd lied to me. Tricked me. So, I arranged to meet her in the human world, to have it out once and for all."

Tiesa's eyes widened, her gold markings creasing. "What did you do? Did you kill her? Oh Pace—"

"I didn't kill her." I smiled in spite of myself. "I fell in love with her."

"You *what*?"

"I fell in love with her," I repeated, forcing myself to meet her horrified gaze. "I've been meeting her as often as I can in the human world."

Tiesa clasped her hands to her mouth. "You didn't. You can't. If your parents found out . . . If Dashuri found out . . . Oh, Pace. How could you?"

The embers of my doused anger sparked. "This is exactly why I didn't tell you. Everything is so black and white for you, but it's not. It's not that simple."

"It's exactly that simple," Tiesa snapped. "You can't fall in love with a Chaos. What about Caitland?"

"The wedding was called off," I said. "You know that."

"Postponed, Pace. The wedding is postponed. If not Caitland, they'll still expect you to marry a Cupid in a couple of years. What will happen then?"

Flames ignited in my gut, my fingers clenching. "I'll cross that bridge when I come to it."

"What about the humans?" Tiesa said, getting to her feet. "Are you still planning on helping them? What does Dariel say about this?"

I stared up at her. I wouldn't tell her about him and Marlowe. That was up to him. Tiesa stared at my face, reading my expression—the set of my jaw.

"He knows," she said. "He knows about you and the Chaos. I was right, wasn't I? There's something between him and that human, isn't there?"

I said nothing. I wasn't going to feed her lies, but it was clear she was spiralling and anything I could say would only make it worse.

She shook her head in disbelief, her white hair swaying. "You've both been visiting the human lands without me, haven't you?"

"Tiesa—"

"Are you helping the humans? Are you sneaking them arrows?"

I got to my feet, taking hold of her arms. "Tiesa. We're not stealing any arrows."

"But you're helping the humans."

It wasn't a question.

"Tiesa." I sighed. "It's complicated. War is coming to the human world. Hundreds of thousands of lives will be lost. If I can do something—anything—to prevent that, I have to."

"No. You don't. The Fates have already decided what will be."

A laugh of disbelief shook my shoulders. "And if the Fates have decided to allow the murder of innocent children, we just have to be all right with that?"

"Yes!" Tiesa snapped. "How are you doubting this? Our entire existence is built on the Fates. Cupids exist to serve the Fates. Chaos too. If you choose to ignore them—to go against them—you're denying your entire reason for being."

"This is pointless." I turned around, pushing my fingers through my hair. "We're not going against the Fates or ignoring them. We're gathering information for the humans. That's all."

"And you honestly think that's not interfering with Fate?"

I shook my head, hating the disappointment in her voice. "Maybe this is Fate. Maybe us helping is Fated."

"And you with your Chaos female? Is that Fated also?"

I stared at my friend, the wall between us almost tangible. "Are you going to tell my parents? Dash?"

"Do you really think I'd do that?"

"I don't know, Tiesa. If everything is as black and white as you say it is, perhaps that's your only choice."

She shook her head. "You're my best friend, Pace. I might disagree with what you're doing, but I'd never betray your trust."

The familiarity of her words echoed painfully in my chest. She hadn't told my parents about the tournaments. The spacing. Even though it went against everything she stood for, she had never once betrayed my trust. The same could not be said for me. I'd doubted her friendship, even when she had given me no reason to. Why? Because I didn't want to hear her words of caution? I'd blamed Tiesa for the wall between us, but now I realised, it had been built by my hands alone.

"I'm sorry, Tiesa. I should have told you." I groaned, pressing my fingers to my eyes. "I just knew how you'd react—what you'd say—and I'm already aware how impossible it is. Not a second goes by that I don't think about it."

She stepped closer, the furrow between her brows folding her golden Hand markings. "You need to end it."

I frowned. "End what?"

"Everything. Whatever is going on with the Chaos. The deal you and Dariel have with the humans. It needs to stop. It's not too late to put things right before you anger the Fates."

"No." I backed away from her. "This isn't something I can just stop, Tiesa. I love her."

"Surely you can see it has no future, though, Pace. I mean, you don't even live on the same side of The Crossing. What will you do? Only see each other in the human world for the rest of your lives? You won't be able to keep it a secret forever."

Even though I'd thought the same words myself a thousand times, they stung coming from Tiesa's lips. "I don't need you to point out how hopeless it is. I'm well aware of that myself. I haven't figured it out yet, but I will."

Tiesa stared up at me. "This will end badly, Pace. It won't work. When you take over from Dashuri, you'll have people with you all the time. You won't be able to sneak off. You're being selfish."

"Selfish?" I echoed. "How am I being selfish?"

"Have you even stopped to ask yourself whether this is fair on her? After your birthday she'll be lucky if she sees you once a month. Does she want a family, Pace? How will that work? You're asking her to make do with the scraps of you." She sighed deeply. "End it now and sure, you'll both hurt, but you'll get over it. Let her find someone that lives in her own world who she can see whenever she wants. Who she can have a life with."

"Get out."

"Pace—"

"Get. Out."

My chest heaving, I turned around, barely hearing the door open and close. My skin felt hot and too tight for my body. *Selfish.* Perhaps it was, but the thought of letting Sirain go stripped the air from my lungs. The thought of her with someone else gripped my heart in my chest, squeezing with iron claws. It wasn't hopeless. We hadn't found a way yet, but we would. We had to.

I leaned against the windowsill, breathing the cool evening air into my lungs. It would be sunset in a couple of hours. Hopefully Sirain would be waiting for me at the cliff. I needed to find out what was going on. My mind swelled with the possibilities of what might have happened between her and Emeric, but nothing made sense. If she wasn't at the cliffs, I didn't know what I would do. I had no way of contacting her. If Sirain stopped going to the cliff, the chances of me seeing her again were near impossible. What if she never left Helle again? It would be over, and I would never know why. A dark sense of hopelessness settled over me. Two hours. The breath I drew caused me to wince in pain.

32
Sirain

I threw the frame onto my bedside table, my heart racing. The flight had calmed me, but now, standing in the castle, I was back to a state of panic. The human's words reverberated around my skull. *I think I might be your father.* It was impossible. I wasn't half human. There would be signs. Breathing was difficult as I leaned on my dresser, staring at my reflection in the mirror. When I was younger, I had wondered about my purple colouring, but as my father had the royal red and my mother's was blue, it made sense that I was a mixture of the two. Now, I thought of that damned painting—the way Emeric's hair and eyes were the exact same shade as mine. The way he and my mother had looked at each other. They'd been together for years. How had they managed to keep their relationship a secret for so long?

Pushing away from the mirror, I wrenched open my bedroom door and flew through my rooms, heading for the stairs. I could barely form a thought as I moved through the castle towards my mother's chambers, hoping against hope she was there. If she was in the throne room, or with my father, there was no way I'd be able to get her alone, and I certainly wasn't going to have this conversation in front of the king.

I didn't bother knocking when I reached her rooms.

"Mother!"

Servants scattered as I flew from room to room, my wings sending flurries of wind through the space, upsetting ornaments, and knocking things from shelves.

"Where is she?" I demanded of a cowering young female. "Where is the queen?"

"Sirain! What are you doing?" My mother's sharp, clipped tones rang out and the servants dropped, bowing their heads.

"I need to speak to you," I said. "Now."

My mother stared at me, her expression unreadable. Her eyes didn't leave mine as she barked her order to the servants. "Leave us."

The servants scurried away, looking relieved to be out of the way of the brewing storm.

"Fold your wings," the queen snapped. "You'll break something."

There was no point drawing it out. I took a shaky breath, holding my chin high. "Who is my father?"

Shock widened my mother's eyes for the briefest second before she regained her composure once more. "Don't ask such ridiculous questions, child."

"I am no more a child than you are telling the truth." I stepped closer, my blood thrumming in my veins. "I met Emeric."

This time the shock that lit my mother's eyes was tinged with sadness. She looked away, no longer bothering to hide her emotions, and I knew. He'd told me the truth.

"That's a name I haven't heard in a very, very long time."

I snorted. "Twenty years perhaps?"

"Dare I ask how you came to meet Emeric?" she asked.

"You've lied to me my entire life," I hissed. "I don't owe you any truths."

The queen sank onto a chair, pulling her long hair over her shoulder with a sigh. "I couldn't tell you the truth. You know that. I couldn't tell anyone. If your father—"

A hollow laugh tore from me. "Which one, Mother?"

"If *the king* found out."

My stomach lurched. She was right. If he found out, he would . . . My breath stuck in my throat. Would he kill her? Would he kill me? He'd throw us in the dungeon at the very least. I'd seen my father—the king—murder someone for not bowing low enough. Perhaps death would not be punishment enough for tricking him into raising another man's child.

"Do you see?" my mother said quietly. "I ended things with Emeric because I knew I had to marry Nemir. It was my responsibility. The Fates had declared it. I thought about running away—Emeric begged me to stay with him. It broke my heart."

I sat down beside her, my head throbbing as I tried to take in what she was saying. "Why didn't you stay with him?"

"I was scared. It would have meant never returning to Helle. It would have meant living a life in hiding because of my wings. I'd only have been free one day a year—"

"Plumataria."

The queen blinked in surprise. "How do you know?"

"Emeric still holds the celebration every year. I thought his obsession with wings was a bit over the top, but now it makes sense. It's all about you." I shook my head. "He's still in love with you, even after all this time."

A tear tracked down my mother's face and I watched in awe. It was the most emotion I'd ever witnessed from her. How closely had she guarded her feelings—her heartbreak—over the years?

"I didn't know Emeric was your father until you were born," she said. "I was so worried your father would ask questions."

I shook my head, the pounding intensifying. "He would have killed us both."

She said nothing.

"Do you have any idea how much danger you've put me in?"

I got to my feet, suddenly aware of every window and every door, panic pulsing through my blood. “If anyone found out—”

“No one can find out,” she snapped. “If they did—if they could prove it—you’d lose your claim to the throne.”

“The throne?” I barked a laugh. “I’d lose the claim to my life!”

I couldn’t breathe. Every part of me ached. The worst part was, I wanted Pace. More than anything, I wanted to be in his arms, telling him everything. But I couldn’t. I’d hidden the truth from him. So many truths. My eyes burned. I turned and ran.

“Sirain!”

Bursting from her rooms, I smacked face first into something black and solid. I staggered backwards, forcing air back into my lungs, my face aching.

“Whatever is the matter, Sister? You look rather upset.” Fin stared down at me, his thin mouth twisted in a cruel smile.

Trying to calm my erratic heart, willing my tears not to fall, I forced a scowl. “Out of my way, Little Brother.”

He moved to stand in front of me, blocking my path. “What’s the hurry? Can’t I show concern for my sister?”

There was something about the way he said ‘sister’ that made my blood run cold. Had he been standing outside the door? Had he heard? We hadn’t been talking loudly and we had been nowhere near the door, but . . .

“I appreciate your concern, Fin,” I said. “But I have somewhere to be.”

His smile widened as he held his ground. No. He hadn’t heard. He just knew I wanted nothing more than to get away from him—to get away from everyone—and he was delighting in preventing that from happening. I had never wanted to stab someone more.

“Move,” I barked.

Behind him, through the large window, I could see the

darkening sky start to take on hues of orange. If I was going to speak to Pace, I needed to get to the cliff. I needed to know if Emeric had told him. I needed . . . him.

"Sirain?"

I turned at the sound of Kwellen's booming tone, relief sweeping over me. Fin tensed, lifting his chin in a failed attempt to combat the height difference. Kwellen was the tallest Chaos I'd ever met. He glanced at Fin, dismissing him instantly.

"The king wants you immediately," he said, turning to me.

Any relief I had felt evaporated like morning mist on a summer's day. "Why?"

Kwellen raised a dark eyebrow. "You think His Majesty discloses his wishes to me?"

It took every ounce of strength I had to hold it together as panic tore at my edges, threatening to pull me apart. "Let's go, then."

Fin sneered as we walked past, clearly unsure who to direct the majority of his disgust towards. I didn't look at him. I had bigger things to worry about. Why did my father want to see me? My stomach lurched. He wasn't my father. Did he know? Had someone seen me coming through The Crossing? Had someone told him?

"Are you okay?" Kwellen asked as soon as we were out of earshot. "You look like you're about to pass out."

"I'm fine."

What I really wanted to do was throw myself against my friend and sob. The thought almost brought a smile to my lips. He wouldn't know what to do. I marvelled at how used to affection I'd become since meeting Pace. My head whipped toward the nearest window. The orange was fading, being swiftly replaced by the shadows of night. He'd understand. Pace would know I'd be there if I could. I blew out a breath and lifted my shoulders. The king did not tolerate weakness.

"Sirain," Kwellen said quietly. "You know you can talk to me, right? If Fin's done something—"

"He hasn't." I reached up and squeezed his arm. "I'm fine. Honestly. And I know."

We slowed to a halt as we reached the towering iron doors that led to the throne room. I stared up at them, my heart slamming against my chest. A part of me, larger than I wanted to admit, wanted nothing more than to turn and run.

"Wait for me?" I whispered.

Kwellen nodded. "Of course."

As I stepped forward, the guards bowed briefly before heaving open the doors. The throne room was empty, and each footstep rang around the stone and metal in a deafening echo. King Hadeon stood before his throne, watching me approach, his face void of all expression. This was the most infuriating thing about my father. When he was angry or disgusted with me, it was almost a relief, because I knew what he was feeling. Most of the time, it was this—nothing.

I stopped at the bottom of the dais, dipping into a bow. "Father."

"The Fates have spoken."

My head snapped up. I didn't dare breathe.

"They have given the first of the Royal Rites," he continued. "Two days from now, you will travel through The Crossing."

My eyes widened.

"Don't look so terrified," he sneered. "A child could do it. The Crossing is not your task."

I bit back my retort, clamping down on the inside of my cheek until it bled. He didn't know. I forced myself to stay rigid even though my knees threatened to sag with relief. He had no idea I'd been through The Crossing countless times over the past few years. I could have laughed.

"What is my task, Father?"

He huffed, his lip curling in disgust. "I doubt you'll be able to do it. I'll give you the chance now to bow down and let your brother take your place in a couple of years. You can live a quiet life somewhere, perhaps produce some smallwings."

I choked on a laugh. "Forgive me, Father, but when have I ever given you the impression that I am weak? When have I ever backed down from a fight? Shied away from a challenge?"

If I didn't know better, I could have sworn something akin to pride flashed across his stony face. "You might fare well in the arena, Sirain, but the Royal Rites are a test, not only of physical strength, but your loyalty to the Fates.

I lifted my chin. "Tell me."

Reaching into his black robes, he pulled out a piece of parchment. It was identical to the small squares given to the Captains and Hands of Fate detailing their missions. I'd seen them dozens of times when accompanying Odio. My heart raced. Would I have to shoot an arrow? This wouldn't be a challenge at all.

"The Fates have control over us all," my father said, staring at the rolled-up paper. "Chaos, Cupids and humans."

My heart stammered at the mention of Cupids. I wasn't sure what to do. Should I feign surprise? Shock? Indifference? Before I could decide, the king continued, oblivious as always to my inner turmoil.

"Your first Rite is a task deigned to show your resignation to that fact. We have no control over Fate. Although we administer its commands, we are still liable to its whims."

Unease swirled in my gut, my skin prickling with nerves, and I bit down on my lip to stop myself from demanding he stop waffling and hand the paper over. The king turned and picked up an arrow from the throne behind him. I frowned. It wasn't the obsidian black of the Hands' arrows. As its shaft gleamed in the torchlight, it looked as though it was cast from silver.

He turned it over in his hands, his dark eyes unreadable as

he pressed the point to his finger. A bead of dark red blood bloomed, and he grimaced. "You are to use this arrow to kill a human."

Everything stilled. The dust motes in the dusky air. My breath. My heart. "I'm to kill a human?"

My father sniffed, shaking his head. "Just listen to the weakness in your voice. Humans are nothing more than pawns of Fate. I knew you couldn't do it."

"I didn't say I wouldn't do it," I snapped. "I'm just surprised. I wasn't expecting the first Royal Rite to be cold blooded murder."

The king narrowed his garnet flecked eyes. "To be Queen of Helle, you must be steadfast in your faith. Ruthless. Uncompromising."

I nodded. "I understand."

With a sigh that clearly said he didn't believe me, he extended the arrow to me. I took it, surprised at its weight. "Which human have the Fates decided must die?"

My father held the paper between his fingers, as though considering. After what felt like an eternity, he handed it to me.

Quietly proud that my fingers didn't tremble as I took the small square of folded parchment, my insides recoiled at the fact that the Fates had decided someone must die by my hand. I had no choice but to accept the Rites. If I didn't, Fin would become Crown Prince. I couldn't let that happen. My father was a ruthless bastard, but my brother was a worse kind of evil. Where the king was angry and impulsive, Fin was cold and calculating. The thought of Helle under his rule made my blood run cold.

I stared at the paper in my hand. If the Fates had deemed this human unworthy of living, there would be a reason. Maybe they were a criminal. Perhaps they were a murderer themselves.

Unfolding carefully, I braced myself for the gold lettering I knew would be on the inside. I read the name, forcing my face to stay neutral, although a scream loud enough to shake the snow from the mountains echoed inside me.

"Two days," my father said, his voice a million miles away. "You can take two Chaos with you. I'm going to assume you'll take Kwellen and Odio."

I nodded, willing the bile rising in my throat to stay down a little longer. "Yes, Father."

"Fine. Come and see me when it's done."

Crumpling the paper in my hand, the silver arrow heavy in my other, I turned and walked out of the throne room. I continued walking past the guards, past Kwellen—who fell into step beside me—and around the corner.

As soon as I was out of earshot, I sank to my knees and vomited on the floor.

33
Pace

Staring out of the small ship window at the gently churning ocean, I tried not to scan the sky for the millionth time. Sirain hadn't shown up at sunset the day she disappeared from Liridona. I'd waited at the cliff the following two days as well, but nothing. I pinched the bridge of my nose, my head throbbing. I'd barely slept since Plumataria. How could I? There was no way of knowing whether Sirain was okay. The helplessness was all consuming and I flitted between rage and despair on an increasingly frequent basis. Somewhere behind me, I could hear the hushed tones of Marlowe and Dariel as they poured over the maps spread on the cabin's table. It was hard not to feel jealous. My cousin could visit Marlowe whenever he wanted. A growl of frustration built in my chest, and I gripped the wooden frame until my fingers ached.

"Pace?"

I exhaled, my shoulders sagging. "Yes, Cousin?"

"She'll be okay."

Closing my eyes, I shook my head. "You don't know that."

Floorboards creaked, followed by a firm hand on my shoulder. "I know I haven't formally met her, but she seems extremely tough. There'll be a reason she hasn't tried to contact you. Be patient."

I clenched my jaw. Marlowe had arranged this meeting with Dariel at sea, with the minimal crew given orders to stay below deck until told. We were discussing strategies for gathering information, but I couldn't concentrate. My thoughts were not only plagued by Sirain's absence, but by my conversation with Tiesa. We'd never fought like that. I leaned forward until my forehead met with the cool glass. The flames of my decision were finally licking at the people around me. I'd been naïve to think I'd escape without consequences.

"Come, Cousin." Dariel squeezed my shoulder. "If nothing else, discussing Newbold might distract you."

He was right. With a sigh, I turned from the window and took a seat at the table, the map of Lord Diarke's realm spread out on its surface.

"The problem with Newbold," I said, pointing to the jagged coastline, "is they seem to be expecting people to be spying by air. Why else station archers along the coast?"

"We can get around that," Dariel said. "We fly above the clouds until we're inland."

Marlowe shook his head. "It's still dangerous. You wouldn't know what you were descending into."

"We'll have to take precautions, then," I said.

Dariel nodded. "Armour."

"Do you think you could get Sirain to help?" Marlowe asked. "The Chaos seem like the type to have access to that type of stuff."

Dariel stiffened beside me. "I'm not sure if that's—"

"If I ever see her again, I'll ask." The words sounded even more bitter out loud than they had in my head.

Marlowe looked at me for a moment, then turned to my cousin. "Have you heard anything from your sister?"

My head snapped up. "You asked Amare?"

"I did." Dariel nodded. "I told her that as part of your studies to take over from Dashuri, you were reviewing as much history as you could."

I pushed aside the revelation that my cousin had lied to his sister. "And what did she say?"

"She said she'll have a look for me. There are vaults that hold ancient texts, but no one goes near them. She's not sure whether they're allowed to leave the island."

I nodded. It wasn't a dead end, yet.

Marlowe leaned back in his chair. "We need to prepare for the worst. Which is why we must focus on Newbold. Lord Diarke is the leading force in this war. The Midnight Queen has more than enough land and money to keep her happy, but he's persuaded her to join forces with him. I don't know whether he's holding something over her or he's just very persuasive. Either way, I know it's him."

"He led the charge in the last war," Dariel explained.

Marlowe nodded, sitting forward and placing his hand over my cousin's. "Lord Diarke is even more secretive than the Midnight Queen. No one I know has ever met him in person."

Tearing my gaze from their joined hands, I focused on the dark mass of land on the map before me. "Did Dalibor join forces with Newbold in the last war?"

"No. My parents reached out to the Midnight Queen and Emeric when Newbold launched its attack, but it was so sudden, everyone was too busy defending their own land. My parents were good friends with Emeric and, although I was only twelve at the time, I remember them being confused as to why he didn't respond to their letters."

I frowned. "That's why Cove was so reluctant to work with him this time."

Marlowe looked up in surprise. "How did you know that?"

"The first time I came to the human world, Dariel had orders from the Fates for Cove, to ensure the meeting went well."

Dariel shook his head. "Then why did the Fates ask the Chaos Hands to shoot an arrow at Marlowe? It makes no sense."

"I don't think the Fates have to make sense," I muttered. "Tiesa would say, this is why we have to trust in them. They see the grand plan, where we can only see pieces. She'd tell us not to question it."

"That may well be true," Dariel huffed, "but if the Fates are steering the course of the war, I want to know their reasons."

I turned to my cousin. "If only my brother could hear you now. The steadfast, reliable, Lord Dariel Dragoste, Captain of Fate, good influence on wayward second princes, doubting his role."

"There's a difference between doubting and questioning," Dariel replied, giving me a withering look.

The doors to the cabin flew open and we jumped to our feet, hands reaching for our weapons. It took me a moment to make sense of what I was seeing in the doorway, the blue sky beyond the cabin casting the figures there in shadow.

Sirain stood in her familiar black leathers, an onyx bow in her hand, but any feelings of relief I felt were quashed as I took in Kwellen and Odio at her shoulders, blades drawn. I hadn't seen them since the storm, and it was jarring to see them now after holding Sirain in my arms as she told me stories of them from her childhood.

"Sirain?" I said, taking a step toward her. "What are you doing here?"

I wanted to rush forward and sweep her into my arms, but I had no idea whether she'd told the other Chaos about us, and it took all my self-control to keep my distance. I allowed myself to look at her, checking her for signs that something wasn't right. She didn't seem injured. When I looked at her face, however, my chest tightened.

"What's wrong?" I asked, my pulse racing at the tension bracketing her mouth. "Sirain? Look at me."

She shook her head, her eyes glistening with unshed tears. "You shouldn't be here."

I took another tentative step forward, aware of Dariel behind me, the sound of his blade sliding from its sheath almost deafening. "Why are you here? Why did you leave? He wouldn't tell me."

Sirain kept her gaze forward, her eyes shuttering. "You shouldn't be here."

"What's going on?" Odio said, his dark eyes flitting between us. "Why doesn't he look like he wants to kill you?"

A low rumble sounded, and for a second, I thought it was thunder. It took me another second to realise it was a growl, emanating from Kwellen's towering figure.

"This is what you've been hiding, isn't it?" he bit out. "You've been meeting with this Cupid, haven't you?"

Sirain refused to look at me, her gaze distant.

"Cousin?" Odio asked, his grip tightening on his blade. "Tell me Kwellen has been eating nightberries again. Tell me that's not true."

Blood roaring in my ears, I moved forward another step. It was impossible to stop myself. I didn't know how to be so close to her and not touch her. I'd missed her so much it ached, and now to see her standing there, on the verge of tears, it was too much to take.

"Sirain," I said quietly. "What's wrong?"

She shook her head, the blank expression she was trying so hard to maintain crumpling just a little. "This is bigger than us, Pace."

"What are you talking about?" I took another step, but Kwellen raised his sword, angling it at me.

"Don't even think about it, Cupid," he snarled.

The air felt like water, every breath, every movement, slow and heavy. "Sirain. What's bigger than us? Why are you here? Why are they here? Why won't you look at me?"

"The Fates have spoken," she said, her voice barely audible over the roaring in my head.

Relief and understanding swept over me as I looked between the bow and Marlowe standing behind the table. "The Fates have ordered an arrow for Marlowe?"

She said nothing. The relief I'd felt flickered and extinguished. It was too simple. Things weren't right. It was daytime. They weren't masked. Sirain reached to the quiver between her wings and pulled an arrow free. It wasn't the glimmering black of Chaos arrows, but a rich shining silver. Horror walked spiked steps down my spine as I realised, the arrow wasn't meant to change a human's mood. It was made to kill. Every muscle in my body tensed as I watched Sirain nock the arrow in her bow.

"Sirain?" I said, my eyes on the arrow. "What are you doing?"

She shook her head, the sadness pooling in her eyes deep enough to drown in. "I wanted to talk to you Pace. I did. I couldn't get to the cliff in time after Liridona, and then I found out what the Fates wanted from me, and I knew there was no way I could ever make you understand."

"What the Fates want from you?" I echoed. "What do you mean?"

"The Royal Rites," Odio said, pointing his sword at me, his burgundy eyes narrowed. "Four tasks. One for each of the four days before her twentieth birthday. This is the first one."

I frowned, trying to make sense of his words. "Royal Rites? What are you talking about?"

"You didn't tell him?" Odio cackled. "Good to know there's still a little Chaos in you, Cousin."

The muscle in my jaw ticked, my hands clenching into fists. "What is he talking about, Sirain?"

"What is he talking about, *Your Majesty*," Odio said with a grin. "You really should address the crown princess with more respect."

The floor swayed beneath my feet, and I was certain it wasn't due to the rocking of the ship. I stared at Sirain in disbelief.

"Crown princess?" I repeated. "Why didn't you tell me?"

"I'm sorry," she whispered.

"Sorry?" I laughed through the pain splintering across my chest. "You're going to be Queen of Helle. How was that going to work? Were you just going to disappear from my life on the day of your coronation?"

"I'm sorry."

"Stop it!" I snarled. "Stop saying you're sorry."

"This is bigger than us—"

"No. It's not." I took another step forward, ignoring Odio's blade now inches from my throat. "Nothing is bigger than us."

A tear escaped, rolling down her pale cheek, as she raised the bow, aiming at Marlowe.

"No!" Dariel shouted.

In the time it took for me to lift my hand to reach for my weapon, Odio was behind me, his blade pressed to my throat. Dariel leapt over the table, wings splayed and sword raised, but Kwellen was already there, his own weapon swinging. I struggled against Odio's vice-like grip, but he pressed the sword closer to my throat.

"Stop struggling, Cupid," he hissed in my ear. "Don't make the mistake of thinking I'll hesitate to kill you."

As the clashing of metal filled the air, I sought out Sirain.

Her eyes were fixed on Marlowe, her bow still raised and ready as silent tears marked her cheeks.

"Sirain," I called out. "You don't have to do this."

"I don't expect you to understand," she said.

A clatter echoed around the cabin, and I tore my attention from her to find Kwellen kicking Dariel's fallen sword to the other side of the room.

"You can't stop this," Kwellen said. "The Fates have spoken."

"Please," Dariel said, his voice breaking as he turned to Sirain. "Please, don't do this."

Marlowe stood against the back wall, brown eyes wide, his twin swords hanging useless in his hands.

"Sirain," I choked out. "If you ever loved me—if anything between us was real—you'll walk away. The Fates can't demand this of you. It's not right. You know that."

Dariel let out a sob as she drew back the bowstring.

"Sirain. Please." I struggled against Odio, a trickle of warm blood sliding down my neck, but the pain was nothing compared to the agony in my chest. If I could just get to her, I could stop her. I could make her see. If she would only look at me.

"I love you," Marlowe whispered, his gaze fixed on my cousin.

The broken sound that tore from Dariel snapped something inside me.

"Sirain," I barked. "If you fire that arrow, there's no coming back from it."

She kept her gaze, unwavering, on Marlowe.

"Look at me," I demanded. "Sirain. Look at me."

Her body trembling, she screwed her eyes shut, and when she opened them again, they were focused on me. My breath caught in my throat at the pain and desperation I saw in their depths, but there was more. Above everything else, acceptance. My heart plummeted. She'd already made up her mind.

"Sirain," I said, willing deadly calm into my voice. "If you fire that arrow, I will never forgive you."

She looked away, returning her focus to the trembling human at the back of the cabin and I watched, unable to breathe, as she took aim. I watched as she let go of the arrow, and with it, everything we'd built between us.

34
Sirain

I was going to miss. From the second Odio had kicked the door open, and I'd seen them standing there, I'd known. The choice was made. My heart slammed against my ribs, trying to break out of my chest, as I tried not to look at Pace. I had to do it. I had to shoot at the human, and Odio and Kwellen needed to witness my attempt. I knew I could ask them to lie for me, but this way, I wouldn't need to. Adjusting my clammy grip on the bow, I locked eyes with Marlowe, aiming straight for his heart. Then, holding his gaze, I shifted my aim. His eyes widened almost imperceptibly, and I knew he'd noticed. If he stayed perfectly still, it just might work.

Pace's words were razor sharp claws, slowly dragging through my flesh. Even after I missed, he wouldn't forgive me. It was the reason I hadn't been to the cliffs. After the Royal Rites, I wouldn't be able to disappear to the human world whenever I wanted, and part of me knew I'd never have the strength to end it. At least this way, he'd hate me. Willing my hands to stay steady as I drew a slow breath, I released the arrow.

A guttural yell filled the air and I watched, the bow still vibrating in my hand, as Dariel rammed into Kwellen, knocking him to the side. Spreading his beautiful white wings wide, the Cupid dived in front of Marlowe. I staggered backwards, air refusing to fill my lungs, as the silver arrow sank into Dariel's chest. He fell to the floor with a thud that echoed in my soul, crimson spreading like fire across his white shirt. I shook my head, my eyes wild, as Pace's heart-wrenching roar thundered through the cabin. He fell to his knees at his cousin's side and hands closed around my arms, pulling me backwards. Everything was muffled, moving in slow motion, as I was tugged through the doorway, my limbs limp and lifeless. I was vaguely aware of Odio and Kwellen shouting. I didn't care. I couldn't tear my eyes away from the broken Cupid kneeling on the floor, his hands covered in blood as he begged and pleaded. I was still watching as he lifted his eyes to mine, disbelief swimming in their tear-filled depths. He blinked, and when his golden pupils focused on me once more, they were filled with hate. The hands around my arms tightened, and as my heart splintered into a million razor edged shards, I found myself lifted up into the air.

"For Fate's sake, Sirain," Odio grunted. "Use your wings!"

I couldn't breathe, watching the familiar oaken ship with its folded beige sails, shrink below me as we climbed higher above the sea.

"I *will* drop you, Cousin," Odio snapped. "Snap out of it!"

"You will not drop her," Kwellen bit back. "She's in shock."

I tried to make sense of their words. Shock? I'd fired the arrow. I'd missed. But I hadn't. Someone made a noise that sounded somewhere between a whimper and a wail. It sounded like me.

"Come on, Sirain," Kwellen said. "Hold it together until we're through The Crossing."

Taking a shaky breath, I spread my wings and shook off my friends' grip, dipping down towards the ocean before swooping back up to join them.

"Thank the Fates," Odio muttered.

I could feel Kwellen's concerned gaze on mine, but I kept my attention forward. I couldn't look at anything—couldn't allow myself to think or feel—until The Crossing took hold of me, pulling me through the pulsating green and purple. When I emerged into Helle, I swooped down to the first clearing I spotted and fell to my knees.

In my mind, I yelled and screamed. I tore up fistfuls of grass, revelling in the pain of the rocks tearing at my skin; letting the tears stream down my face until my eyes were sore. In reality, I knelt. I was an empty shell. The anguish lining my insides worked like acid, eating away at me until nothing remained. This was a pain unlike anything I'd ever felt before. I'd killed Pace's cousin.

The world was grey and muted around me. I wanted it that way. I didn't deserve beauty. Every time I blinked, I saw the revulsion on Pace's face, the cold, hard hatred in his beautiful eyes. I'd broken him. He said he'd never forgive me if I released the arrow, but for this . . . I shuddered.

"Sirain?" Kwellen asked, crouching beside me. "Are you all right?"

I had no answer to give, so I said nothing, my eyes unseeing and unfocused.

"She's not okay," Odio said from where he stood, watching.

"Oh? Really?" Kwellen snapped. "Thanks for pointing that out."

He placed his hand on my back, rubbing with a tenderness I wouldn't have imagined he possessed in a million years. I could barely feel it. I was numb.

"I'm going to go ahead and guess you were doing more than just meeting up with that Cupid," Kwellen said, sitting on the grass beside me.

Several answers formed in my head, but I couldn't find the strength to form the words. What was the point? Words wouldn't undo what had happened. Words wouldn't bring Dariel back. Words wouldn't fix my heart. I had always known it would have to end. After all, wasn't that the reason I hadn't told him I was Crown Princess? I'd thought I was prepared to have Pace hate me. I'd thought it would make it easier. A painful knot rose to my throat from the space where my heart used to be, and I choked it down. Just the thought of him hurting—knowing that I was the cause of that pain—was enough to make me want to curl up in a ball, every inch of me burning in agony.

"Seriously, Sirain." Odio sneered. "I can't believe you were stupid enough to go and fall for a fateforsaken Cupid. How did you think it was going to end?"

Not with an arrow through his cousin's chest.

"Maybe he'll be okay," Kwellen said. "It might have missed his heart."

A fragile flicker of hope fluttered in my chest.

"Don't be ridiculous," Odio scoffed. "Did you see the blood?"

"Odio!" Kwellen snarled.

"What? It's for the best anyway. Think what would have happened if the king had found out?"

I stood, numb and empty, my body a ghostly mass of weightless limbs.

"Sirain?" Kwellen stood, trying to lean into my line of sight.

"We need to go to the castle," I muttered, my voice not my own. "I need to tell my father what happened."

Odio barked a laugh. "What? Tell him you killed a Cupid instead?"

"No. I'll tell him I missed."

"You can't do that," Kwellen said. "If you do that, you'll fail the Rite."

"And that's not happening." Odio shuddered. "I'll die before I let Fin get his feathers on that throne."

Kwellen snorted his agreement. "We'll lie. We'll tell him you did it."

I blinked, my vision focusing for the first time as I looked at my friends. "And what happens when the Fates give orders for him? It's pointless."

Kwellen squinted, scratching his stubbled chin. "Do you really think the king reads the orders? He'd have no idea."

"And even if he did," Odio offered. "We'll say he must have made a miraculous recovery because we saw you shoot him right through his heart."

My head drooped on my shoulders. I'd underestimated my friends. Chaos were a cruel and ruthless race, but when it came to people we cared about—even in our own vicious way—we would die to protect them. I had no idea whether the lie would hold, but it was worth a try.

"Thank you," I whispered.

The flight back to the castle took every ounce of strength I could muster, and as we approached the jagged spires, I wondered whether I'd make it, or whether the desperate weight of my grief would drag me down the rocky mountainside. I barely registered where I was or what was happening as we marched down the stone hallway to the throne room. Kwellen and Odio stayed beside me the entire way, silently offering their strength. Two guards heaved open the doors and I stepped forward, too numb to tremble.

"Those two can stay outside," the king barked.

I felt Kwellen hesitate at my shoulder for a second before their footsteps retreated, the heavy doors groaning shut behind me with a thud that shook my bones.

"Come," my father barked.

Usually, I would hold my chin high and hold his gaze, showing him that I was not afraid of him. As I walked towards the throne, I didn't have the will to be anything other than what I was. Broken. My footsteps echoed around the empty room and with each stride a heavy realisation settled over me. I couldn't lie. The king would see through such a feeble falsehood and lying to his face would incur a punishment much worse than the alternative. The truth, however, would mean the end of everything. I didn't care.

My father met me at the bottom of the dais, his wings flared. Reaching out, he grabbed my chin roughly in his fingers and lifted my face, squeezing until my eyes watered. I stared into his dark eyes, flecks of ruby and garnet glinting like flames around his pupil. His dark brows furrowed as he stared down at me.

"You did it," he muttered. "I didn't think you had the strength to take a life, but you did."

I blinked.

"There's death in your eyes, Daughter. I'm just disappointed you seem to care about it so much." He pushed my face away and I stumbled backwards, ignoring the urge to rub the blossoming bruise.

A movement behind him drew my attention and my blood ran cold as I took in my brother leaning against the black throne, his face void of expression.

"I would perhaps understand it," my father continued, glancing at his hand as though checking to see if my weakness had rubbed off on him, "if the Fates had asked you to kill a Chaos. That you would feel any remorse for a pointless human life is weaker than I'd expected. Even for you."

I stared up at my father, aware that in normal circumstances I would refute his statement—that I would stand up for myself. I couldn't bring myself to care. Everything felt pointless. Against my better judgement, I shifted my gaze to Fin. He smirked at me from beside the throne, a knowing look in his eyes.

"Yes, Sister," he said. "Why would anyone care about a pointless human?"

My blood ran cold; sending icy pinpricks across the back of my neck as his dark eyes flickered with malice.

"Leave," my father said, turning his back to me. "The Fates have announced your second Rite for tomorrow."

I paused, waiting.

"You'll defeat our best warrior in the arena," he said, glancing over his shoulder. "I suggest you go and find somewhere to regrow your spine."

I didn't bother bowing as I turned and strode out of the throne room.

Kwellen and Odio stepped forward, their expressions one of matching concern and I nodded.

"He saw death in my eyes," I said.

They shared a look, but before either could speak, my mother appeared at the end of the hall in a rustle of material and a flutter of wings, causing Kwellen and Odio to drop into deep bows.

"Come, Daughter," she said. "I want to speak to you."

I shook my head. "There's nothing you could say that I want to hear."

Kwellen shifted uncomfortably next to me, and I could have sworn I heard a snort from my cousin.

"Leave," the queen barked. "Everyone."

Hesitation hung in the air for the briefest of seconds before the hallway cleared, including the guards at the door, although I'm sure they didn't go far.

My mother leaned towards me, her voice low. "We need to talk."

"Like I said, Mother, there's nothing I want to hear from you. You raised me on a dangerous lie and nothing you can say will change that."

She pressed her lips together, her eyes searching mine. "Once you complete the Rites—which you will—you will be the next ruler of Helle, no matter what happens. The Royal Rites are binding."

A weak, hollow laugh choked from my chest. "So, you're

saying, if people find out that I'm half human with no Hadeon blood, there'll be nothing they can do to stop me?"

She nodded, her eyes fierce. "Exactly."

"If you don't think that either Fin or my father would kill me without a second's hesitation, then you really need to get your head out of your wings and take a look at what's going on around you." I moved to step past her, then paused, a question rising from the aching depths of my chest. "How did you survive?"

Her brow furrowed. "Pardon?"

"When you left Emeric," I said. "How did you survive the pain?"

My mother looked at me then, her eyes widening for a second before filling with sadness. She shook her head. "You, Sirain. You were the only reason I survived."

She lifted her hand towards me, but I slipped out of her reach and walked away without looking back. I hadn't expected her answer to make me feel better. I hadn't expected a magic solution. My legs were like lead as I trudged up the winding staircase to my rooms, the very tips of my feathers dragging up the steps behind me. All I wanted to do was collapse face down on my bed, but I willed myself forward. Even before I pulled open the bottom drawer where I'd placed my mother's framed feather, I knew what I'd find.

It was gone.

35
Pace

Witnessing Tiesa's grief was almost as painful as reliving my own. My chest was a hollow void as she sank to her knees at Dariel's side; the breaking of her heart almost audible between the creaks of the ship as it rocked gently on the waves. I knew I wouldn't have been able to carry him all the way back to Hehven by myself. If there had been another way—a way to spare her from this—I would have taken it.

In the time it had taken me to fly to Dragoste and find Tiesa, Marlowe had cleaned up the blood and found a sheet to cover him. I noticed the other things too. The way his wings had been carefully tucked in, not a feather out of place. A few were stained pink, where an attempt had been made to remove the blood.

Tiesa's sobs drew me from my stupor, and I dropped beside her, wrapping an arm around her shoulder. She fell against my chest, and I rested my chin on her hair as her tears soaked my top and trousers. I'd told her he'd been injured. The cold lie had torn at my insides, but I knew if I'd told her the truth, she would have never made it to Marlowe's ship.

I lifted my gaze to where Marlowe sat, slumped against the wall, his arms wrapped around his knees and his muted gaze fixed on Dariel. My heart twisted. Just hours earlier I'd watched the two of them, my thoughts tainted with jealousy at what they had. Alternating between broken sobs and silent tears, Marlowe hadn't spoken a word since the light had faded from my cousin's eyes. I forced myself to look at Dariel. His sky-blue eyes now closed; his pale lashes fanned out across his cheek as though he was merely sleeping. I held Tiesa tighter as I recalled the way they'd widened, searching, as life had slipped away from him in shuddering gasps. The memory would haunt me for the rest of my days.

"What happened?" Tiesa choked out.

Her question took me by surprise. I'd almost forgotten I would have to explain, and my stomach rocked as I realised it wouldn't be the last time. I would have to explain to my parents. To Dariel's parents. The truth was not an option, and I couldn't even begin to think of a suitable lie as I knelt, trembling and numb, by his side.

"Pace?" Tiesa said, her fingers clutching my shirt as she stared up at me through red-rimmed eyes. "What happened?"

"Sirain." The word was a sword, twisting in my gut. A knife carving out my heart.

Tiesa sat back, her face soaked with tears, still sniffling. "What does that mean?"

"Sirain. The female Chaos."

"Chaos?" Tiesa blinked, her brow furrowing as she processed my words. "The one you fell in love with?"

I winced. Over the last few hours, I'd replayed what had happened over and over in my head, trying to make sense of it—trying to see something I'd missed. When the door had burst open, I'd been so relieved. But then she'd stood there, a bow in her hand, focused on Marlowe. The way she'd refused to look at me.

I struggled to my feet and walked over to the window, leaning my forehead against the glass. The room was too hot. The air too thick. I sucked in clammy breaths, attempting to calm my ragged breathing. She'd lied to me. Sirain was the crown princess. The next queen of Helle. I closed my eyes. Why would she have lied? Our love was already impossible; stacked against every odd imaginable. What difference would it have made? A growl tickled the back of my throat, my fingers clenching the window frame. There was no use trying to pretend. I wasn't going to be king. There would always be a little more freedom for me. As queen, it was a solid expiry date on our relationship. I swallowed painfully.

"Pace," Tiesa's voice was barely audible over the creaking of the ship. "Why would she shoot Dariel?"

"She didn't mean to," I explained, my exhale fogging the glass. "The arrow was meant for Marlowe."

It didn't make a difference. Human or Cupid; there should have been no arrow.

"How are we going to get him home?"

I turned at Tiesa's question. I'd expected her to ask about Sirain, but perhaps she knew there was no point. That conversation would come later.

"If we wrap him up and use rope, I can take most of the weight." I'd had the whole journey to fetch Tiesa to consider the logistics. "I just need you to take his feet."

Talking about Dariel as an inanimate object knocked me sick. Every time I looked at him, the grief hit me in a fresh wave, my eyes burning as the air turned to ice in my lungs.

"I'll take the ship as close to The Crossing as I can," Marlowe said, his voice little more than a rasp. "If you show me the way."

I stared at the broken man on the floor, his eyes still on Dariel. Of course, he'd told him about The Crossing. How many times had my cousin visited Marlowe without anyone knowing? I'd been so caught up in my own sneaking around, I had no idea. Had they seen each other every day? How many hours had they spent together as they fell in love?

I tried not to think as we worked together to wrap Dariel tightly in sheets. Everything about it felt undignified and wrong. When it came to covering his face, I couldn't do it. It felt so final. Every fibre of my being shouted at me that if we did, he wouldn't be able to breathe. Marlowe took the sheet gently from my clenched fist.

I turned away as he lovingly traced Dariel's features with his fingers, as though memorising them one last time. My jaw clenched and I screwed my eyes shut as I heard him whisper that he would always love him.

"It's done."

I couldn't look.

"Lead the way to The Crossing," Marlowe continued, his voice a hoarse whisper as stood. "I'll tell the crew to get us going. They shouldn't see you, right?"

I shook my head, my wings already unfolding in my desperation to get out of the cabin. I needed to be in the air, away from . . . everything. Opening the door, I shot straight up into the sky, avoiding the towering mast where Sirain had rescued Tiesa. Everything—everywhere—was doused in memories. My chest tightened and I gulped at the cool breeze as it whipped through my feathers. Staring down at the ship as it shrank beneath me, I wished Cove and Shanti were there. I hated the idea of Marlowe grieving alone.

Tiesa reached my side, her expression listless as she stared ahead.

"I'm sorry," I said. "For not telling you the truth."

"About what?" she said, her voice cold.

"About Dariel."

"I understand."

Before I could say anything else, she rode the breeze upwards, looping back behind the ship. The sails were unfurled now, and it was moving at speed, but still not as fast as us. My mind kept trying to push memories of Dariel into my head, but I shoved them back. I couldn't let myself start down that path. Not until we got him home. Before then, I had to come up with a believable explanation for how my cousin had been killed. I wasn't sure how I was supposed to do that, when I still couldn't believe it myself.

"How did this happen?"

The world was a crushing weight on my shoulders as I wondered the same thing. My father stared up at me from where he knelt beside Dariel's body, the sheet pulled back from his face, while my mother's sobs echoed around the high ceilings. Even though I'd had the entire journey to try and think of a plausible excuse—some way to explain what had happened—I had nothing but the painfully jagged truth. I sucked in a breath, but Tiesa spoke first.

"We were on a mission," she said. "Humans spotted us and started shooting. We tried to fly higher out of range, but we weren't fast enough."

I watched, mouth open, as she pulled the silver arrow from the quiver on her back and presented it to my father. I hadn't seen her take it. He stood, taking the arrow, and turning it over in his hands.

"It's definitely of the human world," he said. "This metal is not found in Hehven."

I couldn't tear my gaze from the arrow that had ended my cousin's life. It might not have been made in Hehven, but could it have been made in Helle? I clenched my jaw to keep the question from spilling from my weary lips.

"And what about Pace?" My father turned his attention to

me, his blue eyes reminding me so much of Dariel it felt like a kick to the chest.

Tiesa dropped to one knee, her head bowed. "Please forgive me, Your Majesty. I was so scared, and I knew I wouldn't be able to bring Dariel back by myself. I dragged him somewhere where he wouldn't be found and flew back to get help. I know I should have asked another Hand, but I ran into Pace. He saw how upset I was and insisted on coming. Please forgive me, Your Majesties."

I stared at the top of Tiesa's silvery head, marvelling at the flawless lie as the echoes of it faded around us.

"Is that true, Son?" My mother asked, her golden eyes glistening with tears.

I nodded; not trusting myself with words.

The doors to the reception room we'd found ourselves in slammed open, and my brother half flew, half stomped in, his face twisted with rage.

"Tell me it's not true," he barked. "A messenger said that—"

Dashuri's words trailed off as his eyes found Dariel's lifeless body at our feet, his angered expression slipping to one of devastation.

I jolted as a gentle hand touched my arm.

"Go," my mother said. "You and Tiesa have been through enough today. Go and try to get some rest."

Tiesa stood and my mother embraced her before turning to me.

"What about Uncle Rahu and Aunt Milovat?" I asked. "What about Amare?"

Dariel's parents and sister would arrive soon, and I owed it to them to explain. My heart sank. I wouldn't be explaining. I would be lying.

My mother shook her head. "You don't need to go through it again, Pace. I know Dariel was a brother to you. This is not your fault. Go and rest. You can speak to them at the final flight tomorrow."

She pulled me into an embrace, and it took every remaining drop of strength not to sag against her. With a heavy nod, I turned and left the room, Dash's demands for an explanation ringing in my ears. As soon as we reached a deserted stretch of hallway, I turned to Tiesa.

"You didn't have to do that."

"I think you mean 'thank you'."

"I was going to tell them the truth."

Tiesa sighed, rubbing a hand over her tearstained face. "And what good would that have done? Your parents already think you're reckless and impulsive. How would telling them that you've been sneaking off to the human world for months, losing your purity to a Chaos, make them feel any better?"

"You make it sound so pointless," I muttered. "It was so much more than that."

"Was being the operative word. It's time to move on now, Pace."

I stared down at her. When we'd picked Dariel's body up from the ship, Marlowe had embraced me and told me he was meeting with Emeric in two days' time, and that I should be there. Even though they had long since dried, I could still feel his tears against my skin. I sighed. It would be so much easier to walk away. War could rage for decades in the human world and, other than the orders from the Fates I would undoubtedly see in my new role taking over from Dash, I would be oblivious.

Tiesa frowned. "I honestly thought you would be tearing the world apart right now."

"Excuse me?"

She tilted her head, her green eyes assessing me. "She killed Dariel. The arrow might have been meant for the human, but—" She sniffled, her voice breaking. "She's taken something from us that can never be replaced."

I pulled a hand over my face. "What do you want from me, Tiesa? Do you *want* me to tear the world apart? What would that even look like?"

"I don't know. I just expected you to be . . . something! I thought you'd be swearing to find her and make her pay."

My wings sagged. "That won't bring Dariel back."

Tiesa stared up at me, fresh tears racing down her brown cheeks. I reached for her, and she sank against my chest as her sobs rose to the surface. It was the second time in all our years of friendship that we'd embraced, and that thought alone was almost laughable. Everything I thought I'd known about being a Cupid—everything I knew about Fate—had been called into question since entering the human world. I rested my chin on top of Tiesa's head, searching for the flames of anger she was expecting but finding nothing but jagged emptiness.

Part of me had been furious. I had been ready to tear The Crossing to pieces to get to Sirain, but the anger had fizzled out; doused by despair. She'd lied to me. If she'd told me, perhaps I could have helped her find a way around it. Instead, she'd gone to the human world to kill Marlowe. What if we hadn't been there? Would we be comforting Dariel as he found out Marlowe had been killed? Would Sirain have admitted it was her? Had she even been planning to see me again? It didn't matter. My cousin, my brother—my person—was gone because of her. There was no point tearing the world apart to find her and kill her. As far as I was concerned, she was already dead.

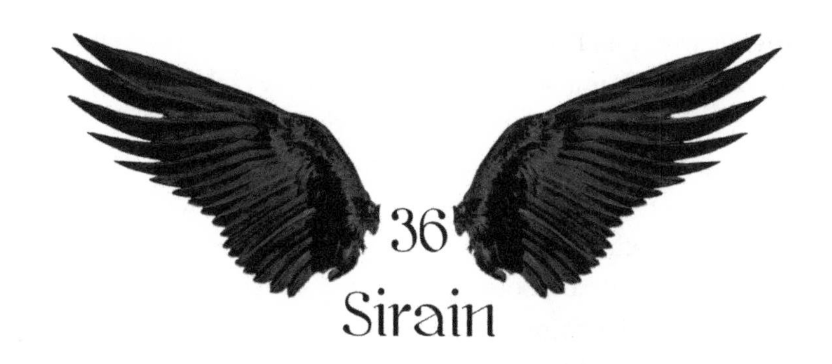

36
Sirain

My sword felt heavier than usual as I slid it into its scabbard. I hadn't slept. Every time my eyes drooped closed, my mind had swum with visions of bloodied feathers and golden eyes filled with hate. I took a deep breath and straightened my spine; fighting the burning sensation at the backs of my eyes as I adjusted my padded leathers and tightened my braid. Of all days, this was not a day to show weakness.

"Sirain?"

"Come in." I looked up as Kwellen stepped into the room, shaking his head.

"I'm sorry. I haven't been able to find out who you'll be fighting."

"It'll be Krieg," I said, turning back to the mirror. "He's the only one besides me who's ever beaten you and if my father won't let me fight you, it has to be him."

"Once," Kwellen sniffed. "He beat me once."

I rolled my eyes. "Tell me about him. Any weaknesses? Things to look out for?"

"Nothing unusual, unfortunately. He's ruthless. Don't expect him to hold back because you're the crown princess."

"Are you joking?" I tried to ignore my racing pulse. "Krieg is friends with Fin. Knowing my brother, he's probably given him a list of every bump and bruise I've had since childhood."

A low growl rumbled in Kwellen's throat. "Bastard."

Wiping my clammy palms on my thighs, my eyes flitted to the drawer that had contained my mother's feather. A profound sense of loneliness washed over me as I realised there was no one I could talk to about it. I'd seen a softer, more protective side to my friends recently, but I still couldn't be sure what they'd say if I told them I was half human. I realised with a heavy tug to my heart that with a human father, I was no longer related to Odio by blood. It was more than trust, though. I was fighting for a throne I had no claim to. Without Hadeon blood running through my veins, I was an imposter. I couldn't expect my friends to stand by me—to face the lethal repercussions if I was found out. It was fine. I'd never had a lot of friends. I was used to being alone. This felt different, though. Colder. More hollow.

"You'll win this."

I blinked to find Kwellen staring at me, his brow furrowed. "Thanks for the vote of confidence. I mean, it's win or die, right? No pressure."

"I wish it didn't have to be today. Your head isn't in the game."

"My head is fine," I lied.

Kwellen stepped forward, placing a large hand on my shoulder. "I need to know that you want to win this."

"What?" I shrugged his hand off. "Are you suggesting that I'd let Krieg kill me?"

He frowned. "I know how hurt you are about what happened yesterday."

"If I throw this fight then not only does Fin get a chance at the throne, but I murdered someone for no reason." I glared at him, my fists clenching at my sides. "I have to win this, or Dariel's death was for nothing."

Heavy silence filled the room.

After a moment, Kwellen nodded, releasing a slow breath. "Okay. I suppose that also means you're not thinking of going back to the human world."

I didn't miss the hope in his voice. "I hadn't planned on it, no."

"Good. Because I remember how hellbent the Cupid was on hurting you after you took his feather. You might have fallen in love with him, but you killed his family. If he ever sees you again, you know he'll run you through the first chance he gets."

Kwellen's words came from a place of concern, but he might as well have punched me in the face. A small part of me had considered going back and trying to explain. If not to the human world, at least to the cliff; but Kwellen was right. Why would Pace listen to my excuses? There was nothing I could say to bring Dariel back. I'd thought about going to see Emeric, but what would be the point? He might be my father by blood, but he hadn't raised me. He knew nothing about me. There was no point letting him into my life when I would lose him as soon as I took the throne. No. It was best to leave the human world to the Hands.

"Come on," Kwellen said. "It's time."

The walk to the arena passed quickly. All too soon, I could hear stomping and chanting permeating the air. My hands repeatedly patted the dagger at my thigh and the blade at my side in reassurance. As we reached the main doors, the guards hauled them open, bowing as we passed. The sun was low, casting a warm orange light on the dark rocky surfaces. I wondered what the sunset would look like from the cliff, and my breath caught in my throat.

"You've got this, Sirain," Kwellen said, squeezing my shoulder. "You're the best fighter I know. You can do this."

I nodded, not daring to look at him as I walked on trembling legs toward the entrance that would lead me onto the main floor of the arena. It irked me that I was so nervous, but this was no ordinary fight. Although Chaos injured each other during sparring, this was a fight to the death. My stomach flipped. I would have to kill Krieg. My fingers gripped the hilt of my sword and I sucked in shallow breaths, trying to calm the nausea. Two lives in as many days.

"I don't understand why I have to kill someone to prove I can take the throne," I muttered.

"Death is chaos," Kwellen said, opening the grated metal door and revealing the dark stone staircase beyond. "It sends shockwaves of events out in ways we might not even see. By causing death, you're embracing that chaos with open arms."

I squinted into the darkness, my footsteps echoing on the stone as we descended. "Do you know what else causes chaos? Love."

"Yes, well," Kwellen huffed. "That wouldn't fill an arena, would it? Besides, who are we to question Fate?"

My jaw clenched. *I* wanted to question Fate. I had a long list of questions for Fate.

The noise from the arena was almost deafening as we reached the bottom of the stairs. A crowd of guards were waiting for us and, for a brief second, I realised I'd expected to see my parents before I walked into the arena. My skin heated. Of course, they weren't there. They would be up on the royal balcony. Why would they come to wish their daughter good luck before she faced death?

One of the guards stepped forward to tell me something, but I held up my hand. "Let's just get this over with."

Filled with purpose, I strode towards the wooden double doors that opened out onto the arena floor, but a large hand on my shoulder stopped me.

"Good luck," Kwellen said, his dark eyes intense, even in the dim light.

For a moment, I thought he might hug me, but he dropped

his hand to his side and stepped back, concern painting his face. I tried to give a confident smile. At least one person cared if I lived or died.

"Cousin!"

A rueful laugh rippled in my chest as Odio shoved guards out of his path to reach me. He arrived at my side, his garnet eyes wild.

"I didn't think I was going to get to see you before you went in," he said, breathlessly. "I've been called on a mission, so I won't get to see the fight. Promise me you'll be alive when I get back."

I smiled. "I'll try."

"You be careful too," Kwellen said, giving him a pointed look.

Looking between the two of them, I frowned. "What do you mean?"

Odio rolled his eyes. "He's telling me to watch out for pests while I'm down there."

It took me a moment to realise what he was talking about, and I stared between the two of them as their meaning sank in. What would happen if Odio ran into Pace and his friends? Would Pace kill him as revenge?

"Don't worry, Cousin," Odio said, surprising me by pulling me to him for a brief hug. "Not only can I take care of myself, but I have a plan."

I opened my mouth to ask what he meant, but someone opened the doors behind me, and I turned, flinching at the onslaught of noise. When I looked back, Odio had disappeared.

"Time to go, Your Majesty," one of the guards said, gesturing at the arena.

Taking a deep breath, I stepped out of the shadows to face the crowds. The arena was packed. The rows of stone seating appeared as one heaving mass of black wings as Chaos roared, cheered, and stomped. I turned my attention to the royal balcony. My mother and sister sat together, their faces not worried, but calm. Or perhaps it just seemed that way in contrast to my father and brother's matching maniacal grins.

My father stood, raising his arms, and the crowd fell silent almost instantly. If I hadn't been waiting to fight for my life, I might have been impressed.

"We are here today for the second Royal Rite," he boomed, the words reverberating around the arena. "The Fates have spoken. Tonight, Crown Princess Sirain Nemir Elda Hadeon of Helle will fight and slay the best of our warriors, embracing the destructive beauty of chaos."

I forced myself to stand tall, remembering Kwellen's words. My hand tightened on the hilt of my sword, and I steadied my breathing as thousands of pairs of eyes watched, wondering whether I'd leave the arena alive.

"The first Royal Rite demanded that the crown princess take the life of a human," the king continued. "By completing this Rite, Crown Princess Sirain has shown that the wishes of the Fates must be honoured above all else. Our lives are intrinsically linked, a finely woven tapestry of threads, all with their own path and purpose. Those threads may fray, they may be cut, but it is all part of the Fated future that is not ours to see. As Chaos, we trust in the vision of the Fates. We give ourselves wholly to their will, without question."

It took everything I had to keep my face neutral. I hadn't expected him to announce that I'd taken the life of a human. My stomach rolled, but I lifted my chin, hoping I looked proud. As the king's words echoed around me, I wondered whether I actually believed them anymore. I didn't want to give myself wholly to the will of the Fates. I didn't want to submit without question. Perhaps it would be easier if I did, but my own thread had already started unravelling from the tapestry.

A roar rippled around the arena, and I turned to find Krieg Arazo striding across the flagstones, his black wings spread, and a long obsidian blade in his hand. Stopping a few strides away, he dipped into a low bow, spreading his arms and wings wide. He looked up with a grin that stretched across his angular face, his dark eyes shining with vicious intent.

Before I could react, he stood and raised his arms to the crowd, his blade glinting in the final rays of the sun. Cheers and stomping filled the arena. Krieg was a Hand. These were his friends. These were the people who attended the raucous parties my brother threw, the ones who wreaked havoc in the villages, causing messes my parents had to clean up. I drew my own sword, scanning the crowd for Kwellen—one friendly face amongst thousands.

"Let's do this, Princess," Krieg crowed. "Your brother has offered me quite the incentive for winning."

My lip curled into a sneer as I turned to face him. I'd suspected as much. "What a shame you won't be winning, then."

There was no warning, no preparation, as Krieg raised his blade and took his first strike. I leapt out of the way; the noise of the crowd drowned out by the roaring of my blood in my ears as his sword sliced the air beside me. Whirling, I gripped my weapon with both hands and struck at him. He parried my blow, the impact ricocheting through my bones, jarring my gritted teeth.

As I deflected the following blow, I spread my wings, flying back a few strides to give myself time to regroup. Krieg grinned a grin that showed all his teeth as he marched toward me, swinging his blade. My gaze was drawn to the balcony behind him, and I instantly wish it hadn't. My mother and Malin were watching with the same nonplussed expression, but my father was talking to someone, completely unbothered that someone was trying to kill his daughter in front of him. It was the figure at the front of the balcony that had pulled my attention, however. Leaning over the stone balustrade, my brother watched intently, a vicious smile on his face. I shuddered. No wonder he and Krieg were friends—or as close to the concept of friends someone as twisted as my brother could fathom. I suspected they made quite the terrifying pair together.

Krieg's attack was relentless, and I dodged and deflected, barely able to find my footing to try and land my own blows. I couldn't figure out whether it was because I was tired or because he was just that good. Sweat trickled down my back and I blinked away the beads that dripped, stinging, into my eyes, not wanting to betray my exertion by wiping them away. Krieg spread his wings and leapt, a shadow of death, as he brought his blade down on me with both hands. I readied my stance, my feet sliding on the worn stone as the blow tore at my muscles. Twisting the sword away as he sliced down, the edge tore along my upper arm and I growled in pain. I stumbled backwards and Krieg's eyes flashed with victory.

As the wound throbbed and blood soaked my sleeve, I wondered whether Pace would care if I died. I shook my head, blinking the sweat from my eyes. This was not the time to think about him. With a roar, I advanced on Krieg, slashing down hard enough to wipe the victory from his face. He scowled as I forced him onto the defensive, my sound of my blade clashing with his, drowning out my thoughts. He flared his wings, leaping out of my reach and I allowed myself a sneer of my own.

A flash of white caught my eye and I turned, but there was nothing. Shaking my head, I swung my sword, advancing once more. Feinting left, I dropped low, my blade slicing across his thigh. Krieg roared and I laughed, despite the worsening throbbing in my arm.

"Is that it, Princess?" He spat. "Is that all you have to give?"

A flicker of white caused me to turn to the crowd again and I stared in disbelief at the figure I found amongst the roaring Chaos. *Pace*? Had he come to see me die? His expression was blank, his golden eyes unfeeling. I blinked, and when I looked again, he was gone.

Krieg spun, his wings tucked tight, and I leapt back out of the way, the tip of his blade scratching a line along the front of my leathers. I stared down at the almost invisible mark, my breathing ragged. If I'd been a split second slower in moving backward, I would have been bleeding out on the arena floor. I needed to focus.

Krieg snarled and his words reverberated around my skull. *Was* it all I had to give? Anger ignited in my gut, a small flickering flame, as I adjusted my sweaty grip and advanced on him. How much had I given already? I slammed my blade into his and he stepped back, his eyes widening a fraction at the rage twisting my face. I'd given my life to the throne—to a father who terrorised me, not caring if I lived or died, and a mother who'd raised me on a lie.

I slashed again, the blow nicking Krieg's shoulder.

I'd given my life to the Fates—taking a life in return with no explanation or reason. The flame in my stomach roared, burning, and gritting my teeth I swiped and hacked with my blade, forcing Krieg backwards.

Is that all you have to give?

I'd given my heart. I'd given every part of myself to Pace and then burned us to nothing, scattering the ashes on the wind.

Burning tears mingled with salty sweat, stinging my eyes, and strands of dark hair clung to my face as I screamed—the rage all-consuming. I raised my blade and brought it down on Krieg's weapon using every last ounce of strength I could muster. His sword fell to the ground with a clatter, and I kicked it away, my chest heaving. Whether the crowd still roared, or it was merely the blood pulsing in my ears, I couldn't tell. I could barely think straight as I swung at Krieg once more. He stepped backwards, but I slid forward, swiping his feet from under him. He'd barely hit the ground, his wings sending up plumes of dust, before I was kneeling on his chest, my blade pressed to his throat.

His dark eyes were wide as he stared up at me, but after a second, they shuttered, his face settling into resignation. "End it," he said. "The Fates have decided."

I barely managed to keep the roar of frustration from bursting from my lungs. "You think the Fates decided this?" I spat. "I've already taken one life this week. The Fates can jump off a cliff."

Krieg's eyes widened. "You have to kill me. One of us has to die."

"Why?" I hissed. "What happens if I don't kill you? Do you think the Fates are going to leave that fateforsaken island and slit my throat in my sleep?"

Krieg's lip curled as he snarled. "If you don't kill me, Princess, I'll be disgraced."

I took a deep breath and drew back my sword. "Yes, well. You'll live."

Getting to my feet, I turned to the royal balcony, prepared for the disgust on my father's face. Before I could lock eyes with him, a cry rang out from beside him. Malin was on her feet, her mouth open in a scream. I was so surprised by the show of emotion, it took me a second to realise why she might be shouting. I spun, my hands gripping my sword as Krieg launched himself at me, a dagger raised above his head and his black wings spread wide like an extension of the evening sky above us.

Piercing through the soft flesh below Krieg's ribs, I watched as his torso swallowed my sword, the weight of his body bowing my legs until I fell backwards. My head hit the stone with a resounding crack, the air tearing from my lungs as his shuddering body slid down my blade, coming to a rest on top of me. Staring up at his fear-filled eyes, blood trickling from his gurgling mouth, I forced air back into my lungs and pushed him off me. I scrambled backwards on my hands and feet, my body trembling. The arena watched in deafening silence until Krieg's large body slumped, his arms drooping listlessly to the bloodied stone floor. Then, they cheered.

Sitting in the middle of the arena, the moon casting a silver glow on the thousands of black wings surrounding me, I watched the building pool of dark crimson trickling between the stones towards me. I'd killed, again. Two lives in two days.

The crowd fell silent, and I stood, knowing my father had commanded it. When I turned to him, every muscle exhausted and my pulsing arm soaked with blood, he was standing, his large white hands gripping the stone railing. The smile on his face didn't reach his eyes, but then, it never did.

"Crown Princess Sirain has completed the second Royal Rite," he announced. "Tomorrow, for the third Rite, she will climb Mount Hadeon and spend the night on its peak."

I stared at him, my expression frozen, as he turned and walked away. Not even a 'well done' or a 'congratulations'. I'd defeated one of the Chaos' best warriors—ended a life—and he'd just walked away. I wasn't sure what I had been expecting. Hatred and disgust mixed with the bile in my stomach, and I sucked in a breath of cold air.

"You did it!" Kwellen boomed, landing in front of me, relief plastered over his face.

I stared up at him, numb from my head to the tips of my toes.

"Come on." He frowned. "Let's get you to a healer. Blood's dripping out of your sleeve."

He gripped the wrist of my uninjured arm and led me from the arena. At some point, someone took my sword from me. People appeared in my line of sight, smiles and words of congratulations wafting around me, but I felt as though I was underwater. The healer peeled off my blood-soaked leathers, warning me that the stitches would hurt. All I could do was nod. There was nothing anyone could do to me that would hurt more than the loss tearing me apart from the inside.

"You did great," Kwellen said, handing me a cup of something hot and sweet smelling. "I knew you'd do it."

I nodded. He didn't mention that I'd tried to let Krieg leave with his life. At some point, I'd have to thank my sister for saving mine. My heart squeezed at the thought. I had vowed to spend more time with her, but I hadn't tried hard enough. If I could prevent her from becoming like Fin, I would. I had to.

"Odio will be pleased you're alive too," Kwellen said, nudging my hand to remind me of the cup there.

I blinked, staring between him and the steaming liquid. Odio was on a mission. He'd said he had a plan. What did that mean? I would have to try and speak to him before the third Rite.

Exhaustion weighed heavy as I considered the task ahead. I'd climbed Mount Hadeon before, but only to get to the top and then fly down. To spend the night, exposed to the elements at the top of the freezing peak, wounded and exhausted, there was a chance I wouldn't make it back down. But of course, that was what the Fates wanted. I sneered. The closer I came to the throne, the closer I came to tearing the Isle of the Fates apart, brick by Fated brick.

37
Pace

Painful didn't begin to describe how it felt being back in Liridona at Emeric's manor. Standing in the room beyond the ever-open balcony, I was plagued by memories of the last time I'd been there. How the night might have gone if Sirain hadn't disappeared. It was so easy to imagine what would have happened if she'd have returned. We'd have danced and laughed, kissing until we couldn't hold back anymore, sneaking off to find somewhere to be alone. It would have been a glorious taste of what life might have been if we weren't who we were. That was the problem, though. We were who we were; doomed from the very first kiss.

Below in the courtyard, servants detached horses from a carriage, and I watched through the window as they led them away toward the stables. I'd barely had a chance to talk to Emeric before Marlowe's arrival had been announced, and he'd excused himself to go and greet him. It felt strange without Dariel. Everything felt strange without him. The pieces of my already shattered heart had turned to dust at his final flight; watching his parents and sister clutch at each other as silver flames devoured his body. I closed my eyes and took a deep breath.

"Pace."

I turned as Marlowe entered the room, Cove and Shanti a step behind. His usually vibrant brown skin appeared grey, his chin coated with stubble. Before I could gather my words, he crossed the room and wrapped his arms around me, ensnaring me in a fierce embrace. Exhaling, I returned the gesture, cursing the burning at the back of my eyes. When Marlowe pulled away, his cheeks were damp. He squeezed my shoulder and turned away, pinching the bridge of his nose. Emeric squeezed his shoulder while Cove and Shanti took turns grasping my arm in the traditional Wendell Islands greeting.

"We're so sorry for your loss," Cove said, her rich brown eyes glimmering with sadness. "Dariel was so special."

A sad rasping mewling sound came from Shanti, and I started, finding the small ruby dragon curled around her neck, its scaled tail nestled under the neck of her shirt.

"He can sense your pain," she said, her smile strained. "He can sense all our pain."

Cove scratched under the creature's chin with a sigh, and it closed its yellow eyes. "Bertie was really fond of Dariel."

I nodded, the lump in my throat rendering me speechless. It was hard to imagine the time my cousin had spent with the humans without me. My chest tightened at the thought of him sitting and laughing with Marlowe, Cove and Shanti. How much had he told them of his life, of his dreams? Perhaps in the end, they'd known him even better than I had.

"Please, sit," Emeric said, locking the door. "Thank you again, Pace, for meeting with us. I understand how difficult this is for you."

I turned a chair around and straddled it, too tired to fold my drooping wings. "Have you received news regarding Dalibor or Newbold?"

"Before we talk war," Cove said. "We need to talk about what happened on the ship."

Leaning forward, I rested my head on my hands. "Must we really? I've relived those moments a thousand times, and I'll continue to do so for the rest of my life. Surely, that's enough."

"We must." Cove waited until I looked at her. "Marlowe told us something that we think it's important you know."

Warily raising my eyebrows, I turned to where Marlowe was standing, slumped against the wall. He looked at me with red-rimmed eyes.

"Sirain was going to miss."

I frowned. "What are you talking about?"

"I should have said something afterwards, but I was so . . ." He took a shaky breath, fresh tears forming in his umber eyes. "Sirain aimed at my heart then looked me in the eye and shifted her aim. It was clear as day. She was telling me to stay still so she could miss."

A sharp pain sparked at my temples, and I screwed my eyes closed as I tried to make sense of what he was saying. "Why would she do that?"

Marlowe shook his head, his face crumpling. Lifting a hand in apology, he unlocked the door and disappeared into the hallway. A heavy silence filled the room as the door clicked shut behind him.

"He doesn't think she wanted to kill him," Shanti explained. "Perhaps she had to make it look like she'd tried, but Marlowe told us he knows, beyond a doubt, she was going to miss."

"Beyond a doubt," I echoed, pressing my fingers to my eyes. "It doesn't matter. She shouldn't have been there. She shouldn't have had an arrow pointed at anyone."

"That might be true, but perhaps there was a reason we don't fully understand." Cove glanced at the door, before continuing. "That's why Marlowe is so upset. He believes that if Dariel had stayed where he was, no one would have died that day."

I stared at Cove in disbelief, the room suddenly too warm. "Are you saying it's Dariel's own fault he died?"

"No!" Cove shook her head, her long braids swishing against her leather waistcoat. "He died because he wanted to save my brother."

"Marlowe thinks it's his fault," Shanti said gently, taking Cove's hand in hers. "He thinks Dariel died because he loved him."

Cove rubbed at her eyes, grief creasing her brow. "We've tried to tell him, but he won't listen. What happened was an accident. A terrible accident."

"It wasn't an accident." I shook my head, my wings lead weights against my shoulders. "Sirain came to that ship armed and ready to kill. She might not have killed who she intended, but the intention was there."

"Did she give a reason for being there?" Emeric asked.

I turned to the older man, a wry smile on my lips. "The Fates sent her."

"Marlowe said it was for something called the Royal Rites," Shanti added.

"Her cousin said there were four Royal Rites leading up to her twentieth birthday set by the Fates," I said, shaking my head. "She lied to me. I had no idea she was the crown princess."

"Did you ask her?" Emeric said quietly.

I stared at the older man. He sat, a long leg resting on his knee, his chin between his fingers.

"What do you mean?"

"Did you ask her if she was royal? Did you ask her if she was next in line to the throne?"

"No." I frowned. "Of course, not."

"Then she didn't lie. She omitted information, but she didn't lie."

"Why though?" Frustration pushed at my edges, too big for

my body and I blew out a slow breath. "Why wouldn't she tell me?"

Emeric's dark purple eyes filled with pity. "If she didn't tell you, there was probably a good reason."

"No reason is good enough to justify what she did. She killed Dariel."

"By accident," Shanti muttered.

Silence fell over the room, punctuated only by the occasional snore from Bertie, who appeared to have fallen asleep around Cove's neck. I leaned forward, resting my head on my forearms. It wasn't just that I missed Dariel, it was as though someone had taken my compass. My whole life I'd looked to him, followed him, and asked his advice. He had been the big brother Dash hadn't. Without him, I was lost, turning in circles, unsure of where to go next. I couldn't see clearly.

Emeric stood and cleared his throat. "I'm going to call for some tea. Would anyone like anything to eat?"

"Wait," I said, lifting my head as a thought burrowed its way to the forefront of my mind. "What happened at Plumataria? What did you say to Sirain to make her disappear?"

"It's not my place to tell you," Emeric said, running a hand through his greying hair.

"Well, Sirain can't tell me, because she's in Helle, possibly murdering more people for whatever the Royal Rites are."

"I can't. It's—"

"Tell me." My wings flared, and my eyes narrowed in frustration. "Please?"

"It sounds like whatever it is, it's an important part of what's been happening, Bickerstaff," Cove said, staring between us. "If you want us to give you some privacy, we can. However, I swear none of us will breathe a word of whatever it is outside of this room."

Emeric turned to her, looking at each person in the room for a moment before settling his weary gaze on me. He sank back down on his chair with a sigh. "I don't even know where to start."

My fingers gripped the gilded edge of the chair. "From the beginning."

"I had my suspicions the first time I saw her," Emeric said. "That night of the storm. She looked so much like her."

"Like whom?" I gritted out.

"Her mother."

I stared at the old man, my mind spiralling. "How would you know that?"

"Many years ago, a Chaos landed on my roof. She wasn't supposed to be there, and I wasn't supposed to see her. But she was, and I did." He pulled his hands over his face. "We became friends, and she would visit often. Of course, over time, it became more than that. We fell in love."

"Plumataria," I breathed. "All the wings you have everywhere. It's because of her?"

Emeric nodded, a wry smile on his face. "Not just the angel fanatic people think I am."

"What happened?" I asked.

"She was promised to the crown prince of Helle. She didn't want the marriage, but her parents accepted on her behalf." He sighed, pain creasing his face. "I never saw her again."

"So, you told Sirain that you were in love with her mother?"

"I told her I think I might be her father."

In a heartbeat, I was on my feet and standing in front of him. Staring down, my gaze flitted from the lingering strands of indigo in his greying hair to the unusual purple colour of his eyes and I staggered backwards, my heart pounding.

"She flew away before I could explain," he said. "I—"

"What more could you explain?" I asked, my eyes wide. "Do you even realise what you've done? The danger you've put her in?"

Emeric hung his head, and I rubbed a hand over my face, my mind reeling.

"What do you mean?" Shanti asked. "Would she be in trouble if her people found out?"

I stalked to the window, unable to filter through the myriad of emotions coursing through my veins. "If Emeric is Sirain's father, it means she has no claim to the throne." I clenched my fists until my knuckles ached. "She might not have told me she was a princess, but she did tell me on several occasions how evil her father and brother are. If they find out, they'll kill her."

"What?" Shanti gasped, causing the small dragon to mewl in protest. "Just like that?"

I closed my eyes, leaning my head against the windowpane. "You've seen first-hand just how ruthless the Chaos are."

Emeric appeared at my side, placing a hand on my arm. "She's made it almost twenty years without anyone finding out," he said. "She'll be okay."

"She's no longer my concern." I shrugged off his hand and stepped away. "Whatever happens to her now is out of our control."

Sinking back down onto the chair, I shoved the rising feelings of unease down into the raw and jagged hole where my heart had been before Sirain had ripped it from my chest. Perhaps this was all Fated. Everything was, after all, wasn't it? My head pounded. Did that mean the Fates knew I'd come to the human world? Did they know I'd meet Sirain? Cold crept over my skin as I thought of the mysterious shrouded figures, knowing everything. Had they known Dariel would die, even as they sent Sirain to kill Marlowe?

Sharp claws sank into my thigh, and I jolted, finding Bertie picking his way up my leg. I watched, wide eyed, as the garnet-scaled dragon wound his way up my body, wrapping himself around my neck. Shanti chuckled and I looked at her in surprise.

"I thought he didn't like things with wings?"

"He must have decided he likes you."

It was hard to see the unusual creature when it was tucked so tightly around my shoulders, but the heat of him was almost unbearable.

"He's so hot," I muttered.

Cove leaned back and folded her arms with a smile. "He's a dragon. What did you expect?"

"You get used to it," Shanti said. "It's great in the winter."

The door opened and I looked up to find Marlowe standing there, his eyes on the dragon around my neck.

"That's what he used to do to Dariel," he said, a sad smile on his lips as he took a seat beside his sister. "I think you remind Bertie of him."

The dragon's tail swung gently, like a soothing pendulum across my chest, and I exhaled, allowing some of the tension to leave my shoulders. It was strangely comforting, and I lost myself in the sensation as Emeric sent for food and drink.

"We're thinking of sending a team to Newbold," Marlowe said, once tea had been poured and plates had been filled with food.

I turned to him in surprise. "With what purpose?"

"To find out what Diarke is planning. Perhaps to force his hand," he admitted, staring intently at the steam rising from his cup.

Emeric nodded, his brow drawn. "I'll give you some of my soldiers for the mission. I'll have my general coordinate with yours."

"No," I said, shaking my head. "You're not thinking straight. Take some time to think this through, Marlowe. You—"

"I can't, Pace," Marlowe said, his expression weary. He looked older than before. "I'd like nothing more than to lock myself away and grieve, but I can't. Diarke doesn't care that I'm broken. The world won't stop turning just because mine has.

The people are restless. They know war is coming and we can't just sit and wait for Newbold to attack. We have to do something."

I ran a hand over my face trying to find a way to stop the inevitable slaughter. "You'll never get past their defences. They almost shot Sirain and me from the sky. How do you think your team will fare better?"

"You said there were watchtowers along the coast," Marlowe explained. "We'll split the team and take out the watchtowers first—"

"That will be construed as an act of war," I said. "And even if you make it past the towers? Then what?"

Marlowe shook his head, the emptiness in his eyes stealing the breath from my lungs. "I don't have any other choice, Pace. We can't sit around waiting anymore. The Chaos are clearly not an option, and I know how you feel about going against the Fates."

I stared at him, my mind scrambling. Marlowe and Cove's parents had died in the last war, and I knew when this one arrived, the two of them would be at the front line, leading their people. I could see Dariel, clear as day before me, his face pleading.

"I've already started training to take over from my brother," I said slowly, my thoughts sliding into something resembling a plan. "I'll be leading the Captains of Fate. Which means, I'll not only have access to orders and missions, but I'll be closer to the Fates themselves. Perhaps I can do something from there."

Marlowe raised his eyebrows. "You'd do that, for us? That's a huge risk."

"Dariel gave his life for yours," I said gently. "He wanted nothing more than to keep you safe, and now that responsibility passes on to me. I owe it to him to do what he can't. If that means going against the Fates, then so be it. They're not playing fair, so why should we."

Just saying the words sent a shudder along my wings, but I shrugged the feeling off, Bertie growling in protest. Surely the Fates already knew. Perhaps the next orders would have my name on them. Perhaps Odio's next arrow would be for me.

We discussed possibilities and logistics until the sun began to sink towards the horizon. As if sensing my wariness of the approaching dusk, Bertie unwound himself from around my neck and snarled in my ear, his forked tongue tickling my cheek. His claws pierced my skin and I winced as he launched himself from my shoulders, his leathery wings spreading as he circled the room once before settling on Cove's. I shivered as I got to my feet.

Shanti smiled. "I told you you'd get used to the heat."

Marlowe stood and pulled me into another lingering embrace that made my chest ache. "Thank you."

"I meant it," I said. "I'll do whatever it takes to keep you safe."

He stepped back, his gaze dropping to the floor. "I miss him so much."

"Dariel's death was not your fault," I said softly, gripping his shoulders. "Dariel would hate for you to think that. Yes, he was protecting you, but that doesn't make it your fault. He loved you. I never saw him as happy as he was when he was with you. Promise me you won't blame yourself."

Marlowe nodded, his eyes brimming with fresh tears. There was only one person to blame for my cousin's death, and she wasn't there to deal with the aftermath of her actions.

After clasping Cove and Shanti's arms, and tickling Bertie under his chin, I turned to Emeric, who unfolded himself from his chair and walked me to the balcony.

"She went looking," he said, stepping out into the dusk with me. "That night. She must have suspected something. I found her in my private office, where she'd already found her mother's feather. I hadn't planned on telling her. If I had, I would have ensured you were there too. I'm sorry."

My jaw clenched, but I inclined my head in acceptance. "It doesn't make any difference now."

"It does, Pace." He stepped towards me. "She loves you, and although you're trying to convince yourself otherwise, you still love her too."

"How I feel doesn't matter," I said, lowering my voice to ensure Marlowe didn't hear. "If today has taught me anything, it's that we'd all be better off if we kept to our own kind. You and her mother didn't work. Dariel and Marlowe didn't work. There was never any chance of Sirain and I having a happy ending. We were delusional to even entertain the idea." I ignored the flash of pain on the human's face and stepped up onto the stone railing. "Give me a couple of weeks to figure out what I can do from Hehven. I'll let you know as soon as I have answers."

Without waiting for a response, I spread my wings, and soared into the honeyed sky. The pull inside my chest that signalled the location of The Crossing had long since become second nature, and I allowed myself to be led toward the faint flickering of green above the sea.

I needed to speak to Tiesa. I wasn't sure how I was going to do it, but I needed to get her onboard. I needed to make her see how important this was. We had it within our power to lessen the devastation the human war would wreak. As the lights of The Crossing folded around me, I swore I could feel Dariel's gratitude wrap around my heart, and I closed my eyes, comforting myself with the idea that he was somehow still with me.

By the time I emerged from The Crossing, dusk had fallen in Hehven, the sky somewhere between charcoal and navy. Both physically and emotionally exhausted, I was so caught up in longing for my bed, that I didn't notice the wall of white feathers until it was right in front of me. I backbeat my wings, my heart slamming against my chest as I stared at Dashuri.

"Oh, Brother," he said, the familiar stain of disappointment on his face. "I had really hoped it wasn't true."

My mouth ran dry as I tried to make sense of the sight of my brother hovering before me. Several Hands were lined on either side, their arrows nocked and pointed at me.

"What are you doing here, Dash?"

"I heard a ridiculous rumour that the second prince of Hehven has been visiting the human world," he said, his arms folded across his chest. "I thought there was no way it could be true. No one, not even Pace, would be that *stupid*."

Panic swarmed me, my breathing quickening as I scrambled for a way out of the situation. "I—"

"Don't try to lie your way out of it," Dashuri sneered. "I'm taking you into my custody."

"Your what?" I balked. "You can't."

"I'm Crown Prince," he said. "I haven't informed our parents of your activities yet, and my Hands here have sworn to keep this between us, for now. It's up to you, Brother. You can come with me, or I can go to our parents and tell them what you've been up to."

I stared at him in disbelief. "Dash—"

The Hands circled around me, their arrows appearing more silver than gold in the dim light. Casting a glare at my brother, I allowed them to herd me toward the palace. A thousand questions swarmed inside my head, and by the time we descended onto one of the rear courtyards, I could barely contain them.

"Broth—"

"Wait," Dashuri said, motioning for me to follow him.

Clenching my fists, I followed, with four Hands behind me, their arrows trained on my back. I wondered whether they would actually shoot me if I tried to fly away. Although, where would I go? Perhaps I could hide out in the mountains or forest until I could get back to The Crossing. My heart sank. I had planned to use my position to help the humans. The chances of that happening were turning to ash before my eyes. My throat thickened. *Ash*. The fire I'd lit was catching up with me, and it burned.

Dashuri led me up a staircase to a corridor in the south wing of the palace and, opening a heavy wooden door, he gestured for me to enter. The room was minimal, with a bed, a dresser, and a washroom. Most likely a guest room for visitors staying during events such as the Festival. It took me a moment to realise that the window had been bricked over, the only light coming from a flickering lamp on the dresser. I frowned, turning to my brother.

"Yes, Pace," he said, closing the door to give us privacy. "This is where you're going to be staying until I figure out what to do with you."

"What to do with me?" I laughed. "You can't lock me up. I'm not an animal."

Dashuri leaned against the door, his face pained. "You've left me no choice, Brother. I knew you were reckless and thoughtless, but sneaking off to the human world, meeting with the humans . . . Do you have any idea how many rules you've broken?"

My breath halted in my lungs. He knew about the humans. "How?"

"Oh, Pace." He shook his head. "I hadn't wanted to believe it, but your reaction has just confirmed it. I suppose that means you also really did lose your purity to a Chaos?"

My face heated as my mouth fell open. "Who—"

"It doesn't matter who told me," Dashuri said, his nose wrinkling in disgust. "It only matters that it's true. You're a disgrace, Brother. I need some time to figure out what to do with you, so you'll stay here until I do."

I opened my mouth to protest, but he opened the door and

left; the sound of the heavy bolt sliding shut like a punch to my gut. Storming over, I slammed my fists against the wood, a roar tearing at my throat.

"Dash! You can't do this! Dash!"

Stepping back, I kicked the door, my chest heaving. I knew there was no point. He'd already gone and there would be at least two Hands standing guard outside. Turning a slow circle, I took in the room, searching for a way out. It may as well have been a tomb. How had he found out? My heart sank as I realised there was only one other Cupid who knew. The Cupid who'd told me from the start that I needed to stop. Betrayal was bitter in my throat as I sank to my knees, staring at the locked door of my prison.

38
Sirain

A brisk wind tore strands of hair from the delicate twists a servant had wound it into, but I couldn't find it in myself to care. I was dressed for my final Royal Rite. The blood red gown clung to my body, flaring out at my knees, where it trailed to the floor in shimmering layers. Pace would have loved it. Staring out at the water, the waves swelling in mounds of orange and blue beneath the setting sun, I shook my hands out to my side and took a deep breath. I hadn't come to the cliffs to reminisce; I'd come to say goodbye.

"I know you're not there, Pace," I said softly. "I'm not going to pretend this is anything other than a thinly veiled attempt to patch up the bleeding mess inside my chest. I'm sorry. I'm sorry I didn't tell you I was Crown Princess. I'm sorry I didn't stay in Liridona and talk to you. I'm sorry I aimed that arrow." I gulped at the air, my heart pounding.

"I don't know if you would have understood, but I didn't give you the chance. I have to do this. I would have done it, if only to keep Fin from the throne, but with what Emeric told me . . . I have to, Pace. This is the only chance I have at surviving. When I'm on the throne, I can try and change things. I don't know how long my father will continue to rule, but at least there's a chance of a better future if I'm next."

I paused, listening to the wind and waves. There was so much more to say, but I couldn't find the words. Staring down at my hands, I inspected the bandages on four of my fingers. Frostbite. Getting to the top of Mount Hadeon hadn't been a challenge, not even with fifteen stitches in my arm. I'd spent the night attempting to shelter between two boulders, inside a frozen cocoon of my own wings, as the snow flurries swirled around me, dusting me white. Shaking and blue-tinged, my thoughts had been a delirious concoction of stolen feathers, deadly arrows, and golden eyes. Above all that, it had been the memory of lying warm and happy in Pace's arms, his soft lips trailing gentle kisses down my neck and along my shoulders, that had got me through the night. Even if the pain of knowing I would never have it again was almost too much to bear.

Reaching out, I trailed my bandaged fingers through the lights of The Crossing, my heart heavy. "I love you, Pace. I hope, one day, you'll find it in yourself to forgive me, and when you think of me, it won't be with hate in your heart. I know that when I think of you, I'll think of your smile. The way your eyes look like molten gold when you laugh. I'll think of rain and waterfalls, and how you made me feel like I belonged somewhere. You were my home, Pace." I drew a ragged breath, willing the tears not to fall. "Goodbye."

Spreading my wings, I tried to piece myself back together as I soared high above the forests towards Hadeon. The castle was lit like a flaming torch, visible from miles away. The lords and ladies from every region of Helle had gathered there tonight for the ball, and as I flew closer, I could make out the silhouettes of people still arriving—some flying and some choosing to preserve their gowns, travelling by carriage.

I swooped around, approaching the castle from behind to avoid questions about where I'd been. Kwellen knew, of course. He'd barely left my side since the ship. When I'd told him I needed to go to the cliff, he'd begrudgingly understood. If anything, I could have sworn I saw relief on his rugged face.

Landing on the cobblestones, I straightened my dress and smoothed my hair, knowing it looked nothing like it had earlier that day. Music poured from the open windows and doors, punctuated by laughter and chatter. The air was pungent with the smell of roasted meat, herbs and spices, and the breeze carried it in eddies around the courtyard.

Stepping through the side doors, I made my way down the corridor to where I'd told Kwellen to wait. He was leaning against the wall, his face set in such a deep frown, I couldn't help but smile as I approached.

"You scrub up rather well," I said, gesturing at his midnight black tunic and pants, the embroidery at the neck and sleeve a similar dark red as my dress.

His face relaxed as he looked me over. "You're okay."

"Why wouldn't I be?"

"You were gone for ages," he said, offering me his arm.

"Yeah well," I muttered, sliding my arm through his. "I had a lot to say."

As we made our way towards the main ballroom, the hallway began to widen, filling with people who bowed and curtseyed as I passed.

"How are you feeling?" Kwellen asked as we approached the large, open doors, a pair of black wings carved into their sprawling surface.

I squeezed his arm. "Just don't leave me, okay?"

He gave me a reassuring smile and led me into the room. The ceiling was bedecked with swathes of black and red material, the hundreds of flames adorning the iron chandeliers casting flickering shadows as the breeze caused them to shift and sway. Almost immediately, someone pressed a drink into my hand, which Kwellen swiftly removed, and clusters of Chaos clamoured to congratulate me on my victories so far.

Although I would rather have been anywhere else than in that ballroom, I wasn't nervous about the final Rite. My father had briefly described what was to happen while I'd lain shivering in the healers' rooms having my body temperature slowly brought back from freezing, and the icicles melted from my wings. For a moment, I'd thought he'd come to see if I was all right. I wondered why, after almost two decades of disappointment, I continued to be surprised by his complete and utter disregard for me. At least he wasn't my real father.

My skin heated at the intrusive thought, and I looked around at the Chaos gathered nearby as though they might have heard. I tightened my hold on Kwellen, causing him to raise an eyebrow. Giving a weak smile in return, I focused my attention on the lord prattling away in front of me.

"Princess Sirain," a young male with jet black hair that brushed his shoulders stepped forward, bowing deeply as he interrupted the elderly lord I was talking to with no remorse. "Lord Drafferth of Nefret."

I inclined my head. "Lord Drafferth, I hope you're enjoying the festivities?"

He smiled, the already severe angles of his face sharpening further. "I am. However, I would enjoy them a lot more if you would honour me with a dance."

Panic fluttered in my stomach. I didn't want to dance. Not without at least five glasses of wine in me. I looked up at Kwellen, who was staring down at the slim lord in distaste. His lips curled in what might have passed as a genuine smile, but it didn't reach his eyes.

"I'm afraid the princess has saved her first dance for me," he said.

I leaned against him in relief, and he tugged my arm closer to his body. "Perhaps later?"

"You can't expect me to believe you can dance properly with

only one arm," Lord Drafferth sneered before turning back to me. "I'd be a much better partner for you, Princess."

Kwellen stepped forward, his smile widening to show his large white teeth. "I think you'll find I can do anything better than you, Drafferth."

The lord pulled himself up to his full height, which still fell woefully short of my friend.

"There are some things you'll find you need two hands to take care of properly," the young lord leered. And just in case either of us missed his meaning, he dragged his gaze down my body.

"Oh, Drafferth. I'm more than capable with just one hand." Kwellen laughed softly, leaning towards him. "Just ask your mother."

Before the lord could respond, Kwellen manoeuvred me to the heaving dance floor and spun me around in a dizzying circle.

As he tugged me back towards him, I placed my hand on his shoulder and laughed. "That poor boy."

"He's an idiot," Kwellen said, as he spun me again. "And I am an excellent dancer."

The music swelled around us, muting my sorrow, and soothing my aching bones as my friend proved he was exactly that. It was the closest I'd felt to happiness since Plumataria, and I grasped at it with both hands. The musicians struck up another melody, but before Kwellen could set us moving again, a cold hand clasped my shoulder, the fingers gripping to the point of pain.

"Mind if I cut in, Lord Devland?" my brother crooned.

He'd mastered the ability to make the prestigious title sound like a slur.

Kwellen raised a dark eyebrow, but I shook my head. "It's fine."

It wasn't fine, but I doubted even my sadistic little brother would hurt me in front of hundreds of people. Even so, my eyes flitted to the head table, where my father sat in flowing black robes, his face the picture of disdain. My mother, who would usually be at his side all evening, was nowhere to be seen.

Kwellen watched, his dark eyes narrowed, as Fin placed a hand on my waist and moved me away. We began to move around the dance floor and my brother pulled me closer, his grip causing my eyes to water.

"I know," he whispered, dipping his mouth to my ear. "I know the truth, you disgusting half breed."

My eyes widened and I looked around wildly to see if anyone had heard—to look for Kwellen—but my brother took us into a spin that made the faces blur around me.

"I don't know what you're talking about."

He laughed, low and cruel. "That's what she said. It should be me on that throne. It *will* be me on that throne."

I could hardly draw a breath, as he clutched me closer. To anyone who didn't know better, it probably looked like an endearing gesture between siblings. I tried to move away from him, but he dug his long fingers in deeper, forcing a whimper from my lips.

"That's what who said?" I asked. "Who's spreading lies about me?"

"You're pathetic," he spat. "Go ahead and finish your Rites. They'll mean nothing when you're dead."

Fin spun me again and when I came to a stop, he was gone. Kwellen was already waiting and took me in his arm as though it had all been part of the dance.

"What did he say to you?" he asked. "You look like you're going to be sick. Please don't be sick on my outfit, it's new."

I sucked in a breath, trying and failing to recall the sensation of being happy just moments earlier.

"He was just being his usual charming self," I lied.

Kwellen frowned but didn't push it. My shoulder and hip

throbbed from where Fin had dug his fingers and I knew there would be ten more bruises on my skin by morning. It wasn't a surprise. I'd known in my heart it was him who'd taken the feather. What unsettled me more than his threat of death was who he'd been talking about. *That's what she said*. There was only one 'she' who knew the truth. I looked again for my mother at the head table and found her place still empty.

"Have you seen the queen tonight?" I asked.

Kwellen shook his head. "I heard she's not feeling well."

My stomach lurched.

"Mind if I cut in?"

I turned at the familiar voice. "Odio."

"The one and only," my cousin said, bowing deeply.

His tunic and pants were a red so dark it almost looked black, accentuating the colouring in his hair and wings. The stripe of hair down the centre of his head was neatly braided, resting across his shoulder, the sides freshly shaven.

"You almost look handsome," I teased.

He clutched his hands to his chest in shock. "I am by far the most handsome Chaos in the room, and you know it. What did your oozing scab of a brother want?"

Odio reached out and touched my shoulder as though he could see the bruises forming beneath the thin layer of red gauze.

"Just congratulating me," I lied. "Are we dancing or what?"

Kwellen gave a half bow before disappearing into the crowd. I knew Odio was the only Chaos in the room he felt safe leaving me with, and my cousin took me into his arms with more care than I would have expected from a hardened ruthless warrior.

"Do you realise, this is the first time we've danced together," he said.

I frowned, realising he was correct. "Probably because at the

Festivals, you're too busy bedding as many males and females as possible."

He grinned, his garnet eyes flashing as he spun me around. "It would be rude not to share this gift."

"Of course."

"I haven't seen you since your fight with Krieg," he said. "Kwellen told me it was spectacular. Congratulations."

My heart clenched. "I don't think 'spectacular' is quite the word I'd choose."

"Well, either way, you won and you're alive," Odio said, his hands giving me a gentle squeeze. "And I'm glad of that."

The music slowed and we fell into a sway.

"How did your mission go?"

He pulled back to look at me. "Which mission?"

I tried to school my face into something resembling neutrality. "Before my fight, you said you were off to the human world on a mission."

"Oh. It was fine. I've been back twice since then. It's busy with the war coming."

I pressed my lips together. The war. Were the Cupids just as busy? What was Pace doing with the humans? Was he still working with them? I took a breath, attempting to clear my head.

"You said you had a plan, before you left. What did you mean?"

Odio smiled. "You worry too much, Your Majesty. You've successfully completed three of the four Royal Rites and proved that you're the toughest Chaos in Helle. Try and enjoy yourself."

"Please," I pressed. "Tell me what you meant, and I'll try and enjoy myself."

Odio huffed a sigh, leaning closer to whisper. "I meant what I meant. You don't have to worry about any repercussions for killing that Cupid. I've dealt with it. He's no longer a threat."

I leaned back, my eyes wide in question. "What—"

Odio spun me away from him and I collided with Kwellen's broad chest. Shoving my hair out of my face, I turned back around, but my cousin had vanished into the crowd. The room tilted.

"Drink?" Kwellen asked, handing me a glass overflowing with red wine.

I snatched it from him, almost downing it in one go, my hands trembling with anger. What had he done? He couldn't mean Dariel was no longer a threat because he was dead. Did he mean Pace? What had he done? My stomach rolled. Had he killed him?

Handing Kwellen my half-empty glass, I moved away to try and find him. I'd barely taken a step, when the music stopped, a hush falling over the room. I halted, turning to find my father standing on the dais at the front of the room.

"Thank you for joining us this evening," he said, inclining his head as he held his arms out to the crowd. "You honour us with your presence. Tonight, my daughter will complete the fourth and final Royal Rite. She will be my undisputed successor."

Watching from the crowded dance floor, I was aware of the Chaos turning to look at me, the motion rippling outward like the petals of a flower. I stepped forward, a path parting before me, and I was grateful for the large presence of Kwellen at my back. A page extended a hand to help me up onto the raised platform and, trying to exude confidence and calm I wasn't feeling on the inside, I walked towards the polished obsidian bowl resting on a narrow plinth at the front of the dais. My father stood beside it, a gleaming dagger in his hand.

He'd described the basics of the ceremony, and at the time, I'd been relieved at their simplicity. I was to cut my arm and fill a bowl with my blood. Compared with fighting Krieg and surviving a night at the top of Mount Hadeon, it had sounded like skipping through a field of daisies. Now, I stared at the size of the bowl wondering whether 'filling' it was an exaggeration.

My father reached for my wrist and held my arm over the bowl. His fingers were cold and hard like Fin's, and I flinched.

"By giving her blood, Crown Princess Sirain shows us—shows the Fates themselves—that she is willing to bleed for Helle. That she will die before turning her back on the Fates. That the very last drop of her blood will fall before Helle does."

His words were met with murmurings of approval throughout the room, even as the very blood he spoke of ran cold. A movement at the edge of the dais caught my eye and I found Fin watching, his arms folded and his trademark sneer marking his face. I promised myself that I would go and find my mother the first chance I got. If he'd done anything to her . . . I looked away, finding Kwellen and Odio standing to the other side of the stage, a mix of pride and concern on their faces. Kwellen gave me a small smile and I exhaled gently. I could do this—this final test.

Taking the blade from my father, I made to slice the back of my forearm, but he wrapped his cold hand around mine, controlling the dagger as he gripped my wrist with his other. I watched, wide eyed as he dragged the blade along the smooth skin on the inside of my arm, creating a deep cut running from my elbow to my wrist. The pain was blinding, and thick crimson blood pooled at the incision, streaming down my arm and into the bowl. I gasped, gripping onto the plinth to steady myself as the king stepped back, his eyes fixed on the stream of blood.

I couldn't ask how much blood I needed to give, not in front of everyone. So, I stood, trembling, as it drained from me in a steady stream. A shiver trailed my spine, the faces in the crowd blurring into a mass of white and black as my heartbeat pulsed slower. *Slower*. I frowned. It had only been a few seconds. Looking down at the bowl, I swayed. It was nearly full. How long had I stood there, the room fading in and out of focus? I turned to look for Kwellen and Odio and found them, their edges melting and their faces a dripping mass of wide eyes and pleading mouths. Were they saying something? I was so cold.

Looking out at the crowd once more, I thought I saw a pair of white wings and my heart faltered. I squinted, trying to bring the figure into focus, but it had gone. Of course, he wasn't there. I chuckled to myself. I'd said goodbye. He hated me. Why would he come to rescue me? I frowned. Did I need rescuing?

Each drip was deafening, and the pain was now a steady throb of agony spreading up my arm and across my chest. I glanced at the bowl again, leaning heavily against the plinth. It was almost full. *So close.* Soon, it would all be over. I would have proven myself worthy of the throne. Worthy of a new start. I was strong. Stronger than my crumpled heart. If I survived this, I could survive anything.

Looking into the bowl, my pale reflection stared up from the rippling pool of blood and smiled. It was full. The throne was mine. My eyes drifted shut as a hand closed over my arm, halting the flow of blood. Then I fell.

39
Pace

I couldn't be sure how many days had passed, locked inside the room. With no windows, it was impossible to tell. I had tried to keep count by the changing of the guards outside my door and the meals that were brought to me, but after a while it had blended into a monotonous blur. I thought perhaps it was close to two weeks. It may as well have been months. After my initial anger had worn off, I'd settled into a routine. I'd exercise after waking until my muscles screamed, then after bathing, I'd eat breakfast. Some books had been left for me, so I'd lie on the bed and read until lunch. Sometimes I'd repeat the exercises or return to reading, depending on how I was feeling. Occasionally, I'd bang on the door until my fists bled and yell until my throat tore. It never did any good. No one ever answered. My food was slipped around the door three times a day, with an arrow aimed at me through the crack.

Most of my time was taken up by thinking—or trying not to. I'd told Marlowe I'd meet with him in a couple of weeks. Would he think I'd abandoned him when I didn't show? The coils of frustration that worked their way through my body at the thought, were the ones that often caused me to try and tear the door down.

More often that I'd have liked, my thoughts strayed to Sirain. Hours had been lost to replaying conversations and turning over my feelings, which often resulted in a pounding headache. I was angry with her. Bitterly so. I could understand, begrudgingly, why she hadn't told me she was Crown Princess. What we'd had was so impossible anyway. At first, I'd considered her selfish, but I knew that even if she'd tried to break it off for that reason, I'd have told her it didn't matter. There was nothing she could have said that would have made me turn away. I knew what I was doing when I lit that match—when I chose her. What angered me was that she hadn't made a stand. The Fates had decreed that she kill a human—kill my friend—and she'd taken them at their word. A lengthy groan worked its way from my lips.

That was what took up most of my thinking time. *The Fates.* I'd always trusted them, but because I wasn't a Hand, it hadn't affected me directly. If the Fates had asked Dariel to kill someone, would he have done it? Would Tiesa? Why were conflicting orders given to Cupids and Chaos? Why did the Chaos have Royal Rites when we didn't? With each passing day, my questions multiplied. The questions had started a long time ago. Ever since that first visit to the human word, the fabric of my belief had been slowly fraying at the seams.

I leaned back against the stone wall, my wings twitching. That was the worst thing about being locked up. It was the longest I'd gone without flying since being a smallwing. I stretched out my wings to their full width and scowled at the thinning patches amongst the innermost primary feathers. Even as I folded them back in, another feather drifted to the bare wooden floorboards. I stared at it, Dariel's deep booming laugh echoing in my mind. *My cousin, the oversized pigeon.*

I sucked in a breath and clenched my hands into fists. Would Dashuri have locked Dariel up too if he was still alive? My heart stumbled. Did Dashuri know what had really happened in the human world? He'd known about Sirain. I wasn't sure how much he knew. He'd mentioned a Chaos but hadn't mentioned her name.

Two weeks of contemplation didn't make the bitter pill of betrayal any easier to swallow. Nothing made sense. Tiesa had lied for me. She'd lied to the king and queen's faces about how Dariel had died. And yet, she'd betrayed me to Dash. I had a feeling she would tell me it was for my own good.

I'd spent my life in blissful ignorance, trusting blindly. Trusting the Cupids I fought with in the tournaments not to tell others of my involvement. Trusting females I spent time with not to tell my parents. Trusting my friends not to betray me. I sucked in a breath, my chest tight. I'd trusted Sirain. There may have been no windows in my room, but I watched the world around me slowly burning, disintegrating into fine silver ash. My trust burned right along with it.

Over the last couple of days, or at least what I perceived as days, something cold and hard had emerged from those ashes. Resolve. Determination. Enough was enough. I thought of how my parents and Dash saw me and my lip curled in a sneer. That version of me was gone. The very idea of that happy-go-lucky prince, dancing on the edge of propriety, seemed laughable. I exhaled and leaned forward onto the floor, sinking into another round of push-ups in an attempt to expend the restless energy that pulsed through my veins.

I was going to get out of there. Whatever it took. The Fates hadn't been fair to me—hadn't been fair to anyone—and I was done playing by their rules. When Dariel had died, Tiesa had asked me why I wasn't trying to tear the world apart. I would. I would tear down everything I knew. But I would do it quietly. Cutting away until I got my answers. Until Dariel and

Marlowe got their revenge. Until I felt something other than . . . This.

Voices sounded outside the door, and I rolled up onto my feet. My breakfast had only been recently cleared away, so I wasn't due another meal for a while. Breathing hard, I grabbed a towel and wiped the sweat from my face, listening to the muffled voices. It opened and Tiesa stepped in.

I stared.

"Pace?" she said, her eyes wide as she looked around my prison.

I held my hands out to my sides. "The one and only."

Her mouth hung open, her Hand markings creasing. "I've been so worried."

Turning away, I strode to the sink, splashing cold water on my face to buy some thinking time. If she wanted to pretend she wasn't the reason I was locked up, then fine. I shoved the sting of betrayal down under the armour I'd been crafting around my heart. I'd already come to terms with what I needed to do to get out of there, but I thought Dash would have been the first person I'd have to convince.

"What are you doing here?" I asked, tossing the towel onto the side, and grabbing a fresh shirt from the dresser.

"I came as soon as I could, Pace," she said, her sea green eyes glistening with tears. "As soon as I found out what Dashuri had done, I told him he had to let you out, but he wouldn't listen."

Crossing the room, I climbed onto the bed, tucking my knees to my chest. "How did you find out?"

"I went looking and couldn't find you. When people said they hadn't seen you, I started to get worried." She leaned against the door, wrapping her arms around her middle. "I had a mission in Liridona. Not Emeric, but one of his generals. While I was there, I found him and asked whether he'd seen you."

I raised my eyebrows. "You showed yourself to a human? On purpose? Tiesa Caracy, you rebel."

"Anyway," she continued, ignoring my scathing tone. "He said he'd met with you and Marlowe two days prior. It was then I started to worry. I figured perhaps you'd got hurt between Liridona and The Crossing. So, I asked Dashuri. I didn't tell him about The Crossing, though. I just asked if he'd seen you and that I was worried. He told me that you were safe."

"I bet he did," I muttered.

I stared at her, trying to find the lie in her features. It had been easy to believe her betrayal when she wasn't standing in front of me, but now, all I could see was my best friend. I frowned.

"Pace," she said, stepping closer. "Are you okay?"

"What do you think?"

Tiesa took another tentative step forward. "When I pressed Dashuri, he told me to let it go, and that all I needed to know was that you were okay."

"But that was days ago, right?" I frowned. "Why did he change his mind?"

Tiesa stared at her fingers, playing with a thin leather bracelet around her wrist.

"Ah," I said, realisation dawning. "He sent for you. Dash asked you to come and talk to me. What does he want you to do? Interrogate me?"

"Pace—"

"If you didn't tell my brother about The Crossing, who did?"

Tiesa's mouth hung open. "You think I told Dashuri? You think I betrayed you? After everything?"

"You're the only other person who knew," I said, refusing to feel guilt at her wounded expression. "Can you blame me?"

"I heard a rumour," she said, hurt flickering across her features. "That one of the Hands was approached by a demon during a mission."

My heart stilled. "A demon? You mean a Chaos spoke to one of our Hands?"

"I don't know. That's all I heard. I don't even know who it was. To be honest, I'd dismissed it as nonsense."

I leaned back against the wall. "It must have been Kwellen or Odio. Why would they do that, though?"

Tiesa looked at me, her brow furrowed. "Maybe they were worried."

"Worried? About what?"

"You."

I stared at her. "What are you talking about?"

"She killed Dariel. Maybe they thought you'd be out for blood."

Tiesa's words piled like boulders on my chest. I thought of the way the Chaos had dragged her from Marlowe's cabin—the look of devastation in her eyes. Had it been fear? Was Sirain scared of me? I pulled my hands over my face. As much as I knew I could never forgive her, I couldn't help but worry about her. It had always seemed that she didn't quite fit in with her family—with Helle. Perhaps it was because she'd never been fully Chaos. There was a good chance she was already dead.

"Pace?"

I peered at her through my fingers. "What?"

"You need to stop."

"Stop?"

"Everything." Tiesa shifted awkwardly, as though unsure what to do with her hands. "Meeting with the humans. Going to the human world."

I stared at her for a long moment. "This is why Dash let you come and see me, isn't it?"

Her pained expression was all the answer I needed.

"Do you honestly think I would return to the human world after all this?" I said, my voice as cold and hard as my armoured heart.

Surprise flitted across Tiesa's face, and she took a small step back, clearly unsettled by my tone.

"I'm sure you'll be happy to hear that you were right," I continued. Staring hard at my hands, I frowned. "I disrespected the Fates and look where it got me. I've lost Dariel, my reputation is in tatters, and I'm locked up like some wild animal. There's nothing left for me in the human world. I wish I'd never asked Dariel to take me."

"I wish I hadn't been right," Tiesa said softly. "I hate everything that's happened. I hate seeing you like this."

My frown deepened and I picked at the scabs on my knuckles, refusing to look at her. If I did, she might see the lie.

"I understand why my brother did this," I say, releasing a long breath. "It's given me lots of time to reflect. Time to think about what life would look like if I hadn't made those choices. Dariel would still be with us and perhaps if I'd stepped up and taken on Dash's role like I was supposed to, my parents wouldn't have forced me to marry Caitland. Things could have been good."

A sharp shard of truth ran through my words. My feelings were a lie, but Dariel was dead because of me. Marlowe blamed himself, but the thread would always lead back to me. If I hadn't made him take me to the human world, he'd still be alive.

"I'm so sorry, Pace," Tiesa said. "We might not be able to see what the Fates have planned for us, but we need to trust in them. There's a reason all of this has happened, Pace. I'm sure of it."

I nodded; my gaze still fixed on my hands.

"I'll try and persuade Dashuri to let you out," she said, backing toward the door. "I'm not sure how much longer he plans on keeping you here. He's still pretty angry."

"I can imagine."

"I'm going to ask them to send a healer in," she said. "For your wings."

I winced. Even tucked in, she'd noticed. My skin heated with shame, the room suddenly suffocatingly small. Dragging in a slow breath, I forced a grateful smile to my face as I looked up at my friend.

"Thank you, Tiesa. And thank you for coming to see me."

She nodded. "I'll try to visit you again soon."

The smile remained on my face until the door closed behind her, then it melted away. There'd been a part of me that had worried she wouldn't believe me. Tiesa had known me my whole life and could spot even a half-truth from a distance. Perhaps I looked that broken. Maybe the idea that I would want to continue tearing at the tatters of my ruined life rather than trying to build them back up was an easier truth to swallow.

Both in my heart and outside this prison, the flames had already devoured everything I held dear. When I'd chosen Sirain I'd worried about hurting the people around me, but now there was nothing and no one left. Dariel was dead. My parents didn't seem to care that I'd been gone for weeks. I wondered what lie my brother had spun them. Sirain was probably dead too. Even if she wasn't, she might as well be. How could you burn something that was already ash and embers? I'd unravelled the thread this far; I would take it to the very end. For Dariel, I'd do everything I could to keep Marlowe and the people he cared about safe, even if I went down in the flames.

I slid off the bed and onto the floor, resuming my push-ups. I would get out of here. I'd convince them all. Then, I was going to start tearing the world apart, rip by rip, slice by slice—right under their noses. A growl rumbled in my chest as Tiesa's words came back to me. We needed to trust in the Fates. There was a reason everything had happened. Perhaps Fate had led me to the humans—had led me to Sirain. Maybe Fate had killed Dariel. But I was done trusting. I was no longer going to stand by and let the Fates decide when and where to align the jagged pieces of my wretched life. Even if I had to grip the Fates by their all-knowing throats, I had questions, and I wasn't going to stop until I got answers.

Book 2 Coming 2022

Pronunciation Guide & Origins

Name	Pronunciation	Meaning	Origin
Pace	PAY-ce (or PAH-chay)	Peace	Italy
Sirain	SIH-rain	Destroy	Philippines
Kwellen	KWELL-en	Torment	Netherlands
Dariel	DAH-ree-ell	Open	Old French
Odio	OH-dee-oh	Hate	Latin
Tiesa	tee-EH-sah	Truth	Latvia
Dragoste	DRA-ghost	Love	Romania
Hadeon	HAD-ee-on	Destroyer	Ukraine
Dashuri	da-SURE-ee	Love	Albania
Fin	FIN	End	France
Maluhia	ma-LU-hee-ah	Peaceful	Hawaii
Briga	BREE-gah	Argue	Portugal
Nemir	neh-MEER	Turmoil	Slovenia
Armastus	ar-MAS-tus	Love	Estonia
Amare	am-AH-ray	To love	Italy
Malin	MAL-in	Warrior	Old English
Amani	am-AHN-ee	Peace	Kenya

Cupids

King Kärlek Dragoste + Queen Freya

King Armastus + Queen Maluhia

Prince Dashuri

Prince Pace

Princess Amani

Prince Rahu + Lady Milovat

Lady Amare

Lord Dariel

Chaos

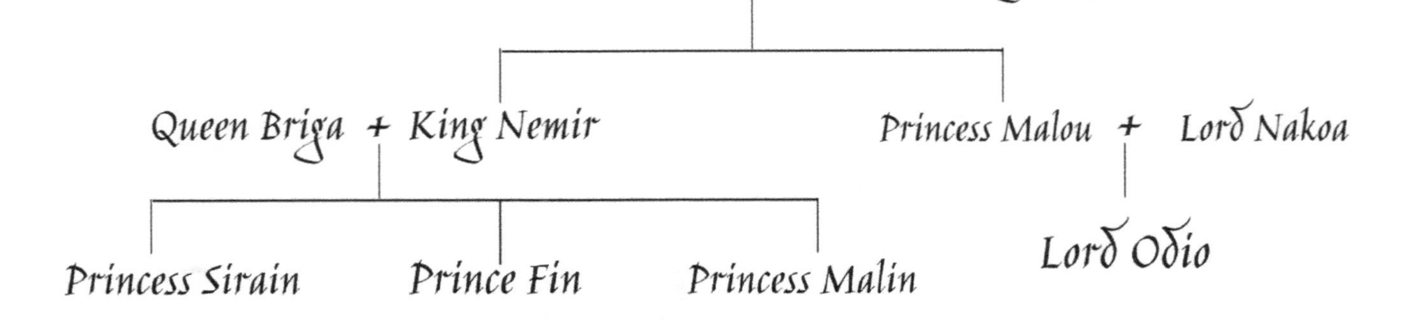
Queen Elda Hadeon + King Nered
Queen Briga + King Nemir
Princess Malou + Lord Nakoa
Princess Sirain
Prince Fin
Princess Malin
Lord Odio

ACKNOWLEDGMENTS

I usually don't know where to start these, but there's no question this time. Miranda and Claire. Without you two incredible ladies, this book wouldn't exist. Your support and feedback have helped me persevere through re-write after re-write, your confidence and love for these characters never wavering. Thank you so much. I hope you're as proud as I am of the final result.

Thank you Emily for the incredible artwork. I had a vision and you brought it to life, even more beautiful than I could have imagined. Thank you Tairelei for the stunning cover design—you were a delight to work with and I'm thrilled with the result.

An enormous thank you to my proofreaders, Claire, Lisa, Gaelle, and my sisters, Lindsay and Natalie. I appreciate your eagle eyes and your invaluable feedback so much.

A huge thank you to my Arrows: the Cupids & Chaos Street Team. I'm honestly so grateful for your support and cheerleading. You're truly the best and I can't wait to take you on the rest of this journey.

Finally, as always, thank you, to you—the reader. I hope you enjoyed Pace and Sirain's journey and I hope you'll return to find out what the Fates have in store in book two.

ALSO BY DARBY CUPID

Crystal - Starlatten Book 1

Rebel - Starlatten Book 2

Legacy - Starlatten Book 3

CPSIA information can be obtained
at www.ICGtesting.com
Printed in the USA
LVHW090152241121
704331LV00017B/415/J